THE HUNTERS

KAT GORDON read English at Somerville College, Oxford and worked at *Time Out* briefly after graduating. She travelled extensively in East Africa where she also worked as a teacher and an HIV counsellor. She received a distinction for her MA in creative writing from Royal Holloway and her debut, *The Artificial Anatomy of Parks*, was published in 2015. Kat has lived in Budapest and Reykjavik and is currently settled in London with her partner and young son.

Also by Kat Gordon

The Artificial Anatomy of Parks

KAT GORDON

The Hunters

THE BOROUGH PRESS

The Borough Press
An imprint of HarperCollins*Publishers*
1 London Bridge Street
London SE1 9GF

www.harpercollins.co.uk

Published by HarperCollins*Publishers* 2018
1

A catalogue record for this book
is available from the British Library

HB ISBN: 978-0-00-825306-6
TPB ISBN: 978-0-00-825307-3

This novel is entirely a work of fiction.
The names, characters and incidents portrayed in it, while at times based on historical figures,
are the work of the author's imagination.

Newspaper article, p.211 © *East African Standard,* 14 July 1934

Selected quotes, p.262-3 taken from Kenya Legislative Council Debates, 1938, vol IV, Defence, col.6

Selected quotes, p.265 taken from Kenya Legislative Council Debates, 1938, vol VI, col.461

Set in Bembo by Palimpsest Book Production Limited,
Falkirk, Stirlingshire

Printed and bound in Great Britain by
CPI Group (UK) Ltd, Croydon, CR0 4YY

MIX
Paper from
responsible sources
FSC™ C007454

This book is produced from independently certified FSC™ paper
to ensure responsible forest management.

For more information visit: **www.harpercollins.co.uk/green**

To my son, Noah, and the Somerville girls, for everything.

Her heart stopped at 20:57 exactly. She had looked at her watch only moments before, and asked the totos to turn on a lamp. She had been reading and hadn't noticed it getting dark until her eyes had smarted suddenly with the strain.

It had been a warm evening – a warm end to a hot, sticky day that had wrapped itself around her, dampening her upper lip and armpits and the backs of her knees – and she was wearing a thin blue cardigan over the white dress. It made her laugh, wearing white, after everything that had happened, or maybe it made her cry. She stopped the totos again and asked for some tea. Her stomach was still delicate. Her whole body had changed since childbirth, in fact. But she didn't like to think about that.

She turned her head towards the door, as if she'd heard a noise outside. A crunch and a low purr, but not an animal's; this was a car pulling up. She wondered for a moment if it was Theo – he often dropped by unannounced. She held the book up. She didn't want to see him. She didn't want to see anyone, except the totos passing in and out of the shadows cast by the lamp.

Through the screen door she could smell the magnolia tree, and the roses she'd planted. The sweetness of the flowers mingled with the sharpness of the limes that the totos used to polish the furniture, filling the room with a powerful haze. It made her feel tired, or was that the sudden quiet? The cicadas had stopped their humming, and she couldn't even hear the water. Peace.

A toto stood in front of her with the cup of tea and she shook her head. She'd changed her mind. She didn't want tea, she didn't want anything. Go back to the kitchen, she said. Or anywhere; just stay out of this room. She closed her eyes.

The bullet went through the book first; she hadn't lowered it. Maybe that was the reason there was so little blood, just a small, dark hole in her chest over her heart. When the totos found her, her eyes were open and clear. They said it almost looked as if she was smiling.

Part One
1925–1927

Chapter One

The station was big and crowded with no benches or stalls, just two signs, one reading 'Mombasa', and the other 'Upper-class passengers and luggage'. Most of it was open to the hot November sun and the flies.

After a few minutes I found a porter, and led him back to my family: my father, mopping his forehead, my mother, tapping her foot, and my twelve-year-old sister Maud, melting against the pile of trunks holding books and clothes and everything else that hadn't been sent on ahead to the new house at Lake Naivasha.

'There you are, Theo,' my father said. He waved our tickets and two pennies in front of the porter, 'Load our luggage into the carriages, there's a good man.'

'Yes, Bwana Miller,' the porter said. He was wearing a thick navy jacket and trousers. As he picked up the first of our trunks I saw he had dark circles under his armpits. He smelled different to the Africans in Tanganyika, less spicy and more sour.

Our carriages were two square compartments with an inter-connecting door and mosquito screens attached to the window frames. I sat next to the window on a green-cushioned bench and my mother and Maud sat with me. Smartly dressed train guards checked our tickets and bowed to my father as he strode around the two rooms, explaining little features here and there. My father was an engineer, now Director of the same railway that in 1896 he'd come out to Africa to build.

I rested my forehead against the cool glass of our carriage window. We'd spent the last two weeks in Dar es Salaam, and if we were still there I would have been stretched out along the jetty with Maud and Lucy – the daughter of my father's friends – soaking up the warmth of the wood beneath us, and listening to the shouts of the men unloading fish and spices along the harbour. In front of us, moored dhows would be bumping gently against each other in the waves, and kingfishers dive-bombing the water in flashes of blue and orange. Across the bay was Zanzibar, home to the sultan. One afternoon I'd taken my father's binoculars out to look at the island, a stretch of brilliant white sand dotted with palms and matched by the whitewashed palace and fort at its edge. To the left I could see an Indian banyan tree, alive with vervet monkeys, and behind that, the shaded labyrinthine streets of Stone Town. Children darted in and out of focus, rusted-red iron roofs sloped upwards, and bedsheets, used in the place of curtains, flailed outwards in the breeze. 'That's the breath of God,' Maud said, when I showed her. I didn't see how Kenya could be better than that.

Along the train, doors began to slam.

'Theo, open the window, please,' my mother said.

'Perhaps we should leave it closed,' my father said. 'It gets quite dusty later on.'

My mother frowned, and he hurriedly waved at me to do as she said.

With the window open the carriage began to smell. Home – Scotland – had smelled clean, like heather, or salt when the breeze blew straight from the ocean. And then in the spring and autumn the rain would come, hammering the earth and releasing the rich smell of peat from it. Africa smelled too much – fishy, peppery, rotting, and smoky all at once – and at first I'd thought I was going to pass out in the confusion. Now I could occasionally make something out: the sour, animal scent of a donkey, or the sweetness of the mimosa that spilled over the white fences surrounding the Europeans' houses. Or caramel, from the sugared nuts a man was selling on the platform.

'That's hardly any better,' my mother said, peeling off her gloves, and I pressed myself against the back of my seat to be further away from her. She was seventeen years younger than my father, and I knew that men found her beautiful. To me, however, she was only unpredictable. Sometimes she would nuzzle me, rubbing her nose against my cheek and gently pulling my hair, and other times she would fly at me, cuffing me around my head. My last tutor had quit when my mother – whose own schooling was stopped at thirteen – overheard me stumbling on my arithmetic and ran into the room to slap me across the face, shouting the right answers. After that I was sent to boarding school.

'When are we going to leave?' she said. 'Can't you have a word with someone, William?'

'Just a few more minutes.'

Maud traced an outline with her finger over the mesh of the mosquito screen. 'Will we come back to Mombasa?'

'Another time,' my father said. 'We're going to The Norfolk Hotel in Nairobi now. You know Theodore Roosevelt stayed there in 1909 on his "African Safari and Scientific Expedition"?' He placed a meaty hand on my neck. 'Your namesake, Theo.'

At fifty-four, my father was the one who resembled Roosevelt, with his moustache and his glasses and his waistcoats. I was slim, short and blond, and my mouth was too large – too thick-lipped – and my nose too wide, my eyes too green and my cheekbones too high to be much like the former President. I was too girlish-looking. The boys at my school had called me *Theodora*; sometimes they'd chased me around the rugby pitch and pinned me down while they took turns to kiss me.

I breathed in deeply; the idea that I'd never see a school again

5

made me want to shout with exhilaration. My mother had already found a governess to take charge of my education. After the incident with one of the rugby boys that last term, and after I'd been sent back early, she hadn't spoken to me for a week, but at least she seemed to realise I was better at home for the next three years. Then there would be university, but I didn't need to think about that yet.

'Will we see any animals from the train?' Maud asked.

Maud had large brown eyes and olive skin; in Scotland they'd called her 'the Spanish Sister', because of her looks and her habit of carrying a bible around. I'd once heard my father tell a friend that Maud had never lied in her life.

'We will,' my father said.

There was a shrill blast of a whistle from the platform, and the train jerked forwards impatiently.

'Finally,' my mother said.

At first the scenery was of dusty bazaars and colourful buildings – pale pinks and greens and glowing whites with towers and domes and covered balconies – or wide roads lined with palm trees and sycamore figs and only a few cars in sight. The blare of shouting reached us through the open window, becoming muffled as we headed out of the centre and the houses turned European: well-spaced bungalows with large, tropically lush gardens. Then came the thatched huts and swampland, African children running alongside the tracks to wave at the train, and then we were out of the city completely. The view changed to brown scrubland and small streams and I turned away from the window, disappointed with what I'd seen of the country so far.

The journey was slow. We had to stop every time a buffalo wandered onto the track, and the train jolted badly. At Voi we stopped for an hour, this time to have dinner by the side of the track, under large hanging lamps and a cloud of buzzing insects. We started with soup then moved on to a rubbery-tasting fish.

'It's good to have some proper food again,' my father said, spearing a large piece with his fork.

I swirled my own piece around its plate, leaving trails of slimy leeks in its wake.

'What's wrong?' Maud asked me. 'Do you miss Dar es Salaam?'

'We were only there for a fortnight,' my mother said. 'You can't be that fond of it already.'

In Tanganyika our supper had been dates, then spiced beef or fish curries cooked in coconut milk and served with rice on a metal platter, with hollows for each dish so we could mix the food if we wanted to. Sometimes, if we were still hungry afterwards, we'd buy food from the *baba lishas* – the feeding men – down by the harbour: grilled cassava with a chilli sauce, samosas, pineapple, custard apples, avocados and andazi, a sweet, deep-fried dough cake. Lucy's parents had joined us on our second night for supper, bringing Lucy too, the first time we'd met. She sat with me and Maud and I tried to talk to her, but she was monosyllabic.

'You made quite an impression,' my mother said afterwards.

'She didn't like me.'

She gave me a funny look. 'Your delusions never fail to amaze me, darling.'

My father pushed away his empty plate, and an Indian waiter in a starched white uniform swooped down and exchanged it for one piled with beef. My mother, who'd just laid down her knife and fork in the middle of her plate, hurriedly picked them up again and continued to pick at her fish.

A cat appeared in the doorway of the station master's office, and sauntered along the platform in our direction.

'Here, kitty,' Maud said, holding out a morsel of fish.

The cat reached my mother and started to rub himself against her leg, purring and arching his back. My mother reached down and scratched his head, and I suddenly wondered what it would feel like to be him, to stroke my face against her long, smooth

7

leg, and have her fingers gently massage the ticklish spot just behind my ears. I looked away from the two of them.

'How much longer before we reach Nairobi?' I asked.

'Oh, sixteen hours or more,' my father said.

'Is it as far as Edinburgh to London?' Maud asked.

'Much further.' He dabbed his mouth with his napkin. 'That's why it took so long to build. That and the lions, of course.'

'The lions?'

'In Tsavo,' my father said. 'Slave trader caravans used to cross the river there, and two lions developed a taste for human flesh. They must have been eating the bodies of dead captives left by the wayside before we showed up.'

Maud put down her cutlery.

'They ambushed the workers at night and dragged them off. After a while most of the workers ran away – we had a devil of a time trying to get them back. The lions ate more than a hundred men until Patterson found them and shot them.' He shook his head. 'He took them home as rugs. Beautiful specimens.'

When we returned to the carriage, the guards had made up our bunks with crisp sheets, soft pillows and blankets. Our parents were in the compartment next door, and I shared with Maud. I lay on my top bunk, unable to sleep. After an hour or so I jumped down and stood by the window.

'What are you doing?' Maud asked.

'Surveying my kingdom.'

She got out of bed and stood next to me, wrapping her arms around herself. 'Do you think there'll be wild animals there? By our house, I mean.'

'Of course there will be.'

'I want to see an elephant. And a tiger.'

'Tigers are in India, Spanish. Africa's got lions, and hyenas. And leopards.' I turned to face her, leaning back against the window. 'You know they live in trees, don't you?'

'Yes.'

8

'And you have to look up when you're in a forest. Otherwise they could drop down behind you and bite you here,' I put my hand to my throat, 'and drag you back up and we'd never find you.'

'They don't eat humans,' Maud said.

'They eat everything.'

'Stop trying to frighten me.'

'It's no fun if you don't actually get frightened anyway.'

'Mother says we can have a dog here.'

'She won't really let us.'

Maud looked up at me, wide-eyed. 'But she promised.'

'When I'm older and I have my own house,' I said, 'you can live with me and we'll get a dog.'

'Are you going to move out soon?'

'Why? Do you want me to go?'

'No. I hated it when you went to school. But I do want a dog.'

I tried to hide my grin.

'Anyway,' she said, leaning her head on my shoulder. 'I won't be able to live with you because you'll have a wife and a family.'

'I'll never love another girl as much as I love you.'

She sighed. 'Liar.'

Just before dawn the next day the train stopped for the passengers to stretch their legs. The light was silvery, just clear enough to see by, and jugs of hot water were produced for the men to shave. The grass by the side of the tracks was still wet with dew, the air so cold it burned my throat. We huddled together, scarves wrapped around our faces so that only our eyes were showing.

'Only six more hours,' my father told us. 'You know, if we stayed on all the way to Lake Victoria we'd have travelled more than five hundred and eighty miles. How about that for engineering? We built this line through swamps, forests, mountains, plains, deserts, you name it. They didn't think we could do it, but we did. And before the bloody Germans, too.'

9

Sometimes I wondered why my father disliked the Germans so much. Maybe, I thought, it was in solidarity with my mother, whose only brother had been killed by them in the War, whereas my father had stayed at home with flat feet. My mother never talked about her brother. I couldn't remember him, but I'd seen a photograph of him in her locket. I thought he looked like her, and like me.

We climbed back aboard and as the train wound its way along the track the sun came out and coloured the landscape outside our window in blushing oranges and coppers and scarlets. Now that we could see better, we realised we were covered in dust from where the desert had blown through the mosquito screen. My mother took out a handkerchief and rubbed at her face, but said nothing, and the window stayed open.

A few hours after sunrise, the air was already shimmering with heat. Maud and I sat with our faces turned towards the view and I felt my stomach knotting with relief and excitement. Overnight, the scenery had turned dramatic – plains stretching endlessly away from us, matched by a colossal, empty sky. Looking upwards I saw it carried on blankly forever, miles and miles of bright blue and nothing else.

The plains, on the other hand, were warm with life. Giraffes clustered around trees, nibbling at the upper branches, and swooping long necks down to nuzzle at their babies, already taller than my father. Fifty or more zebra marched in a long snaking line towards a nearby pond, where a herd of wildebeest were bathing, the mud darkening their spindly legs. One of them raised his head and stared at the train. He had the gentle eyes of a cow, but a horse's long face.

'Look, Theo,' Maud said, pointing.

I saw a flash of white, brown and black – four gazelles running and leaping abreast of each other to rejoin their herd.

'They're so sweet,' she said, clapping her hands.

I pressed my face against the screen – Dar es Salaam had been

10

exotic, but this new Kenya was the Africa I'd dreamed of, the Africa of H. Rider Haggard, and I was impatient to finish the train journey, to start living in this incredible landscape.

Eventually we saw a city on the horizon. It got closer and closer, the buildings on the outskirts made of daub and wattle, or yellow stone, then sturdier brick buildings, then the train pulled into Nairobi, and we piled out with our luggage onto the wide platform, with the station clock swinging from the canopy above us, showing twelve thirty in the afternoon.

'Well,' my father said. 'Are we ready for our new lives?'

In the hotel lobby I saw a framed photograph of the town in 1904 – rows of identical huts along a dirt track and The Norfolk, newly opened. Nairobi had grown since then, but the hotel still looked the same: a long, low building with a mock-Tudor front, surrounding perfectly manicured gardens and a turquoise pool in a courtyard area. Inside, the roof was supported by rows of gleaming white columns and criss-crossing white beams. It was the grandest building I'd been in. I didn't wonder that Roosevelt had chosen it for his hunting trip.

Our interconnecting rooms were homely, decorated in soft greys and caramel browns and furnished with sleek sofas and lacquered dressers. Chrome and frosted-glass desk lamps provided soft pools of light, and slatted doors to the garden kept the heat out. My father tipped the bellboy another penny and closed the door behind him.

'What do we think?' he asked my mother.

She lay down on the bed in their room. 'A soft mattress at last,' she said. 'Maud, come and unpin my hair.'

My sister knelt by the side of the bed removing hairpins one by one until her hair fell in a fiery mane across the pillow. Maud had inherited red hair from our mother, but hers was a dark mahogany colour, not the pure copper that gleamed before us now.

11

I met my mother's eye. 'Can we go for a swim?' I asked. She shrugged, but gripped my wrist as I turned to collect my bathing shorts.

'Look after your sister,' she said.

Maud and I changed and took our towels downstairs. Out of our room, I was painfully conscious of the bruising on my left thigh that showed just below the bottom of my shorts. My mother had been responsible for that, after I'd made too much noise outside her hotel room one afternoon in Dar. She'd had a headache but I'd forgotten, and the fact that I'd brought the beating on myself only made me want to hide the evidence even more, so when we reached the garden path I sped up. By the time I reached the pool I was running. I dropped my towel and sprang forwards, feeling my muscles uncoil after days of cramped conditions, and hitting the water with a smack.

I let myself sink to the bottom, holding my breath until I thought I was going to pass out, then clawed my way back to the surface. Maud was sitting cross-legged by the side of the pool. I could tell she'd been watching for my bubbles.

'One day you're going to go too far,' she said.

We stayed for an hour, racing each other, doing handstands underwater, then drying off in the sun. It was early afternoon when we went back into the hotel and the lobby was deserted. The receptionist was talking to someone in the office – we could hear his voice floating out but not the words. We walked through the room, trailing our fingers over the deep armchairs arranged in groups around it. Our footsteps rang differently across the wooden floors, Maud's slapping as she ran ahead, mine padding softly behind her. I'd been in a grand hotel in Edinburgh before, but that had been stuffy, smaller and darker and filled with elderly people asleep in uncomfortable leather chairs. The Norfolk was nothing like that.

'We should put some clothes on,' Maud said when we'd done a full circuit. 'Someone might see us.'

'Mm–hmm.'

'Are you coming?'

'Later,' I said. I heard her skidding off, but I was already looking at the covered terrace outside the hotel. The same plush armchairs were assembled out there, but two of them were occupied. I felt myself mysteriously drawn in their direction, not minding that the occupants were in a private conversation, or that I was naked other than bathing shorts.

At first I thought they were a young boy and an old man – since only old men wore brightly coloured African shawls – but then I reached the edge of the terrace and saw that the old man was young and blond, and the boy's flannel shirt gave way to a long, white neck, and above that a slim face, half-hidden by a cocktail glass, but visible enough for me to see a woman's painted mouth and elegant nose. More than that I noticed her eyes, which were fixed on me over the rim of her glass; they were the colour of the last moment of an African sunset, when the sky deepens with violets and blackish-blues, and they made me feel hollow. She was the finest, most delicate person I'd ever come across, a living china doll with porcelain skin and wide, doe-like eyes and black hair so shiny it was like an oil slick. When she smiled I felt a surge of energy in my stomach.

He had his hand on her knee, but lightly, as if he didn't need to keep track of it. Her body was twisted towards him, one elbow resting on the arm of her chair and her face propped up in her hand.

When I didn't look away she smiled, and dropped her gaze, then murmured something to the man who turned to look at me properly. He smiled too and called me over, and I felt a flush rising through my body that had nothing to do with the sweltering heat; I fled back inside the hotel, leaving them laughing at my shadow.

That was my first glimpse of Sylvie and Freddie.

Chapter Two

A few days later I was sitting at one of the outer tables on the terrace with my mother and Maud. It was nine pm, the hotel busier now, and the moon was out, much lower and larger in the sky than back at home. A few feet away in the dark was the creaking sound of a calling nightjar and the buzzing of katydids. Each table had a flickering candle to see by and waiters moved silently in and out of the shadows, bearing trays of cocktails and olives. A low hum of conversation filled the air.

'I don't know where your father's got to,' my mother said.

'Mr MacDonald probably invited him for supper.'

She sighed.

'Excuse me…' The voice came from behind me. I turned and recognised the blond-haired man. He wasn't wearing a shawl this time, but a shirt and dinner jacket. His face was half hidden in the darkness, but I could see a gleaming row of teeth and the whites of his eyes.

'Yes?' my mother said.

He stepped forwards. 'I couldn't help noticing you're new here.' He winked at me as he said it, and I flushed as deeply as I had at our first meeting. 'I'm Freddie. Freddie Hamilton.'

'Jessie Miller,' my mother said warily. 'My husband is William and these two are Theo and Maud.'

'*Come into the garden, Maud,*' he said.

'My favourite poem.' My mother smiled and I realised, thankfully, that she wasn't going to be difficult.

'I should congratulate you on two very good-looking children,' Freddie said, and I felt he was looking at me particularly when he said it. 'But how could they be otherwise with such an attractive mother?' He clapped his hand on my shoulder and I started. 'How old are you, Theo?'

'Nearly fifteen,' I said, at the same time that my mother said, 'Fourteen.'

'You make friends so quickly, Freddie,' a woman said, and I felt myself tense under his hand as she came into the light, her eyes even darker and wider than before. I caught a hint of her scent in the air – musky and fruity, and intoxicating, like her voice, which was husky, with an American twang. It was nothing like the voice I'd given her in all the conversations I'd imagined us having over the last few days.

She was so close to me that I could have reached out my right hand and touched her. She was wearing the same outfit as before, with the addition of a small monkey perched on her shoulder. Now she was standing, I could see how long her legs were.

'He's called Roderigo,' she said, and I realised she must have been watching me. 'I'm Sylvie de Croÿ.'

'These are the Millers,' Freddie said. 'Jessie, Theo and Maud.'

'Can I hold him?' Maud asked.

'Of course you can.' Sylvie offered her forefinger to Roderigo, who wrapped his paws around it, and swung him off her shoulder into Maud's lap.

'He doesn't bite, does he?' my mother asked.

'This one's tame,' Freddie said.

'Freddie bought him for me,' Sylvie said. 'He knows a man.'

'You have to be careful who you buy them from. The locals

know we like to have them as pets, so sometimes they wait underneath marula trees and catch them as they fall out, then pretend they've been domesticated for years.'

He still had his hand on my shoulder, weighing on me. I'd come across boys like him at school – popular, witty, larger-than-life. In comparison to them I'd always felt smaller and wirier than ever, with big, clumsy hands and feet.

I cleared my throat, trying to get my voice to sound as confident as Freddie's. 'What makes them fall out?'

'Marula fruit gets them soused,' he said.

'He's so sweet,' Maud said.

'He's very naughty,' Sylvie said, and smiled slowly.

'And what brings you all to Kenya?' Freddie asked.

'That would be my husband,' my mother said.

'He's the new Director of the railway,' I said.

Back in Scotland, our neighbours had been amazed at my father's job offer. Freddie and Sylvie didn't even bat an eye. I shrank back in my chair, embarrassed that I'd tried so obviously to impress them.

'The "lunatic line",' Freddie said. 'That's what they call it around here.'

I'd heard the name too. My father didn't like it.

'Of course it was going to be a difficult project,' he'd said once. 'It was the biggest we'd ever undertaken.' The line had taken five years to construct, and he'd lost many of his Indian workers, shipped over by the British for the job. They'd been struck down by dysentery or malaria, and, in the worst cases, the malaria developed into blackwater fever, where the red blood cells burst in the bloodstream.

'You have to know the symptoms to look out for,' he'd told us. 'Chills, rigor, vomiting. Black urine was the worst. If we saw that, we knew they were as good as dead.'

Sylvie took a cigarette case out of the pocket of her slacks. Her fingers were slim and delicate, but her nails were ragged and unvarnished. 'I took the train when I first got in,' she said. There was a kind of bubble in her voice, like she was holding back laughter. 'My husband was sick after eating that brown stuff they serve.'

'Windsor soup,' I said, surprised. I couldn't imagine Freddie being ill.

She leaned forwards and lit her cigarette with our candle. 'I hear it built the British Empire.' She bowed her head when she was talking, making it hard to tell who she was looking at.

'Oh, here's William,' my mother said.

We all turned to look at my father, who was picking his way around the other tables on the terrace. He knocked into the back of a white-haired old lady's chair, and she glared at him. I wished suddenly that he was younger, more dashing.

'I'm sorry I'm late, darling,' he said to my mother as he reached us.

She tipped her face upwards to receive his kiss. 'Freddie, Sylvie, this is my husband, William.'

My father held out his hand and Freddie removed his from my shoulder; Freddie's nails were in much better condition than Sylvie's – smooth and blush-coloured.

'Pleased to meet you,' my father said. He shook hands with Freddie and Sylvie then mopped his forehead with a handkerchief. Out of the corner of my eye I saw Freddie wipe his fingers on his trousers.

'Would you like to join us for a drink?' my mother asked.

'We'd love to,' Freddie said.

'Theo, Maud, give up your seats,' she said, and we hopped up.

The grown-ups ordered drinks and we hovered nearby, Maud busy cradling Roderigo. It was well after our usual suppertime, but I was still brimming with energy somehow, even with an empty stomach.

Freddie sprawled back in my chair, the ankle of his left leg resting on the knee of his right. He was extremely physical, his

17

hands constantly on the move, tapping his fingers on his foot then on the arm of his chair.

'I can't believe you've never seen Kirlton,' he was saying. 'How can you call yourself a Scot? When we were growing up I thought it was more important than Buckingham Palace.'

'I've never seen Buckingham Palace either,' my mother said.

'Now you're just being contrary.'

My mother laughed. 'So is it still in your family?'

'No,' Freddie said. 'My grandmother sold it, cursed woman. Generations of bad money management. My father even has to,' he leaned forwards, '*work*.'

She smiled. 'I don't believe you.'

'It's true. For the Foreign Office. He was training me up to replace him, but I married an unsuitable woman and came out here to be a farmer instead.'

I felt a thrill at hearing Sylvie described as 'unsuitable' and wished my mother would ask him more about it.

'Well, you're young enough to get away with it,' my mother said.

'You noticed,' Freddie said, grinning.

'You can't be more than twenty-eight.'

'Twenty-five in May, actually. But you can't be more than eighteen.'

'Now you're being cruel,' my mother said.

Sylvie was talking to my father about the railway. People's expressions, especially women's, usually started to glaze over within five minutes of the topic, but Sylvie was keeping up with him, asking him questions. Every time she exhaled she turned away so the smoke wouldn't go in my father's face. In profile, hers seemed sharper somehow, her nose and jaw clearly defined and her lashes long and sweeping. Her eyes protruded slightly, and she kept her lids halfway down, blinking dreamily. She spoke dreamily too; if Freddie was a torrent, Sylvie was like a slow-moving river.

18

'Look, Theo,' Maud said, appearing at my side. 'Roderigo's gone to sleep . . . I think he's snoring.' She put her head down to listen.

'Maud, don't get too close to the monkey's mouth,' my mother said.

'Freddie said he was tame,' I said.

'Mr Hamilton, Theo.'

'Freddie, I insist,' Freddie said. 'Especially as we're countrymen. It's good to hear my name pronounced correctly for once.'

'Was that meant for me?' Sylvie asked.

Freddie took her hand and kissed it. '*You* torture it more than the natives.'

'I'm not surprised if they don't get it right,' Sylvie said, withdrawing her hand. 'They're all terrified of you.' She cocked an eyebrow at him and he laughed.

'Edie's got you pegged,' he said, and turned to my parents. 'Edie's my wife.'

I felt my stomach lurch – as if I was back at school in one of the rugby games, a bigger boy rushing towards me. So they weren't married, or at least not to each other.

'What does she say?' Sylvie asked, smiling.

'That you're a wicked Madonna, slaying the menfolk and defending the vulnerable.' He stood up and drew her up after him, slipping his arm around her back. She went slack and seemed to lean into him, raising her eyes to meet his and smiling that slow smile. I felt myself prickle with envy and admiration, but also embarrassment at my misunderstanding. They were the two most beautiful, exciting people in Africa. Marriage would have been too ordinary for them. Of course they were lovers.

'Look at you –' Freddie said. He lifted his free hand up to Sylvie's face and ran his thumb across her lips. She made a snapping sound, like she was about to bite it, and he moved it quickly, laughing at her. I looked at my parents. They were both checking their watches, and I hoped it wasn't time to go.

19

'Well.' Freddie bowed his head at my mother. 'We should leave you to have your supper.'

My father stood up. 'Yes – we better eat soon. Paid for the food here all week – don't want to waste it.'

Sylvie turned away and I had a sudden dread that we'd never see them again. I took a step forwards. 'Are you staying at the hotel?' I asked.

My parents looked surprised. Freddie and Sylvie looked amused.

'For tonight,' Freddie said. 'I'm driving back to African Kirlton tomorrow, but I'll be in Nairobi again for Race Week.'

'What's that?'

'One of the highlights of the social calendar here,' he said. He looked at my parents. 'It happens over Christmas. I'd be happy to take you around it if you're interested?'

I prayed they'd accept.

'Don't feel like you have to,' my mother said.

'I don't,' Freddie said. He kissed her hand. 'Good to meet you, Jessie, William, Maud, Theo. I'll call for you in a week.'

My mother stood too and they all shook hands.

'Very nice to meet you,' my father said.

'Nice to meet you too,' Sylvie said. She came towards me and reached out her hands. For a moment I thought she was going to touch me, and my legs trembled, but she lifted Roderigo out of Maud's arms instead, then left.

Chapter Three

On Friday morning my father said he'd take the afternoon off to show us around Nairobi. By midday the sun was fierce, and the lobby, where we were supposed to meet, was busy. I escaped into the garden and found my mother and Maud already out there. They were with another couple, a tall, dignified-looking man with thinning hair and a bristly moustache, and a slim, serious woman with dark, bobbed hair and a pretty, oval-shaped face. He was probably a little younger than my father, and she was probably a little younger than my mother. They were all standing on the garden path, and the woman was naming the flowers growing in the beds nearby.

My mother waved me over. 'This is my eldest,' she said. 'Theo, say hello to Sir Edward and Lady Joan Grigg. Sir Edward is the Governor of Kenya.'

'How do you do?' I said.

Lady Joan looked me up and down and smiled at my mother. 'I'm glad we don't have a daughter,' she said, which I thought was an odd remark.

'Joanie's trying to twist your mother's arm,' Sir Edward said to me. When he talked his moustache bristled even more. 'She wants her to help out with the Welfare League she's going to create.'

21

My mother spread her hands helplessly. 'I don't know anything about nursing or midwifery. What exactly could I do?'

'Fundraising.'

'I don't have much experience of that, either.'

'Every woman's had to extract money from someone at some point,' Lady Joan said. 'And it's a good cause.' She nodded at me and Maud. 'You've had children of your own. White settlers think the natives don't feel pain when giving birth, but that's completely ridiculous. We *need* to provide proper midwifery training for them.'

Sir Edward made a show of looking at his wristwatch. 'I think I'll head back to Government House. Leave you ladies to discuss the . . . finer points.'

'No, don't go,' Lady Joan said. She turned back to my mother. 'I won't force you, of course. Just think about it.'

'Well . . .'

'She won't leave you alone now,' Sir Edward said, laying a hand on his wife's arm. 'It's much easier to give in, believe me.' He looked at Lady Joan as if he admired her and she rolled her eyes.

I felt the sun beating down on my head and shoulders, and wondered how much longer we were going to stand around.

'You must come over for supper,' Lady Joan said. 'I can put my case across properly.'

'Do you have any wild animals?' Maud asked.

'I'm afraid not,' Sir Edward said. 'We have lots of dogs, though. Do you like dogs? One of our bitches has just got pregnant.'

'I like dogs,' Maud said solemnly.

'Perhaps we can find a puppy for you,' Sir Edward said.

'Then it's decided,' Lady Joan said. 'Come around for supper and choose your dog.'

'It's very kind of you,' my mother said. 'But we leave for Naivasha in a few weeks, and of course, there's Christmas before that . . .'

'And Race Week,' I said, suddenly more awake. 'Freddie'll be showing us around then.'

'Lord Hamilton?' Sir Edward asked.

'Yes.'

'Did you know him before you came out?'

'We met him the other night,' my mother said, frowning at me.

Sir Edward raised his eyebrows. 'That might be his fastest work yet.'

'I'm sorry?'

'The government officials have a name for that crowd,' Lady Joan said. 'The Happy Valley set.'

My mother looked helpless again. 'I'm not sure I understand.'

'The "Valley" is because they live in the Wanjohi Valley region. The "Happy" . . .' She glanced at Maud and then me. 'I wouldn't really like to say.'

'Freddie's a decent sort,' Sir Edward said. 'He takes his farming seriously. And he's going to be High Constable of Scotland when his father dies. That'll force him to grow up.'

'I liked him,' I said.

'He's very charming,' Lady Joan said, 'and you're very young. But he's not a good friend to have.'

I fixed my gaze over her shoulder so I wouldn't have to look at her properly. I'd changed my mind – she wasn't pretty at all.

'He's *her* third husband,' she continued. 'And I've heard bad things about their new guests – the de Croÿs. I don't believe Madame de Croÿ is a good influence.'

'You don't know her,' I blurted.

Lady Joan gave me an odd look.

'We shouldn't keep you,' my mother said, holding out her hand again. 'And it's very kind of you to invite us over. I know William will be delighted to meet you.'

Sir Edward touched his wife gently on the shoulder. 'Come on, Joanie,' he said. 'We should be getting back.'

'I'll be in touch about the League,' she said.

'Please do.'

They headed off.

My mother turned to Maud. 'Can you run out to the front of the hotel, darling, and see if your father is there yet?'

She waited until we were alone before beckoning me to her and twisting my ear viciously until it couldn't go any further. I bit my tongue to stop myself from crying out. 'Don't be so stupid,' she hissed, and shoved me away. 'Do you want us to have a chance out here or do you want to ruin it?'

I pressed my palm against the ear, trying to stop it throbbing. 'Why can't we have a chance with Freddie and Sylvie?'

My mother started walking away. 'You don't understand people,' she said over her shoulder.

My father hadn't arrived yet, so Maud and I waited on the terrace. I sat with my head against the cool of a pillar, boiling with anger; Maud sat next to me.

'Lady Joan's a bloody old witch,' I said.

'I liked her.'

'She's got something against Freddie and Sylvie, and now Mother's bound to stop us being friends with them.'

Maud turned her face to me, eyes serious. 'Mother only ever does something because she thinks it's right.'

'She does whatever she wants at the time.'

'But she loves us, Theo.'

'I don't –'

'There you are.' Our father appeared before us and I bit my tongue.

Maud was sent to fetch our mother. We piled into the Model T Box Body my father had hired and drove away from The Norfolk, down Government Road and into the centre of the town. After a while, it got too hot with all of us in the front seat, and I switched to standing on the running board, hooking my arm through the door to stay on. Some of the roads had been laid properly, but many were made of a type of crushed gravel and a slight breeze blew its dust into my eyes and mouth. Every time my forearm touched the scorching metal a white-hot pain went through me, but it felt cleansing. My mother wouldn't look in my direction, and I dreamed of catching her attention somehow – throwing myself off in front of another car maybe – and forcing her to see me, apologise to me.

Nairobi reminded me of the frontier towns in the Westerns I'd seen, with hitching posts outside the buildings and troughs for the horses. Only the people made it clear we weren't in America. I tried not to stare at the women wearing skirts and nothing else, carrying large earthenware jugs on their heads.

My father showed us 'railway hill', where George Whitehouse had built his first house. He'd been the chief engineer of the railway, and my father used his church voice when he spoke about him.

'The town was founded as a railway depot,' he said, 'and now it's the capital of British East Africa.'

We turned onto 6th Avenue at the corner where the Standard Bank of South Africa stood. Groups of white settlers were standing on the bank's porch, talking and smoking, and thick blue clouds had gathered around their heads. As we drove past my eyes began to sting.

Further up the road was the post office, with a white flag hanging from the tall flagpole in front of the building.

'A blue flag means the mail ship's left Aden for Mombasa,' my father said. 'A red flag means overseas mail has been received. The white flag means the mail's ready for distribution. Not very sophisticated, but the couriers will find you anywhere – even on safari.'

'Can I send a postcard to Grandma?' Maud asked.

'Good idea,' he said.

The car juddered to a halt in front of the building, and I stepped down from the running board, stretching my back and arms. The sun was almost directly overhead and my skin felt tender from exposure to it. My mother made her way to the shade of a gum tree, fanning herself with the two wide-brimmed, floppy hats that all the women wore out here. She was still ignoring me and I suddenly couldn't bear to be near her.

'Maud, choose a postcard,' my father said, mopping his forehead. 'I need to send a telegram to the Glasgow office, and then we'll head back.'

'Can I stay out?' I asked him. 'I don't mind walking home.'

My father looked to my mother and I felt my heart sink. Out of the corner of my eye, her expression was impossible to read. I scuffed my shoe in the dirt.

'Don't walk in the sunshine,' she said eventually. 'Here, take some money just in case.' She held out some coins and I stepped towards her warily. 'Remember – stay in the shade.'

'I will,' I mumbled.

She surprised me by kissing my forehead. 'And be back at the hotel by four o'clock, or we'll start to worry. We don't want to lose you.'

My anger dissolved into gratitude at how quickly my punishment seemed to be over, and I started down the road with no clear idea of where I was going, relishing the opportunity to explore. Leaving the main streets behind me, I ended up in a more residential area, where most of the houses were bungalow mansions with tiled roofs, smallish windows and verandas supported by brick pillars. Perfectly straight paths ran between veranda and white picket fence, where flowers bloomed in pinks, purples, blues and creams, and in front of each house immaculate green lawns lay like carpets rolled out for important visitors. The road was wide, and dappled in the sun. I thought of the red tenements in Edinburgh, five storeys high and always cold inside, and felt a smile forming on my face.

These streets were mostly empty, but after a while I started to pick up a buzzing sound and, turning a corner, I stumbled on an open-air market. Stalls had been set up displaying all manner of produce: carnations, violets, tomatoes, large brown eggs, limes,

26

courgettes, green bananas, aubergines, sacks of flour and dusty potatoes. People were thronging the aisles, squeezing and weighing the vegetables, and swatting away the flies that hovered at face-height. I hesitated, overwhelmed for a moment, but when I finally ventured in no one paid me any attention until I reached a crossroads in the market and paused, trying to decide where to go. A few shoppers knocked into me, and I felt a tap on my shoulder and smelled amber and peach. 'You're a lone beast, aren't you, Theo?'

It was Sylvie. She was wearing a loose-fitting black blouse with a plunging neckline that ended just above her bellybutton, and black velvet trousers. Roderigo was wrapped around her neck, nibbling her earlobe. I got the impression she was laughing at me in a friendly way, although she wasn't actually smiling. I felt a rush of panicked excitement at being alone with her.

'I see you've found Mr Sand's market,' she said. 'Here every Tuesday and Friday.'

'Oh?' I cursed myself for being so tongue-tied.

'And what are you up to?' she said, with that bubble in her voice again. 'Buying provisions for The Norfolk kitchen?'

'Just looking.'

'Mm-hmm?'

It was hard not to stare at the apricot-coloured skin stretched taut over her stomach. She was still watching me, her head cocked to one side. I tried for the most grown-up conversation I knew, 'Would you like to have a drink?'

Now she laughed for real, throatily. 'Are you asking me on a date?'

Blood thrummed in my ears. 'I'm . . .'

'I'd love to have a drink with you.'

She fell into step with me. My body moved automatically, steering a path through the crowds and towards a bar on the side of the square. Despite all the people around, it was empty, and several of the tables had dirty glasses or overflowing ashtrays on them.

27

She sat in a chair on the porch, and I sat opposite her. When she leaned towards me I saw that she wasn't wearing a brassiere, and her small, firm-looking breasts had dark nipples. My hand was on the table, and for a moment I thought they might brush against it. I bit my tongue, desperately trying to distract myself.

Roderigo scampered onto the table between us, exploring the ashtray, picking up the butts and tasting them before spitting them out onto the floor.

Sylvie folded her hands neatly in her lap and smiled mischievously. 'I've never been taken here for a drink – I hear it's quite unwholesome.'

I jumped up, my face burning. 'We can go somewhere else.'

'I want to stay here.' She laughed at me again and signalled for the waiter. 'I'll have a whisky sour,' she told him. 'And this gentleman will have some wine-and-water.'

The waiter went away without saying anything, but I thought I saw him sneer at me. Freddie would have known exactly where to take her, I told myself, and he would have done the ordering.

Sylvie took out her cigarette case and lit a cigarette. 'Good,' she said. 'Now I can get to know you properly.'

'There's not much to know.'

'Don't be so hard on yourself. People are talking about you already, you know.'

'Why?'

'You're absurdly handsome, Theo.'

I felt my heart beating violently in my throat. I'd never been made to feel handsome by people my own age – it seemed too manly a word – but maybe adults had a different idea of beauty to children and I thought how wonderful it would be to be part of a world where I was appreciated rather than laughed at.

Sylvie gave me her special smile and breathed blue smoke out of her nostrils. 'Freddie noticed it,' she said, 'the first time we saw you at the hotel. He said "Who's that beautiful boy over there?" You were like a wild animal, the way you were watching

28

us with your big eyes. Then you ran away as soon as we'd spotted you.'

Knowing that Freddie thought that made me feel hot and cold at the same time. I flailed around for something to say. 'Sorry.'

'For what?'

'For running away – it's rude.'

'I wouldn't say that.' She leaned back again in her chair. 'Now, I know you were born in bonny Scotland, but have you lived anywhere else?'

'No. Have you?'

'Born in Buffalo twenty-five years ago,' she said, pulling on her cigarette. 'Mother died when I was seven, father remarried.' She parted her lips slightly to let the smoke curl out of her mouth. 'I actually liked my stepmother, but my father was a bit of a kook, so I went to live with Aunt Tattie in Chicago when I was thirteen. Then she decided I was running with some unsavoury characters so she took me to Paris, where I met my husband, the Comte de Croÿ.'

The Comte de Croÿ; I rolled the title around in my head – he was probably old and rich and fat.

Our drinks arrived and Sylvie waited until the waiter had gone before continuing, 'We lived for a little while in Beaufort, his castle in Normandy, but I felt . . . trapped. So he agreed to bring me out here.'

So he was some provincial Frenchman who didn't speak a word of English and ignored her. I remembered Lady Joan's disapproving face when she mentioned Sylvie, and felt a surge of protective anger. Why should she stay with her husband if she was unhappy? If someone younger came along who could make her laugh, and look after her, then why shouldn't she be with them?

Sylvie dropped her cigarette on the floor and ground it out, then scooped Roderigo up in one arm. 'And that's the potted history.' She held her glass up and I chinked mine against it. '*Salut.* Your turn.'

29

'Born in Scotland,' I said, shifting in my seat. 'Lived there until a month or so ago. Both parents alive. One sister.'

'She's charming. She reminds me of my eldest daughter.'

I took a sip of my wine, but it went down the wrong way and I broke into a coughing fit. Sylvie took out another cigarette and lit it, pretending she hadn't noticed. I took a second sip of the wine, trying to calm my throat. 'I didn't know you had children. You don't look old enough.'

'I'm not,' Sylvie said. 'I wasn't. I should have waited.' She drained her whisky sour and gestured to the waiter for another. 'They're both living in France with Aunt Tattie. Great Aunt Tattie now.'

'Oh.'

'They're adorable, but they're . . .' She leaned back in her chair, resting her head against it. 'People. Human beings.' Roderigo climbed back up to his perch on her shoulder and she scratched him behind his ear.

'I suppose so.'

She smiled. 'I mean – they're real. And they're so small and they need you so much, and I couldn't be sure I wasn't going to mess up their lives.'

She looked so beautiful and fragile. I knew I should say something, but I didn't want to disturb her, either.

'I'm sure you wouldn't. You're very nice.'

'I'll give you a tip.' She pulled on her cigarette. 'That's not really a word that women want to be called.'

'Sorry.'

She was laughing at me again, but I didn't mind.

The waiter brought over her second cocktail and we clinked glasses again. I was suddenly, idiotically happy.

'To Africa,' she said. 'And new friends.'

'To new friends.'

When we finished our drinks I tossed the money down onto the table and hurried over to pull out Sylvie's chair for her. Out of the corner of my eye I saw her tip the contents of the ashtray she'd been using onto the floor, and slip the ashtray into her purse. I stopped just beside her, feeling my cheeks flare up.

'Well,' she was saying. 'Now I can cross this bar off my to-do list.'

'Yes,' I mumbled.

She looked up at me expectantly. My mind was racing – maybe her husband controlled the money and wouldn't give her any. Maybe she was keeping it as a souvenir of our drink together.

'I'm sorry,' she said, 'I can't get up with you standing there.'

I looked at her properly and she smiled. I felt her perfume envelop me.

'Let me,' I said, and moved her chair back for her as she stood.

'You're a rarity, Theo,' she said. 'Beautiful people don't usually have beautiful natures.'

My breath caught in my chest, making me feel dizzy. Without thinking about it I offered her my arm, as I'd seen young men do to young women before. Sylvie considered it gravely, then slipped her arm through mine. I knew I would be late back to the hotel, and my mother would probably be angry, but it didn't seem to matter any more.

'Where shall we go?' I asked.

Chapter Four

Christmas arrived a week later. I woke with the sunshine falling across my face. 'Auntie', the white-haired proprietor of The Norfolk, had arranged for stockings filled with oranges, nuts and chocolate to be hung on each guest's door, and we ate the food with the shutters and garden doors wide open, the sky blossoming above us into a rich, cloudless blue. Ten feet away a group of white-bellied-go-away-birds gathered, bleating to each other on the branch of a mango tree. It was a world away from Christmas at home.

Down in the lobby, the staff had decorated the Christmas tree with bells and coloured candles, and guests were drinking glasses of champagne, fanning themselves in the heat. My parents joined them while we went for a swim, staying on the edge of the other groups of children, then we took a rickshaw to the Carlton Grill on Government Road.

By the time we arrived the place was almost full. Other families were already seated and pulling crackers, and the smell of herbs and woodsmoke billowed through the room. My father ordered us mutton chops cooked on an open fire in front of us, the juiciest meat I'd ever eaten. Afterwards, we had Christmas pudding, then climbed back into rickshaws for a ride around town. Coloured lights had been strung up along 6th Avenue, and a man dressed as Father Christmas was standing on the corner, handing out candy canes to passing children.

'Take one for me, Theo,' Maud said. I stretched out my arm as we passed and Santa threw a cane to me.

It was dark by the time we returned to the hotel. A pianist was playing carols in the lobby, and glasses filled with port stood in rows on the bar. Auntie moved between the various groups dotted around the room, smiling, asking after relatives and telling stories of her own. Maud and I gave our mother a tortoiseshell comb, and our father a book. Our presents from them were a pair of new shoes and a whistle each, and when Maud wasn't looking, my father slipped me a few banknotes.

'Isn't this fun, children?' he said, and winked at me.

Maud hung her whistle around her neck. 'It's so shiny.'

'It's not a toy,' I said. 'It's to scare away animals if you come across them in the wild.'

'They won't hurt us,' she said. 'Animals only attack if they're frightened.'

'Quite so,' my father said, looking around. 'Can you see if they've run out of the port?'

'What if they're angry?' I asked Maud.

'Animals don't get angry. Only people do.'

I shrugged, looking away. Several of the other boys staying at the hotel had been given airguns, and were running around the garden with them. I watched them out of the corner of my eye, trying not to give away how much I wanted to join them. My mother must have noticed however, because she took my chin in her hand, digging her fingers into my jaw.

'I hope you're not going to leave us,' she said. 'Christmas is family time.'

'Oh good,' my father said, holding up his empty glass. 'They're bringing it round now.'

★　★　★

33

The next few days were hot and humid, with no sun in sight behind a wall of clouds. The flowers were already wilting at the breakfast table when Freddie appeared beside us. He smelled of pomade and oil, and I guessed he'd just driven into town. He shook hands with my father and me, and kissed my mother's and Maud's hands.

'I hope you're still in the market for a guide,' he said. 'I hear the first race today is a good one.'

'Actually,' my mother said, folding her napkin on the table. 'I'm not sure we can attend. We've been invited to lunch by the Griggs. I'm very sorry to put you out.'

'Ah – our illustrious Governor,' Freddie said. 'Well that'll certainly be a more dignified afternoon.'

There was a silence, and in that moment I hated my parents, and the dull way they lived their lives, even in Africa. If they'd driven him away, I'd never forgive them, I told myself. I wanted to tug the tablecloth off and break everything on the table.

'I'll leave you to your breakfast then,' Freddie said after a while. 'But you'll come and visit when you're settled in Naivasha, won't you?'

'Of course,' my mother said.

'Well that's something.' He winked at me, and I realised with relief that he wasn't angry. He said goodbye and we went back to our breakfast, although I'd lost my appetite and I pushed my porridge away.

'Can I go into town?' I asked my mother. 'I want to see if the market's open.'

'Don't you want to go swimming?' she asked.

'No.'

She narrowed her eyes at me.

'I won't be long.'

'Why not?' my father said. He leaned closer to me. 'Maybe you can go to the bank, too? Look into some investment opportunities?'

'I'll do that,' I said.

'If you're only going that far you should be back in two hours,' my mother said. 'I don't want a repeat of last time.'

I looked at a point just past her left ear. 'I told you I got lost.'

'Don't get lost again.'

As I was turning left out of the hotel gate, I heard someone call my name. Freddie was sitting in his car a few yards down the road, smiling at me. The car was huge: a dark green, open-top Hispano-Suiza with a long shiny body at the front and high wheels.

'I thought you might change your mind,' he said, when I reached him. 'My old man was always trying to force me into that world too. Foreign Office engagements with lots of government bores. So . . .' He smiled at me. 'Still keen to see the races?'

'Yes please.' I took a deep breath. 'I've never been before.'

'And your parents? They approve of you attending with me?'

'Yes.'

He looked at me closely, and I tried to keep my face neutral. He laughed. 'Hop in then.'

I climbed into the passenger seat as Freddie started the engine. The leather was blood-red and soft as butter. As he pulled away from the kerb I turned to face him. Close up, and in the daylight, his skin was smooth and creamy. I had an urge to reach out and run my finger along his cheek, feel the smoothness for myself.

'I like your car,' I said, raising my voice above the noise.

'A wedding present from my wife.'

'It's a very nice present.'

'She's very rich.'

He pressed his foot down on the pedal and we shot away. I leaned back in my seat and felt my body relax.

The sky was a steel grey by the time we arrived at Kariokor race course, although it was still bright and Freddie shaded his eyes as he searched for rain clouds.

'It almost flooded the first time we came,' he said. 'Thank God they built the grandstand a few years ago.'

'I thought it never rained in Africa,' I said.

'In the rainy season it rains a lot,' Freddie said. 'As a farmer, I'm very thankful.' He looked down at me. 'Would you like to see the stables?'

I nodded.

He led me to a wooden shed with five stalls within. A stable boy looked up from sweeping the yard and nodded at Freddie. 'You want to see the horses, Bwana Hamilton?'

'Who's the favourite in the first race?'

'Chongo.'

'We'll see him,' Freddie said, then stopped. 'Is Wiley Scot running?'

'Yes, Bwana Hamilton.'

'We'll see him then – he's a distant cousin of mine.' He kept his face completely straight when he said it and the stable boy didn't react. I wondered if he'd understood, or if he just thought that Bwana Hamilton was mad.

It was gloomy in the stall, with only a small window high up in the wall, and it smelled like damp and a mix of leather, grain, sweat and peppermints. I felt suddenly trapped, being in such a close, dark space, and I closed my eyes for a moment. I could still hear a rustling, snorting sound, and when I opened my eyes and peered around Freddie's back I could make out a dark chestnut stallion picking restlessly at straw in a feeder. He was tall, with an extremely broad, glossy chest and a heart-shaped patch of white on one thigh. I knew horses were designed for speed and grace, but I found it hard to imagine as we stood in the stall – all I could see was the mountainous torso, the knobbly knees and delicate ankles, and I wondered how his legs didn't snap underneath all that bulk.

Freddie moved forwards and patted Wiley Scot on his muscular neck and the horse threw his head back and began stamping his legs. My heart was hammering.

'Be good now,' Freddie said quietly. The horse breathed out loudly, then stopped stamping.

'He's a beauty,' Freddie said. 'Do you ride?'

'No,' I said.

'Never?' He looked back at me. 'I wouldn't have taken you for a city boy.'

'I'm not.'

Freddie laughed. 'You're very mysterious.'

He turned to face the horse again. He looked so natural in these surroundings, but then he'd looked easy and confident wherever I'd come across him. I could picture him at school, mobs of admiring boys following him down the lane and laughing at his jokes. I felt a smile form on my face – I would never have got within five yards of him there, and here we were now, alone as friends.

'Introduce yourself,' Freddie said.

I went to stand next to him, and ran my hand along the horse's flank. I could feel his muscles trembling under his coat, and smell something coming off him that was almost bitter, like the taste in the back of my throat when my mother was on the warpath. The phrase, 'His blood is up', was circling my brain – *this must be what that means*, I told myself, and realised I was trembling too.

I placed a finger on Wiley Scot's nose, between his wet, dilated nostrils, and stroked downwards. He rolled his eyes until they were mostly white, then shook me off.

'He's nervy today,' Freddie said. He pushed his hat back on his forehead, and I followed the bead of sweat that trickled down from his temple to his collarbone, until it disappeared beneath his shirt. I felt sweat start to form in sympathy on my upper lip, and brushed it away quickly with the back of my hand. 'Let's leave him to it.'

As we were leaving the stables, a few jockeys were walking in our direction, and they greeted Freddie, slapping him on the back and nodding in my direction.

'Better watch out, Freddie,' one of them said. 'You might have a contender here for the ladies in a few years. He makes you look as ugly as the rest of us.' Little flecks of spit hit my face as he laughed.

A second one prodded me in the stomach. 'What sort of little gentleman are you then, sonny? Baron? Earl? Little lord?'

'I'm not a gentleman.'

'Good to hear it – a new order for a new world.' He grinned at Freddie. 'No one's told the toffs yet, though.'

'Don't mind them,' Freddie said to me. 'All the jockeys out here are Englishmen, God save them, so they're not very bright.' He was smiling, but his voice was cold. I kept quiet, and the jockeys went on their way, cackling to themselves. When they'd gone Freddie looked me up and down. His expression made it seem as if he'd just thought of something unpleasant.

'Have you seen enough yet?' he asked eventually. 'Not everyone gets to come back here, you know.'

'Thank you.'

Freddie looked irritated, and I wondered if he'd started to find me dull. I was reminded again of school, and suddenly wanted to go back to the hotel and crawl into my bed.

Freddie shrugged. 'Let's go inside,' he said.

The race course was two miles in circumference, with a rickety grandstand near the finishing line, and a small, peeling bandstand in the middle. A band was already playing – the King's African Rifles Band, Freddie told me – and people were mingling in front of them. As the morning wore on the air became increasingly damp and sticky. Small insects darted through the grass, biting whatever exposed flesh they could find, until I felt as if my ankles were on fire. Freddie found us two glasses of pink gin and I had to stop myself from pressing mine against my forehead to cool down. I was amazed that no one was passing out from the heat.

We drank the gin as Freddie pointed out the officials – the

38

timekeeper, the clerk of the scales and the clerk of the course. The drink was less refreshing than I'd hoped, and following what Freddie was saying became quite difficult. His good mood had disappeared completely, and his eyes were constantly scanning the crowds as if he were looking for someone more interesting to talk to.

'There you are, Freddie,' someone said after a particularly long silence between us. 'Edie left – she said to tell you she was too hot and too pregnant.'

A tall, blue-eyed man wearing a beautifully cut suit had appeared at Freddie's elbow. He had a gentle face with slightly prominent ears and his voice was gentle too, with a hint of an accent.

'Nicolas,' Freddie said. 'This is Theo Miller – I believe you've heard of him.'

Nicolas bowed, and I wondered, sluggishly, why he would have heard of me.

'And where's *your* charming wife?' Freddie asked.

'Sylvie? She's been captured by that brute, Carberry.'

I had to look down at my feet to stop myself from staring wide-eyed at him; so this was the Comte de Croÿ, my fat, old Frenchman who spoke no English.

'Another admirer?' Freddie said. 'Theo, you've got company.'

My cheeks burned to hear how obvious I'd been. I wished I could laugh it off, but I couldn't think of anything to say.

'More accurate to say we *all* do,' Nicolas said.

'You French are so damn philosophical.'

Nicolas bowed again and I caught sight of Sylvie over his head. She was walking in our direction. A dark-haired couple were walking behind her, the man looking at Sylvie's behind. I didn't like his expression, or his skull-like face. His hairline was receding, and his eyes were small and close-set. The brunette with him had a rather large nose and pointy teeth, but nice eyes and an open smile, which she turned on me as they approached.

'A word of warning,' Nicolas said quietly to me, 'John Carberry is the devil. Don't listen to a word he says.'

'Hello, boys,' Sylvie said, and I got a wave of her perfume.

'Hello, darling,' Nicolas said.

'Hello, trouble,' Freddie said.

Sylvie shook her head. 'It's hard to be troublesome when you're sober.'

'Surely not?'

'Surely yes.'

'Let me save you,' Freddie said, but Nicolas held up his hand.

'That's my cue, Freddie. You stay here and look after Sylvie.'

'Thank you, darling,' Sylvie said.

Nicolas gave the dark-haired couple a half-bow and left. I was sorry. Freddie and Sylvie were smiling at each other now in a way that felt exclusive, and when he kissed her hand I felt a shiver run along my neck.

I looked over at the two strangers. The man had on a mocking smile.

'Another husband bites the dust, Freddie?' he said. His voice was flat and had an unusual accent.

Freddie straightened up and Sylvie rolled her eyes. Neither of them looked at all embarrassed.

'I didn't expect to see you here, Carberry,' Freddie said, then turned to me. 'John and Bubbles, this is Theo Miller.'

'Maia Anderson,' Carberry said. 'Bubbles is a stupid name.'

Sylvie turned away with an angry expression on her face, and I guessed she had the same reaction to Carberry that I had.

'Where's Roderigo?' I asked her.

'Edie took him to The Norfolk,' she said, and smiled wickedly. 'He kept stealing all the ladies' hats.'

'And wearing them,' Maia said. 'The worst of it was he looked better in mine than me.'

'Baloney. You look lovely.'

'You're too sweet, Sylvie.'

'You know what to do with monkeys who steal?' Carberry said.

'What?'

'Chop their paws off. Same with the natives, they won't do it again.'

Sylvie looked sickened. Freddie raised an eyebrow.

Carberry jerked his thumb in my direction. 'Speaking of natives, don't you think this one here could almost pass for one of them? He's got the thick lips and the crafty eyes.'

'Is that meant to be an insult?' Sylvie said icily. She put her hand up to touch her thick, dark hair, and I wondered if anyone had ever made the same comparison with her.

Carberry leered at me. 'I bet I know what happened. Grandfather probably fucked a slave-girl.'

I'd heard this sort of thing from boys at school, but never from an adult, and my ears burned in shock. I saw Carberry's face crease up with laughter. Maia looked embarrassed.

Freddie put his hand firmly on my shoulder. 'See you around, Carberry.'

There was a moment of silence. I could feel Freddie's fingers gripping me hard.

'Pompous Brits,' Carberry said at last. He took Maia by the elbow and steered her away. She looked back at us and mouthed 'sorry' over her shoulder. I felt Freddie relax.

Sylvie swung around to face us, eyes black in anger.

'I know, I know,' Freddie said, although she hadn't said anything. 'I feel sorry for Bubbles.' He took his hand off me, and I felt a surge of relief – Freddie was still my friend, he'd saved me from Carberry.

'Are you alright, Theo?' Sylvie asked.

'Is *he* alright?' Freddie said. 'I had to physically restrain him, or he might have beaten Carberry to a pulp.'

I looked down and saw my body was shaking, and my hands were in fists. I hadn't even realised.

The races started just after one pm, by which point my head was pounding from the gin and the closeness of the air. I'd no idea what excuse I could give my mother for staying out so long – that was a problem some other Theo would have to deal with. This Theo sat between Nicolas and Freddie in the grandstand, with Sylvie on Freddie's other side. First up, Nicolas told me, was the divided pony handicaps. I could barely watch. The thundering of the horses' hooves as they swept past made my headache a thousand times worse, and I closed my eyes so their blurred forms wouldn't make me feel too sick. I desperately wanted some water, but no one had offered me any, and it seemed childish to ask.

Next was the jumps racing. Nicolas and Freddie argued good-naturedly over whether it was called steeplechasing or National Hunt racing. I dozed off in my seat, and woke even thirstier than before.

The feature race was the Jardin Lafitte Cup, a 1400m course. Wiley Scot was running.

'What about a bet on him, Theo?' Freddie asked. 'A simple win-bet?'

'I don't know,' I said, still sleepy. 'What are the other horses like?'

They laughed.

'Very smart,' Nicolas said.

'A disgusting level of pragmatism,' Freddie said. 'Where's your faith?'

'Will they let me bet?' I asked.

'I'll place it for you,' Freddie said. He stood up and held out his hand. I gave him the notes my father had slipped me on Christmas Day. Freddie counted them, then slapped me on the back.

'You're either a bloody idiot or a confident genius,' he said.

Sylvie leaned over and put her hand on my arm. My skin tingled where she was touching me. 'Don't do it if you don't want to,' she said.

'It's just a bit of fun, darling,' Freddie said to her.

'It's fine,' I said.

She moved closer to me to let Freddie pick his way out of the grandstand, and her thigh came to rest against mine. I prayed I wouldn't make a fool of myself, and tried to think of distracting images – suet pudding, my grandmother's bunions, my father in his undergarments.

'I hear you had a run-in with Carberry, Theo,' Nicolas said on my other side.

'I don't think he liked me.'

'He was despicable as usual,' Sylvie said. She took out a cigarette and Nicolas lit it for her.

'Maia's pregnant, you know,' he said.

'Oh God. The poor woman.'

'What did he say to you?' Nicolas asked me.

'He was talking about my appearance.'

'He did that to me as well,' Nicolas said. 'The first time we met, he insinuated I was a closet homosexual. I said, if only I were that interesting.'

He smiled at me and I returned it.

'You're a hundred times more interesting than John Carberry,' Sylvie said.

Their easy conversation confused me, knowing what I did about Sylvie feeling trapped. Nicolas was the nicest person I'd met, I thought, and I wondered what it was about him that was wrong for her.

Freddie returned with more pink gin for everyone and a ticket for me. 'They're leading them on now,' he said.

I looked over and saw the eight horses being walked onto the course, saddled and draped with rugs to keep their muscles warm. I recognised Wiley Scot immediately. Even from a distance he seemed to be quivering.

'*Bonne chance*,' Nicolas said.

I made the effort to tear my eyes away from the animals to look at him and offer a smile, although it felt more like a grimace. The blood was thundering through my body as loudly as the horses had sounded earlier, but otherwise everything was strangely quiet. The crowd was waiting, tense. When the grooms removed the rugs and the jockeys sprang up into the saddles, I was convinced I could hear the creak of the leather, and the murmurs as the men tried to calm their mounts. Wiley Scot bucked and did a side-step, looking like he was trying to shake his rider off.

'He doesn't want to race,' Sylvie said.

'Of course he wants to race,' Freddie said. 'It's all he knows how to do. He's just picking up on the atmosphere.'

The jockeys were lining up on the other side of the course now like coloured specks of dust; red, green, yellow, and Wiley Scot's in dark blue. Nicolas handed me a pair of binoculars and I trained them on the figures with wet hands.

'They're off,' someone called. People were clambering to their feet around me and I jumped up too. The horses were all clumped together at first, but soon they separated out and I picked out Wiley Scot in third place.

Now I saw the elegance in the horses' movements. Their bodies hardly seemed to move at all; heads and chests thrust forward they cut a streamlined shape through the air as their legs curled and stretched out below, each hoof only touching the ground for a fraction of a second before they were flying again.

'Come on, Wiley Scot,' Freddie shouted near me.

He was coming up on the outside of the horse in second place. Now they were closer I could see the sweat darkening his brown coat, and his muscles rippling with each stride, and my throat began to close up with a lump of excitement and fear. I was keenly aware of the ticket between my fingers, the enormity of the money it represented for me. The ground was shaking and the wind that had sprung up blew back the jockeys' jackets like sails. I tightened my hold on the ticket, half-hoping, half-afraid it would be carried away.

Wiley Scot's jockey kicked at him and he passed the second horse. He was gaining on the horse in first place now, with less than fifty yards to go. I was clenching my entire body, my teeth pressed together as if that would spur my horse on, when I saw the first horse stumble and fall, the jockey rolling off his back right into the path of Wiley Scot. I heard Sylvie cry out just as Wiley Scot leaped gracefully, gathering up his legs to clear the figure in front of him, and then he was galloping past us in a cloud of red dust, his head bent down as if for a charge. I only realised I'd stopped breathing when he passed the finishing post and I found myself gasping for air.

'You're rich, young man,' Freddie said, clapping me on the back as the grandstand erupted around us.

The outside of the Muthaiga Club was pink pebbledash and white stone, turning red and gold in the setting sunlight. Freddie guided me up its colonnaded walkway and paused for a moment so I could lean against one of the ivy-covered pillars. After my win, and with Freddie's encouragement, I'd had several more gins, and now the ground seemed dangerously unsteady beneath my feet. Any thought of getting home soon had long since vanished.

'Come on, I'll give you the tour,' Freddie said.

We pushed through the glass door into an airy lobby with a parquet floor and cool cream and green walls. Freddie continued towards the back; I tried to follow him without falling, Sylvie and Nicolas walking behind me.

'Ballroom,' he said, pointing through a set of double doors. 'Bar – no tall stools allowed. Squash courts here, and golf course at the back.' We stepped through a set of French doors onto a covered veranda, and I had an impression of a perfectly manicured lawn, sprinkled with banana plants, ferns, flowerbeds and avenues of eucalyptus trees. Several people were in the middle of a croquet game, and the thud of the mallet meeting the ball carried over to us as we hovered on the step leading down to the garden. I clutched my head and hoped it would stop reeling soon.

'They call it the man's paradise,' Freddie said. 'No Jews allowed, of course.'

45

'Although they've had to let women in,' Sylvie said. 'The balls were a little lonely beforehand.'

'I think I should sit down,' I said.

'You do that,' Freddie said. He helped me back onto the veranda and into a deep wicker chair then called a waiter over.

'We'll have some coffee,' he said. 'And then some champagne.'

I rested my elbows on the table, propping my head up in my hands and massaging my temples with my fingertips. From the ballroom came the sound of a band tuning up.

Sylvie leaned against the pillar to my left and Nicolas came to stand beside her, one hand resting on the small of her back. Her amber smell seemed more powerful than before and my mind was fugged up with it.

Freddie pulled out the chair next to me and sat down. 'You'll feel better soon,' he said, grinning. 'I remember the first time I got tight – even younger than you. I ended up passing out under my friend's parents' bed. No idea how I got there.'

'I'm sure there was a female involved somewhere,' Sylvie said, and Freddie laughed.

The drinks arrived and I grabbed at the coffee, then swallowed it in four gulps.

'That should do the trick,' Freddie said. I looked up and he grinned. 'What about a game? Played croquet before?'

'Yes.'

'Come on then. The four of us versus the four of them.'

I followed him onto the lawn. A waiter followed with our champagne in an ice bucket and placed it at the edge of the croquet court.

There were two men and two women already in the game, and introductions were made, although I only remembered Hugh Cholmondeley – Lord Delamere – who had a large nose that overshadowed all his other features, and a high forehead covered in papery skin. He looked to be in his late fifties, frailer than my father, but still authoritative.

'Mind if we join?' Freddie said.

'We'll start again,' Delamere said. 'Only just got going, anyway.'

He tossed a coin and Nicolas called correctly. Freddie handed me a mallet. 'We'll be blue and black,' he said. 'Association rules here. You know them?'

The coffee was mixing uneasily with the contents of my stomach but at least it had cleared my head. 'I think so.'

'Good. You play first. Start with the south-west hoop.'

The court was rectangular, with a peg driven into the grass at the centre, and three hoops on either side. Four of the hoops stood almost at the corners of the rectangle, with the two inner hoops on each side slightly closer to the peg. I vaguely remembered having to follow a pattern of the outer hoops first, then the inner hoops, then playing another circuit in semi-reverse before you could hit the peg. My hands felt hot and slippery with sweat. It was a long time to keep upright and sober.

Freddie placed both our balls on the ground near the south-west hoop. I gripped my mallet and swung gently at the blue ball. There was a thunk as it made contact, and I felt a momentary wash of relief, but the ball rolled uselessly to the side of the first hoop.

'Never mind,' Freddie called out behind me.

I turned around, face burning, and handed the mallet to Nicolas, then went to stand with the other players, a few yards away from the first hoop.

Lord Delamere took the first turn for the other side and the red ball sailed through the hoop. 'I hear Black Harries was at Kariokor today,' he said, lining up for a continuation stroke.

'I didn't see him,' Freddie said. 'And I'm surprised – I thought he never left Larmudiac.'

'He sounds like a pirate,' Sylvie said, lighting a cigarette.

'He looks like one too – he's got one hell of a black beard. And he's probably the strongest man in Africa.'

'They say he killed a leopard with a single blow to the head,'

Lord Delamere said. The red ball continued its path towards the second hoop, but stopped just short. Nicolas took the next turn and hit the black ball so it stopped just before the first hoop, dead on; Freddie grinned at me and I tried to return it.

'He loves horses,' he said, 'but he doesn't tame them. He has acres and acres of land, and he lets them roam around, but he doesn't geld them or break them in or feed them.'

'What happens with the horses if there's a drought?' Sylvie asked.

'They starve.'

'He sounds cruel.'

'But they're free.' Freddie caught my eye. 'Don't you think animals prefer to be free, Theo?'

'But Harries *isn't* an animal,' Sylvie said. Her lips were white and pressed together. 'He *knows* they'll starve and it's in his power to do something about it.'

'Don't upset yourself, my dear,' Lord Delamere said. He nodded at the ice bucket. 'What if we distribute some of that champagne, eh?'

The champagne was poured, candles were lit on the veranda and suddenly it was my turn again. I stood to the side of the first hoop and lined up the shot more carefully this time. I managed to get the ball halfway through the hoop but when I went to tap it again Delamere called out, 'No continuation stroke – you haven't run it through.'

I handed the mallet over. 'I'm not helping much.'

'You're helping us,' one of the new women said kindly. She pointed at my glass. 'Here – have a top-up.'

We all moved to stand in a line along the west boundary now, watching Delamere's play. The red ball was already through the second hoop, and he took it through the third and the fourth before his turn was up.

'What do you think of that, eh?' he said.

Sylvie had gone quiet since the argument about Black Harries, but now she swore. 'Fucking goddamn it. Not twice in one day.'

I felt the mood change before Carberry reached us, and my heart sank. The conversation died out. Only Freddie looked comfortable still.

'Ill met by moonlight, Carberry,' he said.

'I thought I'd find you here,' Carberry said. 'Talking about Johnny Bull.'

'You're British too,' Freddie said. 'Or Irish, at least. Have you forgotten, Baron Carberry?'

Carberry took out a cigarette. Sylvie was at the end of the line, and he leaned towards her, taking her wrist in his fingers. 'May I?'

She shrugged, but I felt the revulsion coming off her. I took a long drink of my champagne.

Carberry lit his cigarette on hers, then stood back. 'I haven't forgotten,' he said, blowing smoke out in a cloud. 'But I got my American naturalisation papers six years ago.'

'I hear they were revoked,' Lord Delamere said. 'For bootlegging.'

'Finally,' Sylvie said, crushing out her own cigarette in the grass. 'Something interesting about you.'

Carberry nudged the yellow ball with his foot, sending it back towards the start. 'I can't wait to see your faces when your little Empire comes crashing down.'

Lord Delamere turned purple. 'Look, Carberry –'

Carberry snapped his fingers at a waiter on the veranda and called over, 'Bring me a whisky, boy. And don't bother trying to cheat me on the chit – I can read.'

Nicolas stepped onto the court and picked up the yellow ball, returning it to its old spot. 'Lucky for us I have a photographic memory. Excuse us while we continue play, Carberry.'

'Which team are you on?' Carberry asked Sylvie. 'I'll join you. One of the only good British exports, this game.'

She looked away.

'It's my turn,' Nicolas said. 'Take it if you want.'

Carberry took the mallet Nicolas was offering, held his cigarette in his teeth, and hit my blue ball cleanly through the first hoop and all the way through the second.

'Good shot,' Delamere said reluctantly.

We stayed on our boundary line, watching as Carberry played the blue ball through the third and fourth hoops and hit Delamere's red ball. On either side of me, Delamere winced and Freddie murmured, 'bad luck'. I went to take another mouthful of champagne and noticed my glass was empty.

Carberry lined up the next shot more deliberately than any of his others, taking several practice swings to test the angle before smacking his mallet so hard against the blue ball that the red bounced completely out of court. The blue ball rolled forwards to rest in front of the fifth hoop. Carberry looked up at us, smirking.

'Sorry, old boy. It's just so easy to teach you all a lesson.' He puffed out a cloud of smoke. 'Strutting around as if you owned the place.'

'We *built* the place,' Lord Delamere said.

Sylvie took his arm. 'Don't listen to him, darling.'

Carberry snorted. 'You and your bunch of amateurs. Most of them went back home with their tails between their legs, if I remember rightly.' He came towards us and stopped just in front of Sylvie. 'They've told you about J.D. Hopcraft, of course.'

'Should they have?' She crossed one slender leg in front of the other and I noticed the men's eyes following her movements, especially Carberry's.

'He applied for land on the west side of the lake,' Freddie said. 'But unfortunate things kept happening to his surveyors.'

Carberry put his hand on Sylvie's other arm, smiling unpleasantly. He was close enough to smell the sickly sweetness of booze mixed with tobacco on his breath. 'His first surveyor, or the second, went swimming in the Malewa River,' he said. 'A python took him while he was in the water – held him with its teeth and wrapped its body around him, and killed him.' He inhaled, flaring his nostrils. 'Some people think that constriction breaks your bones, but it doesn't. I've heard two theories: the snake holds you just tightly enough to prevent you from taking air into your lungs, and you slowly run out of oxygen and suffocate. Or the pressure from the constriction raises the pressure inside your body until your heart explodes.'

He pinched Sylvie's arm then withdrew his hand. An angry red mark appeared on her skin, but she didn't react; no one else along the line spoke.

'Either way,' Carberry said. 'The man was gone, and his report went with him, and Hopcraft had to find another surveyor.' He smiled again, showing his pointy eye-teeth.

I turned my head to face the garden. The lawn was blue in the moonlight, and rippling gently. The automatic sprinklers had come on, and the soft hiss of the water soothed my ears. I breathed in the scent of eucalyptus, frangipani, fuchsias, lilies, far stronger now in the cool dark than during the day.

'Why did he go swimming with his report?' I asked Carberry.

'What?'

I raised my voice. 'Why would he take the report in the river?'

Carberry narrowed his eyes and started to say something, but Lord Delamere drowned him out with a roar of laughter.

'By God, he's got you there, Carberry,' he said, and clapped me on the back.

'No one believes the story anyway,' Carberry said, waving his hand dismissively.

'You seemed to believe it,' Nicolas said.

'Just trying to scare the ladies.'

'More champagne for the boy genius,' Delamere said.

Carberry's hands were gripping the mallet so hard they'd turned a greenish-white. 'Don't spoil the brat.'

'You're just jealous,' Freddie said. He and Nicolas and the two nameless ladies raised their glasses to me. Carberry threw the mallet down and stalked off, looking disgusted.

'Our saviour,' Sylvie said to me. She came round Delamere and kissed my cheek, sending a shiver up my spine.

We left the croquet court and sat back down at our table. They toasted me, my head spinning, then we toasted the Muthaiga Club, then Kenya, then the King. The champagne seemed never-ending. The nightly ball started and the ladies, laughing, disappeared to change into their ballgowns. We moved to the bar. More men joined us, more names I didn't catch, and a friendly debate started. Freddie was asked to weigh in, held up his hands and made a joke. I noticed the men all laughed loudest at his jokes. Nicolas draped his arm around my shoulder, and one of the new men gave me a cigar. Delamere was in good spirits, and demonstrated it by shooting at the bottles of spirits on the shelves with his revolver. The bar staff didn't protest; they handed him a fine on a club chit and went back to serving other drinkers.

'Let's have a rickshaw race,' Delamere's son said, or at least that was what I thought he said. Everything was becoming strangely muffled, and the ground had started to move underneath me again. The ballroom doors were open, and through them I could see a blur of colours and movement – pink faces, blue gowns, yellow gowns, black tails, waiters in white carrying silver trays of honey-coloured whisky and golden champagne.

'Boy Genius doesn't look like he'll make it,' Delamere said.

'Jack's gone to get a rugby ball,' someone said. 'We'll have a game in the ballroom.'

'Not before I dance with my wife,' Nicolas said, hiccupping. 'I promised her we'd dance.'

'Well I'm down a wife,' Freddie said. 'So I think maybe I should take our young friend home.'

My head, which had been getting heavier by the minute, finally became too much for my neck and I dropped it onto the bar in front of me.

Water was brought, and hands tipped my head back and held the glass out to me. For a moment I thought I was back in the dormitories at school, and I started to struggle, but then I remembered I was in Africa, among friends, especially Freddie.

The water tasted strange. There was a cry of alarm, then I was looking at the floor and there was a puddle of red and yellow on it that smelled like the inside of my mouth.

'Put it on my chit,' Freddie said, then he was steering me through the bar, while the other men laughed and clapped. I was going to tell him that I was alright, and I wanted to stay and see Sylvie in her ballgown, but I was strangely sleepy, and I must have drifted off while he was loading me into his car, because the next thing I knew I was back at the hotel, sitting in an armchair in the lobby, and Freddie was talking quietly to my mother, who must have waited up for me.

'It's my fault, completely,' he was saying.

'Thank you for bringing him home,' my mother said. Her eyes were rimmed with red, as if she had a cold.

'He'll be fine – maybe a little delicate tomorrow, but he's tougher than he looks.'

'We've been beside ourselves all day – he said he was just going out for a walk.'

'I'm afraid he's been at the races,' Freddie said. 'I almost forgot.' He rummaged around in his pocket and brought out a handful of notes. 'He made a bit of money, actually.'

'Well.' My mother took the handful. 'This might soften the blow for his father a little.'

Freddie laughed. 'I'd better get back.'

'Thank you again.' She put out her hand and he shook it. 'Really.'

When Freddie had left, my mother stuffed the money into my trouser pocket, then leaned over me, her hands resting on my knees. I had a burning sensation in my throat, and tried to keep my mouth closed to stop the smell of sick escaping.

'Can you walk?' she asked me.

'I think so.'

'Good.'

She walked next to me all the way to our rooms. I noticed that I was taller than her now, when she didn't have her shoes on.

At the door she turned me to face her. I flinched as she ran the back of her hand along my jaw-line.

'I suppose you think what you did was daring,' she said.

'No.' I put out my hands behind me to prevent myself from falling. The door was cool under my touch, or maybe I was hot all over. I wished she would let me go into my room.

'You can have a good life here, Theo. I don't want to send you away again – and your school doesn't want you back, either. You know why.'

Beads of sweat gathered along my hairline. I didn't like to think about that afternoon, or the boy – Mark Hennessey – who'd followed me around all year, tripping me up, taunting me. Once he'd made me drink water from the toilet bowl. After the fight, none of the boys would look me in the eye, even the few friends I had. It didn't matter that he'd had me cornered, or that all boys fought. I'd gone too far. I'd been happy when the headmaster had suspended me.

I wondered if I was going to be sick again. 'Can I go to bed now?' I asked.

My mother drew back her hand and hit me across the face. At the last moment I turned so it caught the side of my head, and the jolt seemed to go right through to my brain. I looked at her in time to see her hand fly towards me again and this time I caught it and held it tight, digging my fingers into her wrist.

'Don't,' I said.

Her face was just below mine, her eyes wide open. Both of us were breathing heavily. I wondered if another guest, looking out of their bedroom, would think we were about to kiss.

I let her go and she stayed exactly where she was, arms hanging loosely at her sides now. A few strands of hair had escaped her

54

plait and formed a copper haze around her face. I wanted to apologise, or laugh it off, but the longer the silence went on, the more tongue-tied I became.

'I'm going to bed,' I said, eventually.

'No, it's not too late,' she said. I thought she must be talking to herself because I didn't understand her words, or her voice – gentle, and sad and flat. She hesitated, then reached past me and opened my bedroom door.

I went through it and shut it behind me. My head was thumping and my body felt clumsy with shock. I thought Maud was asleep, but as I slipped under my bedsheets she rolled over.

'I'm glad you're back,' she said.

Chapter Five

Nairobi train station seemed familiar, ordinary even, the second time around. I'd been feeling the effects of my drinking for the last few days, staying in our bedroom with the blinds closed while Maud read quietly nearby. Now, the first thing I did when we entered our carriage was throw the window open.

'Watch out for the mosquitoes,' my mother said, but nothing more. She'd barely spoken to me since the night of the races, although once or twice I'd caught her looking at me with a new, almost uneasy expression. I didn't know what she'd told my father, but it must have placated him, because he hadn't mentioned my absence, and I wondered why she'd protected me, or if she was just holding it over me until I did something else.

'Let's hope the good weather holds,' my father said, as we settled ourselves.

I hoped so too – I knew from reading up about it that Lake Naivasha was called after the Maasai word for rough waters.

I leaned my head against the back of my seat and dozed off. It was fifty-four miles from Nairobi to Naivasha, over three hours by train. Occasionally voices broke through – Maud asking questions, my father pointing out towns – but I woke properly only as we were sliding into our station. My father folded his newspaper and bounded up, beaming.

'Here we are,' he said.

Ramsay, the man my father had hired to build our new home, was late, pulling up in a dusty Buick a long time after the train had left us behind on the station platform. He was a small, squat man with a Scottish burr, and a glass eye.

'We expected you an hour ago,' my father said, frowning at him.

'You're on Africa time now,' Ramsay said. He picked up our suitcases and tossed them into the back seat as if they were made of air. 'The bairns will have to walk. It's only a few miles.'

There was a moment of silence.

'Well –' my father said, doubtfully, but Ramsay was already laughing to himself.

'Just a wee joke,' he said. 'They can sit on the luggage at the back.'

We clambered on top of the suitcases, almost slipping off when the engine started with a jolt, and travelled like that for the few miles to our new home.

Naivasha was much smaller than Nairobi. The main street was only a few shops long, and they were all shuttered. The surface of the road was even more pitted, and I held Maud's hand tightly as the car bounced along. No one was out on the road, although occasionally we saw lights in windows, figures moving through rooms on their way to the dinner table, or to gather around the wireless, check the baby was sleeping.

It was fully dark when we turned off the road and onto a forested drive. The trees were tall and shapeless, muffling the sounds around us. Maud drew closer to me, and I squeezed her, thinking suddenly of the leopards I'd talked about on the first train journey. I thought I heard a soft snap, as if twigs were breaking under a heavy foot, and a low growl, and I was about to ask Ramsay if we could go faster but then the trees were thinning and we suddenly saw the lake spread out before us, glittering in the moonlight. Down by the water was a house, with a large garden sloping downwards to end in a jetty. Ramsay pulled to a stop ten feet from the veranda and we climbed out.

'Here we are,' he said. 'Kiboko House.'

'What does that mean?' Maud asked.

'Hippo House.'

'It's rather dark,' my mother said.

'I'll find the lanterns,' Ramsay said.

While the adults huddled on the porch trying to work the lanterns, I picked my way down to the end of the jetty. Fireflies skimmed the water, lighting up the papyrus that grew thickly beneath the wooden planks, and blue water-lilies on the surface. A rowing boat was tied to one of the posts and bumped against it in a small wave when a dark shape rose out of the water a few yards from me, then quickly submerged again. I backed slowly away.

'Theo?' My mother's voice floated down to me. 'Where are you?'

I turned to face the house. They'd lit the lanterns now and hung them on the porch. Beyond, everything was in darkest shadow, but the house itself was bathed in a flickering orange glow. It was a yellow-stone bungalow with tiled roof, like the houses I'd seen in Nairobi on Market Day. Remembering them led me to thoughts of Sylvie, and I wondered how far we were from her and Freddie at that moment.

I walked back up to join the others as they rattled the key in the lock. Behind us, there was a splashing sound, and a chorus of frogs and ducks set up a complaint. Ramsay was chattering away about the area, pointing into the darkness.

'The cleft over there, that's known as Hell's Gate,' he said. 'Red cliffs. And you'll see Mount Longonot as soon as there's any light. It's a dormant volcano, over nine thousand feet high.'

'Charming,' my mother murmured.

Maud was leaning against one of the pillars on the porch with her eyes closed. Her face was white.

'Tired, Spanish?'

'Yes,' she said.

'We'll be in soon,' I said.

The key made a grinding sound and the front door swung open. Ramsay stepped forwards and held up his lantern. We peered inside. The door gave way straight onto a large cream sitting room with an open stone hearth in the middle and two corridors leading off the room at either end of the far wall. Our furniture had been sent ahead, and now it was all in place: the mahogany secretaire bookcase, the Windsor chairs in elm and ash, the oriental hardwood coffee table, the oil paintings of ships, all looking incongruous in their new surroundings.

Ramsay took us through an arched opening on the left and into the dining room – same proportions and decor – and the small kitchen, where Ramsay's wife had left us a cold meat pie and some bread and apples. Behind these rooms was the left-hand corridor, with three of the bedrooms and one of the bathrooms. My bedroom was cell-like, with white walls, a small chest of drawers and single cast-iron bed. Next door, Maud's was exactly the same. At the end of the hall, our bathroom had a claw-footed tub, toilet, sink and a wall-hung medicine cabinet. Mosquito screens were fitted over all the windows.

Off the other corridor was another small bedroom, another bathroom, then the master bedroom, with two large walnut beds, and silks and drapes on the wall. At the end of that corridor was a small study for my father.

'Excellent,' he said.

'I'll bring the luggage in,' Ramsay said. 'When will your maid be arriving?'

'Maid?' my mother asked.

'Most families bring one with them,' Ramsay said. 'That's who the extra bedroom is for, on your corridor.'

'Ah,' my father said. 'I thought you might have arranged that already, Jessie.'

I saw my mother's jaw tighten.

'Nae matter,' Ramsay said, cheerfully. 'I'm sure I can find one for you – one of the Nairobi families is bound to leave soon. And cooks and drivers and other staff you can hire from the natives. They're able to do that much.'

'Well,' my father said, after a pause. 'We can make do tonight, anyway. Thank you so much for all your help.'

'I'll get the bags,' Ramsay said.

'Theo, you go with him,' my father said, and I followed Ramsay out onto the porch.

By the time I'd carried my suitcase into my bedroom, sweat gathering in the small of my back, he'd already moved all of the others.

'I'll be seeing you,' he said. 'Watch out for the hippos. Meanest creatures alive. And leopards – if they come prowling round at night, turn on the lights and make plenty of noise, scare 'em off. And never leave your windows open.' He nodded at me and went back to his car, whistling.

The next few days were spent exploring the house, the lake and the garden, which was lush with jacaranda trees, lawn and flower-beds. The gardener had planted scarlet canna, frangipani, bougainvillea, and, probably as a nod to potential homesickness, English roses. Our water came from a stone well sunk into the ground one hundred feet from the house. Further away still were the Africans' buildings, round mud huts with thatched roofs where our staff would live.

In the end Ramsay couldn't find us a maid, but he did find Abdullah, who served as 'head boy'. My parents hired a cook, a driver and some low-level servants known as 'totos', who wore kanzus, long brown cotton robes that were the typical uniform for servants in Kenya. None of the totos had their bottom two front teeth. When I asked why, Ramsay said they all had them removed as a preventative measure, so if they developed tetanus – rife in Kenya – and therefore lockjaw, they would still be able to take food in through the gap. The boys walked hand-in-hand, or with arms wrapped around each other. There was something intimate about it that I didn't like to watch, and I turned away whenever a pair came into sight.

My father bought a second-hand Buick that broke down at every opportunity. We broke down on the way to Gilgil, Nakuru and N'Joro, as the road wound in and out of sight of the railway line. We broke down in Gilgil itself, a dusty station that doubled up as a post office, with one Indian duka, as the small retail shops were known, and nothing else. We broke down next to the Kikuyu settlement where African children ran away screaming that the mzungu had come to eat them. But east of Gilgil were the Aberdares, the easternmost mountain range of the Great Rift Valley, and there the car ran as sweet as honey. Climbing up into the hills, we looked down on the valley, with its cliffs and boulders, burbling streams and gushing waterfalls, its silvery forests of figs and olives, and vast, dark green pastures that stretched between our escarpment and Mau escarpment, tens of miles to the west. The soil beneath the car was red, and volcanic, but good for farming, our father told us, which was why so many Europeans had settled there.

The air was cold on the Aberdares, and brilliantly fresh, but descending, we drove through a mist that filled the car with the smoky, pine-like smell of cypress trees.

'It feels like Scotland,' Maud said.

The whole time we were playing and exploring and settling in I was thinking of Freddie and Sylvie, wondering what they were up to, and whether they were expecting us to call on them, as my parents had promised to do. When we went out in my father's car, I kept a sharp eye out for Hispano-Suizas, and one dark-haired passenger in particular.

After two weeks in the new house, Freddie's car pulled up outside as I was reading at the veranda table. Freddie whistled, and I got up, moving forwards as he opened the door for his passenger. An elegant ankle appeared, then a perfectly formed leg. I felt my excitement rising until her mousy-brown hair; it wasn't Sylvie.

The new woman was very small and slight, with a weak chin, small mouth, large nose and high forehead. She was wearing a fashionable drop-waisted silk dress and strings of pearls, and her bare feet were dainty. She was a carrying a pot of geraniums, and shifted them to the crook of her arm to wave at me in a friendly way. She looked a little older than Freddie, who seemed almost boyish next to her.

'Theo,' he said, 'meet Edie, my wife. She insisted on calling on you.'

'I'm the friendly one,' Edie said, and flashed her teeth at me in a smile.

'Theo?' my mother called from inside the house. 'Who is it?'

'It's Freddie,' I called back.

My mother appeared in the doorway. 'How nice to see you again,' she said, shading her eyes from the sun.

'You must be Jessie,' Edie said. She held out the geraniums. 'I've brought you these – you're meant to plant them around your doorway.'

'Thank you,' my mother said, accepting them.

'The smell repels the puff adders.'

'Oh goodness.' She looked down at the pot in her hands. 'The agent never told us about that. Would you like a drink? I'm afraid William isn't at home.'

'Wonderful,' Edie said. 'We brought some champagne for the road, but I finished it a few miles ago.'

'Please sit.' My mother put the flowers down on the porch table and disappeared inside.

Edie grinned at me. 'Freddie, I'm bloody exhausted,' she said, lowering herself onto one of the chairs. 'Can you bring me my cigarettes from the car? Would you like one, Theo?'

'Does that repel puff adders too?'

She smiled again. 'Good, you're funny.'

Freddie brought her cigarettes over and she lit up. 'They've all been talking about you non-stop, you know,' she said. 'Sylvie especially.'

My skin tingled the same way it had when she'd touched me at the races. 'Is she still staying with you?'

'They've just moved out,' Freddie said.

'Oh.'

'They bought a spot nearby – fell in love with it. They'll be building that for a good few months.'

I looked at the table, trying to hide my smile, but I felt it radiating from me anyway.

'Here we are.' My mother appeared again, with Abdullah behind her carrying four glasses of white wine on a silver tray, three full and one half-full. Behind him, Maud trailed, looking sleepy as she was introduced. The half glass was placed in front of me and I looked sideways at my mother, who nodded.

'Cheers.' We clinked glasses. The wine tasted heavy in comparison to champagne. I swallowed it quickly.

'How about a quick tour of the garden?' Edie asked. 'I'm crazy about gardening.'

'Of course,' my mother said. She led the way down from the veranda, looking uncertain. 'I'm afraid I don't know where everything is.'

'The roses are at the bottom of the hill,' Maud said. 'Next to the hydrangeas. The gardener puts coffee in the soil so they turn blue.'

'You show us, darling.'

Maud led us down the lawn and stopped in front of a rose bush. 'This one's my favourite.'

'I can see why.' Edie leaned forward, eyes closed, and sniffed

63

the biggest flower. 'It's so good to be able to bend over without a giant belly getting in the way.'

'Edie gave birth to our daughter on the fifth,' Freddie said.

'Congratulations,' my mother said.

'Nan,' Edie said, opening her eyes. 'She's called Nan.' She put out a finger and gently touched the rose, which bowed slightly then sprang back up. Her expression was blissful. 'Isn't this beautiful?'

'*She's* beautiful,' Freddie said, and kissed his wife. 'And what a pair of lungs.'

'Where is she?' Maud asked.

'She's at home with her nurse,' Edie said.

'Probably making this face,' Freddie said, and scrunched up his nose and eyes.

We laughed, even my mother, and Freddie turned and winked at me. I wished the boys back at school could see me now. They'd never have believed that someone so charming, so attractive, could be friends with me. It was intoxicating, and I almost forgot Sylvie wasn't with us.

'So you've just got these two beautiful children?' Edie said. She moved on to the hydrangeas and repeated the smelling and touching routine. We stood behind her in a semi-circle. Maud watched her with a serious expression.

'Yes,' my mother said.

'You must have been terribly young when you had them.'

'I'd been looking after my little brother for a few years by then – I didn't feel young.'

'And where's he now?'

'In a field in France.'

Edie pulled a face. 'I'm so sorry. That bloody war.'

'He was at university when it started – Edinburgh. His tutors all said he was doing very well, but Percy always had such a clear sense of duty.'

Freddie looked sympathetic. 'I'm sure we would have loved him.'

'Everyone did,' my mother said. She smiled – a different smile to before, but it reached her eyes. I felt dizzy all of a sudden and realised I'd been holding in my breath.

After we'd finished looking around the garden I walked Freddie and Edie to their car. My mother and Maud had already gone back inside, leaving the front door open for me. I could hear my mother calling to Maud from one wing to another, and the cook, in the kitchen, clanging pots and pans together, preparing supper for that evening.

'It's beautiful here,' Edie said, 'Aren't you glad you came?'

'Yes.'

'Africa suits you,' Freddie said.

I opened the passenger door for Edie and she slid in gracefully.

'We'll have a get-together soon,' she said. 'You're invited, of course.'

'Thank you,' I said.

'What's wrong? You don't look very sure.'

'Carberry won't be there, will he?'

She laughed. 'No. I hear you're not exactly firm friends.'

'Someone should shoot him.'

It came out less witty than I'd hoped, and Freddie raised an eyebrow, but Edie laughed louder. 'Not you,' she said, 'or you'll miss all the fun at the party. Do come.'

'As long as you stay away from the gin,' Freddie said, wagging his finger at me.

'And the champagne,' I said.

'Oh darling, we're not barbarians,' Edie said. 'It's a party – of course you'll have champagne.'

Freddie grinned. 'See you around, Boy Genius,' he said.

He started the engine, reversed the car up the driveway, and then they were turning the corner and out of sight.

I couldn't sleep that night, and around eleven I got up to fetch a glass of milk. My mother and father were talking on the veranda, and I paused in the sitting room when I heard Freddie's name mentioned.

'Just turned up,' my mother was saying. 'I don't even know who he was here to see. He seems pretty experienced for a twenty-five-year-old, too experienced for Theo.'

Freddie's face danced before me – his wide smile and straight white teeth, his raised eyebrow and smooth skin. My heart thumped painfully in my side, and I moved closer to the screen door, staying out of sight. It would all be fine, I tried to tell myself – Freddie didn't think I was too young and immature. My mother couldn't stop us being friends if we both wanted to be.

'He's changing.'

'Well that's natural, my dear. I know mothers want their children to stay children forever –'

'You know Theo's different. I don't want him influenced in the wrong direction. Not when I've worked so hard on him.'

'Of course you have,' my father said soothingly. 'But Lord Hamilton seemed alright to me. A little bohemian, maybe. Was he alone?'

'No – with his wife. Lady Joan mentioned her in Nairobi.'

'Not complimentary?'

'Not very.'

'Women never approve of other women.'

My mother's voice changed. 'What's that?'

'Oh this? I picked it up today – MacDonald said every household needs one.'

'I don't want it indoors.'

'It's for the leopards.'

'What if the children see it?'

'They won't know what to do with it.'

'I don't want it indoors.'

'It's for our own protection, my love.'

'It's asking for trouble,' my mother said. 'Hide it.'

'As you wish.' My father must have recognised the danger in

my mother's voice, as I did, because he changed the subject. I silently thanked him for whatever purchase had distracted my mother from deciding to end my new friendship, and went back to bed.

Chapter Six

Miss Graham, our tutor, was tall, with overlapping front teeth and eyebrows that met in the middle. She'd come out to Kenya with a family from Edinburgh, but they'd gone back and she'd stayed out for her painting.

Maud adored her, but I got the impression that Miss Graham didn't like me, and I didn't warm to her either. Three weeks after she started she complained to my mother about 'disturbing images' I'd drawn on my exercise books. They were doodles I'd done without thinking, but my mother sided with Miss Graham, although all she did was look at me coldly and tell me if I wanted to be treated as an adult I had to act like one. I lingered after she'd left, scuffing my shoe against the dining table, reluctant to go back to the classroom. I might have escaped a beating this time, but her words still stung, and the thought of Miss Graham's satisfied look made me rigid with anger.

We woke every weekday for breakfast at eight. Lessons were between nine and twelve, then our mother joined us for a hot lunch. Afterwards, there were more lessons until two, when we had a bath. The totos ran the bath for each of us, which took nearly an hour: first they drew the water from the well – at least ten buckets per bath – then heated it in a cauldron kept in the kitchen hearth. Afterwards, they transferred it from cauldron to bath in ten more trips with the bucket. Sometimes they forgot to heat the water for long enough, and we had to sit in ice-cold water, our lips and fingers turning blue.

In the afternoons, my mother napped, and we would row out onto the lake, or go for a walk, or watch Miss Graham painting. Her fingers were surprisingly delicate when they held a paintbrush. We were silent around her, unless she started the conversation.

'I'll be running out of blue soon,' she always said, as she was choosing a colour for the sky. 'Blue and brown, those are the colours I use most out here.'

'What colours did you use most in Scotland?' Maud asked once.

'Green and grey.'

'Did you ever go anywhere else? What colours are other countries?'

'No, not me,' Miss Graham said. She dipped her brush into the pot of cobalt. 'But the family I was with before were in India for a while.'

'What colour is India?'

'Gold. And orange.'

'What about America?' I asked.

'I don't know America,' she said brusquely.

Two of the totos appeared with the laundry, laughing and whooping. They were younger than me, probably no more than twelve, and my mother must have ordered their kanzus in the wrong size because they were both tripping over their hems. One of them carried the washtub, the rub board and soap banging against its sides as he walked. The other carried a pile of clothes and bedding that was higher than him. When the first toto saw Miss Graham he stopped, and the second crashed into him, dropping most of my father's shirts.

Miss Graham rapped her easel with the handle of her paintbrush; it made a sound like a gun-crack, and the first toto flinched. 'Shall I tell Bwana Miller that you throw his clothes on the ground?'

The totos mumbled something.

'It doesn't matter,' I said. 'They're dirty anyway.'

'You have to instil discipline,' Miss Graham said. 'The natives are awfully lazy.' She turned back to them and made a flapping motion with her free hand. '*Pesi pesi.*'

We'd been out in Africa long enough to know that meant 'get on with it'.

The totos crept past us and sat on the jetty, whispering to each other as they washed our laundry. Maud watched them with a confused look on her face. After a while I went back inside.

If the totos were afraid of Miss Graham, they were even more afraid of my mother. A few times I'd been in the kitchen with them, bothering the cook, when someone had muttered 'Bibi Miller', and everyone had melted away.

Joseph, the cook, was the only person who didn't seem intimidated by her temper. He was a good-natured old man whose fingers were covered in calluses. Once I saw him use his bare hands to take a hot cast-iron dish from the oven and realised where the calluses came from. Two months after we moved in, when my voice began to change, becoming cracked and hoarse, Joseph made me a special hot drink that tasted bitter and grainy.

'You a man now, Bwana,' he said. 'This drink make you into a good husband.'

Joseph could cook anything, but he loved schnitzel and potatoes, which drove my father to despair. For my fifteenth birthday, Joseph made me apple strudel with ice-cream. The pastry was light and flaky, the apples were soft and tasted of burnt sugar and cinnamon. It was the best cake I'd ever had.

After a while my mother had a word with Joseph and he grudgingly started cooking food we were more used to. He could cook anything: meringues, custard flans, layer cake, soups, breads, scones, pies. It had felt strange sitting down to schnitzel and potatoes in the middle of Africa, but no stranger than kidney pie and rice pudding.

Abdullah, the head boy, was gentle in everything. He had big brown eyes and a slight stammer that made him shy to speak. Every evening he put down a prayer mat on the grass and prayed for exactly seven minutes. Unlike the other servants who were all Kikuyus, Ramsay told us, head boys were normally Somalis because they were nobler and stricter. My father liked Abdullah a lot, because he approved of my father's beard that he was trying to grow. My mother liked him because he was a genius at running the house, and Maud liked him because he helped her nurse injured birds she found in the garden. When Miss Graham was on leave, it was Abdullah who looked after us. Soon after we moved in, Maud fell out of a tree we were exploring, and ended up with a small gash on her shin. Abdullah washed the wound, then left us sitting by the well while he hunted through the grass near the woods.

'What's he looking for?' Maud asked.

'I don't know,' I said. 'How's your leg?'

'Bleeding.'

'Do you think you'll bleed to death?'

'Don't – you're not funny.'

Abdullah made his way back to us with something in between his thumb and forefinger. 'This is for you,' he said, as he reached the well.

'What is it?' Maud asked.

'Safari ant.' He showed us the ant, which was squirming in his grip. It was a deep cherry-red colour, and almost twice the size of his thumbnail, with long, pincer-like jaws protruding from either side of its head.

'What are you going to do with it?' Maud asked, biting her lip.

'Maasai use them like this,' Abdullah said. He brought the ant down to Maud's cut, until the pincers were on either side of the

71

wound then pressed them onto her skin. The ant went rigid, the pincers snapped together and Abdullah twisted the body off in a quick, clean movement. 'Very strong,' he said.

We looked down – the head was still hanging off Maud's leg, but the pincers had closed the gash like a makeshift suture.

'How long does it last?' I asked.

'Until skin heals,' he said.

'Thank you, Abdullah,' Maud said. She blushed as he helped her to her feet.

It was April, almost three months after we'd moved in, when Sylvie arrived out of the blue. I was out on the lake with Maud when I saw her sitting on our jetty, legs outstretched in the sun. She raised a hand lazily and I jumped up, almost sending us head first into the water.

'Who is it?' Maud asked.

'Sylvie.'

'You must have good eyesight.'

'Maybe it's because I don't strain them reading all the time,' I said, beginning to row us back to shore.

'I didn't know you could read?'

'Very funny.' I caught sight of a monkey-sized figure scampering between Sylvie and the edge of the jetty. 'Look – she's brought your husband with her.'

Sylvie waited until the boat had bumped gently against the jetty before standing up in one slow, supple movement.

'Is it nice out there?' she asked. 'It looks so peaceful.'

'Do you want me to row you out?'

'Another time.' She was looking straight at me, and I passed a hand over my face, feeling the roughness of new hair growing around my mouth and below my ears. I was glad my voice had finally settled.

'I came to invite you to see our new house,' she said. 'Well – our land, anyway. The house isn't completely built yet.'

I moored the boat and jumped up onto the landing stage. 'Is it nearly done?'

'So the builder promises us.'

I stared at her perfect teeth and those soft-looking lips. She stared back, smiling.

'*Theo*,' Maud called from the boat. 'You know I need help.'

Sylvie laughed. Maud held out her hands and I lifted her onto the jetty. Roderigo jumped into Sylvie's arms and she kissed his head. 'Shall we find your mother?' she asked us.

'Lady Joan came to see her for lunch,' Maud said. 'They're out on the porch now.'

'The Governor's wife?' Sylvie peered back at the house. 'That's lucky – I haven't met her yet.'

I wondered if I should warn her about Lady Joan's opinion of the Happy Valley set, but she'd already started walking, Maud trotting next to her. I hurried to join them.

When we reached the house a greyhound was shivering in the sunlight at the bottom of the stairs, and Abdullah was standing nearby, like a protective parent.

'Thank you for looking after Fairyfeet,' Sylvie said softly to him. She crouched down and stroked the dog's ears, shushing it when it whimpered. 'She's so scared all the time – Nico's almost given up on her.'

My mother came down the steps. 'Good afternoon, Countess de Croÿ.'

Sylvie straightened up again. 'Oh – call me Sylvie, please.' She looked at Lady Joan, who was still sitting on the porch. 'It's nice to –'

Lady Joan cut her off with a wave of her hand. 'No introductions necessary. Are you still with the Hamiltons?'

'We've bought our own place actually – I'm here to invite the Millers to tea.'

'How kind of you,' my mother said. She didn't move, and I realised she hadn't offered Sylvie a drink, or invited her inside, or even shaken her hand. Behind me, I could sense Maud fidgeting, and Fairyfeet still whimpered softly, but otherwise a silence had descended. My mother crossed her arms in front of her chest; Lady Joan raised an eyebrow.

I looked at Sylvie. She'd turned pale. It made her seem much younger, somehow, and helpless, and I felt a wave of anger on her behalf.

'Would you like a glass of wine?' I asked.

My mother caught my eye and shook her head, subtly. I hurried on. 'We don't have champagne. I don't know if Abdullah knows how to make whisky sours – you like those, don't you?'

'You remember.' Sylvie smiled at me, and the colour came back into her cheeks. She looked as if she was about to refuse, then Roderigo broke the ice, jumping out of her arms and onto Maud's shoulder.

'He *knows* me,' Maud said excitedly.

Sylvie laughed. 'He always chooses the prettiest person to sit on.'

'Actually,' I said. 'We were going to ask your permission for Roderigo's hand in marriage. Maud's game.'

'Theo,' my mother said, frowning.

'Maud shouldn't be thinking about marriage yet,' Sylvie said. 'Not for a long time.' She tucked a strand of hair behind Maud's ear. 'You've got much more to offer the world, haven't you, darling?'

There was another pause. Out of the corner of my eye I saw my mother draw herself up as if she had something important to say.

'Sylvie,' she said. 'Won't you join us on the veranda? What would you like to drink?'

Sylvie drove with one hand on the wheel and the other in her lap. She was constantly looking over her shoulder to talk to Maud and drifting across the road, or skidding as we turned corners. Freddie had driven too fast, but at least he'd seemed in control.

74

Cedar trees whisked past in a dark blur, and golden stalks of corn bowed their prickly heads in our wake. Fairyfeet and Roderigo trembled in Maud's lap. We were driving towards the mountains, and I had visions of Sylvie tunnelling straight through them. She was telling us the story of their journey to Africa from France, but her words were snatched away by the wind, so I caught only a haze of dances and sea-sickness and misunderstandings.

Then she was slowing down, turning a last corner and Nicolas was waiting to open a gate in the long hedgerow for us. We drove through and parked sharply, while Nicolas fiddled with the gate, trying to shut it again. I looked around. We were at the edge of a lush expanse of countryside, around six hundred acres or so, with a few thatched huts, gently smoking, dotted here and there in the distance. The Aberdares reared up to our right, a silvery waterfall cascading down their sides, and close by on our left the river moved sluggishly around a bend, where a deep pool had formed.

'Welcome.' Nicolas was walking towards us now, and it was only then that we noticed the smallish ball of yellow fluff, with large, ungainly feet, trotting next to him.

'Is that a *lion*?' Maud asked.

'Our surprise,' Sylvie said, turning in her seat. 'Samson the lion cub.' She looked at me, and I felt somehow she'd wanted to show him to me in particular.

'Say hello to him if you like,' Nicolas said, opening the door for Maud. Fairyfeet took the opportunity to escape, and bounded into the bushes. 'He's very tame.'

We carefully approached Samson, who was sitting a few feet from the car. He was no bigger than a domestic cat, but stockier, with shorter legs. His fur was sand-coloured, and there were brown spots on his head much like a leopard. His eyes were wide and black, and his mouth was open, tongue hanging out pinkly, giving him a quizzical expression. His teeth looked sharp enough.

I felt myself breaking into a smile, just looking at him. Here was a real, live predator. A man-killer.

'Where does he like to be stroked?' Maud asked.

As if in answer, Samson flopped onto the ground in front of us and rolled over, exposing his belly.

'He's a flirt,' Nicolas said, slapping him playfully on his flank. Samson growled, and wriggled from side to side, scratching his back on the rocky surface of the drive.

'We've been cursed with all the naughty animals,' Sylvie said, picking Roderigo up from the back seat of the car. 'Now come see the plans for the house. We're living in the manager's house in the meantime.'

The manager's house was smaller than ours and painted white with green shutters. There was a narrow porch along the front of the house with a table and four chairs set up. Inside was white as well, with red tiles on the floor, and stacks of unopened boxes in the corners. No paintings hung on the walls, but there was some needlework above the fireplace, proclaiming 'Home, Sweet Home'.

We sat around a coffee table near the open front door while Sylvie flitted about trying to find the plans, and Nicolas ordered us a jug of lemonade. Roderigo scampered up a tall armoire, and perched on the top, surveying us calmly.

'Here we go,' Sylvie said, unrolling a sheet of paper on the table and tapping a dark line that snaked across the page. 'It'll face Satima Peak, in the Aberdares, and the back will face the Wanjohi River.'

'Sylvie insisted we live near water,' Nicolas said. 'I don't know what it is about people who grow up in the city. They always worry if there's no water nearby.'

Sylvie stuck her tongue out at him. 'And people who grow up in the countryside worry if they can't see the horizon.'

'If you're talking about your monstrous skyscrapers –'

'Much more practical than your draughty old castles.'

'Our castles – exactly. We need to see the horizon to see who's coming to attack us.'

Sylvie waved a hand. 'Who wants them? Anyway, I love water. I used to think I'd like a burial at sea.'

I remembered the times I'd planned my own funeral as a boy, whenever my mother had been angry with me, imagining myself finally beyond her reach and how sorry she'd be. I knew it was wrong to think about it, even sometimes wish it, so it was surprising to hear Sylvie talk so openly about the things I dreamed about in private. I felt a thrill run through me at the thought of everything we shared, and how brave she was.

'Like the Vikings?' Maud asked.

'Exactly.'

'Enough of that,' Nicolas said. 'You know very well that as Countess de Croÿ you're obliged to lie next to me in some dreadful family vault and haunt the castle for generations.'

'I'm not going back to France, Nico,' she said. 'Not even when I'm dead.' The skin around her mouth and eyes seemed suddenly tighter.

A toto appeared with a tray bearing a jug of lemonade and four glasses, and we watched him pour in silence. I glanced at Sylvie out of the corner of my eye, willing Nicolas to do something to reassure her.

'Well anyway. To the new house,' he said when we all had our glasses, and drank his lemonade quickly.

I brought the glass to my lips. Maud was looking at Sylvie, who was looking at Nicolas, who was looking at the floor. In that moment I thought I could see how unsuited he was to taking care of his wife, how she could have felt trapped by his lack of understanding. Even I knew how much she'd hated France, and we'd only met a few times. I wanted to say something to lift the heavy atmosphere in the room, but I couldn't think of anything.

Samson, who'd been lying in the sunlight on the porch, got up and came indoors. He walked straight over to Sylvie and laid his head in her lap.

'You beauty,' she said.

He snorted air out of both nostrils, looking up at her with wide eyes.

'I told you he's a flirt,' Nicolas said, scratching the cub behind his ears.

'He's our flirt,' Sylvie said. They smiled at each other, and the room seemed calm and happy again even though Nico hadn't apologised. I cast around for something to say, feeling suddenly out of my depth.

'You must like animals as much as Maud does,' I said.

'I always judge a person by how they treat animals,' Sylvie said. 'If they're cruel to them, it's worse than if they're cruel to humans. At least we can understand what's going on – but the animals must be so frightened.' She tapped Samson's nose. 'But you feel safe here, don't you, darling?'

'He's adorable,' Maud said. 'I want a lion cub.'

'They eat a lot of raw meat,' Nicolas said, smiling. 'He's eating us out of house and home. And you shouldn't really separate them from their mothers. He only came to us because he was orphaned.'

'How?'

'His mother was living nearby. I stumbled across her when I was out for an afternoon ride a few weeks ago – she would have attacked me, but my little Somali pony bolted before I even saw her. She was just a yellow streak I caught out of the corner of my eye.' He put down his empty glass. 'I went back a few days later – she'd just had cubs. That was why she was in attack mode.'

'Who can blame her?' Sylvie said, kissing Samson's nose.

'She got used to me after a few visits,' Nicolas said. 'She let me come near enough to see the cubs, although never near enough to touch of course. Then I had to go away for a few days, and when I returned there was an Indian maharajah's hunting party staying on our grounds. They showed me a lioness they'd just bagged.'

Sylvie put her hand on Nicolas's. 'It's not your fault,' she said gently.

He grimaced. 'She wasn't as wary of them because she'd got used to me.'

'You didn't know they were going to come here,' Maud said.

'No,' Sylvie said.

'After that, I'm afraid I wasn't a very good host,' Nicolas said. 'I told them – it's an unpardonable crime to shoot females of any species. Unless they've been attacking the herds or the natives of course. Life out here can be brutal, but we don't need to be. The two cubs were half-starved when I found them.'

'Did the other die?' Maud asked gravely.

'Judah?' Sylvie said. 'No. Nico brought them both home. They slept together in a basket. Then one day Judah was gone, but Samson stayed.'

Samson made a low rumbling sound and licked Sylvie's hand.

'Aren't we lucky Daddy's here to look after us?' she said to the lion. 'Imagine the mess we'd make without him.'

'To Samson,' I said, raising my glass.

We drank again, and Nicolas topped up our glasses. From outside came a low, buzzing sound.

'Sounds like Freddie,' Sylvie said, her face flushing.

It got nearer and louder then, through the open front door, we saw his car braking abruptly to a stop a few yards from the house. He didn't bother to open the car door, just lifted himself up and over it. Sylvie laughed.

'What's this?' Freddie called. 'A party you didn't invite me to?' He ran up the porch stairs. 'Theo – Maud. What a lovely surprise.'

'What are you doing here?' Sylvie asked, leaning back on the sofa.

'I came to see if you'd like a spin.'

'You came all this way without telephoning first?'

'I thought it was worth the risk.' He came into the room and the light changed, as if he was giving off his own. He shook hands

79

with Nicolas, then me, then kissed Maud's hand. 'So what about it?'

'Do you mind, darlings?'

I shook my head, trying to keep the disappointment out of my face. I didn't want either of them to go. Freddie clapped me on the back.

'Nico can drive you back to Kiboko,' Sylvie said. 'Unless you want to stay the night?'

Maud looked at me.

'We should get back.'

'Quite right,' Freddie said. 'We can't keep you out too often – your mother'll start to think it's our fault.' He winked at me.

'Let me fetch my hat,' Sylvie said. She kissed Samson again and pushed his head off her lap. He yawned, and moved to lay it on Nicolas's instead.

She disappeared into the back of the house, and Freddie went to stand by the door.

'I'll have her home by midnight, Nico,' he said.

Nicolas shrugged. 'I'm sure she'll want to stay out later,' he said. He fondled Samson's ears as he spoke, and the lion nuzzled his hand. With Freddie in the house, Nicolas seemed smaller, and paler somehow, even with his pet lion.

'I'm ready,' Sylvie called, reappearing in a floppy hat. 'I'll see you later, darlings.'

We stood, and she kissed each of us on the cheek, then followed Freddie outside. He opened the passenger door for her, vaulted over the driver's door and started the engine. I suddenly felt alone. I realised as I watched Freddie and Sylvie that they belonged together, and it hit me hard in my stomach. They belonged together in a grown-up world that existed alongside my own, but was different all the same. I wanted to be old enough to go with them, but as soon as I got older, they would too, and I trembled with the idea that I'd never catch up with them, never be their equal.

'Let Nico know when you need to go home,' Sylvie called, waving.

'Drive safely,' Nicolas called back.

'I always do,' Freddie said.

Chapter Seven

We visited Sylvie and Nicolas often over the next few months. Sometimes Sylvie would pick us up, sometimes Nicolas, sometimes Freddie. When Freddie picked us up he would let me drive the last mile, struggling up the steep, dusty hill at the start as he encouraged me from the passenger seat.

Then, at the top, the view – miles and miles of grass and bamboo, bordered by the towering figure of Mount Kipipiri to our left, and the cedar-clad Aberdares rolling gently upwards in front of us. Sometimes I thought I could pick out dark shapes moving on the mountainside – the wild buffalo that lived up on the frozen peaks.

Coming down the other side of the hill, I'd shift into second gear and stamp on the brakes, but the car still went dangerously fast. I never worried when Freddie was around though – he made danger seem fun, exhilarating. He would whoop and we'd join in, even louder the faster it was, then all of a sudden we'd be at the bottom, thundering past the shaded spring on our left, and turning onto the private road that led to Sylvie and Nicolas's.

'Chops', their builder, worked on the house for several months, and each time we came a little more had been completed, until eventually we swept into the drive and it was finished – a one-storey stone building in the shape of an 'H', with a veranda at the back, and cedar half-logs covering the walls and roof. Sylvie christened it 'The Farm'.

Inside was a large drawing room with a central stone fireplace and a dining room and pantry leading off it. Both wings had several bedrooms and bathrooms. Unlike ours, their kitchen was separate from the house and cooked food was brought from there to the pantry before mealtimes.

Sylvie had furnished the house with a mix of finds from Mombasa – brass-studded chests, oriental carpets and tall coffee-pots – and antiques from France. She filled each room with flowers from the garden, and the whole house smelled like a blend of hibiscus, jasmine and her perfume.

There was always plenty of food and drink. Sylvie liked to drink champagne from the goblets Freddie and Edie had bought them as a house-warming gift, and we would be allowed a little too. Cocktail-hour started at four or five in the afternoon. The drinks were called 'sundowners' because that's what we'd be drinking as the sun set.

Sylvie made every day special – she seemed so radiantly happy all the time, playing with her animals, and writing letters to Nolwen and Paola, her daughters. She and Nicolas threw extravagant dinner parties where the guests brought tents and camped in the garden for several days so the party could continue. We never slept over, but occasionally one of them would show up to collect us early at the weekend, and we would have breakfast at their house – bacon and eggs, pastries, fresh orange juice and strong black coffee. Afterwards, we'd go for a walk, taking Samson, who was getting restless confined to the garden, along with us. He was too young at first, his legs tired out after ten minutes and he sat down and cried.

'What a big baby you are,' Nicolas said.

Samson mewled pitifully until Nicolas picked him up and we carried him home.

When Freddie wasn't there we had Sylvie's full attention. She loved books, and reading to us, everything from *Treasure Island* to *The Turn of the Screw*. She would braid Maud's hair, asking us about our day, or sing for us in her husky voice, accompanying herself on the ukulele.

'All good daughters of America know how to play one of these,' she said.

'What about the bad daughters?' I asked.

She smiled. 'They know how to play something else.'

She made me feel as if I was funny, and clever, but also like a favourite nephew, which wasn't what I wanted at all, and I half-thought about asking Joseph for more of his drinks. And at the same time, I was glad she thought of me like that so she never kept secrets from me. I wanted to know everything about her; I'd never been so fascinated by anyone else, and it was strange and exciting at the same time.

We played cards a lot – pairs and bridge. I always partnered Sylvie, and Nicolas helped Maud, who seemed to lose interest halfway through each game.

'You're good, Theo,' Sylvie said once, after a clean sweep. 'Nearly as good as Freddie, and that's saying something.'

I wondered how Nico really felt about Sylvie and Freddie, and how openly she talked about him. He seemed resigned to it, but maybe it was just that he was quieter than all his friends. I liked Nico a lot. I could tell he was an outsider, and I felt as if he was glad I'd come along. He was the only one who always talked to me as if I was an adult. Even so, I understood why Sylvie was drawn more to Freddie.

When Freddie was around he had us in stitches with his stories, even when they were cruel. He liked to give out nicknames to people behind their backs. Lord Delamere, who was old, and thought of himself as a natural leader of the settlers and the natives, was called 'The Young Pretender'. His son, Freddie called 'Good Time Tom', because he had a serious streak.

He was good at impersonations, too – never flattering ones – and brought them out at parties. Sometimes the person he was imitating looked uncomfortable, but they never said anything. No one was more sophisticated than Freddie. He didn't drink as much as some of the other settlers – although he was very good at making sure everyone else had enough – and I thought maybe that was how he stayed so witty and articulate.

Women, especially, were drawn to him. In town he'd be stopped by every other female on the street. They giggled at his jokes and brushed imaginary dirt from his broad shoulders. Freddie was attentive to them, but it was different somehow with Sylvie. Once or twice I caught him gazing at her while she sang, or danced with Maud, with such a forceful look on his face I felt breathless without really understanding why.

In late September Freddie arrived at The Farm with invitations to a Kirlton party.

'You too, Theo,' he said, dropping into a chair near me and Sylvie on the veranda. 'But not Maud – she's too young and lovely. Where is she anyway? And where's Nico?'

'Nico's walking Samson.'

'Maud's in Nairobi,' I said. 'Mother took her for lunch with Lady Joan.'

'Ah – Lady Joan.'

'I don't think we're friends,' Sylvie said, stretching in her chair. 'Maybe Maud could put in a good word on my behalf.'

'I don't think Maud has any influence over Lady Joan,' I said.

'Don't write your sister off,' Freddie said. 'She's got an iron spirit – you don't notice it because she doesn't let herself get angry.'

'You're right, as always,' Sylvie said. 'How did you become so perceptive, darling?'

'I'm an observer, like Theo here.'

'What do you mean?' I asked.

'I mean, you're not leader of a pride, are you? You're happy to be a leopard, looking down on everyone from your tree.' He grinned.

'And you're a leopard too?'

'In some ways.'

'Baloney,' Sylvie said. 'If anyone's leader of the pride −'

'Sometimes,' Freddie said. 'Sometimes I like to watch instead. But I only watch those worth watching.'

He went to her side, looming over her. Sylvie looked down, smiling, and Freddie cupped her chin in his fingers, turning her face to him. 'Like you.'

He pressed his mouth against hers and her arms snaked up, wrapping themselves around his neck. I wanted to watch, and at the same time wanted to change places with Freddie, and felt my confusion building in my stomach and groin.

I didn't know how long they were kissing before I heard a padding, and the squelch of wet shoes − Samson must have been led into the river to cool down. Nicolas was suddenly there, on the veranda, raising his eyebrows and smiling wearily at me.

Freddie released Sylvie, and stood up straight again. 'So you'll all come to the party?'

'We'll think about it,' she said, smiling up at him.

'Hope you can persuade your mother, Theo.' He grinned again. 'There'll be plenty to look at.'

My mother and Maud were drinking tea when I arrived at Kiboko.

'Theo,' Maud said, jumping up as she saw me, 'come and meet Scotty.'

'Who's Scotty?'

I followed her to her bedroom; she placed a finger on her lips and quietly pushed open the door. Inside, it looked the same as ever, except now there was a small, furry bundle on the end of her bed, snoring gently.

'He's one of Lady Joan's puppies. Their dog had another litter and they said we had to have one this time because they'd run out of names,' Maud whispered. She sat down next to the bundle and scratched behind its ear. The bundle, a black and tan Gordon Setter, opened its eyes, yawned, then rolled on its back and went to sleep again, paws quivering with each exhalation.

'I think I wore him out,' Maud said.

'You called him Scotty?'

'He wouldn't answer to anything else.'

'What else did you try?'

'Arthur, Mordred, and Merlin.'

I raised an eyebrow.

'Miss Graham's been reading me *Le Morte d'Arthur*.'

'I see.'

'Isn't he adorable?'

'How does Mother feel about him?'

'He's not allowed in her bedroom. But she doesn't mind him, because Lady Joan made her join the Welfare League. You know, that thing she was talking about before. Mother says it'll be good to have something to do. She'll have to go to Nairobi for meetings, so Miss Graham will be in charge.'

'Bloody hell.'

Maud was still gazing lovingly at Scotty. I tickled the puppy under his chin and his paws quivered some more.

'I need to go ask Mother something,' I said.

My mother was in the kitchen with Joseph, planning the menu for the next week. I waited for her in the sitting room, and she came out quickly. 'I hate that job,' she said, joining me on the sofa. 'And it's all for your benefit you know – you're eating us out of house and home. I never knew someone could have such an appetite.'

'I'm growing.'

'Be careful you don't grow outwards,' she said, and prodded my stomach. She was smiling.

'I've been invited to a dinner at Freddie's.'

'Lord Hamilton,' she said automatically.

'Can I go?'

'When is it?'

'Next week.'

'I see.'

She stood up and started straightening things around the room, replacing books and closing drawers. 'Who else will be there?'

I shrugged. 'Their friends.'

'I suppose we should be having dinner parties,' she said vaguely. She picked up a teacup from the side table and examined it. 'Did you know you had German measles when you were little? We thought you were going to die.'

I stared at her, confused.

'I suppose you were too young to remember. The only thing you could take was weak tea. It still reminds me of that time.'

She started walking towards the dining room, cup in hand. Her silhouette made me think of Sylvie, and I was suddenly desperate that she wouldn't let me go to the party. I knew that if I didn't go, I would be even further from the others and it would be too late.

'Can I go?'

'I'm not sure, Theo.'

'I have to, I *have* to go.' I hadn't realised my legs had carried me towards her, or my arm had pinned her against the wall, until I felt a trickle of cold on my hand, and saw the teacup had emptied the remains of its contents onto me.

I stepped back, but the slap I was expecting never came. My mother turned her face away, and I saw a flicker of recognition in her eyes before she did.

'Why are you shouting?' Maud was in the doorway, forehead creased in worry.

'No one's shouting,' my mother said.

'I heard it.'

'You're imagining things. Be a good girl and bring me my book, won't you, darling?'

88

Maud lingered. 'Where is it?'

'I can't remember – have a look in my bedroom first.'

Maud slipped out.

'I'm sorry,' I said. 'It's just a small dinner with friends.'

'Much older friends.' She sighed and looked over my head at something in the distance. A silence grew around us; I would almost have welcomed the slap instead.

'So can I go?' I asked eventually.

She nodded, almost imperceptibly.

'Thank you.'

She kept her eyes fixed above me. 'Be good, Theo.'

Chapter Eight

The evening of the party, Nicolas and Sylvie arrived to pick me up at quarter past six. I'd been ready for hours beforehand and Maud had had to brush Scotty's hair off my jacket several times while I waited. I'd thought my suit was smart, but as soon as I reached their car I saw Nicolas's was much more elegant.

Sylvie was wearing a sleeveless green silk dress with a pearl necklace, and black eye makeup that showed off the clear whites of her eyes and her long lashes. Her hair was set around her face in waves, and pinned back with dark clips inlaid with more pearls. I snatched a look at her long legs, which weren't usually on display. The roof of the car had been folded down, and the goose-pimples on her calves told me there had been a breeze as they drove over.

'Hop in,' Sylvie said.

She'd brought a hipflask of pink gin and gave me a sip as I climbed in behind them. The flask had bite marks on it.

'Samson,' she said, seeing me notice them. 'He thought we were playing catch. We had to chase him all the way around the garden before he'd drop it.'

'And where's Roderigo?'

'Sleeping. He broke into the drinks cabinet this afternoon and got sozzled, the scamp.'

'Went straight for the best brandy,' Nicolas said.

'At least you know he has taste.'

They laughed. Nicolas ground the gears and we rattled off. As we crested the top of a hill, the sun hung directly in front of us like an orange jewel in the sky, then it slipped out of sight.

'We should be there before eight,' Nicolas said.

Sylvie passed the hipflask back to me again. 'Are you excited? Your first Kirlton party.'

'Will it be different to a normal party?'

I saw them exchange looks.

'Quite different,' Nicolas said.

Sylvie held out her hand, palm towards the sky. 'I think it's going to pour down,' she said. 'I love nights like this.'

The air was soft and heavy with the promise of rain. Smells carried further in that atmosphere, and I was dazzled with the mix of flowers and earth and Sylvie. I leaned back against the leather seat and looked up at the stars. They seemed much closer in Africa than anywhere else – vast, white and glittering, so different to the small, dirty-yellow ones you saw in London, or Edinburgh skies.

'Could you light the lanterns?' Nicolas asked me after a while.

I lit two and passed one to Sylvie, keeping the other for myself. The road ahead was black as tar, and from either side came the rustling of unknown creatures. I closed my eyes and sniffed the air, to see if I could distinguish them by smell alone.

'Almost there,' Nicolas said.

'I can't wait,' Sylvie said, looking back at me. 'I feel like screaming.'

Her eyes were bright and I felt their excitement spill over and infect me. 'Do it,' I said.

Her scream was breathy and enticing, and I was overwhelmed with the desire to wrap my arms around her.

'Here we go,' Nicolas said.

I opened my eyes as we turned into a drive. Holding my lantern higher, I saw it was bordered by flowers. Up ahead, the drive opened out into a sloping lawn, at the top of which sat a solid-looking house, its windows flung open and golden light streaming forth from them. The sound of glasses clinking and people laughing carried out to us.

Nicolas braked gently and we eased to a halt.

'What ho,' came Freddie's voice, and I saw his figure standing in the open doorway, waving a bottle of champagne.

Kirlton was large and homely, set against a backdrop of forested ridges and soaring peaks, and already full of guests by the time we crossed the threshold.

'I'm glad you came,' Freddie said to me. 'Would you like a tour?'

'Yes please.'

He handed the champagne to a tall, slim native wearing a pristine white kanzu, with bare feet. He didn't look much older than Freddie.

'Waweru – you're in charge of drinks until I'm back.'

'Yes, Bwana.'

'Theo, Waweru. Waweru's my personal servant – couldn't live without him.'

Waweru inclined his head.

Freddie guided me around a drawing room hung with oil portraits of his and Edie's mothers. Like ours, the furniture was English antique. Wooden beams traversed the ceiling, but none of the walls quite reached that height, so anyone sitting on the beams would be able to look into all of the rooms below.

There was an office leading off the drawing room, and a huge library stacked from floor to ceiling with enormous, leather-bound books. The kitchen was separate to the main house, but several tables had been laid in the dining room, and were gleaming with polished silver, champagne flutes and covered soup tureens.

'We'll eat at eleven,' Freddie said. 'To give everyone time to get nice and drunk first.'

There were four bedrooms, with pyjamas laid out on the pillows and silver trays on the bedside tables holding a bottle of whisky and two tumblers each. The largest bedroom had a walk-in wardrobe, and all of them had their own bathrooms. At the last bathroom door, Freddie paused. There were no other guests around, although I felt infected by the party atmosphere, the noise and number of them. Freddie smiled at me and I was glad we were by ourselves. I leaned against the door.

'What now?' I asked.

'Let me go and fetch some of the others,' he said. 'Edie will want them.'

I started to move away with him, but he stopped me.

'Go on in,' he said, motioning me towards the door.

I pushed it open and stopped in the doorway. The room was huge and made entirely of green marble. In the middle was a large cast-iron bath, and sitting in the bath was Edie. She held a bar of soap in one hand, and a cocktail glass in the other. Steam was rising from the water, but I could clearly see she was naked.

'Theo,' she said. 'So glad you could come. Can you hold my cocktail for me while I work this into a lather?'

I felt my pulse thrum. I stepped forwards and took the glass, my eyes fixed above her head.

'How boring,' she said. 'You've grown – another one to tower over me.'

'Sorry,' I said automatically.

'Nice and firm, though. Scots are always solid. Have a sip if you like. Freddie makes them – they're guaranteed to get you tight.'

I took a sip and had to stop myself from coughing all over the bath.

Edie was soaping herself. I caught a glimpse of long, dark nipples and, some way below them, a thick triangle of jet-black, curly hair. The hair was out of place on her body, which was otherwise neat and milk-white, and I couldn't help staring at it. The only other woman I'd seen naked was my mother, when I was young and I'd run into her bedroom after a nightmare. The memory of her on all fours on her bed, my father behind her, surfaced hazily and I closed my mind to it. I didn't want to think of her, but I remembered that her body had been different to Edie's; I wondered how different Sylvie's would be too and felt the stirrings of something better enjoyed in private.

'We have a log fire just outside the bathroom,' Edie said. 'It heats the drums that store the water. Another of Freddie's inventions. He's so clever, my husband.'

The drink seemed to be working on me, because I was able to meet her eye now, even pretend that this was normal. 'Yes.'

'And how are you? I haven't seen you for ages.'

There was a burst of noise behind me, and twenty or so guests trooped into the room. They all came forwards to kiss Edie on the cheek and Sylvie leaned over to put her arms around Edie's neck and hug her, their breasts touching through Sylvie's silk dress.

'I've missed you, darling,' Edie said, kissing Sylvie's nose. 'You must come around more often.'

'I will,' Sylvie said.

Everyone was talking and laughing. Edie drank more of the cocktail that I handed back to her; I moved to the back of the crowd and found Nicolas. He grinned at me.

'We should have warned you, I suppose,' he said. 'Here – I brought you a glass of champagne. I'm afraid tonight will only get more *scandaleux*.'

When Edie finished her toilette, she rose from the water glistening and poised. Several hands helped her out of the bath and into a towelling robe. Some of them seemed to linger longer than necessary.

'Freddie,' she called. 'Where are you?'

Freddie materialised at my elbow. I looked behind me, and saw a blushing young woman melt back into the shadows.

'What is it, my sweet?' he asked.

'Something dreadful's happened,' Edie said. 'My drink's finished.'

'Let me get you another,' Freddie said. He made his way through the crowd and kissed his wife before taking her glass. Sylvie, who was standing with her arm linked through Edie's, got a kiss too.

Edie kept us in the bathroom while she dried herself, applied talcum powder and dressed in silk pyjamas.

'I always dine in pyjamas,' I heard her say.

'You're not going native on us, are you?' one of the guests said.

'Now now,' she said. 'No native-bashing here. Let's rejoin the rest of the party.'

Back in the drawing room, Freddie was attending to drinks. There must have been at least fifty guests, and he was constantly pouring, stirring, shaking and wiping. All the servants were lined up along the dining room wall in starched kanzus, white for serving food, instead of the usual brown. Two dogs wandered from guest to guest, sniffing pockets and purses. A rangy Englishman with a high forehead and prominent ears, who'd been introduced to me as Jack Soames, was fiddling with the record player, turning the volume higher and higher. Later I learned it was Sylvie's record, sent over especially by friends from America because she loved the new swing craze.

Edie and Sylvie began dancing while young, admiring men held their glasses for them.

'Another champagne?' Nicolas asked me.

'I'll get them,' I said.

I fought my way through the knots of people, and reached Freddie. The young woman from the bathroom reached him at the same time, and slipped her hand into his pocket.

Freddie whirled around, one eyebrow raised invitingly. 'So that's what you're after.'

'Freddie, darling,' she said, and giggled. She was extraordinarily pretty, with very round, blue eyes. She was wearing a black dress that clung to her hips and showed off her ample breasts, an armful of gold bracelets, and she'd painted her lips deep red, so when they were parted slightly, as now, the red made the white of her teeth even whiter.

'You said you'd come and find me again,' she said, cocking her head at him.

'Later, darling,' Freddie murmured. 'I have my hosting duties for now.'

'You have staff.'

'I like doing it myself.' He saw me. 'Theo – what can I get you?'

'Two champagnes, please.'

'Right away.'

The woman gave me the briefest of smiles.

'*You.*'

As Freddie turned around with the two champagne glasses in his hands, a short, moustachioed man steamed forwards and knocked them to the floor with a crash. '*You,*' he repeated.

'Paul,' the woman said, 'what the hell are you doing?'

'Protecting you, Sara,' Paul said, squaring up to Freddie. He was almost a foot shorter, and I tried not to laugh.

'Paul, my man,' Freddie said. 'If you didn't like the champagne, you only had to ask for something else.'

A few of the guests nearest us were quietening down and watching the scene unfold. I thought I saw a pound note exchanging hands.

'I'm warning you,' Paul said. 'Don't touch my wife – I've seen the way you look at her.'

'Of course you have,' Freddie said. 'She's beautiful.'

'*I* know that,' Paul said, jabbing his finger into Freddie's chest. 'She's my wife.'

'We all find her very alluring,' Freddie said. 'Don't we?'

There was a cheer of assent from those watching.

'The thing we don't understand is why she's with you, when you're so damned ugly?'

Everyone in the audience laughed, even Sara. I thought Paul

might explode, and I stepped forwards to block his fist if he swung at Freddie.

Freddie waved me away. 'I hear,' he continued, 'it's because – not wishing to be crude – you're hung like a bloody elephant.'

Another cheer went up from the audience.

Freddie slung his arm around the man's shoulders. 'So you see, you've got nothing to worry about, old chap. One look at my paltry member compared to yours and she'll come running back begging you to roger her senseless.'

The audience stamped their feet in approval. Paul's face turned red, then purple, then faded to a pinkish colour. He broke away from Freddie and turned to face everyone. The noise died immediately.

Paul grinned and grabbed his crotch. 'Want to see it?' he said.

The audience roared. Sara made a little moue of disapproval. Freddie slapped Paul on the back and smiled at me. 'Thank you,' he mouthed.

I flushed.

Freddie snapped his fingers. One of the totos from the dining room broke away and stood in the doorway.

'Two new glasses,' Freddie said. He was so unruffled by what had happened and I felt even prouder that I was his friend.

The toto disappeared, then quickly returned with fresh glasses, and Freddie poured me some more champagne. Paul was centre of a large crowd now, and I fought my way back through it to Nicolas, who was deep in conversation with a tall, angular man in a good suit. Several women in our vicinity were throwing admiring glances at the newcomer. I thought his mouth a little small, his nose a little big and his eyes too close-set.

The two of them were discussing literature. I hung back until Nicolas noticed me.

'Theo – this is Rupert,' he said. 'He knows nothing about writing, but don't let that put you off him.'

'I'm English,' Rupert said. 'We *invented* writing.'

'And the Greeks?' Nicolas asked.

Rupert made a derisory noise. His arms were folded across his chest, and he looked as if it was taking an immense amount of willpower not to tap his foot.

I handed Nicolas his glass.

'Is that other for me?' Rupert asked. He took it before I had time to respond. 'Thanks, Tom.'

'Theo.'

'Another fan of Greek, hmm?'

A bell rang, and Edie announced dinner. I was given a seat at the end of one of the tables, opposite Nicolas and next to a beautiful Russian woman whose name I forgot immediately. A farming neighbour sat on her other side and talked to us about his various crops for the first course. I kept trying to find Sylvie, and eventually saw her on another table, seated next to Rupert. They had their heads bent together as if they were sharing a secret, and I felt my shoulders stiffen. I turned back to my neighbours in time to hear the woman say:

'And now they're saying all men came from Africa, but look how different we are to the natives.'

'I don't believe it,' the farmer said.

'What about Broken Hill Man?' Nicolas asked. 'They found him in Kabwe a few years ago, and they say he may be two hundred thousand years old. Much older than the Neanderthals found in Europe.'

'Still,' the farmer said. 'It's rather hard to credit.'

'We must have come from somewhere,' Nicolas said, sipping his wine.

'But here? It's so inhospitable.'

'We seem to have come back, anyway.'

'It's different now,' the farmer said. 'We have tools, machinery, vaccines, you name it. We've evolved.'

Nicolas noticed me listening and smiled. 'What do you think, Theo? Are white men meant to live out here?'

I'd never questioned it before, and was suddenly embarrassed at my lack of sophistication. 'I don't know.'

'Why shouldn't we?' the farmer said. 'We've brought running water, electricity, roads, the railway.'

Nicolas laughed. 'You talk as if we did it out of the goodness of our hearts. White men came out to Africa because we realised we had a native population we could use as labour. And now we depend on them to build and maintain the foundation of our white culture and they can't know it.'

'Why?' I asked.

'You should never let anyone know how much you need them,' the Russian woman said. 'It gives them the power.' She rattled the ice in her glass. 'That's how you men think, isn't it?'

Nicolas shrugged. 'Why do you think the government officials are so obsessed with maintaining certain codes of behaviour? White culture can't be seen to fall short. It's why Sir Edward and his wife are so disapproving of our little set.'

'Well really – it's not as if we live in squalor.'

'You know, people lived here for thousands of years without British rule. Sometimes, I wonder if we have the right.'

The Russian woman clucked at him, and waved a heavily bejewelled hand. 'You French,' she said. 'You're never happy unless you're overthrowing some government or another.'

'I'm hardly –'

'Ah – here comes the main course,' the farmer said, and the conversation was forgotten.

The food was delicious – chilled carrot soup with *fines herbes mousse*, *moules marinière*, *coq-au-vin*, *crêpes suzette* and cheese soufflés – and the totos topped up my glass whenever it was less than half full. By the time we finished eating, everything was a pleasant blur.

'Now for games,' Edie announced, and we moved back into the drawing room. I found the nearest sofa, and the other guests arranged themselves around the room, sitting, standing or lounging against the walls to watch.

First, Freddie and two men moved a circular table into the middle of the room, then Edie chose eight guests to hold a bedsheet stretched tightly across it. She stood behind one of the guests, holding a feather in one hand.

'When I throw this into the circle,' she said, 'you must all keep it airborne. You may *not* take your hands away from the sheet.'

'How do we do it then?' one of the male players asked.

'Blow,' Freddie said from the sidelines. 'Just think back to school if you're struggling.'

Everyone laughed. Edie held out her arm, and dropped the feather over the middle of the table. The players began blowing frantically, leaning in with their chests but keeping their arms down. Some of the female players were laughing too much to blow hard enough, and everyone watching was laughing too and catcalling. The feather fluttered a foot or so above the bedsheet, strangely hypnotic.

A shout roused me, and I saw that the players were no longer blowing, but sitting back, giggling. Edie was standing behind them, looking satisfied.

'Now,' she said. 'Sophia, you go with Boy, Charles, you go with Francesca, Dushka, you're with Jack, Paul, you take Lilia.' I couldn't tell how she'd come up with the pairings, but everyone else seemed to understand. When she'd named them, she gave each couple a key, and they stood up, giggling harder. They disappeared off into the direction of the bedrooms. The air in the room was vibrating with excitement; I wanted to ask someone what was going on, but I couldn't see anyone I knew.

'Next game,' Edie said. 'We'll need another sheet.'

Another sheet was brought in, but this time it had holes cut into it at various points. Edie chose five men to stand behind the sheet. There was a sudden explosion of clapping from the audience and I saw the men were sticking their private parts through the holes. Edie stood beside each hole in turn and the audience shouted numbers at her. Eventually, it was agreed that the left one was a

100

seven. The next one was a six, then nine, then five, then seven-and-a-half. My throat felt suddenly hoarse, and I realised I'd been shouting just as loudly as everyone else in the room.

Edie chose another five men to go behind the sheet, and the game started again. One of the couples from the feather-blowing game reappeared, looking hot and happy. I lay back on my sofa and let the night unfold around me.

The feather-blowing game was played again with four new couples, including Edie. I must have been staring at it intently, because it was a while before I noticed the young man and woman sharing my sofa. She was sitting on his lap and they were kissing, passionately. She was wearing a dress and the skirt had been hitched up above her knees, while the man had his finger inside her and was moving it in and out at great speed. She saw my eyes on her and made a noise as if to stop the man. I closed my eyelids most of the way, until I could see only dimly through my lashes, and pretended to have drifted off, although I itched to use my hands myself.

Then Sylvie was bending over just as the activity next to me seemed to reach a climax. She kissed my forehead. I was about to tell her I was awake, when I saw Rupert standing next to her. I kept quiet and they drifted off together, holding hands. I imagined them slipping into one of the bedrooms, re-enacting what had just happened next to me. I imagined myself older, and ready, taking Rupert's place, Sylvie astride me, her lips soft on mine and my finger wet and hot inside her. I squeezed my eyelids to keep the picture in, until it exploded in my skull and I felt a warmth spread outwards from below.

The rest of the night was a muddle of red lips parting lasciviously, Freddie wearing a string of pearls, cocktail glasses tipping over, loud music, bare bottoms, shouts, grunting, a cloud of cigarette smoke, then the grey sky of early morning and the chatter and singing of birds, the rustling of treetops in a cool breeze that streamed in through the open front door. Some of the guests had

101

decamped to the lawn. Sylvie was out there too. I could hear her voice and her ukulele.

I sat up, gingerly moving the legs of the man sharing my sofa with me. Sleeping guests were strewn around the room like bunting. The servants were up already – or perhaps they hadn't gone to bed – quietly sweeping up broken glass and mopping up spills and vomit.

I stumbled through the main bedroom, past a bed full of naked, sweaty bodies, shut myself in Edie's bathroom and washed my face, then ran a wet hand through my hair, smoothing it down. I had to look presentable when I returned home. There was nothing I could do about my eyes however; they looked different, older. I was different, older; a man for real.

From behind me a bell rang, high and clear.

'Breakfast,' Edie called, and I realised I was starving.

Chapter Nine

After the party, Rupert began calling on Sylvie and Nicolas at least once a week. He was twenty-six years old, he told us, an English aristocrat recently returned from Argentina.

'Were you farming out there?' Nicolas asked.

'Amusing myself,' Rupert said. 'And running up large bills.'

'I bet you were,' Sylvie said, smiling her special smile.

He wore five gold rings, presents from female admirers, and all his stories involved broken-hearted women and irate husbands. 'Love 'em and leave 'em,' he said. 'That's the only way to do it. No woman's ever going to get her claws into me.' Sylvie sat up straighter when he said that.

When he wasn't talking, he had a habit of tapping his teeth with his fingernails, distracting whoever else was talking, and when he wasn't doing that he was chain-smoking or arguing. He was the opposite of Freddie, I thought, who radiated energy. Rupert sucked it out of everyone.

Nicolas didn't seem to notice anything at first, but after a while his face fell whenever we heard Rupert's Buick pulling up outside the house.

'Freddie is married,' he said to me. 'But Rupert's a bachelor – that's the problem.'

Maud stopped visiting after Rupert began showing up. I understood – watching Sylvie laughing at his jokes, or listening wide-eyed to his rants, made me think I didn't know her at all. It burned me to see Rupert ignore her all afternoon, how it only made her more desperate for his attention.

'It's hard for him, you know, being so much cleverer than everyone else,' she said once, when I pointed out how rude he'd been that afternoon. 'He doesn't think about trivial things. And he's just playing for the audience. He can be sensitive too.'

I wasn't sure he was any cleverer than Nicolas. I could tell there was a competitiveness between them, but Rupert only won more often because he shouted louder.

Freddie didn't seem to mind him. Rupert was good at impressions as well. Sometimes they held entire conversations as other people. Rupert's were more insulting.

'What can you possibly have against Auntie?' Sylvie asked, after a particularly bad one. We were playing doubles tennis on a makeshift court, with sofa cushions marking the lines and a net strung up between two trees. Rupert and Sylvie were playing Freddie and Nicolas. I was ball boy. Roderigo watched from a nearby tree.

'Yes, poor Auntie,' Freddie said, grinning through the squares of the net.

'The bitch gave me a public dressing-down the last time I was at the hotel.'

'That's just her way,' Sylvie said. She was wearing a bottle-green blouse and wide-legged trousers in grey. Her lips were the colour of burgundy and I longed to lick them, to see what they tasted of.

'She is, as Hamlet said of his mother, *A little more than kin, and less than kind.*'

'Actually,' Nicolas said, inspecting his strings, 'I believe Hamlet said that of Claudius.'

'Don't tell me I'm wrong about my own culture.'

'Why not?' Nicolas said. 'You didn't write it.'

There was a tautness to the air suddenly.

'You think you're better than me, don't you?' Rupert said.

'I don't think about it.'

'Well you're just a Frog,' Rupert said loudly. 'A dirty Frog.'

Roderigo sprang out of the tree and leapt at Sylvie, wrapping himself around her shoulders and peeking out from behind her head.

'Calm down, de Trevelyn,' Freddie said. 'It's not good for you to get too excited in the heat.'

'You can bloody piss off.'

'Ru,' Sylvie said. 'Why does it matter if Nico's right about the line?'

'You're taking his side too?'

'Maybe I should ask you to leave,' Nicolas said.

'I'm not leaving.'

'It's my house, and you're insulting me.'

'It's *her* house,' Rupert said, jabbing his thumb at Sylvie. 'She's the one with the money.'

I stood up so fast I kicked one of the cushions into the flower-bed. 'Don't talk about Sylvie like that.'

Sylvie put her hand out to touch my arm. 'Boys, please,' she said. She caught my gaze. 'Don't worry about me so much, darling.'

I collected the cushion, my lungs tight.

Freddie looked stony-faced. 'It's interesting, de Trevelyn, that you always know the nearest source of money. Sylvie – if he tries to touch you up to pay off his gambling debts, don't give it to him.'

'It's just money,' she said defiantly.

Rupert grinned. 'You used to be more fun, Hamilton.'

Freddie shrugged. 'If you say so.'

Nicolas threw his racquet down. 'I'm taking Samson for a walk. I suddenly feel the need for more civilised society.'

'Wait, Nico,' Sylvie said. She passed Roderigo to me and followed

Nicolas to the corner of the lawn where Samson was snoozing in the sun. They were just out of earshot, but I could see Nicolas's face soften as Sylvie touched his shoulder. I picked up the discarded racquet and swatted at a fly with it. There was a tiny, satisfying thud.

'Well,' Freddie said. 'I better get back to Edie.'

'Don't leave on my account,' Rupert said. 'Here – I've got your money.'

Freddie waved it away. 'Spend it on something nice for Sylvie. Or a bottle for Nico.'

Rupert laughed. 'You think I'm a cad.' He picked up the tennis ball and smashed it over the net at Freddie, making him duck.

Freddie raised an eyebrow, but he was smiling. 'I *know* you're a cad.'

'I wouldn't have to worry all the time if my damn parents weren't so tight with the purse-strings.'

'Then it's my gift to you. But be gentle with her.'

Rupert had turned away and didn't seem to be listening. 'My love,' he called. 'You do make the nicest *tableaux*.'

I followed his gaze. Nicolas was standing behind Sylvie, one hand on her shoulder, looking affectionately down at the scene in front of him. Sylvie was kneeling in front of Samson; as we watched she planted a kiss on the lion's nose and he yawned then nuzzled her. I ached to be him.

'What do you say to packing in the game and drinking gin sours instead?' Rupert asked.

Sylvie laughed. 'We never turn down a drink in this house.'

'I'm sorry, Nico.'

Nicolas shrugged.

I accepted Freddie's offer of a ride home.

'That was dramatic, wasn't it?' he said, as The Farm disappeared from the rear-view mirror.

'I don't understand why Sylvie likes Rupert.'

'She's contrary,' Freddie said. 'Take the wheel for a moment?'

I grasped it while he searched his pockets.

'What do you think of him?'

Freddie pulled out a cigarette, lit it then took back the wheel. 'He can be good fun. He never holds a grudge, either. And he's a true-blue at least.'

'What's that?'

'Blue blood, my sort. It's the way we were brought up, you know. No boundaries.' He inhaled deeply. 'Don't feel too jealous – I'm sure it'll blow over.'

'I'm not jealous.'

'Of course you are – that's exactly how I would have felt at your age.'

My ears pounded with blood, and I felt a strange urge to cry. Freddie was talking as if I'd never gone to the party, as if I hadn't changed. 'You don't know everything about me.'

'I know you're what we call a "short-fuse".'

'Oh really?'

'Really. It's the fiery Celt in you.'

I drummed my fingers on my knee.

'Now I've offended Boy Genius.'

'Stop calling me that.'

'I'm sorry, Theo.' He shook his head, then burst out laughing.

'What's so funny?'

'I can't say – you'd just get angry with me again.'

For the first time, I wanted to hit him.

My father had taken a room at The Nairobi Club for nights when he was working late, which seemed to be often. Whenever he did appear we were always impressed by his beard, which had become quite luxuriant, and his nose, which was becoming a very cheerful shade of red. Our mother was busy too, but it seemed to suit her; even the totos seemed more at ease around her. The next time my father came home, she suggested we take a family holiday.

'Somewhere up the line?' he asked hopefully. 'The branch line to Kitale should be finished next week.'

'I was thinking of the coast,' she said.

'Ah, well. That sounds nice,' he said, and buried his nose in the paper.

In the end our mother took us to Mombasa by herself at the end of November. We hired a house overlooking the beach at Shanzu, a quiet curve of the coastline to the north of the city, with dazzlingly clear waters and sand so fine it felt like talcum powder.

The house was basic: plain white bedrooms with cast-iron beds and crosses on the walls, a sitting room with a few hard-backed chairs, coffee table and bookcase, and a small room, empty apart from a tub – in the middle of the floor – big enough to squat in while the servants poured jugs of water over us; this was the bathroom. The veranda was wide and cool, with three large sofas shaded by palm trees.

There was an outside toilet in a small, dark hut that buzzed with flies. The roof was made of grass and, instead of toilet paper, a tall spike running through a stack of cloth strips was placed within reach. My mother's cheeks turned pale when she saw it and I felt for her. Not everyone had adapted as quickly as I had.

We ate at my father's club in Kilindini – fresh fish, quail eggs, watermelon, mangos, white wine and dark coffee – on a hill looking down onto Kilindini harbour, a calming palette of colours. During the day there was the brilliant blue of the Indian Ocean, the shimmering, emerald trails of the fish darting about underwater, the pale blue of the sky and the lush green of the palm leaves. Then, at night, the ghostly phosphorescence following the boats as they slipped quietly out to sea.

I took Scotty for a run every morning along the shoreline and to the harbour. There were boats everywhere, mostly yachts manned by 'boat boys' – totos wearing navy-blue trousers and tee shirts. Scotty terrorised them all, chasing them back onto their decks until I called him off.

The fleas and ticks got to Scotty, making him howl in misery. Maud and I picked them off, one by one. Chigoe fleas, or 'jiggers', were the worst. The males simply sucked blood, like other fleas, but the females would burrow into Scotty's paws, or our feet, feeding off blood vessels underneath the skin, staying there and swelling as they produced eggs. We dug them out with safety pins, and washed the wounds in paraffin, which was stored in reused bottles. In Naivasha, Miss Graham would give us a teaspoon of paraffin with our milk, to disinfect our insides, so Maud put some in Scotty's milk too.

He was supposed to sleep on the veranda, but Maud trained him to wait until the lights were out, then push open the screen door and trot into her room. He slept curled up next to her under the covers, his head resting on the crook of her outstretched arm.

On our last night, my mother knocked on my bedroom door after I had blown out my candle, then came in and sat on my bed.

'How do you like it here?' she asked.

'Very much.'

'It's a long way from Scotland.'

'Yes.'

She was looking away from me. I waited, watching her profile caught in a beam of moonlight. She was fingering the locket around her neck.

'I want to ask you about your friends, Theo,' she started, then turned her face to me. In the bluish light I could see her large eyes and her sharp white teeth when she spoke again. 'I let you spend time with the de Croÿs because I think they're harmless, really.'

'What do you mean?'

'Countess de Croÿ is very young,' my mother said, 'but she understands what it means to be a woman in our world, so I don't think she'll do anything rash. However, the government

109

people disapprove of . . . certain behaviour that they hear about.'

'Do they?'

'You know that as well as I do.'

I thought of the party and smiled. The government people probably couldn't even imagine what we'd got up to.

'Well?'

'People like to exaggerate,' I said.

'So there's no truth to the stories?'

'I haven't heard the stories.'

She put her hand on my leg. 'You haven't done anything, have you, Theo?'

'What are you talking about?'

'I don't mind what your friends do,' she said. 'As long as you aren't caught up in it.'

'Caught up in what?'

'You're only fifteen. One day you'll be grown up and you'll have a good job and make a good husband. You're my son – I want that for you.'

'You don't need to worry about me.'

'Promise?'

'I promise.'

She was quiet for a moment, then she withdrew her hand and left, closing the door softly behind her.

Shortly after our second Christmas in Kenya Nicolas sent a toto to Kiboko with a note.

Rupert disappeared for a few weeks, he wrote. *I thought we'd got rid of him for good, but he turned up again yesterday like a bad penny. He must have had a lucky streak while away, because he claims that I promised to take him on safari and insists we go through with it early February, no matter the cost. Sylvie is joining us for the first weekend – how about you? Do you think your parents could spare you?*

110

I couldn't help feeling irritated that Sylvie had agreed so easily to Rupert's plans when he'd clearly abandoned her to go enjoy himself somewhere else. At least if I went too, I could keep an eye on them.

I went inside to find my mother and show her the note. She read it quickly, then folded it up and handed it back. 'Of course you can go,' she said, surprising me. 'Just remember our talk.'

'I do.'

'Good.' She left the room. I waited, half-expecting her to come back in and tell me she'd changed her mind, but after a few moments I heard her ordering a bath, then closing her bedroom door. I felt a small glow of triumph.

The toto was waiting on the veranda for my answer. 'Tell him I'll go,' I said.

Chapter Ten

My father came home the night before the safari, his car jolting and starting down the drive. My mother was reading in front of the fire; from where we were doing our schoolwork at the dining table I heard her little noise of surprise and stood to look out the window until Miss Graham, at the table with us, tapped my exercise book and I sank down again.

Abdullah appeared from the kitchen with a lamp and passed through the dining room silently; I saw him open the screen door and step out onto the veranda, and heard a low murmur, then my father's voice, much louder, thanking him for the light.

'Come and say hello to your father,' my mother called.

We put down our pencils and went into the sitting room. My father was coming up the veranda steps, rubbing his hands against the fog in the air.

'Father,' Maud said. She went forwards to kiss him, and he beamed down at her. He clapped me on the back when he came into the sitting room, Abdullah following with the lantern, then greeted my mother, who stayed seated.

'I thought I'd have supper with my wife, for once,' he said, sitting down next to her on the sofa, his voice booming and jolly.

We sat on the sofa opposite, trying not to be too conspicuous so as to not get sent back to our schoolwork.

'You're just in time,' my mother said.

'What are we having?'

'Cold partridge, red cabbage and mashed potatoes.'

'Wonderful.' He rubbed his hands together again. 'I think I'll start with a sherry.'

Abdullah poured him a glass and helped remove his shoes, then knelt in front of him and massaged his feet, while my father poured the drink down his throat.

'Your face is very pleasant, Abdullah,' he said.

'Thank you, Bwana.'

'*Good wine is a good familiar creature, if it be well used.* What do you say to that, Abdullah?'

'Nothing, Bwana.'

'It's Shakespeare, you know.'

'I agree, William,' my mother said. 'But we should let Abdullah tell Joseph you're here.'

'Yes, go, go.' My father waved his hand.

Abdullah disappeared in the direction of the kitchen. I turned to Maud, grinning, and caught her staring after him with a strange look on her face.

'What is it?' I asked in a low voice.

'Do you ever wonder if Abdullah minds working for us?' she whispered.

'Why should he?'

'He's just so . . .' She looked at my father's feet, then quickly away again.

'At least he has work.'

My father got up to pour himself more sherry, then returned to his seat. 'Why don't we all eat together tonight? The children can stay up a little later.'

My mother raised her eyebrows, but she didn't say anything.

'How are your lessons progressing?' he asked us.

'Fine,' we said together.

'Good, good.' He pointed at me. 'You'll need good grades to read Engineering, especially if you go to Edinburgh.'

My mouth felt dry with the sudden fear that he wanted to send me away. 'What?'

'I know it's not for a few years. But –'

'How are things at the office?' my mother interrupted.

'Ah yes. Passenger numbers are rising steadily. *Courage and comfort, all shall yet go well.*'

'How nice,' my mother said. She stood up. 'I think I'll have a lie-down before supper.'

'Maud, come sit on my lap,' my father said. 'I want to cuddle my little girl.'

'Don't spoil her.'

Maud sat on my father's lap and circled her arms around his neck. My father hugged her to him, and I felt a brief, sharp pang at how easy they were with each other.

'I'm going on a safari tomorrow,' I said. 'With Nicolas and Sylvie.'

'Who?' my father asked.

'The American woman and the Frenchman,' my mother said.

'You're not going to shoot anything, are you?' Maud said.

'No,' my mother said. 'No guns. You wouldn't touch them, would you, Theo?' Her expression was neutral but I felt somehow she was on edge behind it, and I shrugged to stop her staring at me.

My father took another sip of his sherry. Maud leaned her head away.

'You smell like oil,' she said.

'I've been inspecting the engines today.' He put down his sherry. 'You're almost too big for this now.'

'I'm not,' she said, burying her face in his beard.

'Honestly,' my mother said. 'Maud, go ask Abdullah to make me a cup of tea.'

Maud kissed my father's cheek and left the room.

'You have to be careful not to make her life too soft,' my mother said.

'We're not going to let her want for anything.' My father picked up his drink and took another sip. 'This is really excellent, this sherry.'

My mother shook her head. 'Women –'

'Ah yes,' my father said. 'What would we men do without you, eh, Theo?' He pulled her onto his now-free lap and wrapped his arms around her. 'Your life isn't too hard, I hope. I'd wrestle a hippo if I thought it would make you happy.'

My cheeks were scorching, and I shifted further away from the fire. My mother wriggled a little, then gave up and laughed. 'Theo,' she said. 'Go and see what your sister's up to in there.'

I escaped gladly. As I was leaving, I heard my father murmur, 'Ah, Jessie.'

They collected me just after sunrise. Frost still tipped the lawn and flowers, and Sylvie was shivering by the time I joined her on the veranda. She'd left Roderigo at home for once. Scotty bounded after me and gave her hand a welcoming lick.

'Hello, handsome,' she said.

'Hello,' I said.

'I wasn't talking to you,' she said, but she kissed my cheek.

'Don't bark now,' I said to Scotty, who whimpered softly, then lay down with his head on his paws, watching us go.

'It's going to be completely clear today,' Sylvie said. 'All the better for them to shoot something.' She took my arm. 'Will you hunt?'

'Only if I'm going to eat it afterwards.'

She laughed. 'Exactly what I thought you'd say.'

As we reached the cars, Sylvie frowned at something in the distance. I followed her gaze to the wheeling figures in the sky above Hell's Gate.

115

'Griffon vultures,' she said. 'They're bad omens.'

'Only for rabbits and mice,' I said, opening the passenger door for her.

She climbed in beside Rupert, and I walked to the car in front, where Nico was sitting behind the wheel.

'Good morning,' he said as I climbed in. 'If you can call it that.'

'Good morning.'

He started the engine and we drove off. He was quiet for the first half of the journey, staring straight ahead with eyes creased against the dawn.

'How come Rupert disappeared?' I asked eventually.

'He was in disgrace.'

'Why in disgrace?'

'Ah.' He cleared his throat. 'I'm afraid I may have something to do with that.'

'What happened?'

He fumbled in his shirt pocket with his right hand, keeping his left on the wheel, and brought out a cigarette, then lit it before answering. 'We had a fight at Freddie and Edie's a few Saturdays ago. He was being typically insufferable. Sneering at all the guests. Making Sylvie run after him. I know Freddie can be cruel, but with him it's an armour – Rupert's bad, through and through.'

'Why does Sylvie like him then?'

He pulled deeply on his cigarette. 'My wife is a very fragile person – you know she lost her mother when she was young, no? And her father – there are strange stories about the two of them on trips around Europe when she was an adolescent. She was always beautiful, you see, and a little precocious. She told me once he used to pretend she was his wife.'

'Oh.' I pictured a young Sylvie promenaded on her father's arm as his bride, and dug my fingernails into my palm.

'Anyway – she needs to be loved. And when she finds someone who doesn't love her, all she wants to do is change their mind.'

He shrugged. 'She can only really give herself to someone who breaks her – that's her tragedy.'

'Can I have a cigarette?'

'Of course.' He fumbled in his pocket again and offered me the packet. I took a cigarette and lit it, then inhaled slowly, the way I'd seen Sylvie do. I'd thought I'd known her fully before, but now I could really understand why she was so damaged, so impulsive. And why she'd married Nico, too. He must have seemed so safe.

'What happened after you fought?'

'It got very heated,' Nicolas said. 'Then Rupert went outside and set fire to the servants' houses.'

I coughed violently on the smoke. Nicolas slowed the car and thumped me on the back.

'Better?'

'Yes.' I wiped my streaming eyes with the heel of my hand. 'What happened then?'

'He was fined.'

'And the Africans?'

'They lost their houses.'

'No one died?'

'No. They were all working at the party.'

I took another tentative drag on the cigarette. It was foul-tasting, even bitterer than coffee. I hung my arm over the side of the door, then let it slip from my fingers.

'Sylvie was angry at him then, at least,' Nicolas said.

I fell asleep shortly afterwards and woke when we were already at the South-Western Mau National Reserve. Sylvie was right – it had turned into a beautifully clear day. As soon as we'd finished setting up camp, Nicolas and Rupert left with their rifles and the gunbearers. I stayed behind with Sylvie.

'I have a headache,' she said. 'You don't mind if I lie down for a while, do you?'

'No – I'll go explore.'

We were in a small clearing not too far from a shallow stream, and I wandered down to wash my face. At the water's edge, I saw a petite dik-dik antelope drinking further up. I crouched down quietly to watch, but my presence must have disturbed it. It raised its head, nostrils quivering, and gave the cry of alarm it was named after, then was gone in a flash of brown and tan.

I splashed some water on myself and headed back. Trees grew thickly around the spot we'd chosen to camp, their bark dark grey and cracked with age. Birds perched high up in the branches, chirping to each other, and creamy, sweet-smelling flowers fell at my feet when they took flight.

The remaining totos were preparing supper. I sat in a canvas chair outside my tent, and they brought me a Fortnum & Mason chop box full of cheese and biscuits, mustard, tea, cold sausage, grapes, apples, wine and chocolates. I collected the grape seeds in my hand as I ate, then dug a hole on the edge of the clearing and buried them.

'Gardening?' Sylvie called to me when she emerged from her tent.

'Getting rid of the evidence,' I said.

'We brought the record player. Shall we have some music?'

'Alright.'

She knelt down in front of one of the boxes outside her tent and started riffling through it. I joined her.

'What do you fancy?'

'Anything you like.'

She picked one out and slipped it out of its paper jacket, showing it to me. 'Rupert got me this,' she said. 'I told him Cole Porter was my favourite and a week later he turned up with it.' She bit her lip. 'I know he can't afford to give me presents. His family are so strict with his money.'

'Hmm.' I didn't want us to talk about Rupert. I dared myself to move closer, rub my arm against hers. She started, as if she'd forgotten where she was, who I was, then smiled quickly.

118

'Let's put this on,' she said, and got up.

No one bagged anything that day, but they found elephant spoor a few miles from the camp.

'We'll get them tomorrow,' Rupert said as we sat around the fire after supper, sipping whisky.

The night was clear too, and the stars to the east were glittering in a friendly way. Occasionally the fire hissed and shot long sparks into the air. Outside our circle, we could hear the totos moving about, washing up the dinner things, speaking softly to each other.

'I want to die on a night like this,' Sylvie said. 'Surrounded by my favourite people, good food, a glass of whisky.'

'Better to think about living,' Nicolas said. 'We can't control our deaths.'

'There's one way to control it,' Rupert said.

'Don't joke about that.'

'I'm not.' He swished the whisky around in his glass. 'Frankly, I can't think of anything worse than getting old and boring.'

So Rupert thought about dying too. I was irritated that he was muscling in on something that Sylvie and I shared, even if we'd never shared it out loud. 'Really?' I asked. 'Nothing worse?'

'Really.' He pointed at Sylvie. 'How about you?'

'I'd rather die than have people stop wanting me around.'

'People are stupid,' Rupert said. 'Who cares how they feel about you?'

Nicolas snorted.

'I mean it,' Rupert said. 'Do you think I care?' He stretched his legs. 'How would you do it?'

'Gun,' Sylvie said immediately.

'Very masculine of you.'

'Please can we change the subject?' Nicolas said.

Rupert shrugged. 'You should listen to your wife more – she's one of the only interesting people out here.'

Sylvie smiled. Rupert raised his glass to her. 'Why did you

think I was hanging around all the time? I've never met anyone like you.'

He seemed so serious, and my stomach shifted uneasily. I'd never seen his mask slip before. I hadn't noticed how young he looked, or how dark his eyes were.

'I like the night-time better than the day,' I blurted.

Nicolas laughed.

'You're nocturnal, remember,' Sylvie said.

'What's that?' Nicolas asked.

'One of Freddie's theories.'

'What —'

'Apparently I'm a leopard,' I said. I stole a glance at Rupert. 'He's a leopard too, but only because he likes watching Sylvie.'

'Making you his prey, my love?' Nico said.

'I wouldn't say that.'

'She likes Freddie too much to be his prey,' I said.

'Damn mosquitoes are all over me,' Rupert said loudly. His sneer was back and I hoped he was annoyed enough to act out. 'I thought you knew a thing or two about camping, de Croÿ?'

'You chose the spot,' Nicolas said, swatting them away.

'You didn't object.'

'I've been bitten,' Sylvie interrupted. She showed us the insides of her arms. Livid red dots had appeared on both forearms. 'They always go for me.'

'Looks bad,' Rupert said. He took a long drink of the whisky.

'You make it too inviting for them,' I said.

'Do I?'

She was smiling, but at the ground, not at me. In the glow of the fire she looked lovelier than ever, shadows moving across her face and deepening her eyes. She had a string of pearls around her neck that drew attention to the fine bones in her chest and she fingered them, as if she knew what I was looking at without having to see. I loved her so much my heart hurt and my head felt dizzy. And at the same time I had an urge, so strong it was almost bewildering, to hit her.

On the other side of the fire, Nicolas slapped his neck. 'Got one.'

'Maybe we should go to bed,' Sylvie said. 'Before we're eaten alive.'

'Good idea,' he said.

To my disappointment, Rupert just shrugged.

We crawled into our tents. Outside, I could hear the totos clearing away our whisky glasses, putting more branches on the fire and going to bed. They didn't have tents, just a sheet each to sleep under.

Then the sounds of the forest – the shrieking of insects, the chattering of monkeys and the cry of an African wood owl. Once I thought I heard a lion cough, and my body tensed up, but I didn't hear it again and eventually I fell asleep.

The next morning, I opened my tent flap and lay back under my warm blankets, watching the changing scene.

Dew clung to the grass in fat orbs and when I breathed tiny drops of water swirled in a cloud above my head. At first the sky was a grey strip above the treetops, but gradually it filled with hazy colour, pink, then copper, then golden, then the treetops gleamed gold too, and the birds yawned, shook themselves, and burst into song.

The fire was still crackling softly, and every so often the smoke drifted towards my tent, smelling like autumn back in Scotland, when the gardeners would build bonfires to burn the fallen leaves. It mingled with the smell of mimosa and earth and the coffee that the totos were preparing for us.

Sylvie stood at the entrance to my tent and laughed at me. 'You'll never be a great hunter, lying in bed all morning,' she said.

I pulled on a jumper and crawled out. 'I didn't hear the others leave.'

'They went before sunrise.'

She set out two canvas chairs around the fire and we sat. She kicked off her shoes and tucked her feet underneath her. 'There's something about sleeping outdoors that makes me hungry,' she said.

'Me too.'

She lit a cigarette, bending her long neck towards the flame in her cupped hand. She was most beautiful in the middle of nature, I thought, fresh-faced and bathed in sunlight, her hair swept back from those high cheekbones.

I left my chair and picked some wild flowers, presenting them to her in a colourful bouquet. 'For my lady.'

'Flowers at breakfast,' she said, and sniffed them. 'Heavenly.'

The totos brought us coffee and porridge and bananas and we ate in contented silence. Butterflies danced around our heads in crimson and orange and green. Sylvie looked at me over the rim of her coffee cup, eyes laughing. I wondered at how, just over a year ago, I'd sat with her in the bar by Mr Sand's market, completely tongue-tied.

'I think I might go back,' she said, when we'd finished.

'Why?'

'I don't want to hunt.'

'That's the only reason?'

'Well . . .' She laughed. 'You'll think I'm crazy.'

'The vultures?'

'Yes.'

I wanted to put my arms around her. 'I'll go home with you,' I said. 'I don't want to hunt either.'

She smiled at me. 'Good. We'll take my car. Rupert can drive Nico back.' She stood up.

'Don't we need to wait for them?'

'The totos will tell them where we've gone.'

We left in a squeal of tyres.

'I'm parched,' Sylvie said as we neared Naivasha. 'What do we have to drink?'

I rummaged around and found her some brandy. She took a long drink, and sighed.

'I just had to get out,' she said. 'Do you understand?'

'Yes.'

'I felt that way in France, too.' She took another slug of the brandy and passed the flask back to me. 'Nico's brother married the snottiest little bitch – she was always laughing at my accent.'

'And that's why you wanted to leave?'

She shook her head. 'It was just the same every day. Same people, same conversations, same food and wine. Nico loves it, loves the routine. I never settled into it – there's obviously something wrong with me.'

'I don't think so.'

She looked over at me and smiled. 'You're getting to be one of my favourite people, Theo.'

She dropped me off at the top of our driveway, where the ornamental firs clustered on either side of the road, blocking the view of the house and the lake.

'Thanks for looking after me,' she said as I opened the passenger door.

I suddenly saw her again as a girl disguised as a young bride, and felt my insides tighten, then my mouth was moving before I'd even realised what I was going to say. 'Rupert doesn't look after you, you know.' I stopped just short of saying 'like your father'.

'He cares about me.'

'He's not a good person. Nico told me about the fire.'

She frowned, and I hoped I hadn't dropped Nico in it. 'He promised never to do anything like that again.' She stared down at her hands on the steering wheel. 'He's different when we're alone. I love him so much, Theo, sometimes I think I'm dying. I guess I might as well die if I can't be with him.'

She looked up then, and smiled her special smile. I knew I had to change her mind somehow, that my future happiness depended on it. I felt my heartbeat skip and before I could stop myself I was leaning over and kissing her. Her lips were as soft as I'd always imagined, and she tasted sweet, like the brandy. I thought I heard a quick intake of breath. My body responded and I pressed forwards, but she put her hand on my shoulder and pushed me gently away.

'Goodbye, darling.'

I climbed out of the car, throbbing with tension. She gave me another smile then drove off. I waited until she was out of sight before stumbling into the trees to think about her properly.

Chapter Eleven

For the next few weeks the weather was sunny and cloudless, with the dry smell found only in hot countries – everything dry, especially the baked earth underfoot. The totos moved sluggishly, chopping firewood, hanging up the laundry, scrubbing the dirty kitchen pans. Scotty lay in a shaded corner of the porch, his water bowl next to him and his tongue permanently out. Eventually my mother snapped. 'We're spending the next weekend in Nairobi,' she told us. 'The Griggs want to take us for supper and I can't stand looking at this lake a moment longer.'

The Griggs took us to The Nairobi Club. The members were officials and tradesmen as opposed to the settler crowd at the Muthaiga, and the volume in the dining room never increased above a low hum.

We had fish and white wine. Scotty was reunited with his brothers and sisters and they spent the evening chasing each other around the grounds. Lady Joan and my mother discussed the most recent League meeting; Sir Edward listened politely to my father talk about the railway.

'The natives still call it "the Iron Snake", of course,' my father said. 'One of their medicine men prophesied its coming years ago – had a dream about a black snake coming and all their cattle disappearing. They thought it was a bad omen when we showed up to build it, I can tell you.'

'I remember,' Sir Edward said. '"One day the Iron Snake will cross the land, causing trouble wherever it goes."' He drummed his fingers on the table. 'Deplorably superstitious, poor buggers.'

I was silent all evening, even when my mother mentioned I'd gone on safari with Nico and Sylvie, and Lady Joan said 'Ah', and turned to look at me. Inwardly I squirmed whenever I thought of Sylvie, and the kiss, and wondered if she thought about it still, or if she'd forgotten it completely as soon as she left me. I didn't know which was worse.

Freddie was in Nairobi too and picked me up the next evening to take me back to the Muthaiga Club. It felt both more and less than a year since my first visit.

Faces I only vaguely recognised crowded around us and hands shook mine.

'Have you corrupted him yet, Hamilton?' someone asked.

'He's a big hit at the parties,' Freddie said. 'All the ladies want to know who he is.'

'A *big* hit, is he?'

Freddie grinned and draped his arm around my shoulder. In an effort to put the kiss out of my mind I let him buy me drink after drink. After a while I felt light-headed and benevolent towards everyone, especially Freddie; I could hardly remember why I'd been angry with him before. At some point, the two of us climbed on a table and sang the rest of the bar a Scottish duet. I took the man's part; Freddie did a good impression of a woman. We were singing different words, but nobody seemed to mind. At the end of the song, I grabbed his hand.

'Look – we're like the natives,' I said.

'I'm afraid we smell far too clean to fool anyone,' Freddie said.

'We could pretend.'

'You, my boy, need another drink.'

Later, I saw Carberry in the corner of the bar, sneering at us, and I stared him out.

The night ended when one of the gentlemen started swinging from the chandeliers in the ballroom, several of the bar staff hovering below, ready to catch him in case he fell.

The next morning, I woke early with a thick tongue. The first glimpse of daylight through the blinds sent a flash of pain through my eyeballs.

Scotty jumped onto my bed and licked my face.

'Alright,' I told him. 'I'll take you for a walk.'

I threw on trousers and a jumper and we left the hotel, walking aimlessly through the streets, nodding to people I recognised from the club, who looked as peaky as I felt.

We turned onto 6th Avenue and I headed towards the post office to buy some stamps. I tied Scotty up on the shaded porch and pushed open the door. Scotty started to bark.

'I won't be long,' I said.

There was already a queue inside. I took my place at the back, trying to ignore Scotty. My stomach gurgled unpleasantly.

Flies buzzed around in the heat of the room. I wiped away the sweat that was forming on my upper lip. Ahead of me, an elderly lady was arguing with the clerk; I rubbed my temples.

Carberry came into the post office and stood behind me. I pointedly turned my face away. He didn't seem to mind, and started whistling nonchalantly. The clerk behind the grille looked half-asleep as he counted out the change for the elderly lady. After a while, I realised what Carberry was whistling – *Oh where, oh where has my little dog gone.*

I couldn't hear Scotty barking any more.

'Scotty?' I called. Nothing.

I started to walk towards the door.

'You'll lose your place,' Carberry called after me.

Outside, there was no Scotty.

'Scotty,' I called. Still nothing.

I turned on my heel and ran back to Carberry.

'Where's my dog?'

'Damned if I know,' he drawled. 'You should tie him up if you don't want him to go missing.'

I put my hands on his shoulders and shoved, hard. He stumbled backwards, and I thought I caught a spark of fear in his eyes.

'*Where's my dog?*'

'Don't touch me,' he said, but I could see sweat gathering on his brow.

I ran out of the post office again, and up and down the street, calling for Scotty. Two roads back, I found him in a ditch, his leg bent back at a peculiar angle and blood dripping from his muzzle. Next to him, a large rock was red and sticky; he was completely still.

'Scotty,' I said, crouching beside him in the ditch, 'can you hear me?' I was crying so hard I almost didn't hear the whimper. I wiped my arm across my eyes. 'Scotty?'

He looked at me then, dragging his eyes open through a crust of blood and dirt, and feebly lifted his tail in greeting.

'Good boy,' I said, through my tears. 'Good boy – you're going to be alright.'

I lifted him up, cradling him in my arms, and started to run towards The Norfolk. I could feel his heart pounding against his chest, but he didn't cry or bark; he was a brave dog.

People stared at me as I passed them. One of the boys must have guessed where I was going and run on ahead, because by the time I reached The Norfolk, Auntie was coming down the steps with a blanket and a wet cloth.

'I've sent for the vet,' she said.

We laid Scotty out on the veranda on the blanket, and Auntie dabbed at the blood.

'I don't think the cut is too deep,' she said.

'What about his leg?'

'It looks broken.'

I lifted Scotty's head into my lap, and he licked my hand, the whites of his eyes showing.

'It's going to be alright,' I told him again.

'I'll get some brandy,' Auntie said. She hurried into the hotel. I could feel my insides twisting in anger, and my skin was crawling. It took every effort to remain sitting there and not take off in search of Carberry.

A young, tired-looking man appeared next to me. 'What happened here then?'

'Dr Harvill, you're here.' Auntie came back out with a bottle of brandy and a glass. 'I think Scotty's leg is broken.'

'I don't think he'll want any brandy for it,' Dr Harvill said dryly.

'This is for Theo.'

Dr Harvill crouched down in front of Scotty, gently placing his hand on Scotty's head. 'There, there,' he said. 'Let's take a look at you.'

I gulped down the glass of brandy Auntie poured me and stood up.

'Can you wake my family?' I asked.

'Of course.'

I stood up and walked through the lobby, stopping in front of the fireplace. My head swirled with images of John Carberry, of Scotty lying in that ditch, until I couldn't see what was happening in front of me. I felt my hand close around something cold and heard a buzzing sound from far away, as if people were talking, and my mouth moved mechanically, forming words as if I were taking part in the conversation. Then I was walking again. I pictured Carberry leering at me, and heard the tune he was singing. My feet carried on without instruction, first the right foot, then the left, then right again. They walked for so long my legs felt tired and I could taste metal in my mouth, and my right hand was heavy with the thing I'd brought from The Norfolk. There was more buzzing, and a dark, faceless form in front of me.

129

Then I was round the side of the Muthaiga, and I realised it was a poker dangling from my right hand. Carberry's car was in front of me – green with brown mudguards. It was furthest from the windows, but I took off my jumper, and wrapped it around the poker to muffle the sound all the same. Swinging it as hard as I could, I smashed the headlamps and windscreen, and dented the front. I thought I saw a curtain or two twitch on the first floor, but no one came out, and no one raised the alarm.

After a few whacks, the door to the boot hung half-off, and it was easy enough to wrench off completely with my bare hands. I laid it on the ground and jumped on it until it was completely misshapen. I wished I was jumping on Carberry's face. I imagined the blood spurting from his nose, the sickening sound of bone crunching underneath metal, and a calm descended on me.

I made a few half-hearted slashes on the leather interior, then walked back around to the front of the club. Freddie was leaning against one of the pillars along the covered entrance way. I saw his eyes flick down at the poker in my hand and back up.

'What have you been up to?' he asked.

'Someone's smashed up Carberry's motorcar,' I said.

'Plenty of people with a motive.'

I placed the poker in a bush, and leaned against the pillar next to Freddie's.

'Well –' he said. 'Perhaps I'd better run you back to The Norfolk.'

My breathing was returning to normal now, and I felt a wave of sickness. 'I asked one of the bar staff where the car was.'

'Peter?'

I nodded.

'Let me talk to him,' Freddie said. 'I'll be out shortly.'

I retrieved the poker, still wrapped in my jumper, and waited in Freddie's car. After a few moments he came out whistling.

'Peter doesn't remember talking to you,' he said.

We drove back to The Norfolk in silence. Freddie pulled up

outside it and snapped the engine off. 'Carberry can afford the repairs,' he said. 'Maybe this'll be good for him.'

I untied my jumper from the poker, and shook it out over the passenger door. There was a quiet tinkle of glass hitting the road.

'Thanks for the lift.'

'Any time.'

I felt a surge of affection for him, and guilt that I'd ever felt like hitting him. Freddie liked to tease others, he liked to have a good time, but he would always be there for me. He was watching me carefully now, and I could sense the crackle of tension in him that was in me too, an excitement about what we'd both just done. I kept one hand in my pocket as I climbed out of the car and walked quickly through to the lobby. I handed the poker to a waiter straightening cushions on an armchair and he took it without a word.

Maud was waiting for me in our bedroom, red-eyed.

'What did the vet say?' I asked.

'His leg's broken, but it'll mend. And his face is cut and bruised.'

'He must have fallen into the ditch I found him in,' I said. 'And broken his leg that way. I can't have tied him up properly.'

'What about the bruises?'

'There were rocks at the bottom.' I lay down on my bed. 'Where is he?'

She wiped her eyes. 'He's with the vet now. We can collect him tomorrow.'

'He'll be alright, Spanish,' I said. 'Scotty's a fighter.'

She came and sat on my bed and patted my arm. 'Thank you for finding him,' she said.

February turned into March, and the weather stayed hot and sunny and dry. No rain fell, and the ground turned hard and cracked. On my sixteenth birthday we rowed a boat onto the lake and drank champagne and ate cake out there.

'To our man,' my mother said, raising her glass to me.

131

By late March, dark, gigantic clouds were rolling across the horizon, although they were gone by sunset. The air smelled dusty. After my birthday, my mother had suggested to my father that I could be trusted with the car, and I often took it out for long drives, to the Aberdares, to the Maasai Reserve. I liked to turn off the road and drive onto the plains. All around was flat, scrubby land as far as the eye could see, and dry riverbeds and rocks and deserted villages of Maasai huts. Sometimes I saw an eagle gliding high up above me, feathers ruffling in a breeze that never reached ground level. Other times, there was nothing in sight – no birds, no game, no humans – the world vast and completely still.

I hadn't heard from Sylvie since I'd tried to kiss her almost six weeks ago, and eventually I couldn't wait any longer. Even if she was angry with me, I knew I had to see her. When Miss Graham went to lie down one afternoon, I borrowed the car and jolted down the drive, then turned in the direction of The Farm.

My nerves had been building steadily the closer I got to the house, and I was panicky by the time I arrived. It took a while to realise that Freddie and Edie must be there too – their car was pulled up to the house, and from inside I could hear voices and the sound of furniture being moved. For a sickening moment I wondered if Nico had found out what I'd done and was taking Sylvie away.

Freddie appeared at the door, shading his eyes. He waved at me, and strolled over. He wasn't smiling, and I was suddenly glued to my seat in fear. I could barely lift an arm to wave back.

He poked his head and shoulders inside the car, leaning his forearms on the open passenger window. 'You must have some sort of sixth sense,' he said. 'Come to say goodbye?'

My heart stopped. 'Goodbye?'

'I thought you'd heard. Nico came home early – Rupert carried on to Uganda for the gorillas, but Nico was feverish and he'd lost weight. Doctor said it was malaria and gave Sylvie some quinine.'

'When was this?'

'Five days ago.' Freddie scratched his cheek with his right thumbnail. 'Edie got Sylvie to go for a proper doctor yesterday, and he diagnosed blackwater fever. His urine was turning.'

I swallowed, trying to wet my tongue enough to ask my next question. 'Is she taking him away to recover?'

'Back to France. For good. The doctor said he had to live where there was no chance of contracting it again, or the next bout could kill him.' He withdrew his head from the car and stretched his back. 'Poor sod. They're leaving for Mombasa this evening – come and say goodbye.'

I opened the car door and followed him to the house in silence; I felt as if there was no air left in my lungs to speak.

Sylvie was in the living room with Edie. I thought she looked more beautiful than ever, her eyes wider, her skin smoother, her cheekbones sharper. She was wearing a gold necklace that gleamed against her skin, and a simple black dress.

'Theo,' she said, trying to smile. 'I'm so glad you're here.'

'I've filled him in,' Freddie said.

'It'll be good for Nico to see you.' A lock of hair was plastered to her face in the heat, and she pushed it out of her eyes. I stared at her, trying to drink her in, so I'd have something left when she was gone. If I hadn't got impatient and borrowed the car, I told myself, I might have missed her for good. The thought made me shake.

'Where is he?' I asked.

'In bed. Do you want to see him?'

I nodded.

Freddie walked me to the bedroom. He was solid and sympathetic, and I was suddenly overwhelmingly grateful for his presence.

'How's Sylvie feeling?' I asked.

'You know Sylvie – she's made up her mind, and Nico can't persuade her to change it. But I'm sure she feels bad about leaving him – she's really fond of him, you know.'

I groped for a moment to understand. 'She's leaving him?'

'She's staying out here – or she's coming back, anyway. She'll take Nico to Paris, and get him settled in, treated, that sort of thing, then she'll catch the next boat out. Edie's happy, of course.' He grinned. 'I don't need to ask how you feel about her decision, either.'

He pushed open the door and I went in. The curtains were drawn and at first I couldn't see Nicolas, hidden too by the tears of relief that kept welling up in my eyes. Sylvie was coming back.

Nicolas's breath was coming quickly but evenly, and I guessed he was asleep. I sat at his feet; Samson kept watch too, pacing the room. When Nicolas woke up, Samson moved closer, to where Nicolas could put a hand on his head.

'Theo,' Nicolas said weakly. 'How nice of you to come.' He lay back on his pillow and a coughing fit overtook him.

I filled a glass of water from the jug beside his bed and handed it to him.

'Sylvie's packing for you,' I said. 'Freddie says you're leaving tonight.'

'She always packs for me. She likes to put crushed flowers in to make my suits smell nice.' He patted Samson's nose, and the lion snorted. 'I know my wife loves me, in her own way.'

I looked at the floor. There was silence for a moment, then Nicolas made a sound like a sob. I looked up and saw his cheeks were wet.

'I tried,' he said, but more to himself than to me.

There was a knock at the door, then the other three came in.

'We come bearing gifts,' Freddie said.

'Enter, enter,' Nicolas said. 'I feel like baby Jesus.'

They laughed. Edie parted the curtains to let in some light, and I saw Nicolas scrub quickly at his face then sit up and put on a smile. Samson flopped down at his feet.

We ate in the bedroom. Samson prowled around the room, trying to snaffle little bits of unguarded food. When Freddie went to sit down, Samson snuck up behind him and tried to trip him up as he was carrying the cold chicken.

'*Samson!*' Nicolas whispered. '*Méchante bête!*'

Sylvie smiled and burrowed her face in his mane.

Other than cold chicken, there were devilled eggs then baked ham with potatoes and cheese and salad, and caramel custard to finish. The food was delicious, but Nicolas picked at it, leaving most untouched. 'This is my *home*,' he said more than once.

Freddie kept the drinks flowing. 'Don't think of it as the end, Nico,' he said. 'You can have an adventure in Europe instead. Just think of Venice. Beautiful Venice. And London, and Pamplona. You could even go across the pond to where the savages live.'

'No one ever built a wall to keep *us* out,' Sylvie said.

'Now, now,' Edie said. 'You're both savages.'

'They can't make me leave,' Nicolas said.

'We'd much rather you were alive in Europe than dead out here,' Freddie said.

Sylvie held Nicolas's hand. I felt guilty about the relief that coursed through me every time I thought about her returning.

'Who's going to take care of the animals while you're away?' I asked her.

'We're taking them with us,' she said. 'Samson and Roderigo, anyway. They can live with Nico in Paris so he can have a little bit of Africa in Europe. The neighbours said they'll take care of Fairyfeet.'

Nicolas burst into tears again.

'Let me get everyone some more gin,' Edie said.

Sylvie followed her out. Nicolas started talking as soon as she'd left the room. I thought he was feverish, until Freddie answered him and I realised he'd been speaking French.

'You have to look after her, you two,' Nicolas said, switching to English.

'Of course we will,' Freddie said.

We waited until Nicolas nodded off, then went out into the sitting room. Sylvie looked pale.

'You have to do what's right for you,' Edie whispered to her.

'I know,' she said. She clenched and unclenched her fists, looking around the room at the half-finished packing.

'I'd better . . .' She trailed off.

'I'll do the guest rooms,' Freddie said. 'Take your time out here, you've got hours left yet.'

Edie looked at me. 'Theo – why don't you join me outside for a cigarette first?'

I followed her onto the veranda. Edie lit a cigarette and stood facing the mountains.

'How are you, darling?'

'Alright.'

'It won't be the same without them, will it?'

'No.'

She pulled a face. 'I hope she doesn't divorce Nico. I know Rupert – he won't marry her. His parents will be dead-set against it.'

'Does she have to remarry?'

'If she wants to stay out here. Unmarried women aren't allowed in Kenya.' She blew out a perfect smoke ring. 'They terrify the government even more than famine does. Why do you think I'm hanging on to Freddie?'

'I thought you liked him.'

She laughed. 'Of course I do. But I don't come second to other women. Freddie can fool around as much as he likes, but he's not allowed to fall in love with them.'

'Didn't he fall in love with Sylvie?'

'Everyone falls in love with Sylvie.' She tapped the built-up cigarette ash onto the grass in front of us. 'But she's not Freddie's type – she's quicksilver. Freddie needs constant adoration.'

I remembered the look on Freddie's face as he watched Sylvie, and wondered whether Edie had never noticed it.

'Anyway. I just wanted to check you were alright.'

I nodded.

'Shall we go make ourselves useful then?'

Freddie and Edie took charge of the bedrooms and bathrooms while Sylvie and I covered the sitting and dining rooms. Roderigo scampered between the sitting room and the veranda. After a while Sylvie went and sat on the sofa, and I joined her. We were silent for a while, listening to the creak of the wood as it expanded in the heat, and Roderigo padding around. Sylvie smelled of cigarettes and her familiar perfume. I breathed her in.

'When do you think you'll be able to get back?' I asked.

'I don't know.' She puckered her eyebrows slightly. 'It depends how long it takes to settle Nico in, and sort out any other matters.'

I felt a coldness wash through me. 'Are you going to divorce him?'

She looked away. 'Yes. Rupert's going to London next month to tell his family about me.'

'What if they don't want him to marry you?'

'Then I'll wait until they come round.' She fingered her necklace. 'It's better for everyone. Nico deserves someone better anyway. I hope the girls turn out like him. I'd hate to see anything of me in them.'

I took her hand in mine. 'Don't think like that. I wish there were more of you.'

She smiled. 'We never went out in the boat in the end.'

'We can go out now if you want.'

Roderigo ran to her and she scooped him up. 'I don't think there's time.' She looked around the sitting room as if she was about to cry, but she didn't.

I put my arms around her and she leaned her head on my shoulder. It felt so natural, and I thought again of our kiss, squirming inside that I'd rushed her. I wouldn't rush her the next time. *And if she's never allowed back?* a voice whispered, and I shut it out; if she wasn't allowed back, I'd find her in Europe.

'How about this vase?' Edie asked, coming into the room.

'No,' Sylvie said, detaching herself from me.

137

'It's so lovely.'

'It was my father's wedding present to us.'

Edie nodded and went back into the interior. We both stood and started packing again.

'Where will you go?' I asked Sylvie.

'London. Maybe Paris.' She lit a cigarette.

'At least you'll be able to see your daughters more.'

'I don't like to spend too long with them.' She tucked a strand of hair behind her ear. 'In case they get used to having me around.'

'But you're not selling this place?'

'I'll rent it out at first.'

Edie swept back into the room. 'What about this darling little mirror?'

'Yes,' Sylvie said. She started to tremble all over.

'What's the matter?'

'What's the point of it all, Edie?' Sylvie said.

She looked about helplessly, and Edie hurried over and took her hand. 'You'll be back before you know it.'

'I don't know. What if Rupert doesn't . . .?'

'Of course you will – you belong here.'

I turned away. On the wall in front of me was a picture of two milkmaids carrying their pails through a field, the wind blowing a ripple through the corn behind them. Soon Sylvie would be gone, and whoever rented the house would sit in this room, drinking, reading, laughing. Then another, then another, and the milkmaids would stand in their field forever. I wanted to tear the picture off the wall and throw it out the window; it wasn't fair to keep us apart like this.

I turned back, ramming my hands in my pockets.

Sylvie shook herself. 'I'm being a fucking mope, aren't I?'

'We're all fucking mopes, having to say goodbye to you. Aren't we, Theo?'

I nodded. 'Maud told me off this morning,' I said. 'She said –

Theo, if you don't stop being such a fucking mope, I'll thrash you bloody. Honestly, that girl frightens me.'

Edie raised an eyebrow. Sylvie looked at both of us and laughed, then we were all laughing.

Freddie came into the room. 'What's this racket? I thought we were packing, not acting like donkeys.'

'You're just sore it's not your joke we're laughing at,' Sylvie said, holding her other hand out to him.

'Whose joke is it?'

'Theo's.'

Freddie pointed his finger at me. 'I'll have to keep an eye on you, young man.'

'You do that, old man.'

Edie laughed again. 'Please don't,' she said. 'If he's old, I'm decaying.'

'You're delicious,' Sylvie said, and licked Edie's cheek like a cat.

We opened some champagne, and drank the bottle while we finished packing. We were tight by the time we saw them off in their car, their luggage safely packed up and ready to be collected the next day. Nico lay on the back seat, covered in blankets.

'What will you do until the ship sails?' Edie asked.

'Drink cocktails,' Sylvie said. 'Admire the sailors in their little suits.'

'We're going to miss you like hell.'

'I will too,' she said. 'I'll be thinking of you out here while I'm in grey old Europe, dying of jealousy.'

'Don't die,' Freddie said. 'But by all means be jealous.'

Sylvie kissed each of us in turn, then climbed into the driver's seat.

'I'll see you later,' she called.

The car jerked forwards; I felt an urge to throw myself at it, cling to the door and go with her to Mombasa. I knew somehow that everything was about to change, and not necessarily for the better.

'I'll be back,' she called.

Freddie rested his hand on my shoulder, and I stayed where I was, waving mutely.

'*Write*,' Edie called. 'That's an order.'

Then the car was turning out of the gate and onto the road leading away from the house, and finally it was gone.

Part Two

1933–1937

Chapter Twelve

Through the windows of the New British Hotel, I could see the rain coming down on Princes Street. It was late May, and the sun hadn't set until well after nine pm, but the clouds above had made it dark for most of the afternoon, the grey stone buildings in New Town absorbing the gloom. Even now, with their windows lit up against the night-time, they seemed cheerless; I could imagine exactly how cold they were inside, too, with their high ceilings, and the wind that came through the cracks in the walls.

Inside the bar, there was just the orange glow from the fire, and a small candle on each table. There were four of us, grouped in a vague circle in our leather armchairs. Some time ago we'd lapsed into silence, and now all I could hear were the trams passing by outside, the click of pieces in a game of backgammon being played somewhere behind us, and the crackle of logs disintegrating in the fireplace.

I checked my watch: ten thirty pm. The other three looked up from their glasses: Douglas, George and Ned, my closest friends from my time at university; I wondered if I'd see them again.

'How long to the train?' Douglas asked.

'Half an hour. But I should leave sooner than that.'

143

'It won't be the same without you,' Ned said. 'Who'll provide the women at parties now?'

'You'll be lucky,' Douglas said to him. 'From what I hear, teachers barely make enough to live, let alone enjoy themselves.'

I took a sip of my whisky. Ned was bound for teaching, Douglas the civil service. George was joining an engineering firm. I was travelling back to Nairobi to work for my father. The others claimed to be envious of me, but I could imagine the days in the office stretching out ahead of me, muffled and monotonous, and already felt suffocated. Apart from the secretaries, I would be the youngest there by at least twenty years. If only I could work with Freddie, I thought, and couldn't help smiling to myself. I'd seen him a few times when I'd been back at Kiboko over the holidays, and once in Edinburgh. He'd divorced Edie two years ago to marry a woman called Martha, who'd left her husband for him, too. I'd met him at the Muthaiga at the start of it all. 'It's the real deal this time, Theo,' he'd said, grinning. 'She's a red-head, Martha, like your mother. *Very* passionate. And fabulously wealthy, which doesn't hurt.'

He'd brought her along the next day. She was short, shorter than Edie even, and very slim. Her hair was bobbed and auburn-coloured, framing a round face with delicate features. Her lips and nails were painted a dark, shiny red, almost purple, and she wore emerald earrings that brought out the colour of her eyes. She drank her champagne in large gulps, and I saw some trickle down her chin that she wiped off quickly.

They'd stayed in London during the divorce, and Freddie had driven up from there for a visit, pulling up in a silver Daimler, wearing a very expensive suit. I smiled again. Freddie would never change, at least there was that. And now we were equals, both men together, and he was living only on the other side of the lake, in Mahalbeth, the palace Martha had got in her settlement.

'Did I tell you?' George leaned forwards and tapped my knee. 'I ran into Winnie earlier.'

The other two whistled.

'Behave yourself,' I said, and they laughed.

'Was she heartbroken?' Ned asked.

'She put on a brave face.' George shrugged. 'I can't understand how you could let something that pretty go?'

'Maybe there's someone else back in Kenya,' Douglas said.

'Maybe,' I said.

'There *is*,' Ned said. 'You sly dog.'

I thought of Sylvie, chain-smoking and laughing, kicking off her shoes and draping herself along sofas. She'd written to me last year to say that she'd married Rupert and she was on holiday with a friend in Slovakia; Rupert wasn't with her. Since then I'd seen one more communication that Edie had passed on through Freddie. *Dearest*, it had said, *I'm coming home, I can't stand being away any longer.* She hadn't given any indication of a timeline.

'Any photos of her?' George asked. 'More of your mother will do if not.'

I took another slug of my drink. 'Shut up.'

They laughed again. I'd barely seen my mother since I'd left Kenya. Shortly after Nico and Sylvie had moved away we'd reached a sort of understanding, and she'd mostly left me to my own devices. It was only when I'd come to Edinburgh and been away from her as an adult that I'd realised how afraid I'd been growing up, how unsettling she'd been. Now I was going back I didn't particularly want to see her. I knew she was wrapped up in the League anyway, which Lady Joan had left in her hands.

My father was wrapped up in work too; Maud spent most of her time alone at Kiboko. I was glad to be returning for her sake, although she never sounded lonely in her letters. The thought of her made me feel suddenly impatient to be off, and I tossed back the rest of my drink and stood up.

'Onwards and upwards,' I said.

They stood too, raising their glasses to me, then draining them.

'Let's get you on that train,' Douglas said.

Scarves and coats were collected, and we left the hotel by the door that opened straight onto the station. That, too, was quiet, with only a few families saying their goodbyes, and a porter or two standing idly around. It was so different to the station at Mombasa I almost laughed.

I signalled one of the porters, and told him where to find my trunk in the hotel, then the four of us shook hands.

'I'm sure we'll be reading about your exploits in the papers,' Douglas said.

'I'll be reading about yours,' I said. 'Douglas McFarlane, the Great Reformer.'

He pulled a face. 'I'm a faceless bureaucrat, remember.'

'And I'm a pauper,' Ned said. 'George is a pencil-pusher. It's down to you.'

'Well – if my public demand it . . .' I said.

'Shouldn't you board?' Douglas asked.

My train was smoking and letting out occasional shrieks. We shook hands again and I climbed into my carriage and found my compartment. It was small, and the light was dim, but the sink was clean and it was warm. I unwound my scarf and sat down on the green leather seat.

A train guard knocked on my door. He checked my tickets and handed me a menu.

'Will you be eating in the dining car? It closes at midnight.'

I glanced at it briefly. 'I'll have the sauvignon blanc. And chicken salad to start, then the crab croquettes.'

'Very good,' he said. 'I'll make up your bed while you eat.'

He left my compartment. I locked the door after him and went to the window. I manoeuvred it open enough to stick my head out at the top. The other three were still on the platform, hopping about to keep warm. Ned saw me and waved a white handker-chief.

'Go home,' I called. 'It's freezing.'

They turned to go.

146

'Don't forget to invite us when you've settled in,' George called over his shoulder.

I watched them make their way back into the hotel. I could imagine the rest of their evening: another drink at the bar, then a tram back to the close, running up the steps to stay dry. Then inside, where our landlady would have turned the beds down and left supper in the oven. Soon they would start work, and take up golf, and go to the pub on Friday nights to discuss politics.

Whereas I would be rattling through the countryside all night. Tomorrow I would wake up in London, and tomorrow evening I'd be walking up the gangplank onto the boat bound for Mombasa. If I was going back to join the railway company, I was also going back to sunshine, the Muthaiga, parties, sundowners, savannahs teeming with animals, totos shouting 'Jambo, Bwana' as they went about their business, music and laughter and Maud and Freddie. Maybe even Sylvie.

The rain had changed from fat, heavy drops to a slanting drizzle. My compartment was in an open-air section of the station, and I suddenly realised that my face and hands were soaking wet. I withdrew, and slammed the window shut, just as the train let out its loudest shriek yet and started forwards with a jerk.

Chapter Thirteen

When I arrived in Kenya, instead of going straight to Kiboko as I would have preferred, my father arranged a room for me at the Nairobi Club, and scheduled several meetings with railway officials and engineers to 'ease into it', as he put it. It only took a few lunches to realise working at the company was going to be even duller than I'd thought.

It was almost a month before I was able to escape to Naivasha, catching Maud as she was in the middle of ordering meals for the next week. She ran down the veranda steps and threw her arms around my neck. Scotty followed her, dancing and barking around our ankles.

'I've missed you,' she said.

'I missed you too, Spanish.'

She suited the name even more now after years of sun. Her skin had turned nut-coloured, and at twenty years old she was tall, much taller than our mother, and her smile was wider. The totos called her *Mama Mpole*; 'gentle mother'.

'How was the boat? How's work? Is Father well?'

I held up my hands, laughing. 'Give me a minute.'

She rolled her eyes. 'I thought university helped you think, not slowed you down.'

'Why don't we get out on the lake, have some time to ourselves? You can ask me any questions you like then.'

'Alright. Let me just shut Scotty inside.'

'We should go round to Mahalbeth,' I said, as we stepped into the rowing boat. 'How much do you see of Freddie, now he's so close?'

Maud sat down and arranged her skirt around her knees. 'I don't like it there.'

'Why not?'

'It feels sad.'

'The house?'

She shrugged. 'You'll see. Anyway, don't tell me you still have a crush on Freddie?'

I pulled the best outraged face I could muster. 'How could you suggest such a thing? Am I not the pinnacle of manhood myself, now?'

She laughed.

'What about Edie then? Do you see much of her?'

I knew that Edie had started an affair with Boy Long, a cattle rancher employed by Lord Delamere, soon after her divorce from Freddie, but now she was married to an American, making this her fourth marriage. I hoped this one would last.

'No, not really.'

I fixed the oars in their holders and dipped them into the lake. The sun was out, glinting off the water, but it was small and white, and the sky was perfectly clear, not shimmering with the heat as it did in summer.

'It's going to be a bad winter,' I said.

'I hope not.'

'You should move to Nairobi, Spanish.'

'We don't have a house in Nairobi,' she said, trailing her fingers in the water.

'Where does Mother stay when she's there?'

'She has a room at The Norfolk. Didn't you know that?'

149

'We haven't spoken much recently. Don't you mind her leaving you alone out here?'

'I'm not alone. And the League is good for her – she's always needed something to do.'

'You mean she always hated being a mother.'

Maud shook her head. 'I don't mean that at all. She was always thinking about us. It was being a housewife she hated.' She smiled. 'It is a bit boring.'

'What are you going to do for fun, then?'

'I've been thinking about buying some land. For cattle.'

'Are you being serious?'

'Why not? You've got the railway to look after.'

'I wish I didn't – I'm going to spend most of my days drawing up timetables and looking at freight documentation. Anyway, you don't know anything about farming.'

'I'd hire a foreman. Just think of all the jobs we'd be providing.'

'You shouldn't worry about everyone else so much.'

'I do though.' She pulled her hand out of the water and wiped her fingers dry on her skirt. 'And what are *you* going to do then if you don't like working with Father?'

I grinned, and flicked water at her with an oar. 'Scotty's getting fat.'

'I know. You're not here to take him for a run.'

'I'll come back more often, I promise.'

She lay back, resting on her elbows and looking happy. 'Do you remember rowing out here for your birthday?' she asked. 'Mother looked green the whole way. I don't think we got her in the boat again.'

'I don't know what you're talking about – she had a good time on my birthday.'

'You have such a selective memory.' She shook her head, but she was smiling. 'No, actually, it's not that.'

'Not what?'

'It's more – whatever you tell yourself once in your head, seems

150

to come true for you. You can make yourself believe anything, that's what I mean.'

I wondered if that could work with Sylvie – if I told myself she was coming home to me. I could see myself holding her in her giant bed while she rang for champagne, then nestled further into me, finally mine completely.

'Why are you smiling?'

'Oh, nothing,' I said.

I called at Mahalbeth the next Monday morning, hoping to run into Freddie for the first time since I'd returned. I'd never been to the south-west part of the lake or seen his new house; Freddie had told me it was grander than Kirlton, but when it finally came into view, I realised that had been an understatement, and I stopped the car outside the grounds to admire the whole setting. It was an enormous Moorish palace backing onto the water, with white-washed walls, crenellations, a minaret, and a red-floored courtyard out the front where lemon trees dropped leaves into a splashing, blue-and-white-tiled fountain.

Another car was leaving as I drove up. The woman inside waved languidly at me. She was pale and gaunt and wore elbow-length gloves. When she smiled, I saw her teeth were badly yellowing, making my skin crawl.

Waweru opened the door, and led me through the house and out onto the wide veranda, gesturing to the deep, flowered sofas clustered out there. Martha rose from one of them to greet me. She was wearing a lacy black dressing gown and her hair was tousled.

'Theo?' she said. 'From Edinburgh, right?'

'Yes.'

'I'm so sorry – I did recognise you, I just wasn't sure. What a wonderful surprise. Are you living back here now?'

'I am. Am I interrupting?'

'Not at all.' She plucked at her clothes. 'I've only just got up,

151

really – terribly lazy these days.' She did look more dishevelled than I remembered, but still unusually pretty.

'You don't have guests? I just saw a car leave.'

'Oh, that was no one. An old friend.' She looked at Waweru. 'We'll have coffee.'

He disappeared, and she flopped back onto one of the large sofas and patted the seat beside her; I sat down gingerly. For the first time I noticed a chimp stretched out unmoving on the floor, his collar attached to the wall by a chain.

'That's Jules,' Martha said. 'He's Freddie's.'

'Is Freddie here?'

'He's at some meeting or other. He might be home soon.'

Jules blinked, and tugged on his chain.

'Here.' Martha threw a pack of cigarettes at him. The chimp took two and tucked one behind his ear, placing another in his mouth. 'Can you light it for him, Theo?'

'Does he really smoke them?'

'Yes.'

I leaned forwards and lit the cigarette. Jules took a deep drag, closing his eyes.

'He's our surrogate baby,' Martha said. 'We've been trying for a real one, but none of them live beyond six weeks.'

I shifted in my seat, surprised that she was so open with a relative stranger. Or maybe she was still in shock, I thought. 'Sorry to hear that.'

'That's what Freddie said the last time I told him.' She laughed; it sounded pinched and she stopped abruptly.

Waweru appeared with a tray and placed it on the coffee table in front of us, then disappeared again.

Martha fussed around with the cups. 'Milk? Sugar?'

'Neither, thanks.'

'Just like Freddie.' She went to hand me my drink, then put it down again abruptly. 'Do you want the tour? It's quite special.'

'I'd love it.'

I followed her into the house and around the ground floor, admiringly. The ceilings were high, much higher than usual, and one of them had a night sky painted onto it – hundreds of tiny white stars against a deep, rich blue. Dark beams held up the library ceiling, and a large refectory table took up most of the floor space. The paintings on the wall were all fifteenth- or sixteenth-century religious scenes with plenty of blood and gold, except for one full-length portrait of Freddie.

'I commissioned that,' Martha said.

Outside the dining room was an Art Deco bar, with spirits lined up in front of a gold mirror and a beautiful mosaic counter in red, blue, gold and black. Martha took me through an intricately carved wooden doorway and into several bedrooms and bathrooms until we reached the master suite.

The bathroom was at least eighteen feet long by fifteen wide. The floor and walls were white, and arched windows looked out on the courtyard; they were wide open now, and potted ferns bobbed in the incoming breeze. In the middle of the room, a bath was sunken into the floor, and decorated in black and gold tiles. Lit candles had been placed around it, and the whole room smelled of a mix of cinnamon, honey, tobacco and leather.

'It's beautiful,' I said.

'The gardens are even better,' Martha said. 'Freddie had a pool built overlooking the lake. He put in squash courts too.' She ran a hand through her hair. 'He's President of the Naivasha Club now, you know.'

We returned to the veranda. Through the trees, I could see flashes of azure.

'He sounds busy,' I said. 'I was hoping he was still a farmer of leisure.'

'I just don't want him to get bored,' Martha said. 'I know how much he wants an heir. And he's too clever for his own good.' She sipped her coffee. 'Have you met the new Governor yet?'

'Byrne?'

'That's the one. Much better than Grigg. He's trying to get Freddie into politics.'

'Oh?'

'I think it'll be good for him. He's all fired up about the government proposition to introduce income tax here, thinks it'll drive all the capital out of the colony.'

'I'm sure Britain wouldn't let Kenya collapse.'

'We're not a priority back there. We need more autonomy.'

'I don't think that's too likely either.' I smiled.

She shrugged, looking uninterested suddenly. Keeping up with her changing moods was exhausting, and I tried to remember if she'd been like this when I met her at the Muthaiga. I took a sip of cold coffee, then checked my watch.

'I'm afraid I should be off –'

'So this is where I find you,' Freddie said. He came out onto the veranda. 'How long were you back for before you decided to make a play for my wife?'

'I thought a month was gentlemanly enough.'

'More than fair.'

He grinned at me and I grinned back thankfully; seeing him was just as easy as I'd thought it would be.

'Darling.' Martha jumped up and threw her arms around his neck. 'I've been chilling some champagne in case you managed to get away.'

He laughed. 'Not for me, thank you. It's a little early. And you spoil me too much.'

Martha laughed too. Red spots appeared on her cheeks. 'You deserve it. How was the meeting?'

'Very boring.'

She led him to the sofa and they sat. Freddie lit a cigarette and offered me one. I refused. 'You're looking well,' he said. 'Survived finals then.'

'Don't remind me of them.'

He laughed again. 'Never mind. They don't seem too bad after a while, not after you've had to work for a living.'

'I'm starting to believe it. I hear you're taking on more work though. Martha says you might be getting into politics.'

'It's a good idea. I could be a big fish out here, and at my age I should be thinking more permanently.'

'What do you mean?'

'*Had we but world enough and time –*'

'Trust you to quote Andrew Marvell.'

'Very good.'

Sylvie had read poetry to us sometimes, and once or twice I'd read it to her. She'd been pulling a ribbon through the grass for Samson to chase. Or maybe she'd been grooming Roderigo at the table.

'Did you hear me?' Freddie asked, crossing his legs.

'Sorry, no.'

He grinned again. 'How was Edinburgh for you in the end?'

I shrugged. 'Took me a while to get used to the cold. And everyone rushes everywhere.'

'You should try London.' He looked away for a moment. 'Funny going back there after being away for so long.'

'I can imagine.' I pulled a face. 'Speaking of rushing around – I should really get back to Nairobi.'

'You can't be in that much of a hurry,' Martha said. She called for Waweru and he appeared at the door. 'Two Black Velvets. You *will* stay and have a real drink with me, won't you, Theo, if Freddie won't? It's half champagne, half Guinness.'

'I have to work – I only dropped by to see if Freddie was going in too.'

He looked sorry. 'Not today. But come round soon and we can have a game of squash.'

'As soon as I can.'

'Good to have you back.'

'It's good to be back.'

He stood to shake my hand. Martha stayed seated, looking up at him unwaveringly. When I bent down to kiss her cheek she barely seemed to notice, and I wondered whether Freddie found her as intense and tiring as I did, or if she was more relaxed when they were alone. I met his eye and he raised an eyebrow, as if he knew what I'd been thinking.

''Bye then,' I said, feeling suddenly awkward.

'See you soon, young man,' Freddie said.

My father was pacing my office when I arrived. The room was wood-panelled and brown-carpeted, like the rest of the building, with a stippled glass door leading out onto a dark, narrow corridor that ran the length of three more offices – my father's, Mr MacDonald's and the clerk's. The only furniture provided was a large wooden desk, a hard chair and three bottle-green filing cabinets.

My window faced a wide, dusty avenue, its pavements lined with palm trees and sycamore figs, bee hives hanging from their branches. In the sun, the red-brick and white facades of the buildings opposite looked almost colourless and the people moved sluggishly from one spot of shade to another. If I raised my eyes to the horizon, I could see the blazing silver domes and twin minarets of Jamia Mosque.

I shut the door behind me and took off my coat.

'Where were you?' my father grumbled. 'You shouldn't be on the payroll if you're gallivanting around the country instead of working.'

'I stayed at Kiboko over the weekend. To see Maud.'

'Oh. Mm-hmm. How is she?'

'Same as always. I thought you had a lunch today?'

'No,' he said. 'I postponed. Something else has come up, and I'd like you to join me. Don't sit down – we're leaving.'

At The Norfolk he bounded up the steps and onto the terrace. 'There they are,' he said. 'Oh good, Auntie's taking care of them.'

I peered in the direction he was nodding at, and saw Auntie standing over a table set for three. A man and a woman, a little younger than my father, were sitting down with teacups in front of them.

'How are you both?' Auntie said as we arrived. 'Here, let me move some more chairs around the table.'

'I'll do it,' I said.

She smiled at me. 'Then I'll leave you for now.'

I pulled up two extra chairs and shook hands with the strangers, who'd stood when we appeared. They both had grey hair and glasses, and friendly faces. The man had a moustache and was smoking a pipe; the woman was wearing white gloves.

'You're quite grown up now, aren't you?' the man said to me. He saw the expression on my face. 'You don't remember us.'

I flushed. 'I'm sorry —'

'Don't be silly,' the woman interrupted, smiling. 'You were probably still exhausted after your journey, and you spoke more to our daughter anyway.'

'Her name's Lucy,' the man said.

'Of course, in Dar es Salaam. You're old friends of my father's.'

'George and Sarah Cartwright,' my father said.

'Very pleased to meet you again.'

We sat. My father ordered another pot of tea.

'Are you visiting Kenya?' I asked.

George took out a pouch and started filling up his pipe. 'We're thinking of moving here,' he said. 'The situation in Dar's getting a little too hot for us.'

'You'll have to be more specific, I'm afraid,' my father said. 'Theo doesn't read the papers.'

'It's the new German Chancellor,' George said. 'He wants back the colonies they lost under the Treaty of Versailles.' He tamped down the tobacco in his pipe and lit it. 'And suddenly there's an influx of Germans in Tanganyika.'

'Bloody typical,' my father said.

The waiter arrived with a fresh pot of tea and four cups and saucers.

'Can you bring us another cup?' Sarah asked. 'We're expecting our daughter at any moment.'

I thought I saw George and my father exchange a wink. My heart sank. I hadn't remembered her parents, but I could remember Lucy.

'She's very excited to see you,' Sarah said, pouring me a cup of tea. 'It's hard on her having to move so suddenly. We were hoping you might be able to show her around Nairobi?'

'I'd be happy to,' I said, forcing a smile. Something else to take me away from Maud and Freddie. I wondered how long I'd have to spend with her before I could escape back to Naivasha to squash games and sundowners and trips on the lake.

'Here she comes now,' George said, standing. 'Why don't you move up, Sarah, so the young people can be together?'

We all stood, and I turned to face Lucy, walking towards us. She was wearing a white dress with a cherry-pattern on the body and short sleeves that revealed long, slender arms. She was still blonde, and her hair fell around her face in shiny golden waves. Her eyes were large and clear blue and her lips frosted pink. When she saw me she blushed and stumbled, and I put my arms out to catch her.

'Thank you,' she murmured, blushing harder. I released her, noticing how soft her skin was.

'Lucy, Theo's agreed to give you a tour of Nairobi,' Sarah said. 'Isn't that nice of him?'

'Thank you,' she said again; her voice was breathy. Now she was standing next to me I noticed how clean she smelled: minty, with a hint of roses. I knew my cheeks were as red as hers.

'I'd be happy to,' I said again.

Chapter Fourteen

Showing Lucy around Nairobi took up most of my time that wasn't spent at work. I took her to Mr Sand's market, for a round of golf at the Muthaiga on Freddie's membership, and for lunch at the Carlton Grill. I bought us tickets to an opera held among the peacocks in the Jeevanjee Gardens, where we were the youngest couple by at least fifty years. We attended a ball together, Lucy in a cornflower-blue dress that matched her eyes. Other times, we walked the streets and I pointed out notable buildings, or showed her how the post office system worked, and introduced her to everyone at the railway station. Everywhere we went I felt other men's eyes on us – admiring her, envious of me – and felt a thrill of disbelief at my luck. Other times I couldn't help wondering how much more envious they would be if it was Sylvie on my arm, but thoughts like that were hopeless; there was no knowing where she was, or when she was coming back.

Lucy's parents were kind to me; I enjoyed spending time with them, although they were so solidly English, so different from Freddie and the other settlers. I knew the Cartwrights wouldn't understand Freddie, and I didn't tell them about my friendship with him. Luckily he seemed to be spending most of his time setting up a yacht club in Naivasha, so I didn't have to work hard to keep them apart. Sometimes I felt a pang of nostalgia for the old Happy Valley lifestyle. Maybe Freddie would be around more when he was settled in his new position – whatever that turned out to be, I thought – and maybe then he'd bring everyone back together.

I saw my mother for the first time since my return at a dinner with the Cartwrights and my father. She kissed my cheek, asked about the journey, then spent the rest of the night in conversation with Mrs Cartwright. At subsequent meetings she rarely spoke to me or Lucy, and once or twice I caught her looking at us askance.

Maud lunched with us once, too. She and Lucy seemed to get on well, but it was only me that the family invited to the coast with them in late July, three weeks after their arrival.

'Please come,' Lucy said, slipping her hand into mine.

'Go, go,' my father said, when I mentioned their plans. He beamed at me. 'There's nothing like your first train journey together.'

The house the Cartwrights rented was in Tiwi. It was very grand, with indoor plumbing and a swimming pool in the garden. The beach was peaceful and secluded, with a handful of locals selling fresh fruit and only one other family holidaying there, and the water was warm and clear for miles, all the seaweed caught up in the coral reef at Diani. It was always so hot – I'd never known anywhere else where the heat grew out of the ground and ran up my legs.

We went into town a few times to see a picture at the Roxy cinema, and for a meal on a visiting ship for only a few shillings per person, the metal railing of the gangplank blistering our hands if we touched it. Other times we ate at The Nairobi's sister club, which jutted out over the cool blue of the Indian Ocean, bluer still against the palm trees and the blazing white walls of Fort Jesus. Afterwards we took a boat back to our beach, walking the last half-mile along the sand, Lucy dawdling with me while her parents went ahead, our clothes clinging damply to our skin even though the night-time air was cooler.

Sometimes the two of us stopped to look out at the ocean, and she rested her head on my shoulder. Afterwards, my jacket would smell of roses all night. Once she let me kiss her, so soft and yielding. She tasted different to the way Sylvie had, all those years ago, although I tried to put that moment out of my mind. The smell of her skin close up was different too, soapier, less personal.

Another time she let me put my arms around her waist and run my hands downwards to rest on her pert buttocks. At night I thrashed about in my bed, a few rooms down the corridor from hers, unable to sleep.

'Thank you for being a friend to Lucy,' Sarah said, over our last supper. 'I can tell she's happy here.'

Lucy blushed a deep crimson.

'I don't care what my father thinks,' I told her, as we walked back together that night, 'I'm glad the Germans are moving into Tanganyika.'

'You mustn't say that to my parents.'

'Why not?'

She put her arm through mine. 'And how can I believe you? You were so unfriendly when we first met.'

'I was *very* friendly.'

'You barely talked to me.'

'What are you accusing me of?' I asked. I stopped her by our usual spot, where the forest first crept down to meet the sand. We were quiet for a moment, the waves rushing at the shore and collapsing gently into foam before they reached us, and night-time creatures cooing to each other in the trees behind us.

I wrapped my arms around Lucy and squeezed. 'What are you accusing me of?' I asked again.

'You only like me now for my looks,' she said, disentangling herself and smiling up at me.

'You lie.'

'*You* lie.'

'You're hideous,' I said, 'I swear it's your mind I'm after.'

'Horrible man.'

She let me kiss her, and press myself against her, until a screeching came from the forest and she broke away.

'Just a monkey,' I said.

'We're late already.'

I tried to pull her back towards me. 'Your parents will be asleep by now.'

'They trust me,' she said, staying firm. She took my arm again and we continued walking along the beach. 'You know – I really like your father, Theo.'

'He's not too bad, I suppose. A little obsessed with trains.'

She laughed. 'I think they're romantic.'

'Not when you work with them. What about my mother, then?'

'I remember being so scared of her when we were children.'

'Really?' I smiled in the darkness.

'Yes, really. She was so beautiful – *is* so beautiful.'

'And now?'

Lucy paused. 'She's very nice to me,' she said at last.

'Isn't that a good thing?'

'Women can be nice to people they don't like.'

'Can they be horrid to people they love?'

'Women can hide everything they really feel. Men don't understand that.'

'We aren't always as simple and straightforward as you women think,' I said, and stopped her for another kiss.

I drove up to Kiboko the next Friday evening. Maud was sitting on the veranda when I arrived, a jug of gin sour and two glasses in front of her, and I wondered if she'd sensed I was going to come back. She was wearing lipstick and her hair was down, rather than in its usual bun; Scotty lay under her chair, barking at the ducks when they chattered on the lake. There were new trees in the garden, and the air smelled of figs and lemons.

162

'You're not bad at this gardening, you know,' I said, dropping into a chair beside her.

'Abdullah's been supervising me – he's the genius.'

'Don't sell yourself short. Maybe you'll do alright at farming after all.'

'I have to persuade the bank first,' she said. 'They won't give me a loan for now.'

'How much are you asking for?'

'Quite a bit.'

Scotty growled softly and she reached down and put her hand over his mouth. 'Quiet, you. The ducks have just as much right to be here as we do.'

'He's even fatter than before.'

'Don't listen to him, darling,' Maud told Scotty, then looked up at me. 'You'll have to get your own dog soon.'

'Why?'

'Remember the train from Mombasa – when we first arrived in Kenya?'

'Yes.'

'You promised me you'd get a dog when you moved out.'

'That was only if Mother wouldn't let you have one here,' I said. 'Besides, I've practically moved out already.'

'When you have your own house, then. But it'll be soon, won't it?'

'What do you mean?'

'That's what people think.'

'People think too much about other people's lives. Are you going to give me some of that cocktail or not?'

She laughed, and poured out two glasses. 'I like her.'

'Who?'

'Lucy.'

'Me too.'

'Of course you do. She worships you.'

'She thinks Mother doesn't like her though.'

163

'No one's going to be good enough for you in Mother's eyes,' Maud said. 'Lucy's probably just picking up on that.'

'I think it's the other way around.' I held up my glass. 'Cheers.'

A car rattled into sight up the drive.

'It's Edie,' Maud said, waving. 'She must know you're here.'

We went forwards to meet her. I hadn't seen her for a few years, but at forty she was almost the same as before, with only a few grey hairs and her neck and hands still unlined. She was barefoot, as she'd been the first time we'd met.

'Hello, beautiful people,' she said, hugging us each in turn. 'I can't believe how grown up you both look now.' She stepped back. 'Especially you, Theo. When did you get back?'

'A couple of months ago now.'

'I should have come to see you, but you know how it is. We're renovating, and I have to be there to supervise the builder otherwise he gets all sorts of ideas in his head.'

'I've been in Nairobi for the most part, anyway. I've barely seen Freddie, either.'

'No one sees Freddie these days. His new wife.' She rolled her eyes. 'She put him on a pedestal. How could I compete? My fault for marrying a bloody mummy's boy, I suppose.'

Her voice was affectionate. I grinned at her and she grinned back.

'Would you like a drink?' Maud asked.

'Actually, I just came to give you the news,' Edie said. 'I'm on my way to Nairobi.'

'Now?' Maud asked. 'Is everything alright?'

'Better than alright.'

My fingers and toes throbbed with a rush of blood. 'What's the news?'

She smiled at me. 'Sylvie arrived today,' she said. 'Nico wrote her a letter of recommendation, and the new Governor's granted her the right to stay.'

Chapter Fifteen

Sylvie moved back to The Farm with a minimum of fuss. Noel Case, her new housekeeper, oversaw everything, moving the furniture in from the manager's house, hanging new curtains, buying new sofas.

She's a godsend, Sylvie wrote, in her first letter to me. *So sensible. She's settled the servants' wages – I was behind by years, apparently.*

She seemed to fall quickly back into her old life. She wrote about riding and reading, and walking the new puppies – Minnie the dachshund and Louis the Rhodesian ridgeback. She played backgammon and drank whisky sour cocktails with grenadine and fresh lime. Sometimes Edie would be there with offerings: goat's cheese and pâté from France, dark chocolate from Belgium, cigarettes from Turkey, ham and oranges from Spain.

She only does it to annoy her new husband, Sylvie put. *He thinks I'm extravagant.*

Lucy seemed disappointed when I started spending every weekend at Kiboko. I promised I would be around more in a little while; I didn't tell her I wanted to be available for Sylvie. I waited for an invitation but August came and went without one, and something stopped me every time I turned my car in the direction of The Farm. This would be the first time Sylvie met me as an adult, and I wanted the setting for our reunion to be perfect.

Sometimes Sylvie's letters asked about Freddie, who hadn't been to visit yet. I barely saw him either – he was busy supervising the build of the golf course and lending library for the Naivasha Sports Club. In August, he planned and inaugurated the Hamilton Cup race for his new yacht club. Eventually, in early September, Maud and I received a dinner invitation from him. *It's time to bring Maud into the fold*, he'd scrawled at the bottom. *Sylvie is coming too.*

The day of the dinner party was warm and cloudless. Maud spent the morning laying out and rejecting dresses.

'Don't worry so much,' I said.

'It's my first party with your friends.' She shooed me away. 'Go be unhelpful somewhere else. Oh for goodness' sake, they're all covered in dog hair.' She gathered them up and disappeared in search of a toto.

Sylvie drove over to Kiboko mid-afternoon, and I took her onto the lake. Fifteen minutes out from the jetty I laid the oars down and let us drift.

'After all these years,' she said, trailing her fingers in the water. She was dazzling in a silvery-grey dress and large ruby ring, and from underneath her floppy hat, strands of hair had come unpinned and snaked down her beautiful neck. Her face was slightly rounder than before, and she had dark shadows under her eyes, but her skin was as clear as ever, her mouth as full, her legs as slender. She was wearing the same perfume, and I leaned towards her, drinking it in. I wanted to consume her.

'Champagne?' I asked. 'Cigarette?'

'You're spoiling me.'

'I want you to stay forever.'

'I will,' she said, dipping her head towards my flame. 'I'm going to die here, I've decided.'

166

'Planning ahead?'

'Yes.' She straightened back up, lit cigarette in her fingers. I noticed she wasn't wearing her wedding ring.

'So tell me,' she said. 'Have you met our hostess for tonight?'

'Martha? Once or twice.'

'Edie tells me she's charming.'

I grinned, thinking that probably wasn't the word Edie had used.

'Who else will be there? I expect there've been some changes in six years.'

'I don't know. Carberry's around, unfortunately, but I don't think Freddie would invite him. Or his new wife. People say she's tough as old boots.'

'You'd have to be,' Sylvie said. She took a deep drag of the cigarette. 'Did Maia kill herself?'

'Not as far as I know. The plane crashed.'

'But she was flying it?'

'Yes.'

She shrugged. Her head was wreathed in a cloud of smoke. Through it I could see her half-shut eyes, her lazy look.

'Forget Carberry, anyway. What about your side? How's Nico?'

'He's fine. Married again, to a woman called Genevieve. I love that name.'

'I should have visited him when I was back in Europe.'

'Life gets in the way. I wanted to call on you in Edinburgh, but Rupert was always just about to marry me.'

'Where is he?'

'In Australia, I hope. I paid him to go out there.' She touched her hair. 'How about Freddie? Is he busy?'

'He's getting into politics.'

'Oh?'

'And I don't think Martha lets him run around as much as Edie did.'

167

Her fingers drummed on the side of the boat. 'I suppose I couldn't expect things to be the same this time.'

I ached to take her in my arms, but something inside me told me it wasn't the right time. 'I still love you. That's the same.'

She looked down at her feet, smiling. 'You mustn't let any interested young ladies know you say that to me.'

'Lucy wouldn't mind.'

'So there's a Lucy?'

'Lucy Cartwright.'

'You're all grown up now, darling.' A small frown wrinkled her forehead and I had to resist the urge to smooth it out with my fingers. 'Freddie Hamilton would make a good politician's name.'

'Lucky for him.'

'I wonder what he's trying to prove.'

'He quoted Andrew Marvell at me.'

'That still sounds like him, thank God.'

She laughed suddenly; the lowness of it, the catch in her voice travelled up through my body and I reached out impulsively and brought her hand, palm upwards, to my mouth to kiss. I felt her pulse underneath my lips and my own pulse quickened in sympathy.

'Why don't we live out here?' I said. 'Just the two of us.'

She closed her eyes fully. 'That would be nice. What would we eat?'

'The ducks.'

'And drink?'

'Whisky,' I said. 'We'd tie barrels of it to the hull.'

'You've thought this through.'

'I've dreamed it often enough.'

She laughed. 'Tell me about your lady friend.'

'She's very pretty.'

'Of course she is. Anything else?'

'Very sweet.'

'Would you take her to a Kirlton party, if they still existed?'

I smiled. 'If she was American, she'd play the ukulele.'

'I see.' She smiled too, and I wondered how she always understood me completely. 'Bring her around for lunch next weekend. We'll have duck, since you seem so fond of it.'

'It's a date.'

She opened her eyes. 'You know, I'm looking forward to seeing Freddie. Has he changed much?'

'Not at all. He's got a chimp called Jules who he taught to smoke. Maybe if you bring Samson back from Paris they can be friends.'

'Samson's dead,' she said flatly.

'Oh.' I thought of the ball of fluff he'd been, bounding through the house and tripping up the servants, then the loping adolescent, fearless and friendly, quizzical when guests ran screaming from him. I saw him again pacing Nicolas's room when he was ill, his big brown eyes worried and protective, and felt a pang of real loss. 'How –'

'I can't talk about it.' She looked at her silver wristwatch. 'We should row back.'

The sun was behind the mountains when we arrived, but the pool was gleaming in the light from lanterns strung up on surrounding olive trees. To the right, I could make out the gleaming white walls of the gazebo that overlooked the jetty, and at the bottom of the lawn, I heard splashes and grunting coming from the lake. The hippos were out.

There were twenty of us at the dinner party, scattered between the veranda and the sitting room. Music floated scratchily between the two through the open French doors. I'd hoped Sylvie would stay with me, but Freddie drew her into conversation as soon as we arrived, and an old man with a purple face pounced on Maud. I knew I should be looking after her, but I wanted to watch Sylvie, so I sat by myself on the sofa on the veranda. After a while I noticed Martha watching her and Freddie too, with a pale, intense face; she didn't take her eyes off them until

169

eventually the strange woman I'd seen driving away from Mahalbeth appeared and dragged her off.

Boy Long – Edie's former fling – joined me and we clinked martini glasses. I didn't know him well, but since I'd returned from Edinburgh I'd seen him around town a few times in his Somali shawl and cowboy hat, and I'd always liked the look of him – he seemed young and fun and handsome, like Freddie.

'Was that your sister you arrived with?' he said.

'Maud, yes.' I looked around and saw she was still nodding politely at the purple-faced man.

'Very pretty. And what about you? Your father's the railway man, isn't he? Are you working with him?'

'For now.'

'What would you rather be doing?'

I shrugged. 'I don't have enough money for farming. I could get into law, I suppose.'

'What about politics?'

'I'm not charming enough.'

Boy took out a cigarette case and offered one to me, grinning. 'I can't believe that.'

Jack Soames, the tall Englishman I'd last seen playing with records at the Kirlton party, joined us.

'Women are so bloody obvious,' he said. 'Gwladys Delamere spent the last half an hour destroying Carberry's new wife to me. As if I didn't know it's because Freddie is tupping her.'

I looked over at Gwladys, leaning next to Freddie against a side table. She was Delamere's third wife – now his widow. She'd been described as a great beauty when she'd first come out to Africa, the year I'd left for Edinburgh, but she'd filled out since, and had the beginnings of a moustache. As I watched, she licked the tip of her finger, and rubbed it on Freddie's cheek. Sylvie had been cornered by Martha and her gaunt friend and had her back to the scene, otherwise I knew we would have shared a smile at it.

'Who's the woman with Martha and Sylvie?' I asked.

'Kiki Preston, I think,' Boy said. 'I don't know her well.' He shook his head. 'Lives too fast for me.'

Jack took a long drink of his cocktail. 'You should get out more, Long. You don't want to turn into an old fart like Freddie's new friends.'

Boy laughed and looked at me. 'Here's someone who *really* shouldn't get into politics.'

Supper had been set for nine o'clock, but Soames and Gwladys started on a new batch of cocktails at five minutes to. Freddie shook his head, grinning, and beckoned a toto over.

'We'll be eating later now,' he said. 'Make sure you keep the food warm.'

The toto scratched his head, looking worried. 'Bwana, maybe it burn if cook for longer.'

'It's your head if it does.'

The boy's eyes rolled back to show the whites and he made a clumsy half-bow before running back to the kitchen. Maud looked as if she wanted to run after him. I caught her eye and grinned, but she didn't return it. There was a small 'v' between her eyebrows that deepened when she glanced at Freddie.

'Freddie,' Martha said loudly. 'You can't say that – you know how literal Kikuyus are.'

'Poor buggers,' Boy said to me. 'They'll be gathered round the oven all night now.'

At eleven the cocktails ran out and we made our way into the dining room. The table was laid with blue-and-white porcelain dishes, and vases full of English roses. 'Freddie knows they're my favourite,' Martha said.

Freddie sat at the head of the table, in between the District Commissioner for Naivasha and Byrne, the new Governor. Sylvie sat opposite me in the middle, to the left of Soames; Maud was on his right.

Freddie's neighbour, two seats away from me, tried to interest me in bridge.

'You have the perfect face for it,' he told me. 'Gives nothing away. Like Freddie's. He's bluffed us up to far too high a level before, holding only five points. And then there's his damn memory – he's so good at forcing defence.'

I met the eye of the woman sitting in between us. 'I didn't understand a word of that,' I said.

'Never you mind,' he said. 'We'll train you up in no time.'

Across the table, Sylvie was deep in conversation with Soames. He was sprawled back in his chair with an amused expression on his face, and I remembered how good she was at telling anecdotes. Maud was speaking quietly to her other neighbour, the purple man from before. They were both drowned out by Freddie's story of meeting the Prince of Wales on the ship back to Mombasa.

'He doesn't hold with the Duke of Devonshire's views,' he told us. 'And I agree with him. The colonial office has no idea what it's like to live out here.'

'What's the Duke saying now?' Genesse, Boy's wife, asked.

'He thinks we should be considering the rights of the natives more.'

There was a murmur around the table.

'I'm glad D's dead,' Gwladys said. 'All his work creating the white ideal out here annihilated by a government thousands of miles away.'

Byrne tore off a piece of his bread roll. 'It *is* an African territory, as the Duke points out. Why shouldn't the Africans' interests be taken into account?'

'Because they're baboons,' Soames said.

Maud turned further towards her neighbour.

'*Jack*.' Genesse nodded at the wine toto in the corner of the room. He held the jug of wine perfectly still, staring impassively at a point above our heads.

'The system now seems fair to me,' Freddie said. 'We're obviously cleverer –'

'Are we?' Byrne interrupted. 'Aren't we just imposing Western standards of intelligence on a society that prizes different abilities?'

'Come on, Byrne.' Freddie ran a hand through his hair. I felt suddenly sorry for the Governor. 'Did the natives have an enlightenment period? Culturally and intellectually they're centuries behind us.'

'I don't agree. They've got an extremely rich culture of music, stories, art −'

'Are you seriously comparing a bunch of stick figures with the Botticelli *Mother and Child*?' Soames asked.

'Of course I'm not,' Byrne said.

'He's playing devil's advocate,' Kiki said.

'I'm merely pointing out we can't dismiss their contributions just because they differ from our own.'

'They didn't have an industrial revolution either,' Freddie said. 'We did.'

'Because we had access to natural resources like coal and iron. And our population was growing, so we had a larger labour market −'

'There are plenty of natural resources here,' Freddie said. 'And you could let the native population grow until kingdom come and they still wouldn't come up with an industrial revolution − our brains are just different.' He sat back in his chair. 'You know, the world could do a lot worse than if we were in charge.'

'We?'

'Great Britain. We've got the fairest justice system in the world, the best universities, a history of great political, philosophical and scientific thinkers. We discovered gravity. We gave women the right to vote − can you imagine that happening here?'

'You sure that's a sign of civilisation?' Soames said. Kiki threw a piece of bread at him, booing. It bounced off him and fell in front of Maud but she didn't seem to notice it. She was watching Freddie intently. I could see her hands fidgeting in her lap. I felt a pang of sympathy for her. At university I'd realised this was how adults sorted through ideas and opinions, through

173

debating with others. She probably thought a fight was about to break out.

Freddie caught my eye. I smiled at him. 'And now we have the technology,' he continued, 'so the natives work for us. They build our houses, they tend our crops, they cook and clean for us, and in return we give them clothes and meat, we protect them from enemy tribes and wild animals.' He signalled for more wine. 'We need them, so we should treat them well. But we're not equal, as much as the colonial office thinks they can just pass a law saying we are.'

'It'd be a bloody disaster,' Soames said. 'The crops would be gone, the houses would be falling down. They'd all be living with their eight wives in one mud hut again.'

'Is that so?' Sylvie had been unusually quiet up until now. She took out her cigarette case and leaned forwards to light the cigarette on a candle between us. I hoped she'd look at me, but she kept her gaze downcast.

I took a sip of my wine, suddenly irritated. I resented being so cut off from anyone I wanted to talk to privately, and the general conversation was going in circles. No one seemed to consider the possibility that the Africans might not want everything we'd built for them. I'd spent long enough back in Britain to see that not everyone appreciated being paternalised. 'Have any of you heard of the King of the Wa-Kikuyu?' I asked, remembering a story Douglas had told me once.

'Another bloody jumped-up native?' Soames said.

'He was from Yorkshire actually.'

'What about him?' Freddie asked.

'Apparently he ran away from home at thirteen, and set himself up as some sort of leader of an East African territory. He flew the Union Jack outside his house, and held court there, passing sentences and leading raids against other villages.'

Everyone laughed.

'Good man,' Freddie said. 'What happened to him?'

'The British authorities arrested him.'

'Typical,' Freddie said, pointing at Byrne. 'We come out here – the dreamers, the ambitious – to make our mark and help the country out, and the British government won't let us.'

Byrne held up his hands. 'Don't worry,' he said. 'The colonial office isn't going to pass a law along those lines for quite some time. Especially not if the High Constable of Scotland is breathing down their necks. I told you you belonged in politics, Hamilton.'

'Hear, hear,' Martha said.

'You know, I can't understand you, Byrne,' Freddie said. 'Surely you need more people on your side, not against you.'

'I respect intelligence,' Byrne said, leaning back in his chair.

'Freddie tends to use his *other* brain most of the time, don't you Freddie?' Soames said.

Freddie grinned.

I looked at Maud to see if she was blushing. She was still staring at Freddie, but not with an embarrassed expression. As I watched, she opened her mouth to speak, then Sylvie swore loudly and dropped her cigarette. I pushed my chair back to stand but she waved me down again.

'What's wrong, darling?' Freddie asked.

'I burned my wrist on your candle,' she said. She brought her hand up to her mouth and blew delicately at a small red spot on her skin. 'It's not my day.'

'This is your fault, Byrne, of course,' Freddie said. 'My mother always said it was bad luck to have an Irishman at the table.'

Everyone laughed loudly this time. Byrne held up his hands in mock surrender.

'Freddie,' someone called from my end of the table. 'We want to hear your thoughts on the new German Chancellor.'

Freddie raised his wine glass. 'I've got nothing against the Germans,' he said. 'I met Ribbentrop a few times back in London – seemed very decent – and they say he's a good friend of the Chancellor's.'

175

'Hitler's an ex-con,' one of the officials said. 'That would never happen in a British government.'

'Only because they've never caught us.'

There was more laughter.

Maud leaned forwards until she was directly in Freddie's line of sight. The determined expression on her face reminded me of the one she'd worn at five years old when I'd taught her to swim. 'But surely you don't agree with his principles,' she said.

'I'm not opposed to Fascism,' he said. 'In fact, Protectionism is probably the only way to reassert the primacy of Britain and our Empire.'

'You don't really mean that,' Byrne said.

'I might do.'

'Hitler's established himself as a dictator,' Maud said. Two spots of high colour had appeared on her cheeks.

'She's right,' Byrne said.

'Then the Germans shouldn't have elected him,' one of the government wives said.

'They were frightened about the economy and he promised to revive it,' Maud said. 'But now he's made sure they can't change their minds when it's getting better.' She looked around the table, as if for support, but most guests were shrugging.

Freddie signalled for more wine. 'I'm not for dictatorships, but I don't think we need to worry about Hitler.'

'It'll be a cold day in hell before Lord Hamilton is ruffled,' Byrne said, raising his glass.

Freddie laughed. Maud blinked quickly, as if trying to hold back tears. Sylvie leaned across Soames and squeezed her arm, and a look passed between them that I couldn't quite read.

Two totos appeared and started clearing away our empty plates.

The party continued for another few hours after the meal. Maud stuck close to me, looking tired. Eventually I took her to a corner and held her hand.

176

'Don't feel bad about it,' I said. 'He debates for fun.'

'How can you bear it, Theo?' she asked.

'What do you mean?'

'I mean the people.' She lowered her voice. 'What do you see in them? They're rude and shallow, and it's all old-fashioned, insular rubbish, everything they stand for.'

I was taken aback by the sharpness of her tone. 'Even Freddie and Sylvie?'

'Sylvie is different.'

'Freddie is different too – he just knows what people want to hear.' I looked across at where he was standing, his arm clapped across Byrne's shoulders. Byrne was shaking his head and smiling at something Freddie was saying.

'I can't . . .' She removed her hand from mine. 'The way they treat the Africans, the way they think about them. Doesn't it bother you?'

'Waweru's devoted to Freddie.'

'Theo, you can't really be so blind.' Her face was plum-coloured. 'Not about this.'

'Pardon?'

'I need to go to the bathroom,' she said, and left.

I knew I should go after her, but by the time I'd collected myself she was already out of the room. I moved to an empty corner instead, feeling guilty that she wasn't enjoying herself, and hurt that she'd taken it out on me. Even more than before I wanted to finally get Sylvie to myself; she'd make me feel better, I knew, but the neighbour had caught her now. I heard him explaining the perfect bridge hand to her. Freddie saw me and came over to refill my wine glass as I stood alone.

'She's looking marvellous still,' he said.

'She is.'

'You're aching to comfort her, aren't you? Kiss her little injury away.'

His tone irritated me. I could tell he thought I was chasing

Sylvie fruitlessly. He probably thought she was still in love with him. I wondered if she was, and felt bile rising in my throat.

I looked down at my glass. 'I hate to tell you,' I said, 'but I think your wine is corked.'

He staggered backwards, clutching his chest. 'My dear boy, how could you be so cruel?'

'I'd have a word with your wine merchant.'

He was shaking his head, his eyebrow cocked and his gaze meeting mine. 'Cruel,' he murmured. 'Cruel, cruel, cruel.'

I felt a strange thrill at hearing those words from his lips. 'So now you know.'

Freddie walked us to Sylvie's car when we left. 'It's good to see you,' he said to her. 'How's The Farm these days?'

'Come visit me and find out,' she said.

He laughed and put his arms around her. I wanted Sylvie to push him away, but she lifted her face for his kiss instead.

Maud got into the back. I climbed into the driver's seat and shut the door, but I could still hear them murmuring to each other. I lit a cigarette and let the match burn down until it reached the tip of my finger, then shook it out quickly, wound down my window and dropped it onto the grass.

'Are you two still going?' I said.

They laughed. Freddie released Sylvie and she climbed into the car. 'Are you driving me home?' she asked.

'There are spare bedrooms at our house,' I said.

'Aha,' Freddie said, hooking his hands over the top of the window and leaning into the car. 'Nefarious intentions – I knew it.'

'Thank you for dinner,' I said, winding up the window again. He slid his fingers off just in time, grinning at me through the glass.

'Take care, both of you,' he said, raising his voice. 'You know what Joseph Parry says – *Make new friends, but keep the old; those are silver, these are gold.*'

'And we're the old friends?'

'Old and very dear. Especially Maud – I hope we see a lot more of you now.'

'Thank you for having me,' she said, tightly.

'Any time. Now – hosting duties call.' He flexed his shoulders, like a moving Greek statue. 'Come back soon.'

He headed for the house but his smell lingered, peppery and masculine, and the wave of self-pity that had been threatening since we'd arrived suddenly came crashing down on me.

'I should go home,' Sylvie said, tucking her hair behind her ear. 'Would you like me to drive?'

'I can do it. Some other time for the sleepover then?'

'Perhaps.'

I ground the gears and we bounced off.

Chapter Sixteen

Sylvie wrote to me after the party, confirming our lunch. I showed it to Lucy.

'You'll love her,' I said.

'Will she love me?'

'Of course she will.'

'What should I wear?'

I kissed her nose. 'You look beautiful in everything.'

I drove her up early on the Saturday. She was wearing a bright yellow dress that ended just below her knees, and white gloves.

'How do I look?' she asked me anxiously.

'Lovely,' I said. 'Like springtime.'

'Good.' She smiled. 'I didn't ask – how was your party last week?'

'Very political. I mostly stayed out of it.'

'My parents are always talking politics. I can tell they wish I was more interested.'

I looked across at her. 'You wouldn't throw big dinner parties where everyone was debating all night?'

'No,' she said, smiling. 'When I marry I'm going to spend all my time warming my husband's slippers by the fire, and making him drinks and bringing him the papers.'

I took one hand off the steering wheel, caught her hand and kissed it. 'Your husband's going to be a well-informed drunkard then.'

Sylvie was waiting for us on the veranda when we arrived. She stood up to greet us, setting off Minnie and Louis, and I saw Lucy take in the emerald-green dress with nipped-in waist and loose top. The hem reached the floor, and made a swishing sound as Sylvie walked towards us.

'I thought I'd dress up,' she said, taking Lucy's hand, 'as I know you're so important to Theo.' She smiled at me.

'You look magnificent,' I said, kissing her cheek.

'So do you two – a very striking pair.' She squeezed Lucy's hand. 'Let's have a drink.'

There was a bottle of champagne already out on the table, three coupes, and blue, flowered china. Sylvie poured out the champagne and raised her glass. 'To happiness,' she said.

'To happiness.'

Not far away a tame eland trampled through the flowerbeds and rubbed his twisted horns on the trees.

'He's beautiful,' Lucy said, following my gaze.

'He is, isn't he? It's not home without animals.' Sylvie moved to sit down and I held the chair out for her. 'Thank you, darling.'

Lucy took a small sip of her drink and put her glass back down.

'Don't you like champagne?' I asked, holding her chair out too.

'I haven't eaten anything. I don't want to get tipsy.'

'Let's have the food now then,' Sylvie said, and signalled one of the totos.

I joined them at the table and smiled at Lucy, trying to put her at her ease. She smiled back, but not as widely as usual.

The toto brought out fresh bread, cold duck, a salad of lettuce, leeks and potatoes, and dishes of butter and mayonnaise.

'You remembered the duck,' I said to Sylvie.

'Of course,' she said, and caught Lucy's eye. 'Apparently Theo loves it.'

'I didn't know that,' Lucy said.

'Didn't you?' I said.

'Well – there's red wine, too,' Sylvie said, getting up from the table.

She disappeared inside, and I turned to Lucy. 'Is everything alright, darling?'

'Yes.'

'Are you sure?'

Sylvie reappeared. 'They're bringing it.'

'Thank you,' Lucy said.

'When are the whisky sours?' I asked. 'Sylvie makes great cocktails, darling.'

Lucy chewed a mouthful of bread. Sylvie gave me a look that was part-amused, part-unreadable. No one spoke as the toto brought out a decanter of red wine, or after he'd placed it carefully on the table and gone back inside.

'So you're from England, originally?' Sylvie said eventually.

'Yes,' Lucy said. 'I haven't been back since I was five though.'

'It hasn't changed that much,' I said. 'Still rains all the time.'

'It's changed a lot for some people,' Sylvie said.

'I suppose the clothes are different. There are more cars. Everyone has a vacuum cleaner.'

'What's a vacuum cleaner?' Lucy asked.

'A torture device. Probably invented by a sadistic landlady. You wouldn't get them in Tanganyika.'

'I've never been to Tanganyika,' Sylvie said, 'but I've heard it's beautiful.'

'It is,' Lucy said. 'It was hard to leave.'

'That's where we first met,' I said, taking her hand.

'When?'

'Just before I came to Kenya. I was fourteen.'

'I thought he was very handsome,' Lucy said.

'Were you in love?' Sylvie asked, smiling.

'A little.' Lucy blushed and I kissed her hand.

'When she wasn't busy being terrified of my mother,' I said.

Sylvie raised an eyebrow. 'Did you have a run in with Mrs Miller too?'

I grinned, wondering how my mother would feel about this little lunch, and the company I was keeping now.

Lucy seemed taken aback. 'Did you?'

'She certainly disapproved of me at first.'

'But Theo was fourteen when you met, so you must have been too old –' She turned red. 'I didn't mean old – surely you were just friends?'

'We were very good friends,' I said, surprised and irritated at how graceless Lucy was being. I looked at Sylvie, hoping she wasn't offended.

'I know what you meant,' she said. 'It wasn't that.' She waved her hand. 'And fourteen isn't that young after all. My oldest daughter is eleven. She'll be falling in love soon.'

Lucy paused. 'Theo didn't say you had children,' she said eventually.

'Two girls. They live with Nicolas – their father – in Paris.'

'Do you have photographs?'

Sylvie lit a cigarette. 'I don't, I'm afraid.'

'Oh.'

I picked up my cutlery and speared a piece of perfectly tender duck. Lucy was chewing bread again, looking at her plate.

'Have you seen Edie recently?' I asked Sylvie.

'No. I've seen Freddie though – he finally made it over here.'

'Lucky you.' I'd been trying for a joke, but my voice sounded petulant to me. The last thing I wanted was a long discussion about Freddie.

She looked away. 'Rupert came back too. A few days ago.'

'From Australia?'

'Apparently he was too wild for his hosts out there.' She finished her champagne in one long gulp. 'He wants to get back together.'

I speared another piece of duck savagely. 'Where is he now?'

183

'At a farm in Njoro.'

'You don't want him here?'

'He's drunk all the time. And threatening.'

'Is this your husband?' Lucy asked, wide-eyed.

Sylvie stubbed out her cigarette. 'I suppose you could call him that. We were married for three months before I sent him off to Melbourne. I gave him enough money to stay away much longer than this.'

'What happened?'

'He was always bad,' I said. 'No one knew what you saw in him.'

'When someone's so awful to everyone, and sometimes sweet to you, it makes you feel special. But I wasn't, obviously.' She pushed away her plate. 'The last time we saw each other before the separation, we had a fight – about orchestra conductors, I think – and he threw his drink in my face.'

Lucy's eyes widened further.

'I was wearing a hat with a little veil on it, and this maraschino cherry got stuck in the netting.' She lit another cigarette. 'It was so humiliating – I was just sitting there, soaking wet, with the cherry, and he was laughing, and I thought – he doesn't care about me. He doesn't care about anything but getting his way.'

'Can you divorce him?' Lucy asked.

'I'm asking.'

'We're here,' I said, 'any time you need us.'

'Thank you, darlings,' Sylvie said, taking my hand, 'that means a lot to me.'

I felt my heart give a familiar hiccup and looked over at Lucy. She was staring at something in the distance.

We left around five o'clock and rode home in silence. On the outskirts of the city I pulled over and took Lucy's face in my hands, kissing her.

After a moment she pushed me away. 'Someone might see us.'

'Then why don't we go for a walk in City Park?'

184

City Park was the public park by the Muthaiga, almost ninety hectares of forest, botanical gardens, walkways, open areas, a bowling green, bandstand, maze and a cemetery for veterans of the Great War. In the daytime it was full of people, strolling, riding bicycles or picnicking. At night it was completely deserted, although there were no gates to keep us out.

'It's dark in there,' Lucy said at the entrance.

'I'll protect you.'

She let herself be led inside and in the direction of the pond. Twice something rustled in the trees nearby and she drew closer.

'It's just the monkeys,' I said, laughing at her.

The pond was black and bottomless at night. A frog sat by its edge, croaking at us. It was the green of Sylvie's dress. I gently pushed Lucy up against the trunk of a nearby tree.

'No one's going to see us now,' I said.

She didn't say anything, but her breath was coming very fast.

I kissed her, and after a while she kissed me back. I ran my hands through her hair, and along her throat. It thrummed beneath my fingers.

'Theo . . .' she said.

I kissed her harder. I wondered what would have happened if Sylvie hadn't pushed me away in the car all those years ago, whether I would have known what to do. I took my hands off Lucy's throat and ran them up her thighs instead, up and over her knickers.

'Can I?' I asked.

She nodded.

I hooked my fingers over the waistband and eased the knickers down over her bottom, down her thighs and let them fall around her ankles. I knelt down in front of her and lifted the hem of her dress. Her pubic hair was blonde too, and soft, not tight and springy like others I'd known.

I pressed my face into it, breathing in. Her soapy smell was mixed with another, more animal this time. I put my tongue out and licked her inner thigh. The flesh was firm and tasted of salt.

She twisted above me. 'What are you doing?'

I met her worried gaze and held it. 'Just stay still,' I said, 'I know what you'll like.'

'Theo,' she said again, then looked away.

I licked an outer lip. She was silent now, but she grabbed a fistful of my hair. I parted the lips with one hand and looked at the glistening red form in front of me. I placed my tongue at the bottom, and licked upwards very slowly. I felt her shudder, and she twisted the clump of hair in her hand tighter. I licked again, and again, faster and faster, my tongue flicking around her clitoris until she moaned above me and her legs trembled.

Afterwards, I walked her back to The Norfolk. At the entrance to the hotel she turned to me, blushing.

'You don't need to come in,' she said.

'Can I see you tomorrow?' I asked.

'Yes,' she said, and blushed harder.

Chapter Seventeen

Lucy caught a cold after the visit to Sylvie, and I was banished from her sickbed.

The evenings dragged themselves out without her. Most I spent at The Nairobi Club, reading opposite my father. I watched *King Kong* at the cinema. I didn't see much of Freddie – he was still busy with Naivasha issues and he and Martha were planning a trip to London. I was glad to think Sylvie would be free of him for a while.

She was always home when I called, but jumpy, never as warm as she'd been at the lunch. We drank whisky sours on the veranda, or strolled around the garden on either side of Tam, the eland, while she pointed out suitable burial spots for herself. Noel told me it was her favourite game. During a visit in late October Rupert showed up at The Farm, drunk. Sylvie trembled when he shouted at her, in fear or anger, or both. Halfway through his rant, he fell asleep on a sofa and relieved himself. I picked him up and slung him over my shoulder.

'Be careful with him,' Sylvie said, following me out to my car, Minnie dancing around her ankles.

I bundled him into the passenger side. 'Why do you care what happens to him?'

'He's my husband.'

'You're asking him for a divorce, aren't you?'

She picked up Minnie and cradled her, not meeting my eye. I slammed the door shut on Rupert and he sprawled across the seat. 'Answer me.'

She gave me her special smile. 'Of course.'

'Good.'

She laughed. 'When did you become so forceful?'

I climbed into the car, pushing Rupert into an upright position, and started the engine. 'I want to see you soon.'

'Whenever you want,' she called back.

I drove a few miles from the house before I stopped the car. I leaned across Rupert to open the passenger door, then kicked his body out onto the side of the road. He moaned once, but didn't open his eyes.

'Stay away from Sylvie,' I said, pulling the door shut and driving off.

Halfway home I recognised Martha's car sitting just off the road, and slowed down to take a better look. It was turned onto a small dirt path that led to a forest. From afar the reflection of the trees obscured its inside, but as I got closer I could make out a mass of red hair behind the steering wheel.

I tapped on the window twice. She didn't seem to hear me and kept her eyes fixed ahead on the forest. I circled the front of the car and opened the passenger door. She stirred then, turning her head to look at me.

'Are you alright?'

'Theo.' She smiled. 'I was out for a drive and forgot where I wanted to go.'

I climbed in. Closer up, she smelled faintly of sour milk and my stomach churned against it. 'Do you usually drive alone?'

'Not really.'

'Does Freddie know where you are?'

She slumped back against her seat, dropping her hands from

the steering wheel. 'No. I just had to get out of the house.' She passed a hand over her forehead. 'I'm not feeling too well at the moment.'

'Do you need to see a doctor?'

'No.'

'Shall I take you home?'

'Could you?'

We switched seats. Martha fell asleep as soon as I turned on the engine, head propped up on her fist. Now I had a chance to look at her closely, I could see how pale she was.

As I pulled into the drive she woke up and ran a hand through her hair. Freddie was standing in the open front door and waved to us.

'I think I'll go lie down,' Martha said. 'Thank you, darling.'

Freddie squeezed her arm as she passed him, then came over to the car and leaned in through the passenger window.

'Where did you find her?'

'Not too far from Naivasha. I left my car there to drive her back.'

'I'll get Albert to drive you back to pick it up.'

'Thanks.'

'Don't mention it. How did Martha seem to you?'

'Not very well.'

'No.' He looked at his hands. 'She isn't. I think she's in quite a bit of pain, actually.'

My skin grew hot and prickly with shame as I thought about how competitive I'd felt towards him recently over Sylvie. Of course Freddie had problems too.

'Can I help?' I asked.

He stood up and put his hands in his pockets. The coins inside jingled and I didn't catch what he said next.

I opened my door and climbed out. 'Anything I can do.'

'I was going to collect her medicine,' Freddie said, 'but maybe I should stay with her. Would you mind?'

'Of course not.'

'Thanks.' He started walking back to the house. 'I'll write down the address for you. It's not the usual dispensary – Martha prefers to be discreet about it.'

'Of course.'

The dispensary was on the outskirts of Naivasha, and looked more like a house. The door and window frames were painted pink, and the lawn was emerald green and perfect. From the back of the property I could hear a child shrieking in Swahili. A toto answered the door and silently disappeared inside without telling me what to do. I waited outside.

A man wearing a white coat came to the door. He didn't look much older than me. He had curly black hair and a cheerful expression. When he spoke his accent was thick Irish.

'You've come for Lady Hamilton's prescription?'

'Yes.'

'I've just made it up.' He patted his pockets and found a small brown-glass bottle; I noticed it was unmarked.

'That's it?'

'That's everything. Lord Hamilton's already paid.' He grinned.

I took it from his outstretched hand; inside the bottle was a fine powder. 'No instructions? Does she have to mix it with anything?'

'She knows what to do with it.' He cocked his head. 'Don't worry, she'll be better in no time.'

'Okay.' I slipped it into my pocket. Something about the set-up made me feel uneasy, but I knew Freddie wouldn't hire a quack.

He was looking at me closely. 'Have I seen you around some-where?'

'Maybe. My family lives at Kiboko.'

He snapped his fingers. 'Do you have a sister? Always with her head boy. Very beautiful.'

'I'm probably not the best judge.'

190

'Irishmen can't resist a red-head.' He stuck his hand out. 'Dr Joe Gregory.'

'Theo Miller. And my sister's Maud.'

He grinned again, persuasively, and I smiled back this time. 'I'll remember that. Hope I see you around.'

Of all my Edinburgh friends, Douglas was the only one I regularly corresponded with. He always seemed to enjoy hearing work stories, and he particularly enjoyed hearing about a claim made by a visiting duchess that I'd become embroiled in lately. She'd lost her spectacles on the journey between Lake Victoria and Nairobi and was demanding every train guard be fined as an example. As tedious as it was, at least it gave me plenty of fodder for my letters. *The old bat has a pretty unshakeable belief in her own importance,* I wrote. *She's mostly upset that no one else seems aware of it.*

Believe me, he wrote back, *I know the type. I'm in the civil service, remember.*

I thought the story might amuse Maud too, and decided to spend the following weekend at Kiboko. I hadn't seen her since the morning after Freddie's party, six weeks ago, but she'd apologised over breakfast for snapping at me, and I was anxious to make sure everything was fine between us.

She wasn't on the veranda when I pulled up, and didn't answer when I stood in the doorway calling her name. The house smelled of wood polish and I could see the gleam on the candlesticks over the fireplace from across the room. No sounds came from the kitchen. I caught myself hesitating to go in and tried to laugh it off, but without the usual bustle the house seemed unnatural somehow. I wondered if this was how my mother felt about it, and why she was never around any more.

I pulled myself together, and was about to go through to see if Joseph had fallen into the cauldron when I caught a reflection of movement in the screen door. I turned. Maud was walking back from the servants' enclosure. She raised a hand to wave at me.

'You never let me know when you're coming home,' she called.

'Keeps you on your toes. Have you let everyone go?'

'I gave them the evening off – we've been cleaning all day.'

'I can tell.'

She reached me and I drew her in for a hug. The smell of the polish had clung to her hair, mixed with soap and something earthier. She hugged me back, laughing, then stepped away.

'I'm afraid you'll have to eat my cooking tonight.'

'We've all got our cross to bear.'

She smiled. 'Come and keep me company in the kitchen.'

I followed her through. She started opening cupboards and lifting lids on the pots already sitting on the stove. 'Joseph's left a soup – clearly he has no faith in me either.'

'Soup sounds perfect.'

She lit the hob. 'Find me a spoon, will you?'

I searched the drawers until I found a long, wooden spoon and handed it over. She began stirring dreamily. Now I looked properly I could see she was exhausted. Her eyes were half-closed and she was almost swaying.

'Let me do that,' I said. 'You go and lie down.'

'I'm fine,' she said, stirring more quickly.

'You're dead on your feet.'

'No, I want to stay. I haven't seen you for a while.'

'I've been busy.'

'Drawing up timetables?'

'Something like that.'

She laid down the spoon and peered underneath the cloth covering a nearby tray. 'He's left bread, too.'

'I ran into Freddie the other day,' I said, opening the oven door for her. 'He sends his love.'

'Oh?'

'I didn't tell him you disapprove of him.'

'I know he's your friend.' She slid the tray into the oven. 'And he's very charming.'

'But –'

'But. He has so much power, and he thinks of others so little.'

I grinned. 'He talks a good talk, but he's not Prime Minister. Yet, anyway.'

'Not just politically.' She wiped the flour from her hands onto her skirt. 'He could order his totos to wear rags and bark like dogs and they'd have to.'

'He wouldn't.'

'But he could, because he's got the money and the land and he's in charge. But he's only that way because he was born somewhere else and born with money.' She picked up the spoon again. 'That's what his type don't understand – they blame people who don't have the same opportunities for not doing as well in life, instead of being grateful for their own privileges.'

'Freddie works hard at his farming. They all work hard at it. An aristocratic background doesn't exactly guarantee success there.'

'But it does mean failure isn't a matter of life or death.'

I shrugged. 'Alright, what about Father then? You know we wouldn't be here if it wasn't for the railway.'

'But –'

'We took Kenya and Uganda as territories when they were just a bunch of natives and built the railway so Uganda could have access to the coast for trade. And then we needed to pay for it, so the government encouraged the settlers to come and farm. And *they* needed land, so the government took it from the Africans.'

'I know.'

'If you want to blame the Africans' lack of opportunities on something you can't forget the role he played.'

'I know.'

She looked so bothered I put my arm around her shoulder, smiling. 'Don't take it so badly. If we hadn't done it, someone else would have.'

193

'That's not an excuse.'

'You want to farm, don't you?'

'That doesn't mean I don't want them to have their own land, or be able to farm for themselves. I want to provide employment. I want to give something back.'

'Whereas I want to be filthy rich and married to a beautiful woman.'

She half-returned my smile. 'It's funny, isn't it? How different we are now.'

'Were we ever the same?'

'Maybe not. You were always more fun than me.'

'You mean I was frivolous.'

Maud looked surprised at the change in my tone. I dropped my arm from her shoulder and leaned against the oven. 'Mother thought that too. Or not frivolous – stupid.'

'Of course she didn't.'

'You must have seen how differently she treated us.'

She turned back to the pot. 'I know. But it's more complicated for mothers and sons. Or it is with you two, anyway.'

I stuffed my hands into my pockets. 'You don't understand.'

'*You* don't understand. Do you deliberately misconstrue things? Or can you really not see how people feel?' She bit her lip. 'No, let's stop – I hate arguing with you.' She took a spoonful of the soup and blew on it then held it out to me. 'Tell me what you think. It's supposed to be cream of chicken.'

I tasted it, still angry. 'It's fine.'

'Really?'

It wasn't Maud's fault. She couldn't know what it had been like to grow up with a mother who could turn on her at any moment, but it irritated me that she wouldn't acknowledge that I did. I tried to force a cheerfulness that I didn't feel. 'Creamy and chicken-like. And freezing cold.'

'Oh well. Maybe Joseph was right to doubt me.' She looked away. 'Theo . . .'

194

'What?'

'Nothing.'

There was a silence between us. After a while I held my hand out. 'Come on. Let's go sit outside until we smell burning.'

Christmas came and went. Maud arrived at The Norfolk on Christmas Eve, full of a treehouse that Abdullah was building for the servants' children. Lucy and her family joined us for lunch the next day. She was wearing a white dress with small green flowers on it. I sat next to her during the meal, stroking her thigh with my thumb and enjoying the pink flush that stained her cheeks. My father drank an enormous quantity of wine, almost matched by Mr Cartwright, and the two of them sang Scottish ballads over the Christmas pudding. After the third ballad, Lucy and I escaped into the garden and I gave her the diamond earrings I'd bought her.

'Thank you,' she said, kissing me. 'They're beautiful.'

'Not as beautiful as you,' I said, and she flushed more.

Maud left on Boxing Day to supervise the treehouse. I went to the races with Freddie, Martha, Kiki, her husband and Sylvie, and counter to my first experience there, lost a sizeable amount of money.

'Easy come, easy go,' Freddie said, as we drove from the track to the Muthaiga. I sat in the back seat in between him and Sylvie. We'd got soaked in a downpour just before we left, and my skin felt damp and itchy. Outside the car, the sky was the colour of salt and the puddles on the road were deep and muddy.

'It doesn't come quite as easily for me,' I said, looking at Martha, who was huddled in between Kiki and her husband, in the front seat, head resting on Kiki's shoulder. She seemed much happier and more lucid than the last time I'd seen her, and I was glad the medicine had worked.

Freddie laughed. 'You'll learn.'

Sylvie leaned over from my other side to put a hand on Freddie's leg. 'Darling,' she said, 'there are some things you have to be born with.'

'Is that so?' Freddie said.

'So,' Sylvie said. She ran her hand up his leg, stopping at his crotch, and squeezed.

Freddie raised an eyebrow. I shifted backwards, looking away. The rain worsened, hammering against the car roof, and drowning out all other noise. I could smell damp clothes and body odour, and felt the two of them pressing in on me even more. When I looked down I saw Sylvie had slipped her hand inside Freddie's trousers and was stroking him. I caught Freddie's eye. He grinned at me and I felt myself growing, in spite of everything. Sylvie leaned closer, and her jacket fell open. Underneath her blouse, I could see the outline of her breasts, swinging away from her body.

'Why don't you touch her?' a voice said quietly in my ear. I wondered if Martha had heard, but none of them were looking back. My stomach lurched with anticipation; I knew I was ready now, and I wanted Freddie and Sylvie to know it too.

I reached out and took a breast in my hand, squeezing it. Sylvie looked up and her expression changed. If was as if we were suddenly moving around in each other's brain. I felt her talking to me – about her loneliness, guilt, fear, victory, boredom, lust. I felt savage with knowledge and desire. I wanted to throw her across the seat and tear her clothes off.

'Freddie,' Martha said. 'We're here. And the rain's easing up. I think it's a good omen.'

She turned her head in our direction as we broke away from each other. I adjusted my trousers.

Sylvie smiled brightly. 'Martha, can I steal a cigarette, darling?'

'Of course you can,' Martha said, pulling out her case.

'Thank you,' Sylvie said. She selected a cigarette and put it to her lips, not looking at me or Freddie. Gerry pulled to a stop, then came around and opened Sylvie's door first. She climbed out and walked straight towards the front door. I watched her hips swinging from side to side underneath her grey pencil skirt and felt my excitement returning.

'I didn't think you had the guts,' Freddie said, clapping me on the back.

'You have to stop thinking of me as a boy.'

He started to say something, but I held up my hand to speak first. I wanted him to acknowledge that I was an equal now; something had changed between me and Sylvie, and it was my turn to make her happy. I met his eye.

'Freddie, stop dawdling,' Martha said. 'I'm getting cold.'

I drove out to The Farm the first chance I had. Sylvie was reading when I arrived at midday, still in her pyjamas and even more appealing than usual.

'Hello, Theo,' she said, putting down her book. 'I thought you might come.'

'You look ravishing,' I said, kissing her on the cheek.

'And you look like a ravisher,' she said. 'Join me for a drink?'

'Starting the year with a bang?'

'Start as you mean to go on,' she said, and crossed over to the sideboard.

A breeze arrived from the mountains, smelling of pine needles. It ruffled her pyjamas and woke up Minnie, who'd been snoozing under the table. She barked twice.

'What have I told you, silly girl?' Sylvie said. 'Some things you can't scare away.'

I picked up the dachshund and she licked my face. 'How would you feel about going to the coast for the weekend?' I asked and she barked again.

Sylvie returned with two full tumblers and placed them on the table. Minnie jumped off my lap and disappeared inside.

'What shall we drink to?' I asked.

She sat down again and took a deep breath. 'I've got bad news, darling.'

'What's wrong?'

'I had a letter from Genevieve this morning.'

'Nicolas's wife?'

'He died on Christmas Eve.'

I felt the smile on my face stretch further. 'That's a bit of a ghoulish joke.'

She covered her face with her hands and started crying quietly, shoulders shaking. I wanted to reach out to her, but my arms wouldn't move. 'It's not possible.'

'Look.' She stood up then sat down again. 'No, I burnt it.'

I crossed the chasm between my mind and my limbs and took her hands in mine; they felt as if they belonged to two other people, strangers. 'How did it happen?'

'A septic infection, or meningitis. Or both. I didn't take it in properly.' She shuddered. 'He must have suffered.'

'Don't think about that.'

'I can't stop.'

'You couldn't have done anything about it.'

'It's how I feel anyway.' She shook my hands off, gently, and grasped her tumbler. 'What if we hadn't married? He might never have lived out here, never caught the fever.'

'So?'

'You know it weakened him. *I'm* responsible for that.'

'He loved living out here. And he loved being married to you.'

'*I* didn't love *him* enough though – not the way he needed me to.' She blinked and another tear leaked out from beneath her eyelid. I reached forward and brushed it away with my thumb.

'He wasn't right for you.'

'Because he was kind.'

'Because he was too afraid of losing you.'

She took a long drink of the cocktail. 'Just after our wedding I said to him, I can't be caged, Nico. Don't try.'

'But he did cage you. In France, and with the children.'

'I was a child. I thought I was so rare, and delicate. I thought

198

settling down was too high a price to pay. I broke out of the cage, didn't I? For all it's got me.'

She leaned back with her head against the chair, her body open invitingly.

'You don't know what you want,' I said. 'That's your trouble.'

'I wish I could have said goodbye.'

'I do too.'

'I was so *angry* with him the last time we saw each other. I blamed him for Samson's death. Nico gave him to a zoo in France, to keep the nanny happy. I wanted to bring him back here, but they sold him on to a circus, and by the time Nico found him, he was . . .' She shuddered. 'They'd broken him.'

I felt sick.

'Nico said he had some awful trainer who whipped him half to death. We'd never raised our hands to him – he'd never been afraid before.' She dug her nails into her palms. 'You know what he was like – such a ball of fluff. How could anyone not love him? How could they want him to feel confused and scared like that?'

'Couldn't Nico buy him back?'

'He tried to. Samson attacked his trainer and they shot him.'

Images of Samson floated in front of me – rolling in the grass in the sunshine, sleeping with his face buried in Nicolas's lap, panting his way up the hill after a deer that he'd spotted.

'Nico was there when it happened,' Sylvie said. 'He said Samson died in his arms.' She stood up and walked over to the sideboard. 'I hope Genevieve was there for him.'

'I'm sure she was.'

'It must be awful to die alone. And Nico was never very brave.' She covered her face again.

I stood too, and went to her. 'Let me look after you.'

'I'll be fine.'

'You can't lie to me,' I said, and kissed her hands. After a while she took them away from her face and I kissed her mouth.

'I'll make you feel better.'

'You do, just by being here.'

'You know what I mean.'

She looked so serious I almost laughed. 'Come on.' I led her to the bedroom; she didn't resist.

Inside the room, I guided her onto the bed. My heart was hammering so hard I could feel it throbbing in my fingers and toes. This was the moment. Sylvie seemed almost calm, but I could sense something underneath it; I saw it in her quick blink, in her mouth, which trembled before she pressed her finger against it. I heard it when I took off my clothes, and she let out a sound – half pant, half sigh.

'I've wanted to do this for so long,' I said. I stood in front of her, and let her see me, let her take in the full extent of how I felt about her.

'You think I'm beautiful?' she asked.

'More than beautiful.'

She put out her hand to touch me and I willed my body to keep control. Her eyes were huge and doe-like.

'Why shouldn't we, then?' she said, and the blood that had been swelling my body filled my ears with a triumphant roar.

Chapter Eighteen

It was strangely cool when I arrived at Kiboko a few days later, and Maud was sewing near the fire in the sitting room. I bent down to kiss her.

'You look terrible,' she said. 'Exhausted.'

'Thank you.'

I dropped into a chair opposite her. I'd spent the last seventy-two hours unable to do anything but think of Sylvie. I was more sure than ever that we were meant to be together, even though she'd been frustratingly vague when I'd left The Farm – smiling at me, but making no promises. I needed to tell someone about her, but for some reason I'd held back when I'd seen Freddie. I'd thought of writing to Douglas, but he didn't know her. Eventually I'd realised it had to be Maud, although now I was here, I didn't know how to bring it up.

'How's Lucy?'

'Busy.'

'That's a shame.'

'I suppose so.' I knew if anything more happened between Sylvie and me I should end things with Lucy, but at the same time I didn't want to. She wasn't Sylvie but she was sweet and pretty and loving. But I'd cross that bridge later. 'Where's Scotty?'

She put down her sewing. 'Abdullah's taken him for a walk. He was getting too fat to fit in his kennel.'

'Is there anything to drink?'

She called for two glasses of wine and a new toto brought them to us. He was young and very black, muscular, but with long, pale eyelashes. He carried the tray lightly, as if he was indifferent to it.

'Thank you, Bulawayo,' Maud said.

'Thank you, Mama,' he said.

I grinned at her. 'Cheers, Mama.'

She stopped Bulawayo, who was halfway out of the room. 'Are you staying for supper? We should let Joseph know.'

'I'm staying for the weekend.'

'Bulawayo, tell Joseph there'll be three of us tonight,' she said.

'Three?' I asked.

'Mother's going to be home, too. I had to change the menu.' She smiled for the first time since I'd arrived. 'The women have been teaching me to make chapattis and beans, like we used to have in Tanganyika. I was going to help Joseph, but I don't remember Mother liking the dish much.'

I took a sip of my wine; even though we hadn't mentioned the Happy Valley set, I had the sense that Maud was still holding herself away from me, and the drink tasted bitter. The idea of telling her what had happened with Sylvie seemed impossible now. 'Does she like anything much?'

Maud sighed. 'She likes her work with the League.'

'Doesn't she want you to join it with her?'

'I've got enough to do running this place.' She picked up her sewing again. 'Especially if I manage to find some land to farm.'

'You're nearly twenty-one now. Aren't you supposed to get married and have babies?'

She tied off the thread she'd been using and selected another bobbin. 'I don't know. No one's told me.'

'You haven't met any young men you like?'

She looked at me strangely. 'I haven't met any young men I like.'

'Why not?'

'If this were Scotland or England twenty years ago they'd all have bought themselves a country estate, or an officer's commission. I suppose a few of them might have passed the civil service exam.'

'So what?'

She rolled her eyes. 'But it's not, or maybe they don't have the capital. So they come out here to be gentlemen. Of course they love the lifestyle. But they don't love Africa, not really. I want a normal African life out here, not a pretend-English one.'

'I wonder if Father ever thinks about the normal life he was supposed to have. Normal wife, normal children.' For some reason, Nicolas's face suddenly appeared before me, and I felt my stomach cramp up.

'You're too hard on him,' Maud said. 'He knew it would be different with Mother. Remember Uncle Percy?'

'What about him?'

'He was six years younger than her. And Grandma and Grandpa died when she was eighteen. She must have still been taking care of him when she met Father.'

'So?'

'Not everyone would raise someone else's son — they'd have sent him off to boarding school.' She tucked a lock of hair behind her ear. 'Father's kind like that.'

I left my chair to join her on the sofa. 'How do you manage to see the good in everyone all the time?' I asked, kissing her cheek.

She smiled. 'You talk like there's *no* good in people.'

I opened my mouth to mention Sylvie, but I'd lost her attention. The sound of a car jolting up the driveway floated in on the chill air.

'That's Mother,' Maud said. She tidied away the sewing and opened the screen door.

I heard footsteps on the veranda, and my mother's voice saying, 'Thank you, Maud,' then she was standing in the doorway, a dark shape against the sunset behind her. She kissed Maud, then spotted me and came over. She was wearing a long grey skirt and cream blouse. Her hair was pinned up and I saw a hint of grey in that too that I hadn't noticed in Nairobi.

'How are you?' I asked, standing and kissing her.

'Tired,' she said. 'Does Joseph know there'll be three of us tonight?'

'Yes,' Maud said.

'You're much better at this than I ever was,' my mother said.

She took off her jacket, gloves and hat and handed them to Bulawayo, who'd been leaning against the dining room doorway, staring at us unabashed. 'I see you've started on the wine,' she said.

'Join us?' I asked.

She nodded and I signalled to Bulawayo, who disappeared.

We sat, the two of them on the sofa, me facing them on the armchair.

'And to what do we owe this pleasure?' my mother asked. 'Any news in particular?'

'Just felt like seeing my family.'

'Will you be coming home for your birthday this year?'

'I don't know. It's not exactly a special one.'

'You should count yourself lucky. Not everyone makes it to twenty-three.'

Too late I remembered her brother had died a week before his twenty-third birthday.

Bulawayo reappeared with more wine for the three of us. We chose glasses and I took a long drink of mine.

'You can go now, Bulawayo.' My mother's voice was harder now. 'So, Theo, what are your thoughts about staying on at the firm?'

204

'I'd rather not do it forever.'

'Your father's hoping you'll be his successor. And he's sixty-two – he should be retiring soon.'

'He doesn't have to choose the new Director.'

'He'd like to be involved in the process.'

I finished my wine and called for Bulawayo, who appeared straight away. 'Another glass,' I said, handing over my empty one. I thought I saw him smirk, but it was gone the next second. 'Well, it's my decision, Mother.'

'And when will you make it?' She drummed her fingers on the arm of the sofa. 'I don't understand why it takes you so long to get anything done.'

'Yes, I've always been a disappointment to you, haven't I?'

'Theo,' Maud murmured. 'Don't do this.'

Bulawayo returned with two full glasses.

'Thank you,' I said, accepting mine. I tried not to look at my mother's face.

He presented the second glass to her.

'I haven't finished,' she said, 'take them both away, actually.'

'For God's sake.' The glass stayed upright for a moment through the air, then gravity set in and it tipped the other way, splattering its contents on the floor before hitting the stone hearth and shattering. I lowered my arm. Bulawayo looked blank, Maud, shocked.

'I'm sorry I nagged you,' my mother said eventually, then left the room.

Bulawayo knelt in front of the hearth and started picking up the shards that had fallen outside the fire. My cheeks burned as I watched him.

'Don't do that,' I said. 'It was my fault.'

'I can do it, Bwana.'

'Bulawayo, bring some water, some soap and a cloth,' Maud said quietly.

'Yes, Mama.'

She joined me by the hearth and placed a small crystal into the handkerchief I'd laid out.

'I know you're worried about letting Father down,' she said, 'but he'll understand.'

I took her hand. 'That's what you really think?'

'Of course,' she said, squeezing my fingers.

Relief washed through me that it was alright between us again; I wanted to ask her if she'd felt the distance between us too, then from outside we heard barking and twigs snapping and she turned her head, smiling.

'They're back,' she said.

A few weeks later I was locking up the office when I heard a soft knocking on the outer door. Lucy was standing outside, wearing a red satin dress that gave a warm glow to her throat and face. We hadn't been alone since Christmas, almost a month ago, and I felt a jolt of pleasure, even as I remembered saying goodbye to Sylvie a few days earlier, and how she'd stretched out naked across the bed and smiled her smile at me.

'Hello stranger,' I said. I pulled Lucy towards me, trying to assuage the guilt I was feeling.

'Hello,' she said, letting me kiss her. 'I thought you might like to have supper?'

'There's nothing I want more.'

I felt her body relax in my arms. 'Good. Where shall we go?'

'The Club? Carlton's? You choose. I just want to stare at you all night.'

She laughed. 'Carlton's then.'

We hailed a rickshaw and climbed into the back, sitting close together. I wondered briefly if Sylvie would be jealous, seeing us together like this, then brought my attention back to Lucy.

'Where have you been hiding yourself?' I asked.

'I just wanted to think something through,' she said.

'That sounds serious.' I slipped my hand around her waist and bent my head towards her to nuzzle her neck. She didn't move, but her cheeks flamed up. 'Did you have to think for so long?'

'Did you miss me then?'

'Of course I did. Nairobi's been lifeless without you.'

'You could have gone away at the weekends.'

'I did.'

She looked at me casually. 'Who did you see?'

'I went home, to see Maud. And I saw Freddie and Sylvie and that crowd.'

'Oh.' Her voice was still casual, but I felt her stiffen.

'Sylvie's husband died. Her first husband.'

'Oh my God.' She bit her lip. 'Weren't you friends with him? Was it a surprise?'

'Yes – good friends. And a complete surprise.'

'I'm sorry.'

'Everyone liked Nicolas.'

She took my hand. 'Are you sure you want to go out? We can go to the hotel and talk, if you'd rather.'

'I don't want to talk. And I'm hungry.'

'I want to be here for you.'

For some reason her persistence annoyed me. I turned away to look out the window. 'I don't need to discuss it any more,' I said.

Carlton's was busy as usual, and noisy. Lucy seemed distracted during the meal, and towards the end we lapsed into silence. Afterwards, we stood outside the restaurant, side by side.

'Where now?' she asked.

'Why don't we take another walk in the park?' I said.

This time I spread my jacket on the ground, and guided her down onto it. I hitched up her dress until her stomach was exposed. She lay there stiffly, her pupils large as she tried to catch my eye.

'Do you love me, Theo?'

'Of course I do, darling.'

I kissed her, and gradually worked my way down her body,

207

feeling her chest rise and fall beneath me in quick, shallow breaths.

'This is what you want, isn't it?' she said, when I reached her knickers.

'Yes,' I said. It came out as a growl.

I put my hand on myself, feeling it throbbing with blood, and my restraint evaporated; I was freeing myself with one hand, scrabbling at Lucy's knickers with the other and then I was on top of her. Everything was painful for a moment as I pressed forwards, and I dimly heard a cry from her.

'Shush, darling,' I said.

I was moving inside her, feeling her warmth and a stickiness on me, and I gathered her in my arms, until our bodies were as close as possible and I was fully enveloped. I was whispering in her ear, not knowing what I was saying, and my heart was hammering in my chest as if it was going to burst, then finally the release and a moment of pure emptiness overtook me.

Afterwards, in the rickshaw, I held her in my arms and felt her shaking, as if she was crying, although she was completely silent.

Chapter Nineteen

'They're still complaining in the club,' I said.

'So I hear,' Sylvie said. 'Boy's predicting a riot.'

'Really?' Maud asked.

'Only if Byrne doesn't stop talking about income tax.'

'He won't introduce it,' I said.

Sylvie sat in the middle of the sofa at The Farm with Maud and I on either side of her, the dogs at our feet. She was wearing a black silk kimono with green leaf-prints on it, and a dark red lipstick that left its mark on anything it touched – her cigarette, her glass, my cheek. Outside, the ground was arid and the sky looked like a bedsheet hung up above us to dry out. 1934 was the driest year yet, the local farmers were saying. Water tanks had run out a month ago, at the end of June, and Nairobi was dusty and dirty and irritable. I'd already been escaping to The Farm every weekend since April.

Maud bent forwards to pat Louis. 'Really?'

Sylvie blinked slowly at me. 'Who says he won't introduce it? I didn't know you were getting into politics, too.'

She smelled like sex and I wondered if she'd washed since I'd visited the previous afternoon. I hadn't wanted to clean her saliva off my penis, wash away the memory of her kneeling before me,

209

cupping my balls and squeezing gently. I remembered that afternoon on the lake, how I'd wanted, almost willed this relationship with Sylvie to happen. Now I'd tasted this happiness it was even more delicious than I'd imagined.

'Well?'

I reached for Sylvie. 'I can't think of politics now.'

I saw her look quickly at Maud then she laughed, wriggling away. 'You're changing the subject.'

'It was Freddie, actually. We've been in touch. I brought his letters in case you wanted to read them.'

I searched the pockets of my trousers and pulled out two neatly folded pieces of writing paper. They smelled faintly of pomade. 'See what you think.'

Sylvie lit a cigarette and spread the letter out on her knee. Maud sat back to read it with her.

Freddie and Martha had left for London in April. The day before his departure, we'd run into each other at The Norfolk. 'I have a feeling I'll be even busier when I get back,' he'd said, winking at me. 'I'll let you know my news.'

The first letter told me they'd arrived safely, and set themselves up in an apartment in Westminster.

I'm now a fully signed-up member of the British Union of Fascists, he wrote. *Tom Mosley convinced me, not that he needed to, that the present government is wholly out of touch with the everyday needs of its people abroad. Our economy is still suffering from the Depression and the repeated droughts, and if we're to recover, we need decisive men on the ground, not the endless delays we've had so far. The Blackshirt movement believes in action, rather than talk. Moreover, Tom agrees we need to build up trade within our Empire now that foreign markets are closing against us. Restricting it with mandates and the Congo Basin Treaties will damage us all.*

It's not just the colonies, either, that could do with a shaking up. The BUF is immensely popular here. They see what Mussolini's done for Italy and they would like to see Britain's primacy restored in the same way.

210

I'd replied with news of the general unease. He wrote back, saying he'd be returning in August.

It's time for me to do something important, something good. Mosley *has some pretty influential supporters,* the letter finished, *and I suspect Kenya will be easily won over, especially with the failure of the additional tax this year. The country is effectively bankrupt, and its taxable capacity was reached years ago. The BUF understands that.*

I'd been excited, reading it, but Maud's face turned pale on the last page. 'How can someone so intelligent be such a fool?' she asked.

'What do you mean?'

She scooped an open newspaper from the floor and thrust it at me. 'Look.'

The headline read:

BLACKSHIRTS IN KENYA? SPECIAL DELEGATE APPOINTED.

Underneath, the article started: 'Freddie Hamilton, the Earl of Caithness, who is at present in England, has been appointed delegate of the British Union of Fascists for Kenya Colony. The Earl is reported to be returning . . . with a constructive and energetic plan to convert the Colony to the Blackshirt policy.' I smiled and flicked through the rest of the paper.

A few pages later was news of Germany's 'bloodbath', with Nazi SS officers killing stormtroopers and SA leaders they claimed were planning a revolt against Hitler.

'You can't blame Freddie for this,' I said. 'The editor's the one equating the Blackshirts with the Nazis.'

'Because Mosley admits admiration for Hitler.'

'Look, you have to admit we're still shaky here. Much as I like Byrne, I don't think he's going to help us out of it. Maybe Freddie could do better.'

Sylvie, who'd been quiet, handed back the letter, and wrapped one arm across her stomach. 'Don't fall into that trap, Theo.'

'What trap?'

'Listening to Freddie rather than thinking for yourself.'

My face burned. 'That's how you see it?'

'He's not a god.' She stubbed out her cigarette on the ashtray in between us and stood up. 'Excuse me – I have to fetch something from my bedroom.'

Her smell lingered for a moment, then dissolved with the cigarette smoke. I jiggled my leg to distract myself from thoughts of yesterday again.

'I have to get back soon,' Maud said after a few moments. 'Should we let her know?'

'I'll do it.' I stood up. 'Wait here.'

I knocked on Sylvie's bedroom door and opened it before she could answer. She was sitting at the end of her bed, knees drawn up to her chest. She didn't look at me when I sat down beside her.

'What's wrong?' I asked.

She made to stand up and I caught hold of her arm. 'Don't be angry.' I pulled her back down onto the bed.

'Why?'

'Because I love you.'

She shook her head, half-smiling, then looked away. 'Go play with someone your own age.'

'You don't mean that.'

'I do.'

I kissed her. 'You love me too.'

She looked at me for a moment, then swung her legs off the bed and rose gracefully to her feet. 'I'm thirsty. Cocktail?'

'Do I ever say no?'

She straightened her kimono. 'How's Lucy?'

'Very well, thank you.'

'Does she know when you're visiting me?'

'I never say explicitly.' I'd told Lucy I'd been spending my weekends at Naivasha because it was cooler out of the city. I saw her during the week instead, and she seemed to accept the arrangement.

'Be careful, darling. It's not good to have too much power over someone else.'

I selected a cigarette from the case under her pillow, taking care not to let my irritation show. 'You speak from experience.'

'What if I do?'

I considered her for a moment, and she raised her chin, meeting my gaze. 'Come here,' I said eventually. 'Forget the drinks.'

'I'm thirsty.'

'And I'm half mad looking at you like that.'

When we'd finished we lay back on the pillows. She ran her hand down my torso to my penis, still wet from being inside her, and wrapped her palm around it. I moved in her hand, she withdrew it and licked her palm, looking at me steadily.

I laughed. 'Give me five more minutes.'

'Where's Maud?'

'You're right – we should probably go back to her.' I stood up and started collecting my clothes. 'Shall we go out for a drive?'

'I don't feel up to it.'

'Alright. Can I come next weekend?'

'I'm going away with Edie for a little while.'

'To the coast?'

'Coast, safari.' She rolled over onto her stomach.

'When will you be back?'

'When I'm back.'

I grinned. 'I know what you're doing.'

'What am I doing?'

'You can't make me stop loving you that way. I already knew you were cruel, remember?'

'You have no idea, darling.'

I finished dressing; she wrapped the kimono around herself and followed me back to the sitting room. Maud was upright on the sofa, the newspaper folded neatly in her lap.

'Sorry we were gone so long,' I said. 'Been reading?'

'Yes.' Her cheeks flushed and I remembered, guiltily, how thin Sylvie's walls were.

213

Sylvie crossed to the drinks cabinet, poured herself a drink and turned to face us. 'You know, Maud – you could campaign against him if you wanted to.'

'What are you talking about?' I asked.

Maud shook her head. 'I can't campaign.'

'Protest, then. Start a petition.' Sylvie smiled. 'Just don't make the mistake of thinking you'll be thanked for it – people don't like it when others know what's best for them.'

'I wouldn't do it for thanks.'

'I know you wouldn't.'

There was a moment of silence.

'We'd better go,' I said eventually.

Sylvie came out onto the veranda with us and kissed Maud's forehead. 'Take care.'

'You too,' Maud said. They held hands for a moment, then Maud climbed down the stairs and walked to the car.

'I'll see you soon,' I said, leaning in for my own kiss.

She turned her cheek. 'See you, darling.'

Letters were written to the *East African Standard*, some of which were published. They criticised the Blackshirts' links with Hitler and Mussolini, who were planning, they pointed out, to take over Kenya's neighbours, Tanganyika and Abyssinia.

We all know what would happen next, one reader wrote in. *We would be divided up between them, or, more likely, go to Germany and Herr Hitler. This is our land, will the government let that be undermined by Sir Oswald Mosley and the Earl of Caithness?*

Douglas continued to write to me, letting me know the situation as the civil service saw it. *MacDonald is a strange one,* he wrote. *He built the Labour Party up, only to split it; only two colleagues joined his National Government. He's holding us together in some pretty dark economic times, but he doesn't seem to be able to do anything else. Public opinion is against most of his instincts. I worry that he'll go and someone like Mosley will capitalise somehow.*

I didn't tell him about Freddie. I didn't believe Freddie was wedded to Fascism. He'd jumped on a movement that would have him and that he thought had popular potential. But people like Douglas and Maud didn't understand it would always be about him, not the party. I knew he'd be good at politics – he was a fresh voice, and compelling – but the more I read about the Blackshirts, the more I wished he'd chosen someone else to align himself with. Still, at least Freddie was active. Compared to him, my long, unfulfilling days at the railway office seemed even more directionless and pathetic.

One airless afternoon my father called me into his office. He was standing at the window when I entered, looking down at the station and the gleaming train tracks that led away from it; he held a scrunched-up handkerchief in one hand, as if he'd been mopping his forehead before I came in.

'Your mother tells me you're thinking of leaving the firm,' he said, keeping his back to me.

I leaned against the door, feeling the knob press into my spine. 'Does she?' Clearly she'd got impatient waiting for me to bring it up. I could picture her look of satisfaction as she dropped me in it, and felt a mix of anger and incredulity that she was involving herself in my life again now.

'Is it true?'

'I don't know.'

'Don't stay on my behalf,' he said to the window.

'I don't know what else I could do. I suppose Mother wants me to go into law and settle down with Lucy.'

'She wants you to be happy.'

'She has a funny way of showing it.'

'It's different for you young people.'

'What do you mean?'

215

'It's hard for us, sometimes, to understand the world as it is right now. You have more freedoms than we ever did, but less – security, I suppose.' He mopped his forehead again. 'In my day, you joined a firm for life.'

'I haven't said I'm definitely leaving.'

'I know,' he said hurriedly. 'I just want you to know why your mother might seem worried about your direction.' He looked over his shoulder at me. 'You won't speak to her about this, will you? I don't want to upset her.'

I had to stifle the urge to laugh. 'I'm sure she won't get upset.'

'She's not always as strong as she seems. I was there when she got the . . . news, you know?' He turned back to the window, and I had to strain to hear what he said next. 'She locked herself in her bedroom for days.'

'What news?'

'The telegram. You were just a baby at the time – you won't remember.'

'Her brother?'

'She said it was her fault for not stopping him.'

I stayed silent, not wanting to argue with him. I knew Maud would have felt sorry for my mother, but as far as I could see it was another example of her neglecting me.

My father cleared his throat. 'Well, let me know what you decide.'

'I will.'

Freddie and Martha returned in late August. Freddie sent a note to the office proposing a squash match and I left for the Muthaiga straight away. There'd been no break in the weather and even there the grass was beginning to brown at the edges. The bar was blessedly cool but packed. I saw Freddie immediately. He seemed taller and more dazzling than ever in his squash whites. Beside him, Martha looked shrunken and pale.

'I'm glad you can take him off my hands for a few hours,' she said as I kissed her cheek. 'I'm not feeling too well – probably a bug.'

'Sounds awful,' I said.

'You rest yourself,' Freddie said, patting her head. 'Poor girl.'

The doors to the patio were open, and even more drinkers were outside, starting on their sundowners and buzzing fretfully in the sticky heat. The light was golden, with purple notes on the horizon that reminded me of Sylvie, still away somewhere with Edie.

A constant flow of people greeted Freddie as we walked to the squash courts, shoes squeaking on the polished floors.

'Have they been as enthusiastic about British Fascism as you thought?' I asked.

'I haven't done any campaigning yet,' he said, swinging his racquet. 'I've spoken to a few sympathisers here in Nairobi, to form a base. I'll wait until my speech at the Sports Club in November before I declare my position.'

'You think it'll go down well?'

'I know it will.'

'Even if they don't like the idea I'm sure you'll manage to talk them round,' I said. 'Edie's started calling you The Golden Touch.'

'Good.' He grinned. 'Now, let's see how rusty we both are.'

I played better than I had in months and the score was almost even by the end of the match.

'You must have been down here every day,' Freddie said, as we shook hands afterwards. I was pleased to see his hair was plastered to his head with sweat and his clothes looked darker and more crumpled than before.

'Maybe you're losing it,' I said. 'Your golden touch, I mean.'

'I've had other things on my mind.'

He turned away abruptly and started walking towards the changing rooms; I hurried to catch him up, kicking myself – Martha must be worrying him.

'Sorry to hear she's sick again,' I said when we were in step.

'It's not a bug.'

'What is it?'

'It's a degenerative disease. She's not going to get better.'

My mouth fell open and I shut it hurriedly. 'Sorry,' I said again, wishing I could think of something more comforting.

'Not your fault.' He looked at me. 'Actually, I've been meaning to ask you a favour. Dr Gregory's moved to the Muthaiga area. I know you travel between here and Naivasha regularly. Would you be able to run the medicine back for us?' He pushed through the door to the changing room and I followed him inside. 'I don't really know where I'll be most of the time. And I don't trust the servants with it. Maybe Waweru, but he's got his hands full at the house.'

'Of course I'll help.'

'Thanks.' He busied himself removing clothes from his locker; I got the sense he wanted to change the subject.

'Good to hear you trust *me*.' I took one of the towels and patted down my face. 'The secretaries haven't blabbed about all the paperwork I keep forgetting to do, then?'

'Naturally I trust you.' He grinned. 'Anyway, how's your lady friend?'

I realised guiltily that I hadn't seen Lucy for several weeks. 'She's well.'

He raised an eyebrow. 'Just well? At your age she should be in a constant state of trembling gratification. Stop neglecting her for sports, that's my advice. You might find yourself usurped.'

'That's not going to happen.'

He laughed, and tapped my backside with his racquet. 'Do you think you can recognise when it's real?'

'It's always real. For her and for Sylvie.'

'O-ho.' Freddie cocked his head at me. 'So that's how it is? Good for you.' He rummaged around in the pocket of his suit jacket. 'Here – Gregory's address in the city. There should be a prescription ready next Friday if you're free.'

218

I took the note from him. I half-wished he'd asked more about Sylvie, but at least he hadn't seemed too surprised.

'I'll make time,' I said.

Dr Gregory's Nairobi bungalow was slightly larger than his one in Naivasha, although it was in a less salubrious part of town. I was invited in this time, and stood around the spartan living room for a few moments before he appeared in the doorway, half of his chin covered in foam and a towel slung over one shoulder.

'Sorry – just shaving. No time in the mornings usually. Take a seat. Or do you need to get off?'

'I was hoping to drive back before it gets dark.'

'My boy can fetch the stuff for you then.' He wiped his hands on the towel. 'But maybe next time we can go for a drink? I don't know many people in the city yet.'

'Sounds good.'

'Grand.'

We shook hands, and the toto who had let me in brought me a small box filled with the same brown bottles as last time. As I pulled away from the kerb I saw Gregory through a window on the right-hand side of the building. He was whistling as he shaved.

There were hardly any cars out in the early evening, and the journey was peaceful. The sky was indigo and a September chill was in the air, although the lake was perfectly still when I arrived. After the heat and dryness of Nairobi, it was a welcome relief. I stowed the box in my glove compartment, ready to take to Mahalbeth in the morning, and wandered down to the jetty, breathing in deeply as I passed the African huts. Maud had been planting again, and fresh-looking saplings were tied to stakes not far from the compound, eucalyptus, lime, juniper and peach, their scent mixing foggily together.

Abdullah had finished building a treehouse in the big cedar, and the murmurs of children playing in it drifted down to me. Half a mile down the shore I could see the ungainly outline of

219

some eland grazing, their twisted horns growing from surprisingly petite heads. A heron paddled near them, snapping at fish from time to time. I turned back to the jetty and the boat bumping gently against it. I still hadn't heard from Sylvie, but as I stood there she materialised at the far end in her bathing costume, one shapely leg bent at the knee, the other dipping down so her foot skimmed the surface of the water. I watched her with a smile on my face and she laughed, 'It's cold.' She disappeared when I went towards her, arms outstretched, and I felt disappointed, and foolish.

No one was on the veranda, or in the sitting room. I could hear clanging coming from the kitchen, but otherwise all was quiet.

'Hello?' I called.

My mother appeared in the entrance to her wing, wearing a long navy-blue dress and carrying an empty wine glass.

'Maud's out with Abdullah and Scotty,' she said. 'They're looking at land to buy.'

'When will she be back?'

'I don't know.' She put down the glass. 'Shall I ring for tea?'

'No thank you.'

'Suit yourself. It means not dealing with Bulawayo.'

She was acting as if nothing had happened, and it angered me. 'Father said you mentioned me leaving the firm.'

She clasped her hands together and waited.

'It didn't cause a rift between us, if that's what you were trying to do.'

'How can you think that?'

'I know you've never been on my side.'

She took a step towards me, holding her hands out. 'Whose side have I been on then?' She looked the picture of innocence and motherly concern, and I almost admired the act.

'It doesn't matter.'

'You could be extraordinary, Theo. Successful. I'm only trying to help you, darling.'

'I can do without your help.'

'I'm your mother – I know what's best for you.'

I felt my mouth twist itself up into a smile. 'I do remember my childhood, you know.'

She lowered her arms. I wanted to cross the room and take her by the shoulders, shake that cool look off her face. It was laughable to me now that I'd ever been afraid of her. And yet I had been, and I'd craved her affection too. I was almost as angry with myself for how important she'd been to me, how much I'd let her shape me.

'Tell Maud I'll be on the lake,' I said.

I collected my hat and left the house. At the bottom of the veranda stairs I paused. I thought I heard Scotty's barking coming from the Africans' quarters. We'd had problems before with him wandering in and frightening their chickens. I rammed my hat on, and hurried over. I tried to follow the sound, although it was difficult as there were more huts than ever; a few of the men had taken second or third wives in the last year or so and each wife needed her own hut.

I was near Abdullah's hut when Scotty came rushing out. Maud followed him, laughing. She stopped short when she saw me, and flushed.

'I thought you were looking at land to buy,' I said.

'We were.' Her arms were hanging nervously by her side, as if she didn't know what to do with them, and eventually she folded them across her chest.

'Is Abdullah inside?'

'He was just making tea – do you want some?'

I came forwards. Abdullah had built a small picket fence around his hut, low enough for me to step over, but Maud opened the gate for me instead. Inside the compound, pot plants lined the outer walls of the hut, which was square, and painted an orangey-pink. The thatched roof extended slightly further than the walls, and was propped up by four thin posts, creating a small shaded area, big enough to stand up in.

'Come inside,' Maud said.

I'd never been inside Abdullah's hut, or any of the African huts. The only light came from the open door, and at first I couldn't see anything, then Abdullah stood up and bowed.

'Welcome, Bwana,' he said.

The floor was baked earth, and uneven, and covered in rush mats. In one corner, I saw a mat with a pillow and blanket on it, and guessed that was Abdullah's bed. Other than the bed, he had a small stove, two low stools, a sweeping brush, a full-length mirror propped up against the wall, and two Zanzibari chests. Maud went to one of the chests and withdrew three cups and saucers. I guessed the other would be his wardrobe, and wondered how his clothes were always so clean and neatly pressed.

'Please sit,' Abdullah said, and gestured to the stool.

I sat down, and Maud sat opposite me, our knees nearly touching. Abdullah sat on one of the mats, legs crossed, and poured tea into the three cups. His hands were perfectly steady, but the air in the hut was almost jangling with tension.

'Have you found anywhere?' I asked.

'I think so,' Maud said.

They were trying not to look at each other. Scotty came back inside, flopped on a mat near the door and started washing his paws. I took a sip of my tea, trying not to let the anger that suddenly took hold of me spill out. *At least leave Scotty behind*, I wanted to say. *Or do you want everyone to find out?*

I looked at Maud's bowed head. She'd parted her hair straight down the middle that day, and the skin of the parting was almost translucent white; it made her seem childlike, and my anger faded into sadness for her.

'How long have you been . . . looking?' I asked.

Abdullah seemed to draw himself up straighter. Maud raised her eyes to meet mine. She looked defiant. 'Not long,' she said. 'But I've wanted to do it for years. It was my idea, you know.'

'I know.' I drained my tea and stood up. Abdullah stood up too.

'Thank you for your visit,' he said.

I left without looking at him. Maud caught up with me by the fence.

'Do you know what will happen if people find out?' I asked.

She bit her lip. 'Of course I do. Father would fire him. I tried not to feel this way; I didn't want to put him in danger of that.' She folded her arms again. 'But we love each other.'

I looked away. 'I think you're making a big mistake,' I said to her. 'But I won't say anything to Mother.'

'Thank you.' She came closer and touched my shoulder.

'I'm doing it for my sake too,' I said.

I didn't want to go back in to my mother, so I started my car and turned it in the direction of Mahalbeth. It was fully dark by the time I got there. A few of the windows were lit up, but most of the house was in darkness, and for some reason I felt uneasy looking at it.

I pulled myself together and climbed out of the car. Looking around, I couldn't see Freddie's car and felt a pang of disappointment, but I took the box from the glove compartment and knocked on the door.

Waweru answered. He showed me through to the sitting room, where Martha was curled up on one of the sofas. There were no lights on except for a small lamp on a side table near her that barely lit up her face. She got up slowly to greet me.

'I've got something for you,' I said. 'From Dr Gregory.'

'You're very kind,' she said, holding out her hand.

'How are you feeling?'

She closed her eyes and shook her head. 'There are good days and bad days.'

She kept her hand out and I passed the box over then stood waiting; it took a moment for her to offer me a seat. I perched on the sofa opposite her, and she called for Waweru to bring us two Black Velvets.

'What's Freddie up to tonight?' I asked.

'I don't know. Something at the Sports Club, I think.' She passed a hand over her eyes. 'I'll tell him you stopped by.'

'Will I miss him, then?'

'Maybe. He's got a lot on his plate at the moment.'

'I know – he told me.'

'He'll be very grateful,' she said. She leaned forwards and patted my knee. 'He thinks the world of you, you know? He's always said how helpful you are.'

'I'm glad to do it.'

'I'm –'

I waited for another few moments before realising she wasn't going to continue. Her eyes had glazed over and beads of sweat stood out on her forehead. I stood up hurriedly. 'Maybe I should let you rest.'

'Are you leaving?'

'Afraid so. Give my love to Freddie.' I kissed her hand.

''Bye, Theo,' she said.

I found Waweru in the bar and told him Martha had taken a bad turn.

'I see to her,' he said. 'Goodbye, Bwana.'

I sat in my car for a few moments, wishing I'd stayed in Nairobi. Both Kiboko and Mahalbeth had changed in the space of half an hour, and I felt overwhelmed. I ran a hand through my hair, trying to calm down. At least there was still Freddie and Sylvie.

I turned on my engine, and drove home slowly.

Chapter Twenty

Freddie waited until November, as he'd said, before making his first public show of support for the BUF during a Caledonian Society supper in Nakuru. It was hard not to hear about it in the days afterwards, how he'd torn into Byrne's Budget speech, and attacked the Governor, the Secretary of State for the Colonies – Sir Philip Cunliffe-Lister – and the entire government, pointing to them as the reason the Colonial Empire was 'staggering to the brink of destruction'.

'It was brutal,' Boy told me, when I ran into him at the Naivasha general store. 'Byrne didn't know how to respond. Freddie hadn't shown him his speech beforehand, you see.' He grinned. 'I almost felt sorry for the blighter. Especially when Freddie laid into him as an Irishman.'

'How did the rest of the Society take it?'

'You know Freddie – he had them in stitches half the time. But it's shocked some of the older members. The Mombasa chapter wrote Byrne a letter of apology.'

I took out my cigarette packet and offered him one. 'I wish I'd been there. What now?'

'He's holding a meeting in Njoro next week – wants to explain British Fascism to us other settlers.'

'I'd like to see that.'

'I think we all would.'

The Njoro Country Club was a long building with a green
corrugated iron roof – any rain heavier than a drizzle and Freddie's
voice would be drowned out. I peered up at the sky as my car
bumped down the driveway the night of Freddie's talk. The moon
was completely hidden by clouds, but the air was so thick and
still it was as if I was driving through cotton wool. Even the
weather deferred to Freddie.

I parked in front of the building and made my way slowly
through the arches and into the stiflingly hot interior. There were
two hundred or so people at the meeting, jostling each other for
the hundred or so chairs that the staff had put out, and the parquet
was almost completely obscured. Chatter bounced off the gabled
iron ceiling, and hung mid-air in one big conversation. I stood near
the open French doors to the veranda, fanning myself with one of
the pamphlets that were stacked on a nearby table. I saw Boy come
in, and Edie. Edie blew me a kiss and several of the old men nearby
whistled, but I was too distracted to respond. I hadn't known she
and Sylvie were back, and was suddenly impatient for the meeting
to be over already so I could drive to The Farm.

Someone squeezed my arm gently and I looked to my left to
see Maud.

'Didn't think I'd see you here,' I said.

'It's better to be informed,' she said. 'Why are you here?'

'I want to see him in action.'

She half-smiled. 'Is Sylvie coming?'

'I doubt it.' I nodded towards the front doors. 'Here's the man
of the hour though.'

Freddie came around the side of the room to kiss Maud and
clap me on the back. He was wearing a brand-new navy-blue
suit that sat well on his broad shoulders, and his teeth seemed
straighter and whiter than ever. Martha's face the last time I saw

226

her flashed through my mind, pale and sweaty. It was for the best that she'd stayed at home.

'We missed you at the supper,' he said.

'We heard about it,' I said.

He laughed. 'I'm glad you could come to this, anyway. You're the future of Kenya after all.'

'Don't you think the Africans are the future of Kenya?' Maud asked.

'I think anyone who works hard here, farming and so on, is the future, black or white.'

'That rules me out then,' I said.

He grinned, and made as if to move off. 'Well, thanks for your support. This is a big night for me.'

Maud straightened her blouse. 'I'm not here as support.'

He turned back to us, raising an eyebrow. 'No?'

'The entire point of Fascism is to strengthen the state.'

'And don't you think a strong state would be good for its people?'

'Not at the expense of other, weaker states. Fascism just rewards the bullies and punishes the vulnerable.'

'You make it sound like the British public school system,' I said. Freddie winked at me.

'And what about the BUF slogan?' Maud asked. '"Britain first, Dominions second, Foreigners nowhere". Don't you think it's hateful, pitting us against "foreigners"?'

He shrugged. 'People will always feel more for their own country-men. We're tribal like that.'

'But we've never lived in isolation. People have always been travelling, discovering new lands, moving in.' She clasped her hands together. '*We* moved here.'

'So you think there should be no division between countries? No Britain, no France, no Spain, no Germany. Just one big world?'

'I think we shouldn't be so small-minded. Everyone's the same, aren't they? Why should we hate them?'

227

'People aren't the same,' he said. 'The Germans prize strength and power, and the Swiss prefer peace. The Italians are romantic and emotional, and the Swedish are very serious. We have laws against stealing, and the Maasai think they can walk off with any cattle they happen to come across.'

'But individually, doesn't everyone want to be liked and respected? And be able to eat and wear clothes and keep their families safe?'

'Of course,' Freddie said. 'But there are too many people in the world to care about them all.' Maud made a protesting noise and he held up his hand. 'Hear me out. Our minds can't cope on that sort of scale. That's why we form smaller groups – communities, nations – that we *can* comprehend. And after a while those smaller groups start to forge their own identities. And when you share an identity with a man, you're bonded, you want to help him out.'

Maud frowned. 'So you only want to help out those who remind you of yourself?'

Freddie caught my eye and I couldn't help smiling. 'She's getting better,' I said. 'You might not win this one.'

'Listen,' he said. 'If we build up Britain, she'll be able to help us out here in Kenya. That benefits the natives too.'

'And how will you build up Britain?'

'Ah – you'll have to wait for my speech.' He checked his watch. 'Speaking of which, I should get up there now.'

When he walked to the front the whole room clapped and cheered. He took a moment just standing there, smiling.

The woman on my right leaned over to me. 'Doesn't he look natural?' she said.

'Seems like a home crowd,' I said to Maud.

'They haven't heard him speak,' she said. 'This isn't the Happy Valley set – they're ordinary, decent people. They'll see through his rubbish.'

Freddie started talking and the audience fell completely silent. His voice was strong, always clear and unhurried. The first cheer

228

came when he suggested a union with Tanganyika, Delamere's dream. The woman on my right clutched my arm when Freddie went through the basis of British Fascism.

'We believe in loyalty to the Crown,' he said, 'as a symbol of the strength of our nation, less than half the size of France, one fortieth of America, yet controlling one quarter of the world's land. *That's* the vigorous British spirit we want to encourage.'

The crowd cheered.

'We believe in higher wages, and lower costs of living for the workers that keep our nation going.'

The crowd cheered again.

'We believe in an insulated Empire, which we worked so hard for, and can strengthen us from within through trade. We *don't need* to be at the mercy of other countries and we deserve a government that recognises such.'

Another cheer.

Now Freddie came out from behind his podium and pointed squarely at the middle of the crowd. 'Above all, we believe in freedom, religious and social and physical freedom.' He shook his finger. 'It's been nearly nine hundred years since we were successfully invaded and made subordinate, and we're *damn sure not going to start taking orders from anyone else now.*'

The crowd were on their feet before he'd finished his last sentence. His face was calm, his back straight and shoulders relaxed, and he'd left his arm out, finger still pointing steadily over everyone's heads. The lights had changed without me noticing, so now a spotlight shone at the front, illuminating Freddie with a pure, white glow, while the rest of us seemed dim and fuzzy. In that instant I knew if Freddie took on the government he'd win.

Maud looked sick. 'I can't believe they're eating it up.'

'He's good at it, that's why.'

She touched my arm. 'Let's get out of here, Theo, please.'

'Don't you think you're overreacting a little?'

'Please, Theo.'

As we left I turned around, and saw the whole room pressing forwards, trying to shake Freddie's hand.

The next evening we drove to Edie's for a small supper. I'd hoped Sylvie would be there, but apart from me and Maud it was just Edie, her husband Donald, and two friends visiting from America (Nan, I knew, had started school back in England). When I asked Edie how Sylvie was she waved her hand. 'Don't worry about her, darling. Sometimes she just needs to be alone. I'm sure she'll be in touch soon.'

The meal was served at eleven and it was midnight before we finished. I could see Maud flagging. I turned down the pitcher of cocktail that Edie produced and kissed her goodnight.

'Get home safely,' she said. 'There's a storm coming. And come more often – we miss you.' She opened the front door and a hot wind blew in, smacking our faces. 'What a hideous night.'

We drove half the journey without seeing a single other car on the roads. Maud wound down the window and let her hand trail outside.

'It's like an oven in here,' she said.

'It's an oven out there too.'

'I think I'll have a nice cold bath when we get in.'

'Bulawayo won't thank you.'

'I can draw the water myself.' She paused. 'How's Lucy?'

'Fine.'

'Are you still seeing her?'

'When I'm in Nairobi.'

I looked at her profile. Her expression was neutral, but I'd caught the warning in her tone. Maud always seemed to know when I was doing something I should be ashamed of, I thought, and promised myself I'd spend more time on Lucy soon.

She met my eye. 'Mr Cartwright – he's political, isn't he?'

'I don't know what he does. I always assumed he was an engineer, and that's how he knew Father.'

'Theo – I want to take on Freddie.'

'How so?'

'I don't know. I can't stand for election, but maybe you could? We could run against his ideas – stop them before they snowball.'

'I'd be no good, Spanish. Anyway, are you sure you're not taking this too personally, because of your . . . relationship?'

She blinked. 'Please, Theo – I'm asking for help.'

I opened my mouth to speak then a black shape darted out into the road and I braked sharply, pitching us forwards. The shape continued running, through the light cast by the headlamps and into the thicket on the other side of the road.

'What was that?' Maud asked, rubbing her elbow.

'A deer.'

'They don't normally run in front of cars.'

'Must have been escaping from something.'

'Look.' She grasped my arm. 'Coming out onto the road now.'

Another shape was slinking out of the bushes, grey and mysterious in the shadows. It stopped just before the beam of our headlights, turned towards us, and I saw the tawny, rosette-spotted skull of a leopard.

'What's it doing?' Maud whispered.

The leopard let out a low growl. I felt the hairs on my body stand up in response.

'Drive,' Maud urged me.

I reached over and flicked off the headlights.

'Theo, no –'

The leopard started moving in our direction, shoulders coiling and uncoiling with each step. Sweat dripped down my temples. It stopped just next to my door. At this distance I could see the pink of its tongue push up against its yellow fangs, and the wrinkle at the top of its nose as the face set into a snarl although no sound came out.

'Now we can't see it,' Maud said, moving further away from her window. 'Theo, I'm –'

231

'I can see it,' I said. 'It's next to me.'

'Oh my God.'

'It's not doing anything.'

I locked eyes with the leopard. They were like nothing I'd seen before: real; emotionless; sizing up the quarry. I wondered how we looked to it, if it saw our pale, pulsating bodies as they were, or straight through to the red mass of guts and flesh inside. I tasted something bitter at the back of my throat.

'Theo – we have to go *now*,' Maud said, digging her nails into my arm.

I waited. Apart from Maud's heavy breathing next to me there was complete silence. The leopard lifted its chin, sniffing something in the darkness. The car filled with a green, mossy smell and I felt the tension drain away abruptly. The animal's mouth opened wider in a yawn, then it loped off.

'It's gone,' I said.

'Are you sure?'

'Yes.'

'*Now* can we drive?'

I switched the headlights back on and pressed my foot down on the pedal. We jolted forwards and Maud let out a sigh.

'I'm shaking,' she said.

'You'll be fine.'

'I was *terrified*.' Something in her voice made me look at her. There were two silvery tracks down her cheeks. 'Why didn't you drive off?'

'Don't be upset, Spanish.'

'I'm not upset.' She rubbed furiously underneath her eye with the heel of her hand. 'I'm angry. We could have been killed.'

I put one arm around her and drew her into me. She pushed her face against my chest.

'I'm sorry,' I said. 'I didn't think.'

She sighed again. 'It's the first one I've seen. In all our time out here.'

'Me too.'

'Why did it run off?'

There was a terrific crack in the sky and Maud clutched my arm. The crack was followed by a low drumming sound, then large raindrops began to splatter on the windscreen. I took a deep breath and felt a laugh bubble up inside me.

'It was the storm,' I said.

Since Sylvie hadn't been in touch, and I felt guilty that I'd been neglecting Lucy, the following weekend I made a point of staying in Nairobi to see her. Saturday morning was sunny and unusually cool for early December. After spending half an hour trying to track her down, I eventually found her drinking tea with her parents in The Norfolk gardens. Mr Cartwright greeted me less warmly than usual.

'Will you join us?' Mrs Cartwright said.

'Please,' I said. I nodded at the waiter for another cup and he disappeared.

'How are your family?' she asked.

'They're well.'

'We haven't seen much of them, or you even these past months.'

'I know – I've missed you all.' I smiled at Lucy and she smiled back, blinking suddenly.

'Darling, is something wrong?' Mrs Cartwright asked.

'Some insect just flew into my eye.' She brushed them both quickly with her fingers and fixed her smile on us again.

The waiter brought me a cup and I poured myself some tea. Mr Cartwright watched me closely.

'Lucy tells me you attended one of Lord Hamilton's rallies,' he said eventually. 'I hope you're not throwing your lot in with the Fascists.'

'He asked me to come as a personal favour.'

'Are you close to Lord Hamilton then?'

Lucy stirred in her seat.

'I am.'

'He's a complete buffoon.'

'George,' Mrs Cartwright said. 'You don't know the man.'

'I don't need to. His kind are becoming irrelevant, so now they throw their lot in with anyone who offers them power.'

'Actually,' I said. 'Freddie is very clever.'

'Well, if he is bright, then he's being incredibly manipulative.'

I heaped some sugar into my tea so I wouldn't have to meet his gaze. I was annoyed, not just by what he was saying about Freddie, but also by the conversation in general. I'd been so careful to steer away from politics around them for so long, and now I felt like my hand was being forced. It made me feel reckless. 'Aren't all politicians manipulative?'

Mr Cartwright turned purple. 'Do you fill my daughter's head with this cynical rubbish?'

'Daddy,' Lucy said. 'I told you – we don't talk about politics.'

'Not everyone can hold the same views as you, darling,' Mrs Cartwright said.

He ignored them. 'Don't you have anything to say for yourself?'

'I'm sorry if you're offended, but I haven't done anything wrong. Freddie is one of the best people I know.'

'You can't know many people then.'

My fingers felt tight around the handle of my teacup. 'I know everyone at this table.'

Mr Cartwright looked as if he wanted to spit. 'The more I come across the young, the more I worry about the future. Your generation is shallow, totally selfish, totally unaware of the sacrifices made in the name of your safety.'

'At least we don't hide what we want.'

'You want to know what *I* want?' He looked at Lucy. 'I want the two of you to see less of each other.'

'*Daddy.*'

'Well it's not up to you,' I said.

Lucy stood up and walked away from the table.

234

'Look at what you've done now, the two of you,' Mrs Cartwright said.

I stood up without looking at Mr Cartwright and followed Lucy outside to the front of the hotel. She was waiting for me on the street, her face whiter than ever.

'You shouldn't have argued with Daddy,' she said.

'I didn't start it.'

'He gets upset.' She chewed a fingernail. 'He used to work in Intelligence before the War. He still knows things he doesn't tell Mummy or me, about what's going on now.'

'I didn't realise that.'

'I know. I should go back.'

I took her in my arms. 'Did he really mean we can't see each other?'

'Only for a little while. He'll come around.' She patted my chest. 'I'll write to you.'

I kissed her gently. 'I'll miss you.'

'Will you?'

Her eyes were wide and unguarded, and I thought of the way she often clung to me after I'd taken her and felt a rush of affection for how pure she was, how much she loved me. 'Of course I will.'

'Well . . .' She broke away. 'I'll work on Daddy.' She kissed me and went back inside.

I hailed a rickshaw, then changed my mind and started walking back to the club. Frustration burned inside me, quickening my pace. If I could only see Sylvie, I thought. She understood. She'd take my mind off it all.

I collected my car from its spot and drove at double-speed to The Farm. Noel let me in and told me Sylvie was in her bedroom. I hurried to her.

She was at her writing-desk. She turned around when I opened the door, but didn't stand. After a moment she replaced the cap on her pen and tried to smile.

'I was just writing to you, actually.'

'Really? We must be psychically connected – I've been thinking about you all day.'

'Do you want a drink?'

'Please.'

She stood then and nodded at her bed. 'Have a seat – I'll bring them back in.'

As she went past I trembled with the effort to not reach out and grab her, force her to the floor. All I wanted was to taste her, feel myself inside her. I felt feverish suddenly.

She was back in a few moments. I was sitting on the end of her bed, jacket and shoes removed. I patted the mattress.

'Come sit next to me.'

She handed me my drink, but didn't join me. 'Theo, there's something I want to talk about.'

'That sounds serious.' I put the glass on the floor and took her wrist in my hand, tugging at it to make her fall onto me. She resisted.

'I don't know how to say it –'

'You look beautiful today.'

She put her hand over my mouth. I smelled her skin and felt the blood building up inside me.

'Listen – you're important to me. And you're not losing me, but you've pledged your love to someone else. As did I, in fact.'

I started to say something, but she pressed her hand more firmly against me.

'I think it's time we honoured our word. Otherwise we're just liars.'

She took her hand away slowly. I looked up at her.

'I don't understand what you're saying.'

'It's over. I'm sorry, darling –'

'You don't want me to love you?'

'I do. But not the way it was before. Can't we be friends now instead?'

My mind was still trying to make sense of what had just happened. 'Are you in love with Freddie?'

'No, God no.' She tried to take my hand but I stood up, forcing her to step backwards. It felt as though she'd wrapped a metal band around my chest, squeezing the air out. She looked down. 'You don't want this either, really.'

'Don't I get to decide that?'

'I know things were always difficult with your mother —'

'I don't see what that has to do with it.'

'Don't you?'

She caught my eye and I felt my face flare up. 'You can't possibly think — please don't twist this into an issue. You're nothing like my mother.'

'That was the point, wasn't it?'

Her voice was soft with sympathy, and for a moment I hated her. *I've loved you since the first time I saw you,* I wanted to say. *Don't cheapen it like that.*

I pictured my mother, wherever she was, with that disapproving look I knew so well from my childhood. The thought flashed through my mind that she would be glad to come between me and Sylvie, and then another that I'd be glad if she died right now.

'Should I leave then?' I choked on the words.

'Don't be mad, darling.'

'Don't throw me away.'

'You'll come back soon, when you've calmed down? You'll see — it'll be so much better when you're not tied to an old woman like me.' She was trying to make her voice light.

I couldn't look at her or spend another minute in the room. I picked up my jacket and shoes and left the house barefoot. I threw them in the back seat and drove off without looking back. I half expected her to change her mind and chase after me, but after a mile I realised she wasn't coming.

Chapter Twenty-One

Freddie steered the yacht towards the jetty. It was March 1935, and the autumn winds were hardly out. The sail fluttered briefly as we turned, then fell still again. The lake seemed bluer than ever, its surface smooth as glass, rippling only as we cut through it or when yellow, green and black kingfishers skimmed it in search of food.

'We should do this more often,' Freddie said. 'You know, I can't even remember the last time I saw you.'

'It was before Christmas,' I said. 'At the Njoro meeting.' I'd been lucky to catch him. Usually Martha was alone when I dropped off the medicine, but this time Freddie had met me at the door and suggested taking the boat out.

'That long ago?' He shrugged. 'I suppose I've been busy.'

'Campaigning?'

'Trying to keep the party together out here. Not that it seems to be working. That idiot Mosley's fallen under Hitler's spell. He's calling for their old colonies to be returned to Germany, even after I proposed unity with Tanganyika for ourselves. Makes me realise just how far down we are on his priorities.'

'What did he say about unity when you mentioned it?'

'"Very good, very good." But I'm starting to think he's been

238

promising me whatever he knows I want to hear, with no real intention of carrying through.' He stood up, shading his eyes. 'Hello – we seem to have a greeting party.'

I turned and saw a lone toto at the end of the jetty, hopping from one foot to the other. 'Who's that?'

'Henry – new boy. Kikuyu. He's fourteen, but he's strong.'

'Looks important.'

'It'll be some household crisis or other. They've lost something, or broken something, no doubt.' He picked up one end of the mooring line. 'What I wouldn't give for a good cudgel, sometimes.'

The boat drifted to a stop; Freddie tied it up, not looking at the toto. 'What is it this time, Henry?'

'Bwana Hamilton,' Henry said, eyes round with worry. 'Bibi Hamilton keeps asking for more drink.'

'Give it to her, then.'

Henry bowed, and scampered back up to the house.

'Didn't Gregory say it'd kill her?' I asked.

'Goddamn it, she's half gone already.'

I looked away, trying to hide the surprise on my face.

We followed the toto's path to Mahalbeth. Martha was lying on the ottoman in the indoor sitting room. Her face was waxy, made more so by her hair, which was fanned out around her. When she saw Freddie, tears appeared in the corners of her eyes.

'My darling,' Freddie said. He knelt at her side, kissing her left hand. She placed her right hand on his head, gripping a tuft of hair with what looked like a surprising amount of strength.

'I thought you weren't coming back,' she said.

'Of course I came back,' Freddie said. He kissed her mouth. 'Go to sleep, now. We'll just be outside on the veranda.'

'No,' Martha said, raising herself up onto one elbow. She coughed, a dirty, hacking sound. 'Don't leave me again.'

'Alright,' Freddie said gently. 'We'll sit in here, but you have to promise to sleep.'

'I promise.'

239

We sat on the furthest sofa. After a few moments Henry came back in with a brandy, which Martha drank in one long gulp.

'Thirsty, darling?' Freddie said.

She lay back down and closed her eyes. Soon she was snoring loudly.

'Henry, bring us some wine,' Freddie said.

We went out to the terrace. Jules was tied up outside. When he saw us he picked up his water bowl, an enamel chamber pot, and hurled it at us. It missed by a few inches, splattering water all over Freddie's trousers.

'Surrounded by ingrates,' Freddie said.

Jules started beating his chest and screeching. Freddie knelt down in front of him and caught his hands. 'Jules,' he said. 'I can see you.'

Jules went quiet and put his arms around Freddie's neck. Freddie kissed the chimp's head and sighed, straightening up when Henry came out with two glasses of wine. He seemed exhausted.

'So what now?' I asked, trying to distract both of us. I'd never seen Martha so unwell. It must have been frustration that had made Freddie say what he did in the boat, I thought; he'd probably never felt helpless before. 'Will you stay in the BUF?'

'We'll see. I'd like to stand for Legislative Council. But that's at least a year away, frustratingly.' He joined me on the sofa and we clinked glasses. 'I want to keep the momentum up. Cheers, anyway.'

'Cheers. It's good to have a proper conversation – I can't take much more railway talk.'

'No one talks about Sylvie, you mean.'

'I haven't thought of her for months,' I lied.

Freddie grinned. 'Of course not. And you still haven't resigned?'

'What else is there?'

'You're twenty-four. You've got plenty of options, young man.'

'You have options when you have money.'

'And brains,' Freddie said. 'You talk as if I'm some rich bozo.'

'You know I don't mean that.'

'No, I'm just being sensitive.' He took a sip of his wine. 'Tell me why you broke it off with the delectable Miss Cartwright.'

I looked carefully at him. 'You've met her?'

'No. But her fame is widespread.'

'I didn't break it off,' I said. 'I was banned from seeing her. And I seem to recall it was you who got me banned.'

Freddie raised his eyebrows.

'Her father,' I said. 'He didn't approve of our friendship.'

'And you didn't think to say you wouldn't see me any more?'

'No.' After Sylvie had ended things between us, I'd had a horror of losing Freddie too. They'd played such a big part in my life, I almost didn't know who I'd be without them. I'd written to Lucy saying she should respect her father's opinions and I would too. *I can't abandon my friends*, I'd put. *So I suppose this is goodbye.* I'd avoided being alone with Maud as well, in case she brought up campaigning against him again. At least I rarely saw my mother; the few times I'd sat through dinner with her I'd had to bite my tongue, simmering with the knowledge that she was partly responsible for my losing Sylvie.

Freddie was looking at the floor. 'You know,' he said eventually, 'this wine is second-rate.' He stood up. '*Henry*.'

Henry appeared in the doorway. 'Yes, Bwana?'

'Bring us two glasses of the 1896 Macallan. And one for yourself.'

I raised an eyebrow. 'Expensive stuff.'

'If you can't share it with true friends, what good is it?'

He smiled at me, and my stomach bumped, pleasurably.

Henry returned with the whisky and we chinked again. I took a mouthful, closing my eyes as I savoured it. It was smooth and spicy, with a long, warm aftertaste.

I opened my eyes again. Freddie was laughing at Henry, who was spluttering at the end of my sofa, tears streaming down his face.

'Like it, Henry?'

'Yes, Bwana.'

'Stop telling me what you think I want to hear.'

'Yes, Bwana.'

Freddie held his hand out for the glass and Henry gave it back, meekly.

'It's an acquired taste,' Freddie said. 'You haven't failed any sort of test.' He nudged the toto with his foot. 'Go on, get back to work.'

Henry fled indoors. Freddie grinned at me. 'He's a good boy,' he said, sitting down again. 'I like him a lot. But I couldn't face him as an equal, let alone a superior, in any field – at work or at the club, say. That's what your sister isn't thinking of when she criticises the "benevolent white autocracy".'

'Maud?'

'Hasn't she told you?'

'Told me what?'

'She came to the last Committee meeting. Mostly to argue against securing the white highlands for European settlement only. Outside the townships, of course.' He crossed his legs. 'The natives love her. They don't see the aim of the Empire isn't the exploitation of a few unfortunate souls – it's larger, and nobler than that. We take our responsibility to develop their welfare and mould their way of life very seriously.' He took a sip of his drink. 'Why are you smiling?'

I cradled my glass, looking down at the amber liquid inside. 'I'm just remembering the day we met – I didn't think we'd be here discussing politics all these years later.'

He narrowed his eyes. 'I remember . . .You were wearing brown Oxfords, grey trousers, a white shirt and a pullover knit vest.'

'The first time we saw each other I was in bathing shorts, actually.'

'I'm talking about when we first spoke. The first thing you said to me was "nearly fifteen".'

242

'Possibly.'

'You were fascinating. Not quite pure, not quite wild. And totally naïve.' He grinned. 'We knew we had to have you.'

I hesitated for a second, unsure whether to feel flattered by that or not. Freddie waited for me to react. I raised my glass and he followed.

'To friendship,' I said.

'To friendship.'

Later that week my father knocked on the door of my office. 'Do you have a minute?'

'Of course, come in.'

He sat opposite me, breathing heavily, waving away my offer of a drink. 'It's the stairs – takes me half the day to recover.' He coughed twice into his handkerchief, then folded it and put it in his pocket. 'I want to discuss my retirement with you.'

'I still don't know –'

He held up his hand. 'This isn't about whether or not you'll be taking over as Director. I'd like to leave the railway in a better condition than I found it – some of the stations need a bit of sprucing up. We could build new ones, too.' He shifted in his chair. 'We could make it look really first-class, something other countries would be envious of.'

I looked down at my hands.

'You don't like the idea?'

'I don't know if there's much call for it.'

'Theo.' My father leaned forwards. 'Do you know what Churchill said about the line?'

'He thought it was a brilliant conception.'

'He was right. The Germans were building their own line from Port Tanga, and the people at the top had the foresight to see that the country with the means of transportation would control the African interior—'

'Which was unoccupied at the time. I know.'

243

'Nothing could stop us,' he said, as if I hadn't spoken. 'In spite of lions, famine, war; in spite of five years of parliamentary debate, we kept building. It's more than a train and track – it's a symbol of our enterprising spirit, and our ability to overcome obstacles.'

'I suppose so.'

'Do you really see?' Sweat was forming on his upper lip and he wiped it away. 'We *owe* it to the visionaries, to keep up their good work.'

'Why me, then?'

'I thought you might want a distraction.'

'Yes, of course.'

He was avoiding her name, but I knew what he was thinking. My father had been the most disappointed to hear Lucy's and my relationship was over; my mother had nodded once, asked if I wanted a drink, and never mentioned it again. Maybe Lucy had been right that night on the beach, when she'd hinted that my mother didn't like her. Maybe I should have paid more attention to her opinions. I tried to remember what else we'd talked about: trains – *I think they're romantic*, she'd said.

I looked across at my father – they were romantic for him, too; the big romance of his life. I wondered what he'd thought when he first came out to Kenya, a big empty country with its burnt, dry colours, and scatterings of trees across vast plains of yellow grass; the smell of smoke and spice on the air. I could picture the way he would have looked at the ground in surprise when his whole body shook with the vibrations of a stampede. Building the railway then would have been like building to the edge of the world. My father was a conqueror, I thought, and I understood why he was so proud of his work, even if the settlers laughed at him and the trains were slow and dirty and people were looking to the skies for travel now.

I cleared my throat.

He was playing with his pocket watch. 'Well, what do you say to the grand plan? My legacy?' He blinked suddenly. 'I don't want to force you, of course. I just thought if I can't pass on the directorship to you, at least we could share this.'

'I'd be happy to help.'

'Do you mean it?'

'I do.'

He beamed at me. 'Splendid. We'll have a proper meeting later on this week. Put some plans forwards.' He struggled out of his chair. 'Lunch at the club together today?'

I tried not to let my surprise show. 'Two o'clock?'

'Perfect.'

After he left I walked to the window and rested my forehead against the glass. A few months ago I would have wanted to share my news with Lucy and Sylvie, the strange stirring I'd felt at my father's invitation to lunch, but now they were both gone.

Next to me, a translucent gecko ran halfway down the wall, then paused as if sensing danger, its black eyes bright even in the gloom of the office. With its pale, pointy face, it reminded me of Carberry. I put out my hand, letting the shadow rest on the animal, and the gecko's tail flicked.

I lowered my arm. 'Not today,' I said to it.

My father set up our first reconnaissance at Gilgil. The town was small enough to need only a railway siding that connected to the running line in a loop at either end. Another branch had been built in 1929 connecting to Thomson's Falls, whose cold, clear water drained from the Aberdares and plunged over two hundred feet into a forested ravine.

My father was pacing by the side of the track when I arrived; his face lit up when he saw me, and he waved me over.

'Good, good,' he said, pumping my hand enthusiastically. 'Are you ready to start?'

'I think so.'

'Good.'

The track was just over three feet in gauge, and lay flat on the ground at this point in its journey. Elsewhere it was raised, on bridges over rivers and valleys, or sunk, as at Nairobi, but at Gilgil it was possible to walk right up to the rails. When the train was in the station small African children would appear and pass bright green bananas through the open windows in exchange for the passengers' coins. Even when the train was moving, I'd seen them run alongside, trying to catch the attention of the bwanas and bibis. To the left of the track, the ground sloped away after four or five feet to dense green bush and red and purple hibiscus. Up ahead there was nothing but open land.

We tramped along in silence for a few moments. It was dusty underfoot, and the shins of my father's trousers were covered in a fine layer of reddish-brown. Eventually he cleared his throat. 'I didn't know whether to start here or with Voi. What do you think?'

I looked over my shoulder at the station, a few hundred yards or so behind us. Even from a distance I could see that the paint on the woodwork was peeling, and weeds had sprung up through cracks in the floor.

'Voi is mile one hundred,' my father said. He stopped and fanned his face, which was turning puce in the sun. 'It's mile four hundred and seven here – doesn't have quite the same ring.'

'There's the marshalling yard at Voi.'

'And it's the junction for the feeder to Tanganyika . . .'

I looked back at the station again, shading my eyes against the glare. A cluster of men had gathered in the shade at the edge of the platform. 'On the other hand – all the farmers use Gilgil – everyone in the Wanjohi uses it in fact.'

'Is that so?'

'It's one of the main auction towns. And it's a big area for flax.'

We started walking again, my father clasping his hands behind his back. His expression was thoughtful, and I was pleased – more than pleased, proud – that my opinion mattered to him.

'What about the new town they built around the station for Thomson's Falls?' I said.

246

'What of it?'

'It's a market town – and they've got a big lodge there now for the visitors to the waterfall. They'll all be using this branch.'

'Good point.' We turned around and began the walk back in the direction of the station. Next to us, the rails hummed faintly, and my father checked his watch.

'That'll be the train to Mombasa,' he said. 'Be here in fifteen minutes.' He clapped his hands suddenly, his face breaking into a smile. 'Doesn't it get your blood going?'

'What are you thinking?'

'We could enlarge it by at least half. Or we could build a whole new station here.' He stopped short. 'Maybe we could build a special waiting room for guests at the lodge, they'll all know each other by then.'

I tried not to grin. 'That's taking it a bit far.'

'Have you never noticed how friendly people are on trains?' He tapped me on the chest. 'The sharing of the journey is all, Theo. That's what you young people in your automobiles are missing out on – the chance to make new acquaintances, possibly friends for life. You're all so sealed off in your little ones and twos and threes.'

'It does cut the journey in half though,' I murmured.

He waved his hand to me. 'It's not about the destination. Imagine if everyone thought like that.'

We reached the station and climbed the steps to the platform, passing through the building to the dusty main road out front. A signpost pointed north to Nakuru, and south to Nairobi. The only shade came from the shadow of the duka, with its iron roof. Flies buzzed lazily in the heat around a rotting mango, drowned out intermittently by the sound of a Singer treadle set up in front of the shop.

'Did you tell Maud we'd be here?' my father asked.

'I haven't seen her for a while.'

'Must be a coincidence.'

I looked around and saw her coming out of the duka carrying

247

two stacks of neatly folded brown cloth tied up with string. She caught sight of us and waved. I went to her and kissed her cheek. Her smile seemed uncertain, unless it was my imagination.

'Hello you,' she said.

'Hello yourself. What are you doing here?'

'I buy all the kanzus here. Mr Chaudry's the best dhersie in Kenya.'

The old man at the sewing machine smiled toothily at us.

'I see.'

'What are you doing here?'

'Scouting for station-improving opportunities.'

We both looked at my father, who was scribbling furiously in a notebook, his hat tilted to one side.

'I'm strangely not dreading work each morning,' I said. 'What do you think that means?'

'Whatever it is, it can't be good.'

'Oh well.' I took the stacks of robes from her and she linked her arm through mine. We started walking towards her car.

'If you're going to be working up here, will you still be staying in Nairobi?' she asked.

'Probably.'

She nodded. I couldn't tell if she looked disappointed or relieved.

'You can come visit me.'

'Maybe. The loan's about to go through now. But it would be nice to see you all.'

'Us all?'

'You and Father. And Mother of course. She was asking about you the other day.'

'Asking what?'

'How you were.'

I shrugged. 'I'm fine, if she's really interested.'

'I had supper with her and the Cartwrights a few weeks ago.' She squeezed my arm gently. 'I'm sorry – I shouldn't have brought them up.'

'You still see them?'

'From time to time. Mr Cartwright's helping me prepare for my first public speech.'

'When will that be?'

'Before the next Committee.'

'Oh yes.' I looked down at her. 'Freddie told me you went to the last one to thwart him.'

'I'm surprised he noticed me over all the people agreeing with him.'

I couldn't help smiling. 'Why are you fighting him so hard? He's not even elected to Legco yet – he doesn't have any real influence.'

'Of course he does.' We reached the car and I tossed the robes through the open window. She leaned against the hood. 'He's a public figure. What he says matters. When he talks about Africans needing patriarchal benefits and being intellectually inferior to us, people believe him. And then they treat the Africans a certain way at work, or on the street. Their lives are affected every day by what white people like Freddie say about them. And some people say worse, that they're all thieves, or they'll attack white women if you give them a chance.' She looked down at her feet. 'Have you ever noticed how scared of them some people are?'

'Maybe you're too fearless,' I said. 'How's Abdullah?'

Her face flushed. 'We're happy.'

'Are you?'

'Yes.'

'Where is he?'

'We don't shop together any more. Last time a woman came into the store after us and shouted at the storekeeper for letting Kikuyu in there with white people.'

'But Abdullah's not even Kikuyu,' I said.

'They don't see the difference. They just see a black man in funny clothes and say "savage".' She shook her head. 'I almost lost my temper.'

249

'Careful now. You'll get a reputation as a firebrand.'

She rolled her eyes. 'Don't worry about me.'

'Of course I do.'

'Well I worry about you. You're my big brother. Even if you are a dunderhead.'

I grinned. 'I hope you're not this foul-mouthed when you're speaking up for the Africans.'

She laughed. I kissed her again and she climbed into the car.

'I'll come see you soon,' she said. 'And you come home. It *is* still your home, you know.'

''Bye Spanish.'

''Bye Dunderhead.'

The next few months were taken up with travelling to other stations along the line to report back on their conditions. My father's enthusiasm was catching, and I found myself arriving at dusty, tin-roofed out-of-the-way places with visions of grand stone buildings and bustling markets springing up around them. I sketched plan after plan every night at the club, surprised by how vivid my imagination could be.

I didn't see Sylvie, except in passing at the club, or the market. I heard from others that Rupert had finally signed the divorce papers and gone back to England, where he was locked up for killing a pedestrian in a drink-driving case. I felt a grim satisfaction whenever I thought of him behind bars. To celebrate, Sylvie had bought herself a beach house in Tiwi and a bungalow next door to the Muthaiga. Boy Long found me buying a newspaper from the duka in Gilgil and told me she was driving Noel crazy, disappearing to her other properties without letting Noel know, then suddenly turning up at The Farm again.

'The first time it happened, Noel called the police. Thought she'd killed herself,' he said. 'Wish I'd been there to see her breeze back through the doors to all the fuss.'

'She's always been irresponsible,' I said.

'We went for a drive the other day, too, and she started arguing with me about Edie. She bloody jumped out the car while it was still moving. I'm telling you – she's half-cracked. We were going uphill, so it was pretty slow, but she still scraped her knee and tore a hole in her cardigan.' He lit a cigarette. 'I shouted at her and she just shrugged and said "What did you expect?" I could have wrung her neck there and then.'

Maud was busy too, with the cattle and the land she'd bought, producing milk and butter and growing rice and mealies. She wrote in June, saying she was planting orchards now: peach, plum, apricot and quince, and wanted to start a jam business; Abdullah was overseeing the gardening.

We're up at first light, she put, *and it never stops. I wish I had Abdullah's energy, but sometimes all I want to do is sleep. Bulawayo got into a fight with one of the other totos, and Mother wanted to get rid of him – she says he's a troublemaker – but I knew he struggled to find work before we took him on, so I talked her out of it.*

There was a tsetse fly scare, but none of our cows have been affected. Apparently we're in an 'unclean' area, meaning there's fever in the land itself, and we have to dip them – Massiti, the foreman, showed me how. I've learned so much from him already. The best thing about the farm is all the extra jobs it's created for the locals. The other day I was invited to a spear throwing contest – the men all stand in line, with their spears in hand, and a barrel hoop is rolled in front of them and they have to throw to send their spear through the hoop as it rolls past. They take it very seriously. When are you coming home next? Scotty has arthritis.

Towards the end of August, I received a letter from Lucy, telling me that she'd got engaged to someone called Bill.

I thought I should let you know, she wrote. *We're thinking of a summer wedding, maybe December. Nothing big. I hope you're well.*

The next time I went back to Kiboko Maud tried to talk about Lucy to me, but I cut her off.

'I'm fine,' I said. 'We were never a good match anyway.'

'Of course not,' Maud said. She hugged me for a long time before I went to bed.

Chapter Twenty-Two

Every Friday my father and I took lunch at the club to discuss progress on the legacy project. The third Friday in November I arrived first and took our usual table in the corner. I was going through my list of stations by priority when he appeared beside me, put a copy of the *East African Standard* on the table and took the seat opposite.

'I've ordered the wine,' I said.

'Good. Your friend's making the news.'

I looked down at the headline. Freddie had left the BUF and was standing for the Kiambu constituency in the general election.

'I thought he might.'

'No harm in having friends in high places.' He ran his fingers through his beard. 'How often do you see him?'

'Fairly often.'

'Good. Let's try to get him on board, hey?' He opened his briefcase. 'What if we go through the budget today?'

'Fine by me.'

A waiter brought over the wine and uncorked it while my father perused the menu. After he'd decanted it he lingered, eyes downcast, until my father looked up.

'Bwana Miller?'

'Yes?'

'You have someone here for you.'

'Show him over,' my father said. He took a sip of wine and smacked his lips appreciatively. 'And then I'll have the steak.'

'For me too,' I said.

He bowed and left. A policeman was shown to our table, wearing the standard khaki shirt and shorts and carrying his helmet. The noise level in the room dropped for a moment, then got louder. The policeman clicked his heels.

'One of the porters has been arrested and he's asking for you especially, sir,' he said. He had a faint blond moustache and very pale blue eyes. He looked younger than me.

'For me?' my father asked, wiping his mouth with a napkin.

'We've got him down at the station – don't rush, sir. I can wait outside. Just come out when you've finished your meal.'

'We'll come now, I think,' my father said, pushing back his chair.

The policeman drove us to the station, apologising for interrupting our lunch. 'He was caught stealing,' he said. 'Thinks you can get him off.'

The police station was a squat, one-storey building painted white. Inside, a ceiling fan sluggishly moved the hot air around and a fly traipsed across the front desk. There was a strong smell of whisky hanging about and very little natural light. The porter was sitting handcuffed on a bench in the waiting room, his eyes puffy and bloodshot. When he saw us, he stood up quickly and started babbling. Another policeman, an older one this time, pushed him back down onto the bench. No one else seemed to be around.

Our policeman led us to stand in a semi-circle over him. 'Do you recognise this man, sir?'

'Yes,' my father said. 'He's Peter, our head porter at The Nairobi station.'

'Bwana Miller,' the porter said, looking up at us. 'I'm a good man – please tell them, Bwana Miller.'

254

'We've told him there's nothing you can do,' the second policeman said. 'He was caught red-handed.'

'What did he steal?'

'A loaf of bread.'

'I have big family. Sometimes I don't have money for food.'

'You had a job,' the older policeman said. 'You should have been grateful for that.'

'I very grateful,' the porter said; he started crying. 'Please, Bwanas, I have big family.'

Sweat glistened on his temples. The whisky smell seemed to get stronger and stronger on the warm air, and I had to fight the urge to be sick.

'What will he get?' my father asked.

'Five years, probably.'

'That seems a bit much, doesn't it?'

'It's what they normally get.'

'Is there anyone I can write a letter to?'

'I doubt it.'

My father tugged his beard, seeming distressed. 'He *is* a good man, I can vouch for that.'

The policeman shook his head. 'The judge won't go easy on him in case they all think they can get away with it.'

The porter was still crying, a bubble of snot hanging from his nose. He tried to grab my father's hands and the policeman nearest him smacked him away.

'He's a good employee,' I said.

The first policeman looked sympathetic. 'It's out of our hands now, sir, but we thought we should fetch you just in case he kicked up a fuss.'

'I'm sorry, Peter,' my father said. 'We'll keep the job open for you. Do you have any sons you can send me while you're away?'

'One son, Bwana Miller.'

'How old?'

'Seven.'

'We'll give him a job.' My father mopped his forehead. 'And we'll see what we can do about a pension or something of that sort for you.'

The second policeman prodded Peter. 'Back to the cell now.'

He stood up obediently. 'Thank you, Bwana,' he said, not looking at us.

The first policeman showed us out. 'I wouldn't go through with that pension,' he said. 'It'll just make trouble for them with the other families.'

Outside, my father stopped at the bottom of the station stairs. 'That was rather unpleasant, wasn't it?'

'Yes.'

'I wish I'd been able to do more.'

'I'm not hungry anyway.' I looked at my watch. 'Why don't I try finding Freddie, see whether he can do anything?'

He looked relieved. 'Good idea. I'll head back to the club.'

'I'll see you there.'

Freddie wasn't at the Muthaiga, but one of the bar staff thought he'd gone for a meeting at The Norfolk. I ran into him there in the lobby. He looked pleased, and I guessed his meeting had gone well.

He listened to my account, then pulled a sympathetic face. 'Sorry, Theo. I don't know what I can do.'

'I don't know either – have a word with Byrne? He must know the police chief if you don't.'

'Byrne won't want to get involved. The man was caught stealing.'

'It just seems a bit disproportionate, don't you think?'

He put his arm around my shoulder and steered me to one of the tables on the covered terrace. 'It's irritating when these junior officers start throwing their weight around, but it's the law. I really don't see how I can try to get this poor bugger's charges dismissed. If I do a favour for one native, they'll all expect it.'

'That's what the policeman said.'

'It's true, even if your sister won't hear it. Individually you can

256

sometimes reason with them, but in a group, they're a nightmare. They don't think the same way as us, Theo. They're not logical – it's the way they're educated, or not.' He looked away. 'Try to forget the whole thing. No use worrying about something you can't control.'

I thought about asking how much Rupert had been fined for setting the Africans' huts on fire that time. But I didn't think Freddie could have remembered that, or maybe he hadn't heard about it at the time. Even so, it irritated me that he seemed so reluctant to help and I wondered for a moment how seriously he took me or my job.

'I really am sorry.'

I shrugged. 'You know politics better than I do. I suppose if you don't think we can help, we probably can't.'

'I don't.'

'Thanks for listening anyway.'

'Any time. How about a drink now you're here?'

'I have to get back.'

He smiled at me. 'Well – don't be a stranger. Hopefully I can be more useful next time.'

I forced myself to smile back.

I'd started spending the weekends visiting Maud, driving back on Fridays after lunch and arriving in the cool, green light of late afternoon. I'd follow her around on her daily tour of inspection, measuring the saplings in the orchard, overseeing the building of higher stockades for the cattle after lions had taken two of them, talking to Massiti about the crops. After we'd finished she would visit the workers in their huts, Scotty at her heels. Several more had sprung up since we'd bought the land and the compound was getting crowded. The women sat in the entrances to their homes, stirring beans or rolling out the dough for chapattis, and children played in the dirt with cars Joseph made for them out of wire and bottle tops. Sometimes the older children ran up to us with gifts of raw sugarcane or wild honeycomb that we ate on the veranda until our fingers and chins were sticky with the stuff.

'I never want to leave,' Maud said, 'how could anywhere else be better?'

Our family spent Christmas at Kiboko for the first time, so Maud could organise celebrations for the workers. The totos put on a nativity play, and Joseph accompanied them on the concertina. All the adults were given a glass of sherry and Abdullah handed out sweets for the children. Even Bulawayo seemed to enjoy himself, singing and laughing like everyone else.

After the meal, the four of us pulled crackers and played games by the fire. My father opened a bottle of champagne and we toasted the success of the farm, and the plans for the railway.

'I couldn't do it without you,' he said to me.

'To Theo,' Maud said.

'And Maud – you'll be sixteen in no time,' my father said. 'I'm sure some young fellow will be glad of that.'

'I turned sixteen years ago,' Maud said. She was laughing, but her eyes were worried. 'Are you feeling well, Daddy?'

'Of course, of course.' My father waved her away. A little champagne slopped out of his glass. 'Been working too hard. Anyway, what had I been going to say? I couldn't do it without you, Theo.'

I saw my mother watching us over her glass and wondered for a moment what she was thinking, if she felt triumphant at all about the change in my attitude to work, or took credit for it, even. I shrugged off that idea before it irritated me too much.

'I'm enjoying myself,' I said, and my father's eyes looked shiny for a moment.

I was still busy at work, but I made sure I continued the run between Gregory's bungalow in Nairobi and Mahalbeth, even though the medicine seemed to be losing efficacy. Once or twice

258

I found Martha drifting through the rooms, wearing only a dressing gown and with her hair unbrushed, but for the most part she seemed invisible. Waweru wouldn't speak about her – out of loyalty to Freddie, I supposed – and the totos seemed afraid of her. Freddie was hardly ever at home, and I hadn't seen him in months by the time I ran into him at the market one afternoon in March. He smelled the same as always, but his clothes were even smarter and his nails even neater. The weather was muggy, and he alone was cool among all the fans and sodden handkerchiefs.

'Let me buy you a drink,' he said.

We drove to the Muthaiga in his car, the leather of the seat burning hot.

'I should check on Martha,' Freddie said. 'Did you know we'd bought a bungalow opposite the club?'

'So that's why I never see you in Naivasha. Which one?'

'No name – it's got a red door, if you ever need to find it. It's no Mahalbeth, but it's convenient for the campaign.'

'How's that going?'

He grinned. 'Pretty well, I think. I'm up against another two candidates, but I seem to be pulling in front of them.'

'Good.'

'I think I can really shake it up, if I get in. Make a mark, and all that.'

'I'm sure you will.'

'What's happening with you? Still beavering away at Lunatic Line HQ?'

'Actually, yes. My father's retiring next year and we're working on a project to improve the stations, build new ones. Improve the look of the whole thing.'

'Oh?' He turned his face to me. 'You seem more enthusiastic.'

'We understand each other better now.'

'Maybe you should stay, then.'

We pulled up outside the Muthaiga. Freddie turned off the engine but didn't get out. He was staring at something in the distance.

'What are you planning now?'

'I've just had an idea. If I'm elected, would you be willing to come to a Council session, give them the benefit of your expert knowledge?'

'I'm not very good at public speaking.'

'You don't have to be,' he said, 'half the members aren't either. So will you? I know I don't deserve it, but it'd be a huge boon to me.'

'I –'

'Do it for me,' he said, holding his hands out in a mock prayer. 'For the good of my career.'

I laughed. I felt my chest expanding. This was the first time that Freddie had needed me in particular, the first time I and no one else could help him. 'I suppose so.'

'Great.' He slapped me on the back. 'Nothing like hearing it from the horse's mouth.' He opened his door and pulled a face. 'You know, I was going to show you the cottage, but Martha's probably in the bar. She spends most of her time there telling members' fortunes with cards.'

'Maybe she can do mine.'

'She tends to go in for the dramatic, just to warn you. You'll probably meet a tall, dark stranger who stabs you in your sleep.'

'I've been meaning to ask you, actually.' I cast about for a delicate way of phrasing it, and couldn't find one. 'Are you sure Gregory knows what he's doing?'

He raised an eyebrow.

'I mean – she seems to be getting worse by the day.'

'I know.' He drummed his fingers on the steering wheel. 'It's not fair. But she isn't in pain now, anyway, and that's a relief. Are you coming?'

'You go. I feel like stretching my legs for a moment.'

'Alright. I'll get drinks.'

I turned right and walked out of the club grounds and back onto the road. Diagonally opposite was a white-walled bungalow

260

almost hidden by a clump of trees. I strolled over to it and paused outside, looking down the path at the red door. This wasn't where he threw parties, or discussed politics with officials, and I suddenly had a strange urge to see inside the real Freddie.

Other than the sound of a lawnmower a few houses away, and a family of turtle doves cooing and scratching in the tree next to Freddie's front gate, the road was quiet. I checked both directions before walking up the garden path and around the side of the house.

No one was in the garden, and the back door opened easily. The inside of the house smelled of Freddie and something sickly sweet. Most of the windows were shuttered, and it took a moment for my eyes to get used to the dimness. I was in a sitting room. More of Freddie's family portraits hung on the walls, and a pink-and-grey-striped chaise longue took up most of the middle of the floor. I peered closer at the walnut coffee table in front of the chaise longue and saw it was littered with empty brown bottles. I could hear a muffled ticking, and the floorboards shifting and expanding in the heat, but no footsteps. No one came to see who I was.

I wandered through the rooms, hands in my pockets. The decor was simpler than Mahalbeth, and the rooms smaller. Freddie's bedroom had a full-length mirror by the window, a wrought-iron bed, a small bedside table and a row of in-built slatted cupboards along the far wall; I opened all the doors, looking in at his freshly pressed suits and the polished shoes lined up neatly below – one pair of shoes for each suit. Ten silk ties hung in the last cupboard. I pulled one out slowly, enjoying the cool feel of the material against my fingers, then stood in front of the mirror and knotted the tie carefully around my neck. The blue suited me, I thought. Maybe if I could help Freddie with work, he'd need me to move in with him. I pictured myself living in the bungalow with him, sharing some of his clothes – not all of them, his jackets would be too wide in the shoulders for me.

261

I sat on his bed, noting how firm the mattress was. If I lived with Freddie, maybe Sylvie would spend more time around the corner at her cottage here, maybe the black dog would finally leave her. It must be difficult for her to grow old, I thought. She was so beautiful that that was all people could see at first. She'd never be sure if people really liked her beyond her looks, until eventually they were gone.

All her flirting and her changes of mind weren't some sort of tease, but a test, I suddenly thought. If I passed, there was the promise that we'd work it out somehow, and it'd be all the sweeter for the wait. I grew hard thinking about it, and my fingers snaked up to the tie, playing with it, tightening it. I'd noticed that with the satisfaction I was getting at work, I'd found a new confidence, and now I knew what I could do with it. I could see the three of us dining together, playing cards, bathing together. I would be the one in charge; Freddie and Sylvie would look to me for pleasure, for help. Not just with work, but in private. Imagining it brought on a sudden uncontrollable warmth that ran downwards through my body, and just as suddenly a jolt of panic when I realised Freddie would be wondering where I'd got to. I jumped up and straightened the bedsheet, hiding all trace that I'd been there. I stuffed the tie into my pocket, left the house by the back door and joined Freddie at the bar. For the rest of the evening, I could feel it rubbing softly against my upper thigh.

The April elections arrived, and Freddie won comfortably. Edie met me coming out of the post office, carrying the paper with the results, and grinned.

'Page four. And guess the headline.'

'Prospect of war?'

'When is it not? I don't believe I'll notice the difference if we do actually go to war.'

The subject of war continued. At the opening debate of the first Legco session, members discussed frontier raids, air raids and how to prepare for both. 'Our duty is to provide for our own internal security,' the paper quoted one member saying. 'Sufficient in the event of external aggression to hold on until we can be reinforced.'

There were plans to set up a 'Tanganyika League' that would oppose the handing over of the territory to Germany. The Legion of Frontiersmen was revived, and Freddie was put in charge of volunteers, uniform design and finance. He set up a rifle club and persuaded me to visit.

'You're not a bad shot,' he said afterwards.

'A friend at university taught me.'

'Why don't you join the Legion?'

'I promised Maud I wouldn't. Our uncle died in the war.'

He smiled. 'Never mind. As long as you're still willing to help out on the railway issue.'

'I am.'

'Good. And how *is* your rabble-rousing sister?'

'She's worrying about the land; the crops are half the height they should be, apparently.' More than that, a third of the cattle had recently been found killed and picked clean, despite the stockades, and a hippo had blundered out of the lake and attacked the servants' huts. On top of everything, some of the trees in the orchard were diseased or the soil was poor, and her jam business was struggling.

Freddie shrugged. 'It happens. Tell her "chin up".'

After that I didn't see him for months, until the third Legco session was called in September, when he appeared at the office.

'As I said,' he said. 'We just need your expertise.'

I walked after him into Memorial Hall. The building was two storeys high and made of grey stone with tall windows that somehow let in little light; the inside was muted, green carpet and brown walls. It felt oppressive. There were seventeen other members of Legco gathered around, chatting and laughing, ten Europeans, one Arab, two Africans and four Indians. Freddie seemed to know them all.

263

'Nervous?' he asked me.

'A little.'

'Don't worry – you won't have to talk much. Just answer a few questions I put to you.'

I sat at the back of the room until the minutes of the previous day had been read, then Freddie called me forwards and introduced me to the assembly.

'Theo here is the son of the Director of Kenya and Uganda Railways and Harbours,' he said, 'as well as having worked himself in the Nairobi office for a few years. I think everyone would agree that Theo knows what he's talking about, yes?'

There was a murmur of assent. I sat in the chair Freddie gestured to, in the middle of the room facing the benches, and crossed my legs. My head felt hot, and I quickly wiped my forehead with the back of my hand. Freddie smiled at me.

'First off – can you tell us exactly how much the taxpayers of this country pay for the railway?' he asked.

'I don't know exactly.'

'But you do know that we pay more than Uganda?'

'That sounds right.'

'And why would that be?'

I uncrossed and re-crossed my legs. 'The majority of the track is in Kenya,' I said. 'More maintenance is needed on this side. And there are more branches, more stations, more employees.'

A few members nodded their heads; most looked bored.

'That sounds reasonable,' Freddie said. He smiled at me again. 'Who works out the railway estimates?'

'Our finance director, with help from my father.'

'What sort of person is this finance director?'

'I beg your pardon?'

He smiled further. 'I only ask, because each year it seems to me the estimates are significantly more than can possibly be needed . . . Given the visible results.'

My ears thrummed with blood. 'You think the taxpayers are paying too much?'

'I don't know where their money is going,' Freddie said flatly.

I tried to catch his eye, but he turned away to face the assembly, who were looking slightly more interested. The air in the room felt closer than before and I had to resist the urge to wipe my forehead again.

'It is always a matter of great admiration to me,' Freddie said, and paused. 'Admiration' was loaded with sarcasm, and I saw a few members grin. '. . . How he is ever able to get away with these estimates with only an occasional and gentle kick from Council.' He threw his hands up in the air theatrically. 'Which he can, of course, and does, in fact, almost entirely disregard.' He turned back to point his finger at me. I recognised most of these tricks from his BUF days and the buzz in my ears increased. 'Tell me, what will our money be spent on this year?'

'There are plans to improve existing stations,' I said carefully. 'And build new ones where necessary.'

'I see. Now, Theo, what would you say is the primary industry in Kenya?'

'Agriculture.'

'And do you think these hardworking farmers care about beautifying the railway?'

There was a ripple of laughter among the Council.

'I suppose that depends,' I said, forcing a smile, 'on whether they're farmers with a sophisticated aesthetic sensibility.'

Another ripple. 'That's it, Mr Miller,' someone called. I kept the smile plastered to my face, trying to catch Freddie's eye. I didn't understand what he was trying to do, but I had to believe the goal wasn't to humiliate me and the railway. He'd turn it around, or give me a chance to defend myself.

'Let's say they're not,' Freddie said. 'Or they are, but for some reason they're more concerned with the transportation of produce.'

He shrugged. 'Isn't it more sensible to provide refrigeration plants, so the railway is in fact *assisting* our primary producers? Increasing their efficiency?' He shrugged again. 'It seems right to me, to help them make back the extortionate amount of money they're pouring into the thing.'

'It's not a bad idea.'

'Why haven't you discussed this then?'

'I'm an engineer,' I said. 'Not a politician.'

'We can see that,' Freddie said. 'A politician would never give credence to his opponent's idea.'

There was another ripple, louder this time.

'Kenya and Uganda Railways and Harbours mustn't get above itself,' Freddie said, raising his voice. 'The railways should serve the public, not master it.'

I looked at the nodding faces and felt my stomach cramping. 'Maybe you should practise what you preach.'

'Meaning?'

'Is all this out of concern for the farmers, or are you trying to make a name for yourself?'

'I would have thought my name was pretty well established.'

'Government's always been happy to let us get on with it until now.'

I looked at Freddie; he raised an eyebrow. 'That's my point,' he said. He turned away, but I caught his words anyway, 'Things are changing.'

I found him at the Muthaiga a few hours later. He was sitting at the bar with Martha; her face looked fat in the half-light. The room was empty otherwise.

'Theo,' he said, when he saw me. 'I'm sorry – but I believe everything I said.'

I stood a few paces away; I didn't trust myself to get closer to him. 'Why didn't you tell me that's what you wanted me for?'

'Because you wouldn't have come.'

266

'Of course I wouldn't. You humiliated me. And you've ruined my father's plans.' I bit my lip, wanting suddenly, absurdly, to cry. 'It'll crush him.'

'The points needed to be made. The railway is a massive expense, and it's not helping anyone.'

'Not like you, Freddie,' Martha said in a sing-song voice. 'Always helping everyone.'

'Darling,' he said. 'How many have you had today?'

'I can see why she needs them,' I said.

'It's politics, young man. It's not personal.'

'Don't call me that.'

'I said I'm sorry. Can't you see the bigger picture?'

'You mean your career?'

Martha passed her hand over her eyes. 'I don't feel well, Freddie.' She started to topple over and I reached out and grabbed her wrist, pulling her back upright. It was fleshy under my fingers, and spotty, and now I was closer I could see spots all over her body.

'Heroin sores,' Freddie said, following my gaze.

The hairs on my arms stood on end at the flatness in his voice, and I looked down at Martha's wrist, still clutched between my fingers. 'When did she start using heroin?'

'Kiki Preston introduced her to it years ago.' There was silence for a moment, then Freddie laughed dryly. 'What did you think the medicine was?'

I felt sick. 'You knew?'

'Don't torture yourself too much – if you hadn't helped, someone else would have.'

'Why didn't you try to stop her?'

He shrugged. 'She's an adult.'

I felt shame, then fury that he'd been able to trick me so easily into helping him. I gripped Martha tighter.

'Do you know why you're doing this to yourself?' I asked her. She looked at me with blurry eyes.

267

'You're doing it because of him. He's cold and he uses people. He's killing you, Martha.'

'Let me go,' she said quietly.

'He's probably sleeping with Sylvie again, and he won't look after her either.'

'For God's sake,' Freddie said to me. 'I thought you'd got over your little obsession.'

I dropped Martha and kicked at a panel in the bar. There was a sharp crack and the wood splintered underneath my foot. Martha shrieked.

'I don't want to see you again,' I said to Freddie.

He raised his eyebrow. 'In that case you might have to leave Kenya,' he said.

'Or you might.'

He looked at me for a moment, then burst out laughing. 'Come on,' he said, 'let's be friends again. I'm sorry I humiliated you. I won't do it again.'

'No, you won't,' I said, and walked away.

'Theo,' he called after me. I heard him push back his bar stool.

'Freddie, don't leave me,' Martha screamed.

'Theo,' he called again. 'Don't be childish.'

I pushed through the Muthaiga doors and started walking down the drive; I didn't look back.

Chapter Twenty-Three

My father's railway plans were put on hold in order to channel the money towards refrigeration plants. He retired quietly, and MacDonald took over the directorship. I was busier than ever at work, although it had lost all satisfaction for me. Now I had no one to share my success with, it didn't seem to matter. I felt foolish for ever thinking Freddie and Sylvie had even cared in the first place.

Maud wrote to me to say Scotty had died in his sleep; she'd buried him in the garden. *I read out a poem, and Father said a few words, she wrote. Come home soon and see us. It's so quiet without him here.*

It was a warm night when I left Nairobi and the crickets were out, blaring. I had an overwhelming urge to find them all and drive over them, hear the crack of their bodies being crushed, and the blessed silence afterwards.

Maud was still up when I arrived.

'It's getting worse,' she said when I came in, lowering the book she'd been reading. She was wearing a plain black dress and I saw new shadows under her eyes.

'What is?'

'Everything, I suppose. We can safely say the rains have failed this year.'

269

'There'll be other years.'

'But not enough money.' She closed the book and stood up. 'And one of the totos has leprosy – we've never had it here before.'

'Oh God.'

'I don't want to fail them, Theo. I've been writing letters to the newspapers, to Parliament, but all the money's being diverted in case of war.'

'You can't help it.'

'But they're so dependent on us. If we'd devolved even a little bit of power before now, given them more land, maybe they wouldn't be dragged down with us.'

'But we didn't.'

'No, poor them. Bulawayo's been talking to the others – Joseph told me. He's been saying they'll be sent off to fight, the white masters will send them to die first.'

'Cheeky devil.'

'Is he?' She started pacing in front of me. 'We've done it before. I tried to tell him I wouldn't let them take him, any of them. I said we needed them here more than they were needed to fight. He listened to me, but I don't know if he believed me. And now he won't talk to Joseph – he keeps saying Joseph is making trouble for him.'

I put my arms around her, stopping her in her tracks. 'Never mind Bulawayo, anyway. How's Father?'

'He keeps asking about you, how it's going in the office.'

'MacDonald's alright.'

'I'm worried about him.'

'He's pretty dour, but he'll settle in.'

'Not MacDonald.' She pushed me away, but I saw her lips twitching.

'I'm going to bed, Spanish.'

'Do you want a drink before you go?'

'Not tonight. How about we take the boat out tomorrow?'

'We'll see.'

There was a shuffling sound behind me. 'Is that you, Maud?' My father tottered into the sitting room in a white nightshirt. I was shocked by his appearance. His eyes were dark, and swivelled disconcertingly, but the rest of him was the same colour as his clothes.

'What are you doing up?' Maud asked.

'I heard voices. Who's this?'

'It's Theo, Daddy.'

I looked down at my feet, a vein throbbing in my forehead. This was all Freddie's fault, I told myself, and hated him even more.

'Theo,' my father said. 'You must be the man of the house now, look after your sister and your mother.'

'I will.'

Maud crossed over to him and took his elbow. 'Let's not worry about that now. We should get you back to bed.'

He allowed himself to be led away, but turned his face to me. 'We'll show them, won't we?' he said. 'Never let them tell you what to do, son.'

'I won't.'

Maud came back a few minutes later, rubbing her eyes.

'How long has he been like this?' I asked.

'A few days.'

'You should have told me.'

'You're busy. And I hoped he'd get better. Sometimes he is.' She sank down in front of the fire, holding her hands out to the flames, and I felt a fierce rush of love for her.

'I shouldn't have left you to cope alone.'

'I want to do it. It's just hard watching him slip away.' She looked at me despairingly. 'And then there's you, too.'

'What about me?'

'You're almost twenty-six now, Theo. If you'd married Lucy and bought your own house I wouldn't have to worry about you being lonely. At least Father has us.'

271

I felt my mouth twisting involuntarily. 'Well – too late now. Get some rest.'

My father's cough came through the walls all night. The next morning Maud shook me awake. 'He's got a fever,' she said. 'Can you drive for the doctor?'

I was halfway to Naivasha when I recognised Dr Gregory's car coming in the opposite direction. I thought of how he'd lied to me, how he was providing Martha with heroin, and almost let him go past, but I knew Maud wouldn't forgive me if something happened while I was trying to find someone else.

I flagged him down. He wound down his window, grinning; I didn't return it. At least I didn't have to be friendly.

'Of course I'll come have a look,' he said, when I described my father's symptoms. 'How long has he been this way?'

'A few days, my sister says.'

He followed me back to the house and climbed the steps unhurriedly. Maud was waiting for us inside. She rose as soon as I opened the door.

'I met Dr Gregory on the road,' I said.

'Thank you for coming, doctor. Can I get you a drink?'

'Not for me, no.'

She rose. 'Then I'll show you to Father straight away.'

'Good idea.' Gregory rolled up his sleeves.

He was in with my father for half an hour and came out shaking his head. 'Where's your mother?'

'In Nairobi.'

'I think you'd better tell her to come home.'

The funeral was small and quiet, with fewer than ten of us there. The December sun was out, bleaching the sky around it from deep blue to light. A slight breeze had started up, and the ankles of my trousers flapped occasionally, sending cool gusts up my legs. I stared at the other graves, at the crumbling headstones closest to us. Out of the corner of my eye I caught the minister fidgeting, and a shadow passing over the ground. I looked up to see an eagle overhead, wings barely moving.

'Theo.' My mother was standing at the head of the grave; I'd almost forgotten where we were. 'Would you like to throw first?'

I stepped forwards. A shovel was sticking out of a pile of freshly turned earth, waiting for me. I grasped it, looking around at the few faces. My mother looked back opaquely. Maud smiled encouragingly. I scooped up a small amount of earth and tipped it into the hole. It hit the coffin below with an uneven thud.

'Now you, Maud,' my mother murmured and I handed over the shovel.

Afterwards, the other mourners shook our hands silently and left. We three turned away and began walking towards the cars parked outside the church.

I recognised Sylvie's car before I saw her. She was leaning against the bonnet wearing a black silk blouse and black trousers, carrying a bunch of lilies in her arms. Her hair was longer, but she still wore it piled on top of her head, showing off her long neck.

She came forwards to meet us. 'I'm so sorry for your loss,' she said.

'Thank you,' my mother said. She was fingering the locket around her neck, so Maud stepped forwards to take the flowers from Sylvie.

'They're beautiful,' she said.

'Can I drive anyone?' Sylvie asked.

'I haven't arranged for any food or drink,' my mother said. 'We should have given them something to eat, to thank them for coming.'

'It doesn't matter,' Maud said, looking across at me.

'You get in the car,' I said to her and my mother. 'I'll join you in a minute.'

Sylvie waited until they were out of sight before brushing my shoulder. 'If there's anything I can do—'

273

'What are you doing here?'

'I thought you might want to see a friendly face.'

'That's really it?'

'I don't know.' She squeezed my hand and I flinched involuntarily, before collecting myself. 'I suppose I need a friend too. I feel trapped. But I did come for you.'

'Why trapped?'

'Let's not talk about it.'

'No, let's. Distract me.'

She pursed her lips. It made her look young, and I wondered suddenly if that was why she did it. 'I miss looking forward to life. Now half of it's gone already, and I haven't done anything.' She gave a little sigh. 'Freddie's right – he's trying to make his life mean something. It can't all be cocktails and fucking.'

I heard a laugh escape me. 'You do know he's only out for himself, don't you?'

'Is he?' She looked at me out of the corner of her eye. 'Didn't they teach you Classics at school? No one can have everything they want – the gods don't let that happen.'

'Can I ask you a question?'

'Yes.'

'Was I always just a play-thing to you?'

'Theo –'

'I know you used me – both of you – and I'm sick of it.' An ice-like feeling had started in the base of my spine and spread upwards. I was dimly aware that I'd stepped forwards and Sylvie had stepped back, and my arms were either side of her, leaning against the car so she was pinned up against it, but I couldn't feel the metal underneath my palms, or her breath on my face. Her eyes widened.

'Stay away from me,' I said. 'I can't promise not to hurt you otherwise.'

'You wouldn't do that,' she said softly.

I turned my face away and looked out at the pale sky and the

274

fields in the distance, at the coffee workers picking red coffee cherries from their trees. From where I stood, the leaves on the branches were tinged with blue, and rippled in the breeze. The workers were faceless as they moved slowly through the avenues, tossing the cherries into sacks on the ground. It seemed fifty years ago that I'd lain in Freddie's Muthaiga bungalow and pictured the three of us together.

'People change,' I said.

The following Sunday my mother insisted on a family lunch at Kiboko.

'Your father would want us to be together,' she said.

Maud spent most of the morning with swollen eyes. Abdullah didn't say anything, but before lunch I saw him bring her a small brown paper parcel. She waited until he'd left the room to unwrap it, then sat with her head bent forwards, staring down at whatever was in her lap.

I went to sit next to her. 'What is it?'

'Father's pocket watch. The one the office in Edinburgh got him when we left.' She picked it up and opened the case, then stroked her thumb across the glass. 'Do you remember it broke soon after we got to Dar? Abdullah's mended it.'

'I didn't realise he knew how to do that.'

She looked up at me. 'Do you want it? Father would have given it to you, wouldn't he?'

'No.' I closed her fingers over the watch. 'You keep it.'

'Thank you,' she said quietly.

Lunch was silent, and I drifted off, toying with the good napkins laid out on the table.

Halfway through the meal my mother pushed back her chair and left the table without a word. Maud put her hand on my arm.

'Why don't we go for a drive?' she said.

'No thanks.'

'Do you want pudding?'

'No.'

'I suppose I shouldn't ask what the napkins did to deserve their fate either.'

I looked down at the stained and crumpled material in front of me. 'Sorry.'

'No – I don't know why I put them out.' She stood up. 'Let's just go to sleep early. Tomorrow will be easier.'

'Always optimistic, Spanish.'

'Someone has to be.'

'And you were right about Freddie – you've been smarter than me all along.'

'I'm not sure about that.' She rubbed her eyes. 'I couldn't understand what people saw in him, but then, I didn't really know the hardships the farmers were facing.'

'And now you do?'

'I do. Of course they were angry and inward-looking – and Freddie was promising them a fresh start.'

'That he never delivered.'

'Maybe that's for the best.' She shook her head. 'But I should have asked them how they felt.'

'Don't tell me you're –'

'Listening to people doesn't mean agreeing with them.' She bit her lip. 'They should be allowed to say what they think, that's all. And then they have to accept my right to criticise their views too.'

'Did Freddie do that?'

'Theo –'

'What?'

'Don't think about Freddie too much – it won't always be his world.'

I beckoned her over and pulled her onto my lap. 'You know I love you, don't you, Spanish?'

'Of course I do,' she said. She wrapped her arms around my

neck. 'I'm glad Father took the job out here. Even if it is hard sometimes.'

'Me too.'

'When the farm failed I felt as if I'd failed too. But, you know, there's no reason not to try again. There's so much I could do. And if it goes wrong – if it goes wrong for the hundredth time, I just need to go to my room and cry, and then start again.'

I squeezed her. 'You never give up, do you? So what's the new fight?'

'The ivory trade.' She tucked a strand of hair behind her ear. 'The totos showed me an elephant that was killed for its tusks last week. It was awful – that great, big creature dead, with blood all over its face where they'd sawn them off. And all for what? So people can show off their exotic piano keys and billiard balls?'

'Be careful, Spanish. People make a lot of money from ivory.'

'Then they can make money other ways. Organising tours of the parks. If people see how gentle and majestic they are, they wouldn't want to waste them any more. They're part of what makes Africa so beautiful.'

There was a noise behind us. Maud turned and smiled.

'Bulawayo,' she said. 'Don't you think Africa's beautiful?'

I twisted my head to look at him. He seemed even taller and firmer than when I'd last seen him. He didn't return her smile.

'Not for everyone, Mama,' he said. 'White people don't understand Africa.'

Chapter Twenty-Four

We crossed paths outside the Carlton Grill. It was a hot January night, and a blast hit me as I left the restaurant. I paused for a moment to choose between a nightcap at The Nairobi or the Muthaiga.

My shirt was clinging to my skin, and I tugged at my collar for air. Down the road I could hear restless dogs barking, and the peacocks screaming from the Jeevanjee Gardens. Through the heat came the smell of spices and grilled fat from the restaurant behind me, and a hint of roses from the couple who had just stepped out of a rickshaw in front of me. The smell made me think of Lucy, and then, as if thinking about her had conjured her up, there she was in front of me.

She was wearing a dark green skirt suit, with a double-breasted jacket, and her hair was pinned up, making her look much older than I remembered, but the swell of her belly and the glow to her skin lessened the overall severity.

The man she was with was tall, with prominent front teeth and ears. They were laughing and he had his arm around her shoulders. They were going to walk right into me, but at the last moment I stepped aside and they went past, not seeing me.

I watched her go. Freddie had cost me her, too, but the blame didn't lie wholly with him. It lay with me as well and my pathetic desire for acceptance. I'd used her and discarded her the way Sylvie had done to me. Even though she seemed happy I felt sticky with shame.

It was nine thirty when I reached the Muthaiga, even hotter than before, and the sky had a red tint to it. Gregory was sitting by himself at the bar, sipping whisky; he waved me over.

'Since when did you start coming here?' I asked him.

'Freddie sorted me a membership a few days ago. Grand, isn't it?'

'For services rendered, I suppose,' I said, turning away.

'Stay,' he said, catching my arm. 'We can have supper.'

'I've already eaten.'

'Sit with me anyway – I don't fancy going in there alone.' He finished his whisky.

I shrugged. 'Alright.'

We entered the dining room. Freddie was sitting at a table in the middle of the room. He was with June Carberry, who'd I'd met once or twice, a friendly bottle blonde with a long, sharp nose and hooded eyes. Some of the women called her a 'chorus girl' behind her back because of her clothes, but if she knew she didn't seem to care.

There were two others at the table. I guessed they were Ivy and Jim Brandon, more new arrivals. Jim was much older, with slicked-back dark hair that was greying around the edges, and a stiffly upright posture. Next to him, Ivy sparkled – all blonde hair and jewels and very red lips. Both men at the table were staring at her as she talked. Most people in the room were too.

'Beautiful, isn't she?' Gregory said as we sat down. He caught the waiter's eye. 'I'll have the cured salmon in honey mustard with toast, then the beef tenderloin.'

'And to drink?'

'A champagne cocktail for me.'

'For me too,' I said. 'Nothing to eat.'

'Very good.'

'God, I like it here,' Gregory said, then nudged me, nodding in the direction of Freddie's table. 'Something's up.'

Brandon was standing awkwardly, glass raised. 'To Ivy and Freddie,' he said loudly, so the words carried across the room to us. 'I want to stress that there are no hard feelings, and I wish them only the very best together. To Ivy and Freddie.'

The rest of the room was quieter now, and the other members of his table were completely still. After a moment or two Freddie raised his glass and the rest of the table followed suit. I played with the knife in front of me. So he'd moved on to someone else. Sylvie had moved on too. It was only me who'd been left behind. And Martha, I supposed, and felt a pang of sympathy for her. She must have realised by now that Freddie had used her.

Brandon sat down again and the room returned to normal. Gregory tapped my hand. 'The Brandons have only been married two months,' he said. 'You'd think he'd put up more of a fight.'

'Freddie always gets what he wants in the end.'

'Lucky bugger.'

I shrugged, trying not to let him ruin my night too.

Gregory's salmon arrived, and the cocktails. We clinked glasses.

'I'm sorry about your father,' he said. 'There wasn't much I could do by the time you called me in.'

'Could you have saved him if it had been earlier?'

'I might. I'm actually a damn good doctor. Top of my year at Trinity.'

'How come you're out here, and not in Harley Street?'

'No contacts. Rich people like their doctors famous, not academic. Deplorable. But there it is.' He smeared the mustard over the toast and took a bite. 'Thank you, for sitting with me.'

'My pleasure.'

'I hate eating by myself, don't you?'

'I quite like it.'

'I suppose you're one of those silent handsome types. Still waters, and all that.'

I sipped my cocktail. 'And what type are you?'

'Normal.' He took another bite of toast. 'Dependable. Women don't seem to be drawn to that, sadly.'

I'd been purposely avoiding looking over at the foursome, but now they all stood up and started moving towards the door. Freddie and Ivy were holding hands, Brandon trailing after them with a slight limp. The expression on his face made me turn away.

'We're going to the Clairmont,' Freddie said to June as they passed within earshot. 'Take the old boy home.'

Brandon flushed helplessly. June linked her arm through his. 'Come on, Jimski,' she said. 'We'll go to the bar first.'

They left. I signalled the waiter and asked for another cocktail, desperate to drink away the scene we'd just witnessed.

'How are things with you?' Gregory asked. 'How's your sister?'

I tried to calm myself. 'She's having to sell the farmland.'

He looked sympathetic. 'It was brave to try it in the first place.'

'I don't know if she feels brave right now.'

'I suppose not.'

I tried to muster some conversation of my own. 'How are *you*, anyway?'

'Not too good either.' He pushed his plate away. 'Just one of those weeks. I know I've got to toughen up a bit – you can't save everyone, and all that.'

My cocktail arrived. I drank it quickly and ordered another. 'Who was it?'

Gregory stared at me. 'Didn't you know?'

'Know what?'

He leaned forwards and took my arm. 'It's Martha. She died a few days ago.'

'What?'

He closed his eyes. 'It was pretty awful. She was completely covered in abscesses by the end, and the whole house stank of

281

vomit.' He opened his eyes. 'She was obsessed with the idea that no one would come to her funeral. She kept making me promise to attend. I think she knew what was happening.'

I disentangled my arm but he didn't seem to notice; he kept staring at me earnestly.

'Where was Freddie?'

'Not there.'

'Of course he wasn't.'

Gregory blinked nervously. 'It can be hard, living with an addict,' he said. 'Freddie tried to make her as comfortable as possible.'

I laughed. 'Is that what he told you?'

'Why?'

'You know, she wasn't always an addict, doctor.' The rage that had been simmering inside me threatened to boil over. Freddie was going to get away with it. He'd driven Martha to her death, and there would be no consequences at all for him.

'Are you alright?'

'Excuse me. I need to go lie down.'

I circled the house, then crouched in the bushes where I knew the neighbours wouldn't be able to see me. It wasn't a comfortable spot – the ground was hard and cracked. Every time I shifted I sent up a spray of dust that the wind blew back into my throat and eyes. Cicadas were chirping all around me, and I had to strain to hear the sound of the road. After a few minutes I sat down against a tree. Above me in the sky, I picked out the Southern Cross, glowing against the blackness. It was Freddie who'd taught me about the stars.

He arrived two hours later, when the lights in the surrounding houses had already gone out.

I heard a car door slam, footsteps along the gravel, and the front door open and close. Then lights came streaming out, puddling in squares on the grass. I waited for a moment then got up and walked to the centre of the lawn where I knew I'd be seen.

He opened the back door and stood for a moment in the doorway. The alcohol was making my head feel heavy, and I was suddenly aware of how ridiculous my position was. Freddie could call the police at any moment and I'd be charged with trespassing. I wanted to say something reassuring, but my throat seemed to have seized up.

Eventually he stepped back into the room, leaving the door open. I followed him in, shutting it behind me.

'It's melodramatic,' he said. 'But effective.'

I leaned against the door, feeling foolish. 'What do you think I'm here for?'

'I really couldn't say. I thought you'd dropped me as a friend.'

'Can you blame me?'

'I said I was sorry.' He looked at me and smiled. 'Look, Theo, is this going to take long? I've got work tomorrow.'

'Of course. Your important work.'

He was quiet for a moment. 'I'm not just in politics for my ego, you know. I really want to help our community, our producers.'

'Very noble of you.'

'Farming is bloody hard work. Maud knows that now. And sometimes it's more trouble than it's worth.'

'Some farmers have the money to keep going when the crops fail.'

He looked angry. 'You don't know what it was like for me.'

'No?'

'When they fail for the fifth year in a row,' he said, 'and the money's disappearing, and the servants are lazy and you're dragged into some ridiculous case of a miscarriage being the result of "black magic", rather than just a medical complication . . .' He shrugged. 'It gets hard to remember why we're here in the first place, me as well.'

'Why don't you go back then?'

'Because I'm a gentleman. I've been educated to expect a certain way of life that doesn't exist at home any more.' He turned away and walked over to the sofa. 'Out here there's still a semblance of paternalism on our part, and deference on theirs.'

There was something so naked and unapologetic about his selfishness that I almost admired it. 'Your sort only thinks of people in terms of their use to you.'

He shrugged again.

'You admit it, don't you, that you used me?'

'It didn't hurt you.'

'And Martha? It didn't hurt her, either? Gregory told me how she died.'

'I didn't force the drugs on her,' he said. 'Kiki did that for me.'

I came towards him. I could smell pomade and sweat and leather. 'You didn't try to stop it, either. It suited you to have her like that.'

He raised an eyebrow. 'She was certainly a trial by the end. Although she taught me I had to make a name for myself – I should thank her for that. Not that it wasn't already in me, but she brought it out. Edie would never have thought to push me in that way.'

'Is it that important?'

'Of course it is. I'm not going to be just another goddamned nobody, like Delamere, marrying a few silly women and kow-towing to the Maasai. I've got to *be* somebody, Theo. I've got to make my mark. My rank demands it, if nothing else.'

'D was your friend.'

He laughed. I'd never found his laugh grating before, but now I felt it along my spine.

'You don't get it,' he said.

'Because I'm not a gentleman?'

'Exactly.' He shifted impatiently from one foot to another. 'We're just different people, Theo. I'm sorry.'

I closed my eyes. I tried to remember Freddie when I first met him, charming my parents and sharing a moment with me and Wiley Scot before the races. The way the other men listened to what he had to say, how funny he was. His defending me against Carberry. I'd thought we were friends, that I knew and understood him, that I could grow up to be like him. I'd wanted that so desperately I'd let him come between me and Lucy, and even me and Maud for a while. I'd let him ruin my father's plans for his legacy. I'd let him dictate my life, and it was suddenly too much to bear. And now I had to live with the guilt of making Martha worse, killing her even.

'Let me give you a tip,' he said. 'Forget Martha. You think too small, young man. What does she matter in the long run?'

I opened my eyes and almost recoiled. I could see every little detail on Freddie's face: the pores around his nose, the individual strands of his hair. His smile was mocking. I didn't know how I'd ever found it appealing. His eyes were puffy, too, and the skin underneath them was bruised, as if from countless sleepless nights. He stuck his hands in his pockets and blew out his cheeks, as if he was bored of our conversation.

'You know —' he said.

My arm moved as if by itself. It wasn't easy to aim when we were so close and I misjudged and caught him on his shoulder.

Freddie stepped back, his expression surprised. My ears were still singing with blood. I barely heard the hiss of air as my fist sailed towards him again or the soft thwack as it entered flesh. Then he was falling backwards; a spool of saliva joining his mouth to my knuckles. It stretched, glinting in the light like a spider's web, and I had a momentary thought that I could use it like a rope to pull him upright again, then it snapped and his head hit the coffee table.

There was silence again, filling the house like sand in an hourglass.

I tasted salt and metal, and wiped my mouth with the back of my hand. Tiny smears of red appeared on my skin and I rubbed them quickly onto my trousers. I breathed deeply, three times, trying to steady myself.

285

He was lying crumpled between the sofa and the coffee table, eyes open but not focused any more.

'Freddie?' I said, as quietly as I could.

Nothing.

I knelt beside him. 'Freddie? Are you alright?' I put my hand out to feel for a pulse and drew it back, then steeled myself and placed two fingers on his neck. Nothing moved underneath the skin. I pressed harder, desperate to find a flicker, but met only the hardness of his windpipe. I let out a cry, and immediately bit down on it. My heartbeat was so fast it was almost a hum. I couldn't look at him any longer. I took him by both wrists, hating the soft feel underneath my fingers, then manoeuvred him into a more natural sleeping position. As soon as his face was hidden, I felt better, and my heartbeat started to return to normal.

'Fuck,' I said.

It hit me suddenly that he was really dead. I stood up, but immediately felt myself falling and clung to the back of the sofa as if it were a life-raft, gently guiding myself down onto its seat instead. The body shifted as my feet came into contact with it and I imagined I could smell it, a hot, sweet smell, although it couldn't have started decaying already.

I had to get out of there, I told myself. Any of the neighbours might have heard the fall, might come checking to see if Freddie was alright. Except it was the middle of the night, and Freddie had barely made a sound. I tried to remember if we'd raised our voices at all, but my head was swimming and I couldn't think. I was afraid that someone was already outside, and could see the whole scene through the windows. I sprang up and ran to the light-switch, flicking it off. Moonlight flooded the room. I whipped around, checking each window for a face pressed up against the glass, but there was nothing.

I had to leave some time, though, and the sooner the better. *What about the body?* The body was evidence that Freddie hadn't died naturally. Or was it? He could have got drunk and fallen over.

286

I made my way to the drinks cabinet on the far wall. I seized one of the bottles and brought it back, then turned him over. In the darkness his skin seemed almost ghostly white. I crouched down and raised his limp head with one hand, trying not to acknowledge the stickiness beneath my fingers. With my other hand, I unscrewed the bottle and tipped most of the contents down his throat; I dribbled some onto his shirtfront as well to be thorough.

I returned the head to the floor and stood up. Freddie wasn't a big drinker. What if the police knew that?

I sat down again on the sofa. Something about this wasn't right; I didn't know what checks the police could do, but it didn't seem safe, leaving him there like that.

I put the open bottle on the coffee table. *Fire.* Fire would destroy all traces of my visit. It had to have happened naturally though; I looked over my shoulder at the open-plan kitchen at the other end of the room. I was in luck; Freddie had a gas oven.

I crossed the floor and turned on the gas. If enough built up, a spark from a cigarette could set it off, so that's what I'd do. If anything survived, it had to look as though Freddie had turned it on in a drunken haze, then forgotten about it. I went into the front of the cottage, keeping the lights off. My eyes had already adjusted, and I moved about easily. I opened Freddie's wardrobe, as if he'd come in to take off his clothes. Then I went into his bathroom and smeared some toothpaste on his toothbrush; I brushed my teeth for a moment, to work up a lather on the brush, then left it on the side of the sink, as if Freddie had been disturbed halfway through.

I went back into the main room, holding a handkerchief over my nose. I rumpled Freddie's shirt and hair at the front, and moved him back into the original position he'd fallen in. I searched his pockets and found his cigarette case and selected one. I didn't know if I'd left it long enough, if there was enough gas in the air to cause an explosion.

I was suddenly tired; I didn't have the energy or the will to go through with this. All I wanted was to be back at Kiboko with Maud. She was safe. I felt tears building up and pinched myself hard; I couldn't fall apart now. It doesn't matter if the gas has built up enough, I told myself. Leave, before you go mad, and go home.

Keeping the handkerchief in place, I checked underneath the sofa and behind the cushions to make sure I hadn't dropped anything. I crossed the room to the hallway door. Freddie had come home, got drunk, turned on the oven, maybe drank some more, then started getting ready for bed. While he was brushing his teeth he remembered what he was going to put in the oven. He came back into the sitting room, thought he'd have a cigarette while cooking and *boom*. He tried to run to the back door, tripped on the rug and fell, hitting his head on the coffee table.

I went back and turned over a corner of the rug to make a tripping hazard. Hopefully the fire would get rid of all of this anyway, but it didn't hurt to create a story.

I returned to the doorway. My fingers lingered over my lighter. Once I flicked the cigarette into the room, I reckoned I would have a second or two to sprint down the hall to the front door. I measured the distance with my eyes; I could do it.

I lit the cigarette, tossed it in the direction of the kitchen and ran for the front door.

My ears were ringing, and I felt, rather than heard the explosion. The floor seemed to tilt beneath me, then I was at the door, rattling the handle. It jammed. Sweat gathered at my temples and I thought for a moment I would have to bust it down with my shoulder, then I managed to wrench it open and spilled out.

I ran as quickly and as quietly as I could to the road. I turned in the direction of the Muthaiga, then stopped short. I couldn't risk picking up my car and being seen. I'd have to get back to Kiboko another way.

I started jogging in the direction of the edge of town. It was eerily quiet – no birds, no animals, no wind through the grass. I knew the milk boys would be along soon though. Then the sky would turn a silvery grey, as if the darkness were being drained away, and eventually pink and then blue. Everything was different, but life would go on.

Behind me the cottage was burning, although the fire hadn't spread to the front yet. If I looked over my shoulder I could just make out a faint glow on the air. I wondered if anyone had heard the boom. No lights had come on, as far as I could see.

I turned off the road and started to walk faster. I needed coffee and a bath, and to sleep for most of the day.

It took four hours to walk to the outskirts of Limuru Town, where I hitched a lift from a farmer. It was past quarter to eight when he dropped me at the end of the driveway. I slipped into the house quietly. Maud was already up and moving around in her bedroom; I got into bed fully dressed and fell asleep.

I woke a few hours later. I could hear Maud on the veranda, and another voice out there too, a woman's. They were both talking very quickly in hushed tones. I took a moment to steel myself. Sleep had done nothing to the pounding in my skull.

'I must have overdone it at the club last night,' I said, as I stepped out, 'I don't think I've felt this rotten for years.'

Maud and Edie looked up at me. Two untouched cups of tea sat on the table. Both their faces were white and drawn.

'Theo – Edie has bad news.'

'I wanted you to hear it from me,' Edie said, turning her cheek for my kiss. 'I know you haven't been speaking lately, but . . . And you might need to look after Sylvie.'

'What's happened?' I asked.

'It's Freddie,' she said, taking my hand. 'His cottage at Muthaiga caught fire last night.'

I squeezed her, feeling my heart pounding so fast it was almost a vibration inside me. 'How? When? Is he alright?'

She shook her head, and Maud let out a sob behind me. 'He's dead.'

I felt my legs give way beneath me.

Part Three
1937–1938

Chapter Twenty-Five

The city mortuary was a squat building in grey stone near The Nairobi Club. I hurriedly parked Maud's car outside. Behind the front door was a long corridor with a strong smell of formaldehyde clinging to the walls.

It was easy enough to find Sylvie. She was in a small room at the end of the corridor, standing up against the slab where a body lay stretched out. The room was tiled in white; a dirty-looking window high up in the wall let in grey light, and a single bulb hung low from the ceiling. There was a large ceramic basin in one corner, and an even stronger smell of formaldehyde, but no officials in sight. Sylvie was swaying gently with her eyes closed. She was dressed all in black – black silk blouse, black trousers, and a black hat with netting. Gwladys was there too, looking even puffier than usual. She scowled at me when she saw me come in.

I cleared my throat.

Sylvie opened her eyes and smiled at me. 'I knew you'd come.'

I hadn't seen her since my father's funeral, and my body trembled with suppressed rage. I wanted to wrap my hands around her throat and at the same time throw myself at her feet.

'How are you, darling?' I asked, kissing her forehead, then

moving to stand next to Gwladys. Just below my line of sight I was aware of a white mound, but I couldn't face it yet.

'Sad,' Sylvie said. 'But I suppose no one's ever enjoyed life as much as Freddie did.'

Gwladys sniffed.

'There was heart trouble in his family, you know,' Sylvie said, looking back down.

'They think he had a heart attack?' For a moment I wondered if I'd dreamed the whole night, and my body felt suddenly weightless.

'He fell trying to get away from the fire,' Gwladys said. 'That's what they're saying, anyway.'

'He could have had a heart attack first,' Sylvie said.

'I suppose so,' I said.

Gwladys narrowed her eyes at me. 'You know, I wasn't aware you and Freddie had made up. Just here to gloat?'

I shifted, smiling at her, then dug my heel into her toes. 'So sorry,' I said, shifting away again quickly. 'Am I standing on your foot?' Gwladys sneered at me, but she stayed silent, and I caught a flicker of unease underneath it all.

Sylvie caught my eye. 'How did you hear?'

'Edie told me.'

'Everyone loved Freddie.'

'Not everyone,' Gwladys said.

'He's still handsome,' Sylvie said. 'Don't you think, Theo?'

I looked down at the body properly for the first time. He was neatly arranged, arms tucked underneath the white sheet covering his body so that only his shoulders, neck and head were visible. He was still dressed, the green of his uniform matching the waxy green of his skin, and for a moment I wanted to loosen his collar, thinking it might be too tight for him. His head was propped up on a cinder block, and his eyes were closed. If not for his hair, which was far more tousled than he'd ever have allowed, he could have been asleep. There was still blood on his face, and dark stains around his ear. I felt my blood start to thrum in panic.

'I thought he was caught in a fire?'

'They managed to put it out pretty quickly,' Sylvie said. 'What happened here?' She reached out and touched my forehead where I'd scratched it waiting for Freddie in the bushes. My breath beat against my ribcage in response.

'I caught myself on a branch last night. I was a little the worse for wear.' If Freddie's body was this intact, would they be able to tell he'd died before the fire?

'Where were you drinking?'

'The Muthaiga.'

'Did you see Freddie?'

'We didn't speak. He was with the new couple; I was with Dr Gregory.'

Sylvie stayed quiet. She was looking at me from under her lashes and I was suddenly gripped by the fear that she knew I'd gone to the bungalow, that I was involved.

Gwladys looked at her watch. 'They said we could have half an hour.'

Sylvie leaned forwards to kiss Freddie's lips. 'Goodbye, my love,' she said.

The three of us left the mortuary, blinking as we stepped into the daylight. Nearby, a lone bird chattered to itself in a eucalyptus tree.

'I'll see you later?' Sylvie asked me.

I nodded. She squeezed my hand and wandered off. She hadn't asked me if I was upset. I felt an ache inside me for the fourteen-year-old boy who had first met her and Freddie, and another surge of anger against her.

Gwladys walked me to Maud's car and we leaned against it, facing the building we'd just left. I lit a cigarette and pulled hard on it, trying to disguise the bitter taste in my mouth. Gwladys's face was contorted, as if she was trying to decide which was more distasteful, talking to me, or withholding gossip.

'She was doing some strange things in there, before you showed up,' she said eventually.

'Such as?' If Sylvie had worked out that I was involved, could I trust her to keep it to herself? I imagined the police arriving with serious expressions and handcuffs, and my body flooded with adrenalin and shame.

'She kissed Freddie.'

'That doesn't sound so strange.'

'It was the way she did it. I heard her say something too.'

'What?'

'*Now you're mine forever.*' She looked sly. 'Something's off with the whole picture.'

For a moment I thought my knees were going to give way. The last thing I needed was Gwladys poking around, trying to stir up the rumour that there was foul play involved.

'I think you're reading too much into it.'

Gwladys shrugged.

'Anyway, I need to get back to work.'

The sun was out, and fluffy white clouds scudded across a deep blue sky, but I drove back to the office in a cold sweat. At the top of the stairs I paused to take a breath, and experienced a curious sensation, as if my brain had slipped down to the back of my skull, and the rest of my head was trying to follow it. I felt myself swaying slightly, and grabbed hold of the banister. I stayed like that for a few moments before I was able to walk in a straight line again.

Maud was sitting in one of the chairs across from my desk. She turned her head when I entered my office and smiled at me.

'Edie gave me a lift,' she said. 'I needed to come into town anyway and I thought I should check on you. You left so quickly after she told us the news.'

'I was in shock, I suppose.' I dropped a kiss on her forehead. 'I've seen him at the mortuary now. He's really gone.'

'It's so sad. Did you see Sylvie?'

296

'Yes.' I shook my head, as if to clear it. 'What did you need to do in town?'

'Speak to someone in Legco about poaching.'

'How's that going?'

'Slowly. No one seems to want to talk about a ban.'

'I told you.' I sat down in my chair.

There was a knock on the door and my secretary put her head around it.

'Some policemen are here to see you, sir,' she said.

Maud looked up at her then quickly back down.

'Show them in.' She backed out, and I cleared my throat. 'They probably want to question everyone connected to Freddie's death.'

'Are you connected?'

'I was at the Muthaiga last night.'

'Are you alright?' Maud asked. 'It's just routine, isn't it?'

I felt my stomach tighten. 'They might think I was back rather late.'

'When did you get back?'

'You didn't hear me come in?'

'No – was I awake?'

'Yes.'

Maud bit her lip. 'When did he die?'

'Just before three.'

There was a knock on the door, and two men came in. One of them, slightly older, with a square jaw and bushy eyebrows, introduced himself as Assistant Inspector Arthur Phillips.

'I've been talking to the neighbours,' he said. 'And I have a few follow-up questions for you regarding the night of Lord Hamilton's death.'

'I'll help if I can,' I said. I'd expected to feel terrified, but now they were standing in front of me, I felt a kind of euphoria. 'Sit down. Can I offer you a drink?'

'Thank you,' Phillips said, pulling out a chair. 'A whisky would be fine.'

Maud poured him a glass and silently offered one to his partner, a younger man with a short ginger moustache and a shiny forehead. He shook his head and remained standing.

Phillips took out a notebook. 'Are you sure you want to stay, Miss?'

'If it's fine with my brother.'

I nodded.

Phillips shrugged. 'Firstly, then, can you confirm how you spent the evening?'

I crossed my legs and clasped my knee with my hands. 'Of course. I ate alone at the Carlton Grill.' My voice was calm, measured.

'Can anyone corroborate that?'

'The waiters. And I saw Lucy . . .' Phillips looked up from his notebook. 'I don't know her married name. She was Lucy Cartwright before.'

'You spoke to Lucy?' Maud asked.

'No, she didn't see me. But I was leaving as she went in.'

'Carry on,' Phillips said.

'Then I took a rickshaw to the Muthaiga. I ran into Dr Gregory there, and sat with him while he ate.'

'Very good.'

'Afterwards, I'm not sure . . .' I lowered my gaze, 'I'd had a lot to drink.'

'Can you tell me what time you left the Muthaiga?'

'I don't know.' I poured myself a glass of whisky too. 'Can you tell me why exactly you're asking this? I thought Lord Hamilton died in a fire.'

Phillips flicked back a few pages in his notebook. 'A neighbour has testified that he saw someone matching your description enter the property a few hours before Lord Hamilton came home. He didn't see when you left.'

I felt, rather than heard, Maud's sharp intake of breath. I had a feeling Phillips noticed it too.

I pulled an embarrassed face. 'That's right. I went to see if he was in.'

'He wasn't?'

'No. I circled the house and looked through the back windows but all the lights were off. So I left.'

'Straight away?'

'Yes. The neighbour must have missed me.' I gave him a regretful smile.

'What did you want to talk to Lord Hamilton about?'

I took a sip of my drink. My hands were cool with sweat and I held the glass tight in case it slipped. 'I wanted to give him my condolences. His wife died a few days ago.'

'Were you close to his wife?'

I wondered if he knew about the heroin. My mouth was dry, despite the whisky, and when I spoke next my voice shook.

'Not particularly. I used to go to dinner parties at theirs. And I felt sorry for her, of course. She was very ill.'

Phillips looked apologetically at Maud. 'Sorry you have to hear this, Miss Miller.'

'I'm alright, Inspector.'

'Well . . .' Phillips cleared his throat. 'Did you see Lord Hamilton on the road?'

'No. I went straight back home.'

'When did you get back?'

'It was still dark.'

'How did you get back?'

'I hitched a lift. I didn't catch his name, and I can't remember exactly where he picked me up.' Phillips raised an eyebrow. 'I think I've mentioned already I'd had a lot to drink.'

'Can anyone say what time you got in?' He looked at Maud. 'Were you there, Miss?'

'Yes.'

'Do you remember what time your brother got in?'

She put her hands on the desk. 'I do remember. He woke me up, crashing into the furniture.'

I ducked my head, trying to control my breathing.

'It can't have been later than three o'clock.' Maud said. 'In fact it was quarter to three. I remember checking my watch.'

Phillips glanced back at his partner, who nodded. I didn't look at Maud.

'That certainly seems to check out,' Phillips said, standing up. 'We'll keep in touch if we need to follow up on anything.' He made a half-bow to Maud. 'Thank you for the drink.'

I watched out the window as they crossed the street to their car. They looked back up at the building at the same time. I waved. It felt obviously false and they didn't wave back.

'I'm glad that's over,' Maud said, straightening her skirt.

I came back to the desk and put a hand on her arm. 'Thank you.'

She looked away. 'Why did you go there?'

'To talk to him. I did in fact – he came home before I left.'

'Theo –'

'No one saw us together. It was deserted.' I left my chair and knelt in front of her. 'I'm so sorry, darling.'

She picked a piece of lint off my shirt. 'Will I have to lie in court?'

'No, I promise.'

I caught her gaze and held it. The thought came to me that this could all be over if I told the truth. But no one would understand why I'd done it. Not even Maud.

She gave me a half-smile. 'I suppose I should go meet this representative now.'

Chapter Twenty-Six

I heard from Edie that she'd given a statement to the police the day after Phillips visited me.

'As if anyone would want to kill Freddie,' she said. We were standing together in the post office queue. She pulled a sympathetic face. 'I suppose some people resented him. But when it's obviously an accident, to try to make it into *murder* . . .'

'What did you say to Phillips?'

She grinned. 'I'm afraid he was rather shocked by my outfit, or lack of it.'

I raised one eyebrow.

'High heels, of course,' she said. 'And a cigarette holder. Otherwise nothing.'

The ears of the man in front of us turned a deep red. 'You're very cruel, Edie,' I said.

She laughed. 'I had to have some fun with him. I was furious.'

'Why?'

'How dare he come to my house, grubby little man.' She patted her hair. 'It's all so sordid, the whole thing, and I don't want it to . . . *get in* to everything.'

'He's only doing his job.'

'Oh, you're so composed all the time.' A grille opened up and she squeezed my arm and sashayed forwards.

Despite what Edie thought, I was far from composed. I was already seeing policemen in every shadow, and jumping every time the telephone rang. The inquest was set for seven days after the fire, and time seemed to split the closer it got. Each minute seemed to drag, while each day sped past, carrying me onward to the verdict.

On the morning of the inquest I woke after a long, disturbed night. My hair was plastered to my skull, and my eyeballs felt sunken in their sockets. My suit was hanging up in the corner of the room. I looked over at it, remembering the time I'd gone through Freddie's clothes in his bungalow. I could have laughed at how hopeful I'd been back then, how naïve.

I thought about staying in bed all day, but it was better to get it over and done with, to know rather than remain in the dark. I called down for coffee and rolls, then got up and washed and headed to the Muthaiga.

June Carberry was at the bar, looking hot and annoyed. My skin turned cold when I remembered she'd had supper with Freddie at the Muthaiga that night, and I wondered whether he'd seen me, if he'd mentioned our falling out. Maybe I hadn't managed to hide my anger when they'd walked past, maybe June knew I had a motive. I wouldn't have put it past Freddie to have laughed about me to the others, how personally I'd taken it when he used me in front of Legco.

I cocked my head at her and she nodded and came to join me at my table. 'Exciting, isn't it?' she said.

'If you say so. Drink?'

She nodded.

I signalled a waiter and ordered two brandies with soda, then signed the chit. She lit a cigarette.

'How come we haven't done this before?' she asked, as if there was more to our meeting than chance. Her voice was husky from the smoke.

'I try to avoid your husband.'

'Why?'

'He tried to kill my dog.'

'He did?' She laughed. 'Well, bastards will be bastards.'

'So you know what he is.'

She nodded. She was still smiling.

'It doesn't bother you?'

'Nothing bothers me, honey,' she said.

I believed her.

'How did you meet?'

Our drinks arrived, and she took a long gulp. 'In a club, I think. He picked me up – I was only seventeen, you know, and I wanted an adventure. We got married almost straight away, and then he brought me here.'

I looked at my cocktail. So she'd only been a little older than I'd been when I'd first arrived. Carberry must have held the same appeal for her that Freddie and Sylvie had for me. The thought made me tired somehow, and I wished I could just lie down in the Muthaiga bar and go to sleep, forget everything that had happened.

'Do you ever wonder how different your life would have been if you hadn't married him?' I asked her.

'Never,' she said. 'You make your bed, don't you? It could have been worse. I could have ended up like Sylvie, for instance.'

'What do you mean?'

She leaned her elbows on the table. 'I mean, why is she pretending to have lost her marbles?'

'Is she?'

'Everyone else can see it even if you can't.' She took another gulp. 'Maybe she's not guilty, but she's doing a damn good impression of someone who is. Mood swings, jumpy, won't look anyone in the eye. Keeps quoting scripture.' She giggled.

I tapped my fingers on the glass before me. 'You think it wasn't an accident?'

'I think something happened that night.'

303

My pulse quickened. 'Why? Did Freddie say something?'

'Like what?'

'I don't know. Did he say he was meeting someone later?'

'No, nothing. It's just intuition.' She ducked her head and looked up at me with heavily kohled eyes. 'But what do I know?'

She couldn't have been more obviously flirting with me if she tried. My name must not have come up that night then, I thought, and felt a surge of relief.

'Another drink?' I said, mostly to steady my nerves.

'Alright,' she said, too quickly.

I signalled for fresh cocktails. June wriggled in her seat, looking pleased with herself. On the other hand, maybe she was toying with me. Maybe she was just attracted to violent men. My pulse, which had been starting to return to normal, sped up again.

'Better late than never,' she said suddenly.

'Pardon?'

'Us drinking together.'

'Oh. Yes.'

The waiter appeared with the brandies and we held up our glasses in a toast.

'To Freddie,' June said.

My skin crawled. She was grinning, and for a moment I felt like getting up and running out, but instead I fixed my face into a smile. 'To Freddie,' I said.

The building housing the courtroom was a pile of yellow stone and pillars. Inside, the decor was faux-Edwardian: dark wood panelling, with a glass dome in the ceiling and a muffled atmosphere. It was busy but not full. Sylvie arrived, still dressed in black, her hair in loose waves, and made her way around the gallery to where I was sitting next to Boy. The air in the courtroom was a strange red colour, giving her a fiery halo as she stood in front of us.

'Blood in the sky,' she said. 'It's for Freddie.'

'What are you talking about?' Boy asked.

She gripped the back of the seat in front of her and I knew it wasn't just a show, as June thought. I felt a rush of fear that she was going to out me. I held my breath. From outside came the muffled noise of cars. A fruit-seller went by with his wares, reciting them in a sing-song voice: pineapples, mangoes, guavas, bananas.

'It's his favourite time of day,' she said, and sat down.

Boy gave me a meaningful look.

The coroner appeared and proceedings began. They started slowly, with the coroner explaining what an inquest was in law, and how it differed from a trial. 'Most importantly,' he repeated more than once, 'it is a fact-finding inquiry, rather than deciding issues of blame or guilt.' His voice was high-pitched and grating, and I saw several spectators wince or cover smiles.

He went on to read out several statements – one describing the results of the autopsy and the injury sustained to Freddie's skull, one from Brandon describing their dinner at the Muthaiga, and one from Freddie's neighbour, who 'thought he had seen someone enter the garden of the deceased, and hadn't seen him leave'.

The room was warm and my throat was dry. I tried to swallow and found my body strangely unresponsive. I willed time forward. The coroner's voice was monotonous and he took long pauses to look through the papers in front of him.

'What're the odds it was an aggrieved husband?' Boy murmured to me during one of the pauses.

I tried to force a smile but I could feel how unnatural it was and my lips seemed to have stuck against my teeth.

The coroner must have heard people talking. He tilted his face up at us, pushed his glasses back up his nose and raised his eyebrows expectantly. I looked round the gallery – everyone else seemed bored, or asleep, but I could feel him building up to something. I slipped my hands into my trouser pockets so Boy wouldn't see them glistening with sweat. Then the coroner shrugged, looked away, and the moment was gone. He squeaked on for a few more minutes about the presence of alcohol in the deceased's system, the fact of his late wife's recent demise, and the unfortunate circumstance of the gas oven having been left on. My head swam in the heat. Finally he called out the verdict – accidental death. The investigation was closed.

I made my excuses and escaped to the corridor. The red-haired policeman who'd accompanied Phillips to my interview was standing outside the bathroom, scuffing his shoe.

'Verdict?' he asked.

'Accidental death.' I tried to smile; it was a little better than my earlier attempt.

'Must feel like a let-off.'

'What?'

He scratched his chin, grinning. 'Only joking. Besides – you had an alibi, didn't you?'

'My sister.'

His grin widened; it made him look even younger. 'Bit disappointing for us, of course. We always like to have a suspect on hand.'

I wondered how I was still upright. 'Sorry I couldn't oblige.'

'Never mind.' He stood aside to let me pass. 'Did you want to go in here?'

I made it to the toilet just in time before I was sick everywhere.

I drove back to Kiboko a few days later. Maud was having tea on the veranda when I arrived. She'd hung baskets of bougainvillea and honeysuckle up on the outside of the house, and the smell of it trailed through the air in wisps. I dropped a kiss on her forehead and sat down next to her.

'The coroner ruled it an accident,' I said. 'So you definitely won't have to testify in court.'

'Good,' she said. Her skin was clear and almost golden, but there

306

were dark circles under her eyes, and her mouth seemed slacker than before. I'd hoped to reassure her, but she still seemed weighed down, and it occurred to me that maybe she'd suspected me all along, and that was why she'd lied to the police. But I'd been afraid that Sylvie knew, and June, and even the coroner, and nothing had come of any of my fears; I was being paranoid, I told myself.

Still, I couldn't bear the thought that she might know what I was capable of, and cast around for a question to change the subject, in case she asked me more about that night, and in case I couldn't hide the truth from her any longer. 'How's the gardening going?'

'I haven't done much recently.'

'Why not?'

'I've been having these headaches,' she said, pressing her fingers to her temples. 'And I feel sick all the time.'

'You're not coming down with something, are you?'

'You could say that.' She picked up her teacup. 'I'm pregnant.'

I felt my fingers and toes smart with a rush of blood. 'What?'

She flashed me a half-smile. 'It's a bit of a surprise, I know.'

'Does Mother know?'

'I can't tell her.' She shook her head. 'She – you won't tell her either, will you?'

'Of course not. What are you going to do?'

'I'll hide it for as long as possible.' She leaned her elbows on the table. 'We've talked about my going somewhere else to have it, then bringing it home and saying it's Abdullah's sister's baby, and she died.'

'So you're going to keep it.'

'If you can call that keeping it.' She wiped her eye quickly with the heel of her palm. 'I don't want to pretend my baby is someone else's. I want to have it here in the house.'

'Maud –'

'I know. But Theo, it's my baby. I can feel it already in there, and I can't describe it . . .' She leaned back in her chair. 'I feel like a lioness, like I'd kill anyone who came near it.'

Abdullah appeared and started clearing away the tea things. A look passed between them, and they smiled at each other. It was so exclusive, so full of something that I couldn't recognise at first that I felt suddenly lost. All this time, I'd been following Freddie, wanting to be more like him, and he'd never been as happy as Maud seemed now.

Abdullah went back inside. Maud sighed.

'I want you to be happy for me, Theo,' she said. 'I'm proud to have his baby.' She placed a hand on her stomach and let her fingers flutter over it. 'There's no bad in him at all, do you know how rare that is?'

All I could think of now was Sylvie, doe-eyed and playing with the dogs, or brushing her hair in front of the mirror, curling up naked in bed with me. Sylvie in her dark moods, when the air seemed heavy; in her light moods when she laughed all night. Her generosity, secrets, backgammon, whisky sours, Sylvie being scolded by Noel for her carelessness, her smell, her hand slipping into mine. I'd never protected her, the way Maud and Abdullah did instinctively with each other. I'd always thought about the way she made me feel, not about her. I felt a gnawing pain inside. Maybe it hadn't just been her using me. Maybe we'd been as bad as each other.

I took Maud's hand and squeezed it. 'Very rare.'

Her eyes filled with tears. 'Thank you.'

'I think it'll be hard, but I think you'll do the right thing. You always do.'

She tried to pull a suspicious face. 'What have you done with my brother?'

'Oh, he's around here somewhere.' I stood up. 'Darling, there's someone I have to see. I'll be back for supper. You don't mind, do you?'

'Not if you're coming back.' She smiled at me, and I hugged her fiercely.

'I promise.'

I made it to The Farm in no time at all, still unsure of what I wanted to say to Sylvie. I climbed the steps and rang the bell with a nervousness in my stomach that reminded me of the first time I'd seen her.

'I'm glad you're here,' Noel said when she opened the door to me. 'She's feeling a little under the weather.'

'What's wrong?'

'It's the shock, I think.'

I crossed the house to the garden, where Sylvie was sitting in the sunshine, making a garland of flowers. She'd had the table moved from the terrace, as if to take breakfast on the lawn, but an untouched cup of coffee sat by her hand, and a plate of toast, with only a small bite missing. An unopened book was lying at her feet, and underneath the plate, I saw an unfinished letter.

'Darling,' I said, kissing her cheek, 'you need to keep your strength up.'

She lifted her face to the sun, closing her eyes. 'This is my food now.'

'You can't live on sunshine.'

'I could if I were a flower.' She opened her eyes again and let them travel around the flowerbeds. Her pupils were dilated. 'Look at all those colours,' she said dreamily, 'they're so *vivid*.'

'Beautiful.'

She turned back to her garland-making, humming. 'I wonder if it would be peaceful, being a flower.'

'Depends on the gardener, I suppose.' I pulled out a chair and sat opposite her, watching her fingers at work. 'May I have some coffee?'

'Help yourself. Just be quiet for a little while, will you?'

It was warm. I removed my jacket and hung it on the back of my chair, then stretched out my legs. Birds chattered from a nest in the terrace roof, their songs mingling with the sound of the river washing gently over stones and through reeds. All thoughts of prison cells, and the grey claustrophobia that came with them,

309

seemed ridiculous now. I poured myself some black coffee, took a sip and rested the cup on my stomach, breathing shallowly so as not to spill it.

'You must have good stomach muscles,' Sylvie said, not looking up.

'I suppose I do.'

'You're lucky you've never had children in there – they change your body.' She brushed a fallen rose petal from her lap. 'I used to have such a perfect figure . . . Never had to do anything with it.'

'You've forgotten I've seen it. It's perfect still.'

She smiled secretively.

'Have you finished your crown?'

'Yes.'

'Let me see it on.'

She placed it gingerly on her head. She seemed suddenly so young, so innocent, in spite of everything.

'Magnificent.'

'I must show Freddie,' she said.

For a moment I thought I'd misheard. 'You mean wear it to his grave?'

She looked at me as if I'd gone mad. 'He's not dead. He's only been gone a few weeks, and there's no actual fighting at the moment.'

'Where?'

'Egypt.'

'Sylvie – there was a fire. Freddie didn't make it out.'

'He's not dead, Theo.'

'We went to his funeral.'

She took another bite of the cold toast. 'You must have dreamt it. He joined up, and they've posted him out there. He writes to me.'

My head felt fuzzy. 'Do you have any of his letters?'

'He told me to burn them after I'd finished reading them – sometimes he writes things he shouldn't.'

310

'What does he say?'

'He talks about the war, when it's going to happen. He wishes he was back here with us.' She played with her crown. 'He didn't volunteer to go – they needed him.'

I tried to return her smile, but my face felt tight; his death had clearly pushed her over the edge. I looked down at the lawn, and for a moment I saw his limp body stretched out between us like an accusation.

We lapsed into silence. After a while, Noel came to the door and called to us. 'Minnie's had another accident, dear – shall I call the vet?'

'No.' Sylvie stood up. 'She hates the vet. I'll clean it up.'

'I can do it – you just finish your breakfast.'

'What's happening with Minnie?' I asked, when Noel had disappeared again.

'She's old.' She pressed her hand against her stomach. 'I can't bear it, seeing her suffer.'

'Poor darling.'

'Life can be so cruel sometimes.'

I had nothing to say to that.

Before I left I found Noel mopping the floor in the corner of the bathroom. She pulled a sympathetic face at me. 'She was in one of her odd moods, then?'

'How can you tell?'

'Your expression.' She got out her cigarette case. 'I don't think she really believes it – it's more that she's trying to talk herself into it.'

I hunted in my pockets for a matchbook, then lit her cigarette for her. She took a long drag and closed her eyes to exhale, her face relaxing. I realised she was cleverer than I'd given her credit for – but then I supposed running Sylvie's household would keep anyone on their toes.

'Can I ask you a question?' I said. 'What did you hear about Kenya before you came out to work for Sylvie? Back home, I mean.'

She laughed. 'They think we're the dissolute old guard out here, agents of our own downfall.'

I played with my matchbook, tapping it against the back of my hand. 'Freddie told me one time that he didn't belong there any more.'

'Why not?'

'He said it'd changed too quickly. He'd been raised with certain expectations and suddenly they were outdated.'

'I didn't think he could be so perceptive.'

'Was he right then?'

'Do I think the world is changing? Yes. And people like Freddie find it hard to change – why would they want to? They've had it so good for so long.'

'I suppose so.' I remembered his face as he fell, and blinked quickly to get rid of the image.

Noel stubbed out her cigarette. 'Anyway, I'm sure she'll get better. Just give her time.'

Chapter Twenty-Seven

Even though Maud's bump was barely showing, Abdullah made most of the trips into town to post letters and pick up fabric. Once or twice she asked me to deliver letters personally to companies in Nairobi, and once some copy to the *East African Standard* on the declining numbers of elephants in the Aberdare area. I read a paragraph that compared the white settlers to a plague wiping out indigenous species, and wasn't surprised when the newspaper refused to publish it.

She was more tired than usual, and more sensitive. The next weekend I stayed over we went down to the lake before breakfast. A fine mist lay across the water like a blanket, slowly rolling away with the sun. The air smelled mossy, as it always did after the rains.

Emmanuel, one of our totos, was coming back with the laundry.

'Don't tell me he's been washing the clothes in the mist,' I murmured.

'Good morning Mama, Bwana,' he said.

'Good morning,' Maud said. She stopped, and put her hand on his arm. 'Emmanuel, remind me I have Josephine's chapatti board.'

'You keep it, Mama.'

'No, please – it was kind of her to lend it. I'll get it for you today.'

Emmanuel shook his head. 'Better no, Mama.'

'What's wrong? Is she ill?'

'Mama, I don't see Josephine no more.'

'Why not?'

He shifted the laundry basket. 'She wouldn't give me sons. I have new wife now.'

He looked so serious I tried not to laugh.

'But, Emmanuel . . .' I glanced over at Maud and saw she was close to tears. 'What about your daughters?'

'They stay with Josephine. I don't see them either.'

'How do you think that will make them feel?'

'It's her fault, Mama. She know I need sons.'

Maud took a deep breath. 'Emmanuel, you mustn't – just because –' She stopped, and turned away.

'Go hang the laundry up,' I said.

'Yes, Bwana.'

He left, and I drew Maud towards me. Her shoulders were shaking.

I stroked her hair. 'So the natives get bored of their wives. Why are you so upset about it now?'

'Poor Josephine. It's not fair. And those poor girls.'

'That's life, Spanish.'

'Is it our fault? First we come and say we're in charge, behave like us, then the missionaries come and say God is the only thing that matters, make babies for God, and all the while white husbands are swapping wives and no one's any worse off for it.' She pulled away from me and rubbed her eyes with a clenched fist. 'And it's their culture, anyway. What right do I have to say ours is better?'

'So don't.'

'But the women, Theo. How can I just stand by and say nothing? This place –'

'What about it?'

'Sometimes it breaks my heart.'

314

'You can't save everyone, Spanish. Come on.' I dried her eyes with my handkerchief. 'Let's have breakfast.'

It was Edie who told me about Sylvie's overdose. I was in Naivasha, loading refilled paraffin bottles into the car, when she found me.

'How did it happen?' I asked.

'She took almost a whole bottle of pills.'

'I mean – how was it *allowed* to happen?'

'No one knew she'd try anything like this.'

I wanted to scream. 'Where is she now?'

'At Nairobi hospital.'

'When did she try?'

'Yesterday. Noel sent a note saying Sylvie couldn't come because she'd tried to kill herself, so I got a medical team from Gilgil and we drove over and they pumped her stomach. She kept saying sorry.' Edie's eyes filled up and she blinked. 'She was saying sorry to be such a nuisance, and I was saying sorry for saving her.'

'Why would you be sorry?'

'She wanted to go.' She rubbed her eyes with the heels of her palms. 'Goddamn it, I can't do it again, Theo.'

I drove to Nairobi at top speed. When I reached the hospital I smelled paraffin, and realised the bottles had smashed along the way.

My mother had once taken us to the Native Hospital when she'd been running an errand for Lady Joan; all I could remember was the cold and filth of the corridors, and the crowding in the wards, over two hundred beds in a very cramped space. The European hospital was small by comparison, only thirty-one beds, and the floors and linen were spotlessly clean. White doctors and nurses moved quickly through the corridors, their shoes squeaking on the linoleum.

Noel was waiting outside the room. She burst into tears when she saw me and buried her face in my chest. I let her cry for a moment, then moved her away, impatient to get to Sylvie.

'Is she awake?' I asked.

'Yes. You can go in if you want.'

Sylvie was sitting up in bed. She was wearing dark blue pyjamas and cherry-red lipstick. The collected works of Poe was open on her lap but she was looking out the window. She turned her face when I closed the door behind me and smiled at me.

'Hello, darling,' she said. 'You've heard about my accident then?'

'It's an accident now?' I crossed the room to her side and took her by both arms. 'Don't lie to me.'

'I'm not.'

I wanted to shake her. 'I saw Edie.'

'Oh.' Her smile widened.

'You said you wanted to go.'

'It was all the drugs talking – I took too many sleeping pills by mistake.' She shrugged off my hands.

I sat down on the bed and dropped my head into my hands. I could feel the sweat cooling around my hairline, and my heart slowly returning to normal. I could have cried with relief. Edie had made a mistake – Sylvie was fine, cheerful, even.

'You promise it was an accident?'

'Of course.'

I turned to look at her. 'You can't leave us.'

'And why not?'

'Because we want you around.' Her hands were lying on the bedcover, and I put my right over her left. 'Doesn't that make life worth living?'

'Silly boy.' Her voice was warm. 'Our life out here isn't real, is it?'

'That doesn't mean you can't carry on.'

'But what are you carrying on for?' She drew up her knees and hugged them to her chest. 'You can't understand it – you're not a woman. We have this thing inside us that makes us alive, it makes us love, it makes babies; it makes us special. But it doesn't last forever, not like the thing inside a man that makes him alive.

316

So we know at some point, when something isn't really living, it isn't real, it's best to let it go.'

'I don't understand what you're talking about.'

She closed her eyes. 'Freddie would know how to put it. Maybe I'll ask him to write it down in his next letter.'

I felt my heart sink. She opened her eyes and smiled at me. 'He always knows what to say, doesn't he?'

'He does.'

I kissed her hair, and she rested her cheek against my shoulder. 'I'm going to sleep now. Will you stay?'

'Try to keep me away.'

'Lie next to me then.'

She turned onto her right-hand side. I shifted to lie behind her, and fitted my body into her curves. I could feel her heartbeat; when she fell asleep I laid the back of my hand against her cheek where her eyelashes grazed it.

I kissed her hair. 'It's going to be alright,' I whispered, and she frowned in her sleep.

Noel left Nairobi early to prepare The Farm while I stayed on to collect Sylvie after she was discharged. The Matron and I stood over her as she sat on her bed, looking confused. The Matron had to repeat herself several times.

'Take these pills for the pain, and these ones if you're feeling sad. Not too many – they're not sweets, even if they are a pretty colour,' she said. 'Are you listening, dear?'

'Yes,' Sylvie murmured. She turned her eyes on me. They were even bigger than usual. 'I just want to sleep forever.'

'Everyone feels grotty after something like this. You're just the same as everyone else, remember that.'

She leaned on me as we walked out to the car and fell asleep before we'd reached the outskirts of the city. It was cool outside; I kept the windows rolled up so she wouldn't catch a chill and drove carefully, avoiding all the holes and bumps in the road. Once,

317

Sylvie murmured something in her sleep, but I couldn't understand it.

The eland was standing in the pyrethrum by the road when we turned into the drive. He raised his head and stared at us with his cow-like eyes. Sylvie woke with a start.

'You're getting so big now, my love,' she said. He blinked slowly at her.

Noel and the totos were standing in a semi-circle by the front door. I helped Sylvie out and she made a small curtsey.

'I love you all,' she called to them. 'And don't worry about me – Matron said I'll be fine.'

Noel came forward to support her on the other side, and we tottered indoors. We laid her down gently in her bed and a toto brought forward a tray of tea and toasted buns and hand-picked flowers.

'We'll keep the windows open, darling,' Noel said. 'Look at your wonderful garden – that's a nice view, isn't it?'

'Very nice,' Sylvie said, but she didn't move her head to look.

Chapter Twenty-Eight

In early May, three months before Maud was due, my mother found me in the Nairobi Club, reading on the sofa by the fireplace.

'Will you drive me up this weekend?' she asked. 'I haven't seen Maud for such a long time.'

I folded my newspaper. 'I wasn't going to go back this weekend.'

'Please, Theo. Otherwise I'll have to get Abdullah to pick me up.'

'Alright,' I said. She looked as if she was going to sit down next to me, so I stood up.

'I've got a few bits and pieces to go through for work,' I said. 'When shall I pick you up?'

'Three o'clock Friday outside the front here?'

'That sounds fine.'

I kissed her on the cheek and went upstairs to my room. I dashed off a letter for Maud, letting her know we were coming and when.

We could say you're ill, and confined to bed, I wrote, *although she might get suspicious.*

It rained heavily in the morning, and the drive down that Friday was slow, with hardly any other cars on the road other than an old Bentley driving slowly behind an African who walked ahead with a stick, checking for pot-holes in the puddles. Occasionally my mother asked me about work, but I was distracted, trying to come up with a plan as to how we could keep Maud's secret from her. Unless she'd already heard something; I couldn't remember the last time she'd visited Kiboko, and wondered why the sudden interest in seeing us.

The sun, when it appeared from behind the clouds, had a milky quality to it, and when I turned into the drive the lake seemed darker, more impenetrable in its light.

Maud was waiting for us in the sitting room. She seemed thinner and paler than before; even I could hardly tell she was pregnant. My mother kissed her, then held her face in her hands for what seemed like a long time.

'I'm going to wash and change,' she said eventually.

'Would you like tea?'

'Yes, I would.' She kissed Maud again, looked back at me with a strange expression, then left the room.

'How are you, Spanish?' I said when tea was laid out on the veranda.

'I've been better, I suppose,' she said, fumbling for her cup. 'I can't keep anything down. I thought it would go away after a while, but it's been getting worse.'

'I can hardly see a bump.'

'I wear a corset,' she said. She looked at the garden over the rim of her cup. 'I think some of the servants know. Joseph keeps making me special broths.'

I grinned at her. 'He's probably trying to turn it into a man – he did that for me.'

She smiled back. 'I hope it won't disappoint him too much if it's a girl.'

I took her hand in mine. 'Please move to Nairobi. You need proper doctors around you.'

She shook her head. Bulawayo came out and she withdrew her hand.

'Bulawayo, can you ask Joseph if we can have some sandwiches with the tea?' she asked him.

He leered at us.

'Did you hear?' I asked.

'Yes, Bwana.'

'So why aren't you following orders?'

He took a step forwards. 'You no better than us,' he said, and spat on the veranda floor.

I almost caught him, but he was too quick, and he disappeared inside.

'Leave him,' Maud said, putting her hand out as I went to follow him.

'He can't get away with that.'

'I know, it's awful. But they don't trust us any more.' She pushed a lock of hair out of her eye. 'Can you blame them? Even if we give them votes and representation, they'll never be equal in their own country.'

'You think Bulawayo is concerned with that?'

'He'd have to be blind not to be. We built all the social institutions, and we built them to serve us. We've embedded our interest in every fabric of society. The Africans started to realise this a long time ago.'

'What would you suggest?'

'I don't know.' She played with the sugar spoon.

'What's wrong? You always have a plan.'

She pulled a face. 'The last few months have been harder than I thought.'

'You're tired—'

'It's not that. Before, when I was fighting the politicians, at least some of them thought they were doing some good, even if I didn't agree with their methods. Now, talking to businesses . . .' She shrugged. 'They don't see the elephants as living beings. It's about money, everything else is secondary. How can I appeal to them?'

321

'Are you giving up?'

'How can I? The people in power won't just give it up volun-
tarily. It suits them to keep things this way. We have to fight for
change. Think of the suffragettes.'

I tried to meet her eye. 'You're not doing anything stupid, are
you, Spanish? Nothing dangerous?'

'Of course not.'

'Promise me.'

'Yes.' She pushed her chair back. 'I'll go ask for sandwiches
myself.'

My mother joined us a while later and watched Maud pick at
her food with a hard look on her face. After Maud excused herself
to go and lie down we moved into the sitting room in silence.

'Your sister isn't good at keeping secrets,' my mother said eventually.

'How can you tell?'

'It's making her ill.' She lay back against the sofa. 'What's
happened?'

'Nothing.'

'It can't be nothing.'

Clanging and singing came from the kitchen. Abdullah padded
around the house overseeing the cleaning with a worried look
on his face. 'I'd like a glass of wine, please,' I told him, and he
brought me one. I took a long sip.

'Where's Bulawayo?'

My mother looked up to Heaven. 'I saw him leave the
compound a while ago. He's too big for his boots, that boy.'

She screwed up her eyes. The fine lines around them bunched
up as she did, and I realised with a jolt that she was almost fifty
now. Apart from her hair, which had turned silver, and a loosening
of the skin on her neck, she could have passed for ten years
younger. 'What about you, Theo?'

'What about me?'

'You seem quiet too.'

322

I shrugged. 'I suppose Freddie's death affected me more than I thought.'

'My poor darling.' She put her hand on my knee. 'Sometimes I wonder what sort of a world we've exposed you to. Maybe we should go back to Scotland.'

'I'm twenty-six. We call that shutting the stable door after the horse has bolted.'

'I suppose you're right.' She rearranged her skirt. 'It feels strange to worry about Maud now – it always used to be you who kept me up at night.'

'I'm as healthy as an ox.'

'That's not what I'm talking about.'

'Then what?'

She paused. When she did speak her voice was quiet. 'You know, I didn't realise how much I'd love you until you were born. It's frightening, loving someone that much. I was completely fascinated. And then your sister came along – it's funny, you look so much like Percy, but I see him more in Maud. You're more like me.' She brushed my hair away from my forehead. 'That worries me too.'

'Why?'

'You inherited my temper.'

I shifted along the sofa to be closer to the fire, suddenly cold. 'If you're trying to tell me something, I don't understand it.'

'I know you think I was hard on you, as a child. That's why. I wanted to bring you up to be a good person, and I had to rein you in.'

'You're joking.'

'No.'

'Did you never think that you made it worse?'

'Look at you now, darling.'

I laughed once. 'Quite. Maud and I turned out differently because you treated us differently.'

She shook her head slowly. 'You were different anyway. Maud

323

was always easy, always happy. You were difficult. And I was so young.' She pressed the back of her hand against her cheek. 'It made me feel so guilty. And you cried all the time – sometimes I just left you crying, and went out for a walk. I couldn't bear how unhappy you were.'

I shook my head trying to get rid of the image. I was tired and felt almost like crying now, for my younger self, how abandoned I must have felt. Then Maud had come along, and loved me unquestioningly from the start.

'You two must look out for each other,' my mother said.

I found Sylvie sitting on the floor of the sitting room, Minnie sleeping in her lap. She didn't look up when I came in.

'Hello, darling,' she said. Her voice was even lower than usual.

'How are you doing?' I asked. 'Have you been outside today?'

She shook her head quickly.

'Yesterday?'

Another shake.

I knelt by her side. 'Tell you what,' I said, taking her chin in my fingers and turning it gently towards me. 'Why don't we go dancing? I'll take you to the 400 Club.'

She blinked. 'No.'

'What about a late supper? We can have bacon, eggs and beer, then go for a swim.'

She batted my hand away gently. 'I don't want to leave the house.'

I looked at her closely. Her lips were swollen, as they always were after bouts of crying. 'What's wrong?' I asked.

'I've done it.'

'Done what?'

'Killed her.'

'What are you talking about?'

She nodded at her lap; the dog was lying perfectly still.

I caught my breath. 'Minnie? Why?'

324

'She was so frightened all the time.' Her face almost crumpled but she held it together. 'She didn't know how to go on living, but her body wouldn't stop.'

I put my hand on Minnie's head; it was still warm to the touch. 'How did you do it?'

'I gave her Nembutal.' She took a deep breath. 'In some pâté. She licked it off my fingers . . . She was so trusting.' She picked up the little body and cradled it in her arms, crying properly now. 'I had to do it. You understand that, don't you?'

'The vet would have done the same.' I put my arm around her shoulder and after a moment she snuggled into me, smelling like peaches and salt. 'I'm sorry I wasn't here.'

Her sobs subsided after a while, and I kissed her hair. 'My poor darling. Where will you bury her?'

'Under the irises.'

'Do you want me to help?'

'Could you?' She kissed the top of Minnie's head.

We dug a small grave in the iris beds. The milky sun had given way to a soft, indistinct moon. Sylvie changed into a black cotton dress and stood at the head of the grave holding a candle. I gently heaped the earth back on top of the cold body. My hands were shaking and I was thankful for the darkness. Afterwards, the servants came forwards with glasses of wine and wrapped blankets around our shoulders as we stood on the lawn. Sylvie went without shoes. I saw her curl her toes into the grass and loved her for it.

'You know, I used to think they were dead people,' she said, nodding at the stars. 'I wonder what they look like close up.'

'Not as pretty.'

'Everything looks better from far away. Even Rupert. I can't think badly of him now that he's in England. Isn't that strange?'

I didn't want to think about Rupert. 'I wonder what our friends are doing right this moment.'

'Boy will be sitting on his veranda, drinking.' She slipped her hand in mine. 'Edie will be surrounded by admirers in some bar or club in Tiwi. Or maybe she'll be reading naked in her hammock.'

I looked over and saw she was smiling.

'Gwladys is reading romance novels in the sitting room,' I said. 'And Dr Gregory is busy saving the life of a young boy who stepped on a puff adder.' I took a sip of the wine.

'Freddie is writing me a letter from Egypt,' Sylvie said. 'In his tent, by candlelight. He'll be telling me about the food, and how awful it is. Tinned pork and beans every day. And about all the sand.'

'And Nolwen and Paola?'

'They'll be in bed, I hope.' She pulled the blanket around her shoulders with her free hand. 'But they'll be able to hear Paris outside – the cars, the pigeons on the rooftops. The music from the clubs.' She hummed a line from *Imagination*, quietly.

I tilted my face upwards. 'Funny to think that we're all under the same sky,' I said. 'It doesn't feel as if they're too far away.'

'The world's getting smaller all the time,' she said, knocking back her wine. 'Some day we'll be able to get from London to Nairobi in one afternoon.'

'Probably.'

She dropped my hand and started walking back towards the terrace. 'Then how will we pretend we're all so different?'

I started to follow her before I saw Noel at the window of her bedroom, beckoning to me.

'I'll be in in a minute,' I called. Sylvie lifted her arm in a wave without looking back.

I waited until she'd gone in before crossing the lawn to Noel. She opened her window a fraction.

'Can she hear us?' she asked.

'No.'

'I have to show you something.' She turned away from the window and rummaged around in the drawers of her dressing table. When she turned back her face had lost its colour underneath the sunburn.

'I found it under her pillow,' she said.

I looked down at the shiny black object in her hand.

'When?'

'The other day, when I was making up her bed. I don't know if she's noticed it's gone.'

The two of us peered down at it.

'It looks so small,' she said, then cleared her throat gently. 'Should I put it back?'

'No.' I knew it could be for burglars, or leopards, but I couldn't stop thinking about her sitting in her hospital bed, promising me she'd taken too many pills by accident. 'I'll keep it safe.'

Noel held out the gun and I wrapped it in my handkerchief. 'No one else knows?'

'No.'

I bit my lip. I hated the thought that she was suffering enough to—

'Well.' Noel looked around. 'I feel better with it out of here.'

'Me too,' I said, forcing a smile. 'See you soon.'

'You too.' She closed her window and pulled her curtains shut.

Chapter Twenty-Nine

I was woken by a gentle tapping on the door. I fumbled for the cord on the bedside lamp and snapped it on. The small golden pool lit up the contents of the bedside table: a half-drunk glass of water, a blunt pencil, an unread book of poetry and my alarm clock, showing three in the morning. The rest of the room was a fuzzy black.

The tapping came again. I threw off my sheet and hurried to the door. One of the porters was waiting outside with a letter on a silver tray.

'For Bwana,' he said.

I recognised Maud's handwriting at once. The note was short: *The baby's coming. Please get here as soon as you can.*

'Did someone bring this?' I asked the porter.

'He waiting outside in car.'

'Tell him I'll be right down.'

I closed the door, threw on a jumper and trousers and took the stairs two at a time.

Abdullah was waiting behind the wheel in the darkness outside. His eyes seemed whiter and rounder than usual.

'How is she?' I asked.

'She was crying when I left,' he said, his voice cracking.

'She needs a doctor.'

'She says no doctor.'

'I know someone. Take us to the Muthaiga first.'

Gregory's lights were still on when we pulled up. I ran up the garden path and pounded on the door. He came to it with his shirt half-unbuttoned and a toothbrush in his mouth, and looked at me warily.

'You're needed in Naivasha,' I said. 'Please can you come with me?'

He removed the toothbrush. 'I've been sitting with a patient for almost twelve hours—'

'It has to be you.' I took hold of his elbow. 'You can sleep in the car.'

He sighed. 'Let me get my coat and bag.'

He disappeared for what seemed like hours, then reappeared looking more presentable, if no more awake.

'What's the problem?' he asked, as I led him back to the car.

'My sister's having a baby.'

'I see.'

Abdullah opened the doors for us and we climbed into the back. He got into the front seat and started the engine. His shoulders were high and I could see the muscles at the back of his neck straining. Gregory looked at Abdullah as the car jolted forwards, then at me and quickly away again.

'I know we can count on your discretion,' I said.

After a while, Gregory bundled up his coat to use as a pillow, and fell asleep. I stared out of the window feeling sick. Abdullah was driving faster than I knew was possible. The trees were a blur and I could hear pebbles clattering into their trunks. A ditch ran alongside the road – once or twice we veered close to it and I felt my stomach drop and pressed my back against the seat.

The sky was lightening by the time we reached Kiboko. Abdullah braked sharply outside the house and Gregory opened his eyes.

'We're here, then?' he said.

'Yes.'

'Show me the patient.'

Inside, the house felt still, the air thick. African women moved quietly in and out of the rooms with bowls of water, some of them stained red. The smell reminded me of that night in Freddie's bungalow, and I paused on the threshold, my feet suddenly heavy.

'Is she in the back?' Gregory asked.

I nodded.

'You stay out here. You won't want to see this.' He stopped one of the women. 'You, come with me. Everyone else out.'

The women gathered up the bowls and rags and left just as quietly. Gregory disappeared into Maud's room. For a moment I heard her voice, asking where I was, and his reply, then the door shut.

Abdullah stood in the middle of the room rocking back and forth on his heels, his face turned towards the back of the house.

'Sit,' I said, and we both perched on the edge of the sofa. I tried not to think of what was happening in there, all the blood.

'Drink?' I asked. 'I think we need one.'

'No thank you, Bwana.'

'I'll have one, then.' He stood to fetch it for me, but I waved him down and made my way to the sideboard. My hands shook as I poured out the whisky.

Maud's cry came from the back of the house, followed by Gregory's voice, low and muffled. I tossed back my drink and made myself another. I came back to the sofa, shivering.

'Where are all the totos? They've normally lit the fire by now.'

'I tell them not to come today,' Abdullah said. He moved to the fireplace and began piling up the logs.

Another cry floated out to us. It seemed to end on a whimper, and I felt my hands ball into fists. 'I hate the waiting,' I said, and felt my throat close up around the words.

Abdullah carried on positioning logs, his back stiff.

Gregory came out, wiping his hands on a rag. 'She's almost

330

fully dilated,' he said. 'It won't be long now. Good – you're building a fire. They'll both need to be kept warm afterwards.' He didn't meet my eye, and I stopped him as he turned to go.

'Will she be alright?'

'She'll be fine.'

After that things seemed to happen in a blur. I was dimly aware that Abdullah got the fire going, and began boiling more rags. From time to time the woman in with Gregory and Maud came out with a bowl of bloody water that she tipped away outside. Maud's voice came through the walls occasionally, and Gregory's too, then suddenly there was a third, higher-pitched and louder, piercing the air for a few seconds before stopping short.

Gregory appeared again in the doorway. 'It's a boy,' he said, running his hands through his hair. 'He looks pretty healthy to me.'

I blinked, feeling the shame and relief of the tears building behind my eyelids, and turned my face away. 'Thank you,' I said.

Abdullah was standing near the fire. 'Thank you, Bwana,' he said.

Gregory wouldn't look at him. 'You can go in to see her,' he said.

I went in first while Abdullah fetched more rags. Maud was propped up in bed holding a bundle in her arms. She smiled when she saw me.

'He's beautiful, isn't he?' she said.

I peered down. I hadn't expected much but Maud was right. He was a faintly waxy grey, but his skin looked soft and he was chubby, with a full head of black hair, dimples in his cheeks and large, brown eyes that seemed to recognise me.

'Look at our boy,' Maud said.

I turned. Abdullah was in the doorway, his eyes full of tears. Maud passed me the bundle and I handed him over silently. Abdullah kissed his nose and fingertips. Maud lay back, shining.

'Josephine, can you ask the doctor if he needs to rest, or eat?' she said.

331

I hadn't noticed the woman in the corner before. She came over to Maud and smoothed the hair away from her face then took her hand. 'Yes, Bibi,' she said. 'You need sleep, Bibi.'

'I can't,' Maud said.

'I look after baby.'

Maud squeezed her hand and Josephine left.

I crossed the room and kissed her on her forehead. 'Well done,' I said. 'I'm proud of you.'

'I didn't think I could be this happy,' she said, looking up at me. There were smudges around her eyes.

'Josephine's right – you need sleep.'

'Don't fuss.'

'Are you warm enough?'

'Maybe another blanket. It's in my wardrobe.'

I opened the wardrobe door and retrieved the thick blue blanket Sylvie had given us one Christmas from the top shelf. A folded sheet of paper drifted out with it, and fluttered to the floor. I couldn't make out the writing on the inside, but I could clearly see the outline of a company stamp, with a crown in the middle, in the bottom left corner.

'Don't look at that,' Maud said sharply.

'Something important?'

'Something private.'

I thought I caught her and Abdullah exchanging a look. 'I won't.' I picked up the letter and replaced it in the wardrobe, suddenly feeling redundant. 'I'll drop Gregory back if he doesn't want to stay.'

'You'll be back soon though, won't you?' Maud said.

'Yes.' I covered her with the blanket and kissed her again. 'What are you going to do about Mother?'

'I can't think about that now.'

'Of course not. What about a name? Have you thought about that?'

'We thought Solomon.'

'I like it.'

'Good.' She smiled.

I nodded to Abdullah, who nodded back, and left the room. Gregory's head was resting on the back of the sofa, chin tilted upwards. He started when I spoke, and stood up.

'Shall I drive you back? Or do you want to spend the night here?'

'I should go back,' he said.

'Thank you. Again.'

'It's my job.'

'Maud seems well.'

'She's very brave.'

I stuck my hand out, and he shook it awkwardly.

Over the next few months I took whatever chance I could to get back to Kiboko. Being with Maud and Solly made everything else fade into the background, even thoughts of Freddie and that night. It got harder to visit as the threat of war loomed, however, and I was caught up in work, planning the transportation of munitions and inspecting the stations and trains for blackout potential.

'Now the Italians are occupying Abyssinia they keep arming the Mandera and Moyale to raid our side of the border,' Boy told me at the Muthaiga one evening. 'We'll have Abyssinian refugees coming out of our ears soon.'

'I heard.'

'They're threatening to close the wells to our tribes in revenge for us harbouring anyone who manages to make it away. But what are we supposed to do with the poor buggers? Leave 'em to be slaughtered?'

'I can't imagine Legco are happy about all the extra mouths. Food's scarce enough.'

Boy pulled a face. 'That's Legco – they think of everyone in terms of what they consume, or the space they take up in the hospitals and schools. They can't just exist as a human being.'

I grinned at him. 'Have you always been this compassionate?'

'It's the bloody children,' he said. 'You find them wandering around, half-mad from what they've seen. There's something wrong with you if it doesn't break your heart. And they've got nowhere to go. At least we get to leave.'

'What are you thinking?'

'Getting out, staying put. Can't make up my mind. Another drink?'

He came back from the bar with a man I hadn't met before; the newcomer was short and fat, with ginger hair and moustache and a big smile.

'Mr Miller,' he said, shaking my hand enthusiastically. 'My name's Sullivan. I've had the pleasure of meeting your sister.'

'Are you in politics?'

'Nothing so exciting.' He looked deprecating. 'I work for a little export company. She's been stepping on quite a few toes, you know. But it's hard to be angry with someone so charming.' He beamed at me.

I remembered the piece of paper hidden in her wardrobe, and a cold feeling took hold of my insides. 'You say you met her in person?'

'I do a lot of work in the Naivasha area.' He inspected his fingernails. 'I just wanted to put a face to the name. I like to do that.'

'What's the name of your company?'

'The Imperial Africa Trading Company.'

'Your company stamp wouldn't be a crown, would it?'

He made a half-bow. 'Not very original, I suppose.'

Boy grinned. 'Word is Sullivan's a spy.'

'Not a very good spy if my cover was so easily blown.' He chuckled, looking at us as if expecting us to join in.

'Are you drinking with us?' I asked.

'No, no. I've taken up enough of your time.' He shook my hand again. 'Pass on my regards to your sister, won't you?'

'Will do.'

'See you around, then.'

I spent the rest of the following day on edge, worrying about how isolated Maud was out by the lake, and left early to drive to Kiboko.

She was pottering around the garden when I got there. The sun had set and the sky was a pale purple. Someone had lit the lanterns for her to see by. She accepted a kiss on the cheek with a tired smile.

'It makes me happy to see you out here,' I said, putting my arm around her shoulder.

'Yes.' She brushed her hand across her cheek, leaving a smudge of earth. 'I've been very boring recently, haven't I? Sleeping all the time.'

'You're never boring.'

'You have to say that.'

'I mean it.'

We started walking towards the lake and she leaned into my shoulder. 'Solly's getting so fat these days – all he does is eat.'

'Lucky bastard.'

She laughed.

'Spanish – have you thought about what you'll do if war does actually break out?'

'Stay here.'

We reached the top of the jetty. I picked up a stone lying in the grass nearby. 'What about Solomon? What if it's not safe any more?'

'This is his home.' She disentangled her arm from mine and pulled her cardigan around herself. 'What would happen to it if everyone who could just abandoned it?'

I threw the stone. It skimmed the water three times and disappeared with a hiss. 'You can't do the country any good if you're dead, you know.'

'And what about the Africans? Where would they go? We have to stay and fight for everyone.'

I tried to smile. 'I'd rather you were fighting for them somewhere safer. Writing letters from Scotland, say.'

'Are you leaving?'

I thought of Sylvie. I knew she'd never leave either. 'Probably not – there'll be more need of the railways than ever if it happens.'

Maud pulled the cardigan tighter around herself. 'Well, let's not discuss it then. I go where you go.'

'You're a real mule, you know that, don't you?'

'Funny, Abdullah says the same thing.'

I smiled down at her. The mention of Abdullah made me feel better. He could protect her when I wasn't here, I told myself.

'Poor man,' I said.

She took my arm again, laughing. 'Let me show you your nephew. He's sitting up already at four months old. He must be some sort of genius.'

Chapter Thirty

I'd promised Maud I'd visit every weekend, but the next week MacDonald sent me to Mombasa, and I didn't get back until the following Saturday evening. It was unusually cold and dark, and I couldn't face the drive. I sent her a telegram apologising, and went to the Muthaiga instead and joined Boy in smoking and drinking whisky on the veranda. Just before midnight the skies opened and the rain drove down on the tiled roof above us, rebounding to land a few feet from where we sat.

'You never think in Britain you'll lie awake listening out for this,' Boy said.

'There are lots of things we do here that we couldn't have imagined in Britain.'

He grinned and selected another cigarette. 'True.'

'I like it better on the plains.' I took a sip of my drink. 'The rain, I mean.' Sylvie and I had driven out in storms before to hear the earth responding to the water like a sounding board, filling all that open space. Maybe it was the American in her that needed that vastness, that felt claustrophobic in Europe.

Boy pointed his cigarette at me. 'That's because you love drama. Me, I love the rain in the city, cars going through puddles, umbrellas opening. Very small-fry.'

'I didn't realise you were such a psychologist.'

'No one ever thinks of the cattle rancher.'

I drained my drink and stood up. 'Well – see you around.'

'See you around.'

I drove back to my rooms, bone tired. I could understand why Sylvie didn't want to leave Africa. Europe was never home to her, and she hadn't lived in the US for more than half her life now. But I didn't know how safe she was here, or anywhere for that matter. I didn't know how much she was enjoying life. And I couldn't stop thinking about Minnie lying dead in her lap.

My head was pounding so much I barely made it into my room. I peeled off my wet jacket and shoes, and flopped onto my bed still wearing the rest of my clothes. I must have fallen asleep straight away, but it wasn't a deep or restful sleep. I woke up a few hours later, cold and wet, convinced I could hear bombs falling nearby. I listened out for a few moments. When there was nothing, I got out of my clothes and under the covers and fell back asleep.

My headache was still there the next morning, and I stayed in bed all day trying to soothe it. It was still there on Monday, but at the back of my skull now, and I went to work thinking I could distract myself somehow. Maud hadn't replied to my telegram, and I wondered if she'd been disappointed, or just too busy with Solomon.

Work was quiet. The secretaries' footsteps were muffled in the corridors and the clack of their typewriters seemed to come from far away. I closed the blinds in my office and spent the week preparing a report. The weather was sultry, and my headache wouldn't leave me. I ate alone in the evenings, too tired to make conversation. Instead I planned what I'd say to Sylvie over the weekend. I'd made her ill, and now I had to make her better.

Friday morning dragged itself out slowly. I finished the report and handed it to the secretaries to copy and file. MacDonald was in my father's old office, smoking, and dictating to his assistant. He saw me hovering outside and waved me in.

I stuck my head around the door.

'You want to leave early?' he asked.

'If that's alright.'

'Go.' He stubbed out his cigarette. 'Get some sleep. We're gonnae be busy soon enough.'

I picked up some things from my rooms, and the car from outside The Nairobi. After the heat of the last few days, it looked like rain again, and I spent a few moments attaching the hood, before getting behind the wheel and taking a breath. My hands were shaking for some reason, and my vision was blurry around the edges. I thought about calling off my trip for a second time, staying in bed, but I knew I couldn't. I started the engine and pressed my foot down on the pedal.

The drive was uneventful enough, although the further I got from Nairobi, the tighter my chest started to feel. I hadn't planned on what I'd do with Sylvie.

I'd thought about spending the afternoon with her, then coming back to Kiboko for supper, but as I approached Naivasha I found myself turning off. More than anything, I realised, I wanted to see Maud, have her lay a cool hand on my forehead and bustle around me getting tea and broth and a compress. I felt a wave of affection for her and a pang of jealousy that Solomon would grow up with her as his mother.

The police cars were parked at the top of the drive, almost hidden by the trees. I drove past them, my heartbeat doubling, then pulled up outside the house and switched off my engine. Phillips was on the veranda. He came towards me and I felt my headache worsen, until I thought I was going to be sick. Perhaps a new witness had come forward, or they'd found fresh evidence on the grounds. Phillips looked serious. He stopped a few paces from the car. For a moment, we looked at each other through the windshield, then I climbed out and tried to smile.

'Is everything alright? No trouble in the compound?'

He looked surprised. 'No.' He was playing with his hat. 'I assumed you'd been told; I'm sorry.'

'Told what?'

His eyes flickered towards the house. 'We were only called out this morning.'

It was only then I noticed the figure on the veranda covered by a white sheet.

'Was it Bulawayo?' I asked.

'Who's that?'

I could imagine how guilty Maud would feel if he'd done anything. I started towards the house. Phillips tried to reach out and take my arm, but I swerved and he missed.

'Who's Bulawayo?' he asked.

I sped up and took the steps two at a time. The screen door was hanging off its hinges. There was no sound coming from inside.

I called out Maud's name. Another policeman appeared from nowhere, blocking the entrance; he wasn't the same one who'd come to interview me with Phillips; he was shorter and had a thin moustache.

'Sir —' he said, looking over my shoulder.

Phillips was beside me. He took my arm, and I let him this time.

'Mr Miller,' he said. 'I'm so sorry to tell you, but your sister was shot last night.'

'That's ridiculous,' I said. 'I don't know who you've found, but I want to see Maud.'

'She's been taken to the morgue. I asked one of my men to get in touch with you to identify her.'

He was still holding my arm; we both looked down at it, and he let go, seeming embarrassed. I stepped back and turned on my heel, surveying the garden; for a moment, I expected to notice that this wasn't Kiboko, that I'd taken a wrong turn somewhere.

'Who's under the sheet?'

Phillips led me to the white mound, and I saw now that it wasn't one figure, but three. I felt my legs go weak.

Phillips drew back the top of the sheet. I looked at the faces then at Phillips. I wanted to explain that I knew them, and I didn't.

'Do you recognise these men?'

I nodded.

'Do you have names for us?'

'Abdullah our head boy, Joseph our cook, and Kamante, one of our totos.'

I made my way back to the veranda steps and sat down. Phillips stood in front of me. My head felt like it was about to explode.

'What happened?'

He shifted from one foot to the other. 'From what we understand, three gunmen broke in after dinner, and shot your sister. She was sitting in the armchair at the time. The bullet went right through the book; she most likely died instantly.' He shifted back to the first foot. 'They killed the only other person in the room – your head boy. We're unclear on whether anything has been taken.'

So Solly hadn't been with her. I tried to slow my breathing down, and found my gaze dragging itself back to the shapes to my right.

'And Joseph and Kamante?'

'Apparently they ran after the gunmen, and were shot out here.' He cleared his throat. 'Another toto hid in the woodpile and saw everything. He roused a few of the natives in the compound, but no one thought to fetch us until the morning.'

'Did you find any letters in my sister's bedroom?'

'Letters?'

'She was trying to stand up to the people running the ivory trade out here – I know someone wrote to her about it. I think they threatened her.'

341

'We didn't find anything in her room, but we'll look into it.' Phillips seemed uncertain. 'It's more likely to be a case of robbery. There are many people out there who think the law doesn't apply to them.'

I felt a sudden revulsion for him, for Kiboko, for the bodies underneath the white sheet. I couldn't wait any longer to look for Solly, even if it meant explaining who he was to the police. I had to be sure he was safe – nothing else mattered now.

I stood up.

'Do you mind if I go inside?'

'Are you sure you want to?'

'I just want to see –'

Phillips looked doubtful. 'Don't touch anything.'

I had to stop myself from running through the house and into Maud's bedroom. Other than her bed and normal pieces of furniture it was empty. No police, and nothing there to show Solomon had even existed, no cot, no blankets, no toys. I leaned against the doorframe, my mind whirring. I wondered if she'd hidden him, before I remembered Phillips saying she'd been shot straight away.

I didn't even want to consider the possibility that the gunmen had taken him, or what they would do to him if they had. I felt my heart throb imagining how desperate Maud would have been right now.

I stumbled outside and across the lawn. One of the African children was skulking by my car. I leaned against the bonnet, and she took my hand silently, tugging at me and looking up with big eyes.

I followed her to one of the smaller huts in the compound. The woman who had been there at Solly's birth came out, wiping her hands on her skirt.

'I have little bwana,' she said.

My throat closed up and I couldn't speak for a while; the woman waited in front of me, her face turned to the ground.

342

'What happened, Josephine?'

'Before police arrive I bring him to my house. He's a brave boy, not crying.'

'Thank God,' I said, and then couldn't stop saying it.

She waited for me to finish, still staring at the ground.

'Do you think you could look after him for a few days?' I said, when I was finally able to get the words out. 'My mother doesn't know —'

'I can look after him.'

'Do you need food? Does he need food?'

'I have milk,' she said.

I wanted to thank her, but it seemed so inadequate, so I nodded, and turned on my heel.

Poppy knocked on my window as I was sitting in my car. I wound it down. 'Do you need me here?'

'Maybe you could come to the morgue tomorrow?' He looked away. 'I'm sorry again.'

I started the engine and reversed up the drive. I must have driven to Sylvie's without thinking, because the next thing I knew I was lying with my head in her lap, sobbing uncontrollably.

Chapter Thirty-One

We buried Maud the week before Christmas, in the orchard underneath a plum tree. I watched the men fill the grave, patting the earth with their shovels. In January the fruit would fall above her, soft and waxy and the colour of bruises; I thought she'd like that. Then I remembered she wouldn't like anything ever again, and for a moment I couldn't breathe. Images of her flashed past me, worsening the pain in my lungs: Maud as a toddler in Edinburgh, laughing when I pulled faces at her through the bars of her cot; Maud crying when I was sent to boarding school; Maud standing next to me in our train compartment, looking out at the African night and refusing to be scared of the leopards; Maud teaching Scotty to shake paws, roll over. Maud in the garden, talking to the flowers to make them open up; Maud with the children in the compound, kissing their sticky faces. Maud sitting on the veranda and promising me she wasn't doing anything stupid, the stubborn tilt of her chin when she told me we had to fight for change.

The Africans came and stood behind us, at least a hundred of them. They didn't speak, not even to each other. Afterwards, they melted away, until only one woman was left. She came forwards timidly, holding something in her arms.

'Bwana,' she said. 'I bring him now?'

I'd been avoiding facing the issue of Solomon's future during the last few days. He was sleeping now, his long eyelashes quivering with every breath.

'What is she talking about?' my mother asked.

Josephine held him out. I met my mother's gaze.

'Your grandson,' I said. 'Maud's baby.'

Her eyes flashed. 'You're lying.'

I shook my head. Josephine handed him to me and I drew back the blanket to show her. 'Look at his expression.' It was true. The frown between his eyes reminded me so much of Maud that my heart caught against my ribs.

My mother took a step back. 'Take him away.'

'Where to?'

'Anywhere.' She half-turned away while I handed Solomon back to Josephine, and I felt a jolt of guilt that I hadn't prepared her for him. Of course the news was hard to take today. She'd thought she was saying goodbye to Maud for good, and Solly would be a constant reminder of her.

'Can he spend one more night in your house?' I asked Josephine.

'Yes, Bwana.' She didn't look surprised.

My mother started walking back to the house. I caught up with her on the veranda.

'We can't leave him with Josephine forever,' I said. 'She's got children of her own to feed.'

'We won't.' She pushed open the screen door and we stood in the doorway. None of the totos would set foot inside, and the house seemed dead without their noise. My mother went to the sofa and sat down facing the hearth. I stood in front of her.

'Give it a nudge,' she said, nodding at the dying fire.

I picked up a poker and stirred the embers around. A few logs crackled back into life and the sweet smell of woodsmoke filled the room. My mother held her hands out to the flames.

'It was always cold in here,' she said.

'I suppose so.'

She moved to the floor, and I sat next to her, leaning my back against the nearest armchair.

'I'll sell the place,' she said. 'If anyone wants it. You can buy somewhere in Nairobi with the money.'

'And Solomon?'

'Do you have to keep using his name?'

'What else should I call him?'

'I just –' She looked at her hands. 'I didn't think my daughter would keep that from me.'

'I'm sorry,' I said. 'But you know now.'

'I do.' She shook herself. 'We'll take him to the orphanage tomorrow.'

'You're giving up your own grandson?'

'I didn't know about him until five minutes ago.'

'You're in shock,' I said. 'You'll feel differently tomorrow.'

She unpinned her hair and it fell down her back in a thick rope. 'I'm being realistic, Theo. What kind of a life could he have with us? Or us with him? Do you think our friends in Nairobi will welcome him with open arms?'

'Then we stay here. The Africans wouldn't reject him.'

'They would – they have their own rules. Maud did something neither side can forgive.'

Her voice was calm, and my stomach felt suddenly tight. It wasn't shock. She was coldly contemplating giving him away, just as when I was a baby, she'd looked at me and made the decision to teach me through fear. 'She thought he was worth the risk.'

'Because she didn't understand the world she lived in.' My mother shook her head. 'If you'd had a baby with a native no one would bat an eye. Women aren't extended the same privileges.'

'So people would have talked –'

'She would have been an outcast. She was spoiled, and it was her fault – that's how people would have seen it.'

I balled up my fists, then buried them in my pockets. I was

suddenly overwhelmingly angry that it'd been Maud who died, and my mother who lived, and had to fight the urge to hurt her. 'We buried her less than an hour ago.'

'What's that got to do with it?'

'How can you talk about her like that?'

'I thought you understood. You make hard choices for those you love. Especially those that are part of you.'

'Like your grandson.'

'I don't *have* a grandson.' She stood up suddenly and looked down at me. I noticed for the first time how bright her eyes were. 'I had a daughter, and she was an angel, and I won't let anyone say anything different about her.'

My anger left me as suddenly as it had appeared.

'I didn't know you felt—'

She closed her eyes. She was standing over me, and I knew I should reach out and take her hand, but my arms were too heavy to move.

'You're a man. I shouldn't expect you to understand,' she said softly. 'The rules aren't the same for us.'

'I do understand.'

I looked away, and felt, rather than saw her shake herself. 'Stay here and get warm – I'll start supper.'

I kept my face turned to the flames until she'd left the room, then stood and made my way outside to the jetty and the boat. I lay in the middle of the lake, looking up at the birds wheeling above me through the late afternoon sky. Even though it wasn't cold yet, I felt an iciness seep through my skin and into my bones. I closed my eyes, breathing in the smell of damp wood, and listened to the water lap gently against the sides of the boat. For some reason my mind drifted back to the day we'd spent out here on my sixteenth birthday. Maud and my mother had sat at either end while I rowed. Maud had twisted herself in her seat, so her upper half was facing outwards, elbows on the rim of the boat and chin cupped in one hand. Her hair had been up

347

in a ponytail that had bounced when she turned suddenly to point at a giraffe disappearing into the trees along the shore, and when she shook with laughter when the champagne spurted all over me.

I'd wanted to fish that day, but she'd begged me not to. Then when I'd gone ahead and caught a fish after all, I'd stared at it jerking violently across the bottom of the boat, eyes wide open as it suffocated, and hadn't been able to go through with the kill. I'd picked it up instead and dropped it back into the water. The three of us had watched it sink for a moment, holding our breath, then a shiver seemed to run through the silver body, and it had darted away. Maud had linked her fingers through mine and squeezed my hand.

I screwed my eyes shut even further. For a moment, I could almost believe that when I opened them she'd be with me again, body half-twisted in her seat, looking out at the water. The thought made my chest ache with happiness, and grief, knowing even as I imagined her there, she was really a mile or so away, deep in the ground.

I opened my eyes. The edges of the clouds had turned a burnt pink. My coldness had left me. My mother was right, I couldn't let her memory be ruined.

The sun set quickly as I started rowing back to shore, dropping out of sight behind the mountains, and the lake turned cold and black. It was strangely quiet on the water, except for the splash of the oars. After a while I questioned if I was going in the right direction. I stopped and wiped my forehead. Thoughts of hippos swimming unseen beneath me made my hairline prickle with sweat, and I wondered if I should risk a shout, to see how close I was to land. Then I saw a yellow glow to the right of where I'd been steering and headed for that. For a long time it didn't seem to be getting any closer, then suddenly I could make out the shape of Kiboko up the slope of the lawn. My mother was waiting for me on the jetty. She'd brought a lantern and laid it at her feet, so her face was in darkness as I looked up from the boat. I could see her arms clearly, though, and the goosebumps that dotted her skin, and realised she must have waited for me for nearly an hour.

For a moment, neither of us spoke. She was the first to break the silence.

'Supper's ready,' she said.

The lights were on at The Farm, although it was dawn already. Sylvie opened the door to my knock. She was in her green dress, the one she'd worn for lunch with me and Lucy all those years ago, and her hair was pinned, her lips and her cheeks rosy pink.

'I knew you'd come,' she said.

She took me to her bedroom; it was filled with flowers, lilies and roses and forget-me-nots, and their smell mingled with her perfume. She was standing perfectly still at her dressing table, but I could sense the restlessness coming from her in waves. Outside the window, the eland ambled past keeping to the shade, and the river flowed away from us in liquid gold.

'It's such a nice day,' I said. 'How are you feeling?'

'I'm fine.'

'I like your hair like that.'

'I call it Clouds on a Mountaintop.'

I looked around the room. Brown paper luggage tags had been tied to various items of furniture, the dresser, the mirror, the bed. I could make out Sylvie's writing on them.

'Are you moving?'

'No.'

I turned over the tag attached to the floor lamp where I was standing and saw the name 'Edie'.

'You're giving it all away?'

'I don't need it,' Sylvie said. 'Any of it.' She clasped her hands together and tried to smile.

'What's wrong, darling?' I asked her.

349

She was quiet.

'Should I call the Matron?'

'Do you remember Samson?' she said, looking at me properly for the first time. 'Do you remember how I blamed Nico for giving him up?'

'Of course I do.'

'I felt awful about it afterwards, you know.'

'You were right,' I said, moving towards her. 'Samson belonged with you out here, not in a zoo, or a circus.'

'But we spoiled him,' she said. 'We made him think he was one way, when he should have been another. And then it was worse when he learned what lions are. He was dangerous.'

'Does that make you feel differently about him?' I tried to take her in my arms and she looked as if she was going to struggle, but she went limp instead.

'No,' she said. 'He was a wild animal – I knew that. We shouldn't have treated him as a toy.'

I kissed her chin. 'Don't think about it too much.'

'I can't help it,' she said, and ran her fingers through my hair. 'It's all our fault. Now go away and leave me in peace.'

'Let me say goodbye properly first.'

I kissed her again, on her mouth this time, and she kissed back. I let her go and she smiled at me, still that same shy, wicked smile.

'I do love you, Theo. Remember that.'

'I love you too – more than anything.'

'I know,' she said.

'Everyone loves you.'

'I know.'

The smell of lilies followed me all the way to the car.

Chapter Thirty-Two

From the stern of the ship I could see the buildings along Mombasa's shore. After years of being scorched by the sun, their white and yellow paint was flaking off like the burnt skin of the fish cooked and sold near the harbour.

Below me, white foam hissed upwards as we cut through the turquoise water and small dhows carrying spices and salt slipped out of the way and off to Zanzibar, birds wheeling and screeching above them. An early evening breeze had started up, and was gently bending the heads of the palm trees. I checked my watch. It was past six o'clock, and the sun was touching the red roofs of the old town; the whole skyline looked on fire.

I let myself grieve the fact that I hadn't persuaded Maud to leave earlier then pulled myself back from the edge. I couldn't think about that night too much, couldn't go over it and over it in my mind, imagining her last moments, wondering what she was thinking. Was she afraid? Did she know it was coming? I didn't believe it was bandits, didn't believe Bulawayo had anything to do with it, even if he had disappeared, and no matter what Phillips said. What would be the point? If I'd found the letter I might have been able to prove something, catch the killer, even, but someone had got rid of it. I had to let it go.

351

I could get used to the cold and the rain again, and there would be plenty of need for engineers in Edinburgh. It would be safer. It would be difficult too but, then, it would be difficult anywhere.

I'd burned her chair the morning I'd left. I wondered what my mother had thought when she found the charred remains, what she was doing now, if she understood the note I left her, especially the last line: *I'm not sorry we came out here, but it's not home any more.* For some reason I was sure she would.

I left the railing and turned towards my cabin. I didn't need to watch it disappear. Maybe it was never home. Maybe we weren't supposed to conquer Africa. Actions had consequences, after all.

I smiled to myself as I opened the cabin door. The nurse was in the chair I'd brought on board specially, the one that matched the cot. She was feeding Solomon, who was looking up at her with absolute determination in his eyes, milk fog obscuring everything else. He was so unashamedly greedy it was a pleasure to watch.

I wondered if he'd remember her, her warmth, her smell, the feeling of safety she must have given him. Maybe one day I'd write down what happened to them, so Solly could know his mother.

The nurse offered up the baby.

'He's finished,' she said. 'Do you want him?'

I took the little body in both hands, cradling him against my shoulder. I'd have to learn to do this naturally. I was responsible for a whole other person now.

Something stirred inside me, an image of my younger self sitting at a table, Freddie's hand clamping down on my shoulder as he introduced himself to my family. Life could turn on moments like these. Maybe it would be easier to live in denial, like Sylvie, but I couldn't do it; on the other hand I couldn't live in guilt, either.

I wasn't the person who had arrived in Kenya over twelve years ago, and I wasn't the person who had returned eight years later. I wasn't innocent, but I wanted to be good. I wanted to make Maud proud.

Historical Note

While Theo and the Miller family are completely fictitious, many of the characters and places in The Hunters are based on actual historical events and figures. When researching the period, I came across the story of Alice de Janzé (who became the inspiration for Sylvie), a beautiful heiress living in the Wanjohi Valley in Kenya who kept a lion cub as a pet, shot her lover, Raymond de Trafford (the inspiration for Rupert), and later married him. She conducted an affair with Josslyn Hay (a base for Freddie) and was rumoured to have shot him too (this time fatally) before killing herself.

I was immediately drawn to her as a character, to her privilege and her self-destructive quality, and the more I read about the crowd she ran with – dubbed the Happy Valley set – the more I saw those elements appear in all of them. Their lives seemed impossibly glamorous and hedonistic, filled with endless cocktail parties and sexual shenanigans, but also sad and seedy, tainted with drug addictions and stale relationships and sadism. It made me wonder how fulfilled they were out there, and whether they saw their situation as I did, as a desperate, doomed attempt to impose the already outdated culture of 'the aristocracy' onto another society.

I could imagine at the very least they would have felt disjointed and in limbo, which is something I wanted to communicate in the novel. These were people who had been raised to expect a certain status in their native countries, who were struggling to come to terms with the gradual erosion of the lord-peasant relationship, accelerated by changes introduced by the first world war. Kenya must have seemed a respite from this change, a civilisation that harkened back to Britain's bygone era of feudalistic countryside life.

No wonder then that Josslyn Hay fought so hard to preserve white entitlement (as Freddie does), arguing in favour of securing the white highlands for European settlers only. He appears to have considered – as did many settlers and officials at the time – the Africans to be childlike, in need of paternalising and moulding, a view that sits uncomfortably with 21st century readers.

On the other hand, the Happy Valley set were held in contempt by government officials in Kenya precisely because they acted as if unaware of their 'responsibility' to educate and lead the Africans by example. As I have Nicolas comment, if white culture were seen to fall short, the Africans might not accept its "superiority". Codes of behaviour were to be followed when coming across Africans in a social setting, and every opportunity to prevent this from happening seems to have been taken, such as creating whites-only spaces (social clubs such as The Muthaiga were a prime example of this). The Happy Valley set openly flouted the codes with their drinking, fighting, torrid affairs, and general bad behaviour. It seemed to me the perfect situation to explore corruption and resistance, and thus Theo and Maud were born.

Some of the details I came across in my research seemed ready-made for fiction. There was a real life instance (although not in Kenya) of a woman being shot while reading, and the bullet penetrating her book; Josslyn Hay really did have a chimp who smoked cigarettes and drank water from an enamel chamber pot; the sex games at Kirlton are all examples of those that Idina (a model for Edie) and Josslyn Hay played with their guests; and stories about the King of the Wa-Kikuyu, 'Black Harries' – who is so cavalier about the lives of his horses – and the unfortunate surveyor who was taken by a python when swimming, are all true (or reported as such). Secondary characters such as Delamere, Gwladys, Carberry and Kiki Preston, and all the various pets, have retained their own names. Of course, there is no evidence to suggest that a teenage boy was befriended by the set.

I also changed key dates and events for various reasons. Unlike Freddie, Josslyn Hay's body was found in his Buick in the early morning of January 24, 1941; he had been shot at close range. The papers were quick to suggest a love triangle between Hay, Diana Broughton and her older husband, Sir Delves Broughton. Scandal ensued, somewhat embarrassingly for the white community, who probably felt the shooting did nothing to improve their public image. Broughton was suspected, as was Alice de Janzé. There was even a theory that Hay's killing had been authorised by the British government, who were uneasy about his ties to Oswald Mosley and to the BUF. Broughton was arrested, and after a lengthy trial, acquitted. The murder remains unsolved to this day.

Acknowledgements

There are a number of writers whose careful research and outstanding storytelling was invaluable when I was trying to get a sense of the Happy Valley set and their lifestyle. If any reader would like to know more about Josslyn Hay and Alice de Janzé – the real Freddie and Sylvie – and Josslyn's mysterious death, I cannot recommend the following enough: *White Mischief* by James Fox; *The Temptress* by Paul Spicer; *Child of Happy Valley, a memoir* by Juanita Carberry with Nicola Tryer; and *Tarred with the Same Brush* by Frederic de Janzé – the real Nicolas – with a special mention to *The Life and Death of Lord Erroll: The Truth Behind the Happy Valley Murder* by Errol Trzebinski. A few of Freddie's speeches quote a line or two from Joss directly, and those excerpts and the newspaper extract on the Blackshirts in Kenya were found in Ms. Trzebinski's excellent biography. Getting the period details just right was helped immensely by reading Elspeth Huxley's *Pioneers' Scrapbook: Reminiscences of Kenya, 1890 to 1968*, and for a background on the politics, I found Dane Kennedy's *Islands of White: Settler Society and Culture in Kenya and Southern Rhodesia, 1890-1939* extremely comprehensive and thought-provoking. I also recommend *The Africa House*, by Christina Lamb, for its rich and fascinating account of colonialism in action in another part of Africa.

I would like to thank: my editor at Borough Press, Holly Ainley, who impressed me from the first with her passion for the novel and her thoughtful, nuanced editing. She is also a great partner in crime for a new mum at her first party away from the baby.

Everyone at Borough Press, for their enthusiasm, their talent, and for making me feel so welcome.

My amazing agent, Caroline Wood at Felicity Bryan, who is patient but firm and always right, it turns out.

The following writers: Carolina Gonzales-Carvajal, Emma Chapman, Liz Gifford and Liza Klaussmann. For re-reading manuscripts a million times, and for loving the book before anyone else saw it.

My friends and family, for their unending support. I'd like to mention Valur Anarson and Edythe Mangindin in particular. I wrote this book when my partner and I were living in Reykjavik, renting their old apartment, and they became family away from home for us.

And finally, my men. My brilliant partner, Tom Feltham, and our beautiful son, Noah Gordon (on that note, it turns out there is someone I'll give up chocolate for). You guys make every day the best day ever.